ALSO BY LINDA LADD

A Love So Splendid

Forever, My Love

Lilacs on Lace

White Orchid

White Rose

White Lily

A Love
So Fine

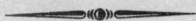

Linda Ladd

A TOPAZ BOOK

TOPAZ
Published by the Penguin Group
Penguin Putnam Inc., 375 Hudson Street,
New York, New York 10014, U.S.A.
Penguin Books Ltd, 27 Wrights Lane,
London W8 5TZ, England
Penguin Books Australia Ltd,
Ringwood, Victoria, Australia
Penguin Books Canada Ltd, 10 Alcorn Avenue,
Toronto, Ontario, Canada M4V 3B2
Penguin Books (N.Z.) Ltd, 182–190 Wairau Road,
Auckland 10, New Zealand

Penguin Books Ltd, Registered Offices:
Harmondsworth, Middlesex, England

First published by Topaz, an imprint of Dutton NAL,
a member of Penguin Putnam Inc.

First Printing, January, 1999
10 9 8 7 6 5 4 3 2 1

Prologue

6 Sept. 1807
Liverpool, England

My dear Libby,

I hope this letter finds you well and happy. I cannot begin to make you understand just how much I miss you and all our friends back home. Even Mrs. Gladstone's frowns of annoyance! Does she still peer over the garden wall when you receive guests under the rose arbor? My, I really cannot believe that I miss even that persnickety old battle-ax, but perhaps that will reveal to you the extent of my loneliness.

We reached landfall at Liverpool yesterday on a cool Thursday evening and took lodging at a dockside inn. It was a rather shabby accommodation but clean enough to tolerate. The bed linens were fresh, in any case, but the drunken sailors in the taproom sang their bawdy ditties until three in the morning. Knowing you, dear Libby, you would have enjoyed the entertainment and perhaps even joined them, I suspect, if given the least provocation!

I am filled with nervousness and anticipation over the prospect of meeting my betrothed husband for the first time. As you remember quite well, I'm certain, I have spent the entirety of the last few months gazing at Lord Lasserthon's miniature, but still I find myself filled with apprehension. What if I do not care for him or find his character less than fitting? Worse, if I cannot abide him, what shall I do? My life shall surely be doomed.

I know you shall say I should be a dutiful wife to Raymond as you were to dear John, God rest his blessed soul, the dear man, but you knew him so well before you exchanged your vows. In truth, he was your mentor and best friend long before you agreed to become his wife, whereas I, on the other hand, have never laid eyes on my bridegroom, other than this tiny portrait I now wear around my neck. Well, in any case, I shall know how well we are suited within three days. I will write again when I arrive at Lasserthon Manor.

Be well and know that I am your ever faithful friend,

Henrietta

11 Sept. 1807

Dearest Libby,

I am here at Lasserthon Manor, set up in great comfort in a rather lavishly splendid bedchamber, certainly one much grander than I am accustomed to! I have met my future husband at long last, and I will not leave you in a state of suspense. The truth is that I find my betrothed quite admirable of character and handsome of face, which, of course, I know should not, and does not, take precedence in the eyes of a wife. However, his appearance does transcend in the most glorious way the likeness of him I carry in my silver locket. Of course, we've only just met, but I am truly relieved and find the manor house here in Yorkshire quite warm and cheery though surrounded by great stretches of desolate heaths and moors. It seems at times, as I look out my bedchamber window, where I now sit composing this missive to you, that I've been transplanted into the midst of an immense, rolling sea of hills and bogs. And the fog is strangely clammy and enfolds the house nearly every night with its wet gray mist. The butler is quite startling at first glance, a hulking giant of a man, whom I've designated the politest gargoyle this side of China, but in truth is quite harmless and kind to all.

I am informed the wedding is to be simple, at the Anglican church in the village of Lasserthon, just a stone's throw down the road. I am pleased, for I was quite dreading any gala affair where I would surely be the only stranger among the villagers.

I promise faithfully that I will write more of my observations later, but I am very tired from the journey and the excitement of meeting my intended. (He seemed very pleased with me—I say this with a blush rising in my cheeks—but his response did lessen my anxiety, for we both know that, unlike you, Libby, I am quite plain in appearance, though I realize I do have my own God-given talents and blessings, of which I am eminently grateful.)

I will write again soon and describe to you every detail of the nuptials. I can be reached at the post marked on the outside of this letter. Please write soon and tell me all the news that has transpired in Philadelphia since I set sail. Is the newspaper still gaining in popularity? I do miss our discussions over your editorials, though at times they became quite heated, especially when we were criticized for espousing the rights of women to hold property in their own name. I've not had time yet to send off a note to the Duke and Duchess of Thorpe, but I will do so soon. I am eager to meet your parents but have said nothing yet to Raymond concerning them, out of respect for your wishes.

I know I shall linger at the posting box daily, so eager am I to hear from you.

Fondly, Henrietta

29 Sept. 1807

Dear Libby,

I do so wish you were here. Could you not find leave soon to pay us a visit? I realize that you are busy training Thomas Rathbone to run John's printing establishment for you, but I do so desperately long for a friend in which to confide. I've met so few people, but there is one woman with whom I especially enjoy spending time. She is the wife of the local justice of the peace. Her name is Evelyn Landers and quite a lovely woman, but as you are well aware, there could never be anyone who could take your place in my heart.

Raymond and I were married by the parish vicar, the Reverend Joseph Curtis, with only his wife, Betty, and a few of Raymond's close friends standing as witnesses. I am not sure what I think about my husband, dear friend. I feel most disloyal for even mentioning his shortcomings in my own hand (what if he should find this letter and read it! I should certainly die from regret and humiliation!). But I will say, he is kind to me, though I am finding it hard to adjust to my wifely duties and do not find them enjoyable in the least. I console myself with the memory that you confided the same after your wedding to John. It's just that I find what is required of me entirely distasteful and alien to my modest nature. I fear I may never become accustomed to it. Oh, I do wish you were here, Libby. Please come to visit, I beg you. Perhaps you could visit your parents, the duke and duchess, while you are here in England. Please consider it. I truly need to see you.

Affectionately, Henrietta

16 Oct. 1807

Oh, Libby, you simply must come soon. I am beside myself with boredom and, yes, I must tell you, despair. I have begun to find this manse gray and cold, like a prison. And the fog, it is always with us, pressing on the windows until I feel I am entombed in a mausoleum. I am stricken with melancholy and thoughts of America more than I ever thought I would suffer.

I find myself walking for hours outside in the swirling mists in order to escape the sheer tediousness of the house, though I am most careful to avoid wandering into the moors, which are dangerous and vast with many perilous bogs, making it quite easy for one to lose one's bearings and become lost.

I much prefer to stroll into the village, where I can enjoy a visit with Evelyn. In truth, she is the only person I seek out now, although I cannot bring myself to truly confide my troubles to her, as I am so comfortable doing with you, dear friend. Oh, I do need you to advise me, Libby. You have always had the gift of intuition (of which I am sadly lacking) and could tell me what I should do when I am distressed and confused.

Raymond is often absent, busy with his accounts and tenant farms, and I fear I no longer please him. He is quite cold and remote at times, only to become warm and faultlessly attentive when his mood turns for the better. He's especially jovial of late, now that he's invited an old friend to stay at Lasserthon Manor.

Our guest is an earl—Julian, Lord Edmonton—and is said to be quite wealthy and well placed in society. He comes from the Rainville family. Are you acquainted with them? I'm sure your parents must be, though I've not contacted them to inquire about him. As for my own opinion, I cannot yet decide what to make of Lord Edmonton. He is quite handsome in a rather dark, unsettling fashion and possesses quite a knack of intriguing everyone around him. At times I find him utterly shocking, both in his words and his deeds.

Most disturbing to me, however, and, Libby, you know better than anyone how reticent I am when in the company of gentlemen, he has the unacceptable habit, in my eyes, of behaving in an overly familiar manner with the ladies. It is quite disgraceful, in fact, and I must include myself among his chosen victims. On several occasions he has quite obviously inveigled to separate me from the others present, only to insult me with rude, completely inappropriate inquiries as to my personal relationship with Raymond. I suppose I am waxing silly, but of late I have become rather afraid of him. I do not trust him, though I am reluctant to mention the fact to Raymond since he and Edmonton are old friends and have become quite inseparable in the last few weeks.

I shall carry this missive myself and meet the post, as I have done with all my correspondence to you, for fear that someone might get hold of it. I know I should be

quite ashamed of myself for these unkind remarks I am
sharing with you about my husband and his friends, but,
Libby, I am so desperately unhappy here. Please come
soon, if only for a short stay.

                    Your loving but unhappy friend, Henrietta

    The man was careful to hide himself behind the velvet drap-
ery. He stood at one of the highest windows in the manor,
looking down at the cobbled driveway. He was waiting for
Henrietta to appear. She was late with her daily stroll. He
didn't mind; he was a patient man. The wait would be worth-
while. The time had come for her to disappear forever. He
felt a rising tide of anticipation, a warm, soothing, liquid excitement that flooded his blood. He always felt this strange,
dark excitement when the time was at hand to take a woman.
And Henrietta had become special to him. She'd come alone
to this house, so young, so incredibly vulnerable and easy to
manipulate. She was his for the taking, but he had to act soon,
today, or he might not get another chance.

    It was almost dusk over the moors. The afternoon light
looked dirty, obliterated by patches of mists rising from the
barren hills that rolled out toward the horizon. The inclement
weather should help him subdue her. She couldn't see him
coming or she might draw attention by screaming. He had it
meticulously planned. He had decided to take her long ago,
so every eventuality was covered. The time had come at last.
The mists would hide the fact that he was following her. More
important, no one would question the reason for her disappearance. The fogs, they'd say, and shake their heads in sorrow. Poor dear little Henrietta. She was so young, so sweet, and
now she was dead. He grinned at the irony of it all.

    Where was she? Suddenly impatient, he shifted from
where he leaned against the wall. Was she hesitant to brave
the foggy conditions? He was alarmed at first but relaxed almost at once. She'd take her walk, all right, if for no other
reason than to get away from him. She fled the house every
chance she got nowadays, usually into the village, where she

thought she'd be safe from him. But she was very wrong today.

When he caught a movement below, he saw her. He smiled. She moved down the steps and paused at the bottom, where the brick driveway began. She was wearing a cream-colored cape and carrying a market basket over her arm. Her head was uncovered, despite the threat of rain. When she turned and glanced up at the house, he stepped back but watched her through the lace curtain. He saw the dark bruise on her cheekbone. She'd told everyone she'd tripped and fallen against the door. He knew better, and so did she. She started off down the drive, so unaware, so unprepared for what was about to happen. He smiled again but only a faint curve of his lips. He was even more eager than he'd been the last time. Henrietta was such easy prey, for him, for everyone who knew her.

Turning, he strode with long, purposeful strides toward the door. Henrietta would never step foot inside Lasserthon Manor again, not if he had anything to do with it.

12 Dec. 1807

Dear Mrs. Liberty Thornhill:

It is with great sorrow and regret that I pen these words to you. I have sorrowful tidings that will no doubt bring you great shock. Unfortunately, I fear there is little way to soften such a devastating blow. My wife, Henrietta, is missing, and now feared dead. God rest her soul, she was taken from us nearly a week ago Saturday.

My heart is heavy with guilt since I was not able to protect her. Although I had often warned her about the perils of the moors, she did not heed me. And on that last day, she walked into the wilds by herself and was lost there in the darkness and fog. Although we immediately launched a massive search with the justice of the peace and many volunteers, we were not able to find her. I do not wish to upset you, but there is no easy way to apprise you of her disappearance and probable death. Though we have yet to find her remains, we did happen upon the tan cloak she was wearing when last seen. Due to its ripped, bloodstained condition, we now fear she was killed by a pack of wolves while trying to find her way back to the manor.

I am totally distraught, as I know you must be. I am well aware of the deep friendship you shared with my wife. I am advised by my London solicitor, Sir Johnston Gillings, that our dear Henrietta has bequeathed all her worldly possessions to you. We will await your reply as to your wishes concerning dispensation of your inheritance.

With my deepest and most heartfelt regards, I am yours,

Raymond, Lord Lasserthon

Chapter One

It had been almost four months since Libby Thornhill's dearest friend had been reported lost on the moors near her Yorkshire manor. In a letter from Henrietta's husband, Lord Lasserthon, Libby had been informed that Henrietta was feared dead after her blood-soaked, tattered cloak was found far out on the moors. Attacked and killed by wolves, was Lasserthon's mournful explanation, but the only problem with Lord Lasserthon's theory, as far as Libby was concerned, was that she didn't believe a single word of it.

Determined to find out the truth, she had put her business affairs in order and sailed to England from her home in Philadelphia. Now she rattled down the graveled entrance road of Lasserthon Manor, where Henrietta had arrived as a new bride less than a year ago. She gave a deep sigh of pure relief when the wheels hit the cobbled driveway and the hulking coachman finally brought the drafty hired carriage to a rocking halt on its squeaky, jouncing springboard. The contraption obviously dated from well before Libby's birth, twenty-six years ago, and she would be very pleased to step out of the slow torture chamber, and even more pleased she'd never have to set foot in it again.

Stretching her muscles and massaging the sore spot at the base of her neck, Libby leaned forward and peered through the rain-spattered door glass. A tall granite structure rose before her, slate in color—at least she thought so, but it was very dark outside. Only the lighted windows glowed yellow in the mist, but she could tell that the house was grander in size than she'd expected for a country estate. As Henrietta had intimated, it had a stark, intimidating facade. At the moment it looked downright eerie as a thick carpet of fog crept like a slinking gray house cat along the ground, pluming upward in clammy, groping fingers of mist as if intent on strangling the two white Corinthian columns supporting the domed portico.

The sheer loneliness of the house made Libby want to shudder. Or was that because she'd arrived in the place where Henrietta had died? A thick lump began to form in the back of Libby's throat, and she felt anguish hit her, hard and quick, as if she'd been struck by a doubled fist. For months now, while she prepared her personal affairs for this journey to England, she'd sought to temper the sorrow, to control the anger she felt—with Henrietta for getting herself killed and with herself for not being there when Henrietta had cried out for help. She missed her still, every day, and had from the moment her dear friend had sailed away. Now she would never see her again. She felt the need to weep but quickly suppressed the urge. She'd cried bucketfuls when she'd received the news. Now she wanted answers. She wanted the truth.

The coach shook slightly as the driver finally bestirred himself enough to climb down and see to his passengers. Not used to hired conveyances and the less than professional drivers usually assigned to them, Libby waited, thinking how terribly fearful Henrietta must have been when she'd arrived at this lonely, godforsaken place all alone, knowing no one. Her father had not taken that into account, had not even bothered to hire a suitable companion to accompany his poor daughter to her new home. All he'd considered was bringing an English title into the family. He'd been a greedy, unloving man, and Henrietta was the only child he had to barter for his vainglorious needs. He was dead and gone now, and Libby did hate to speak ill of the dead, but he had been wrong to send his daughter so far away. Libby would be eternally grateful that her own parents had loved and nurtured her and allowed her to choose her own husband, though her father had initial misgivings because John had been so much older than Libby.

She remembered Henrietta mentioning her fears in one of her early letters, how nervous she'd been when she journeyed over these endless, dreary moors. The village of Lasserthon was even more isolated than Libby had expected. There was one thing, however, that she knew for certain. Henrietta would have known better than to waltz away on her own into dangerous, unfamiliar terrain. She'd said so herself in another letter, when she'd mentioned that she was afraid to wander out on the moors.

Libby's fragile jaw took on a hard, stubborn slant, a mannerism familiar among her friends and family. If nothing else, she had determination, or grit, as her dear husband, John, used to call it, rest his soul. Though Lord Lasserthon purported Henrietta had ventured off alone, Libby knew better. What's more, she was fairly certain she could prove it, if given half a chance.

Henrietta had possessed many wonderful attributes, but the impulsive desire to explore dangerous territory was not one of them. In truth, that might be something more to Libby's liking. Timid, sweet-natured, and accommodating, Henrietta had been an absolute prisoner to convention, often scolding Libby for her penchant of traveling on foot about the city in search of social injustices about which she liked to write. Henrietta was religiously devout, and Libby was quite sure she would have become a missionary in time if not for her father's desire to marry her to an English earl.

For weeks now she'd pored over Henrietta's letters and had come to the conclusion that there was more to this affair than met the eye. She was sure that Henrietta had been the victim of foul play. Perhaps even murder.

Libby shook her head, knowing such suspicions were outrageous. Still, her stomach knotted; she couldn't help it. She knew all was not right; she knew it in her heart and with all her intuition. And if that was true, if someone had dared to harm Henrietta, Libby would never rest, never, until she brought the culprit to justice.

She closed her eyes, and images flooded her mind like swelling waves hitting a seawall, mental pictures evoked from Raymond's letter, and she pictured Henrietta's cream-colored cloak, the one they'd chosen together for her trousseau, ripped, darkened to crimson with her own blood. Henrietta had worn it on the day she left Philadelphia. Inwardly Libby could still see her shy friend waving from the ship's rail, dabbing tears with a white handkerchief, that same cloak fluttering around her ankles in the fierce harbor winds.

Libby shook her head, as if the motion would rid her of such painful thoughts. What in the devil was that drunken sot of a driver doing anyway? Stabling the horses before he remembered he was supposed to open the door for her? Impatient with him—and impatience was one fault Libby readily owned up to—she pulled her rabbit-lined royal blue cape closer around her and fastened the woven frogs at her throat. She had no proof, of course, and that's one thing John had taught her from the beginning, before they were wed, when she was still apprenticing at his printing office. Never accuse anyone of anything unless you have the facts to prove what you say. Libby's nagging suspicions weren't enough, nor were Henrietta's letters. But if there was even a shred of evidence to support her theory, she wouldn't stop until she found it. If only Henrietta had written down more about her fears, been more specific about what had been going on at Lasserthon Manor!

On the opposite seat, her maid, Alice, asleep and curled into a warm little ball, was beginning to stir. Libby paid her little attention, thinking that although Henrietta's letters had hinted that all was not well, she hadn't exactly pointed a finger at anyone. She'd been desperately lonely and unhappy in the months preceding her death, and that sorrowed Libby more than anything else. She'd also mentioned, however, that her bridegroom was moody and hard to understand, and that many of his friends unnerved and frightened her, especially one Julian, Lord Edmonton. Perhaps that made both gentlemen unmannerly boors, but it didn't make them killers.

"Oh, thanks be to heaven, 'ave we come to the place at last?" Alice had come awake. She pushed herself upright and blinked myopically at Libby. Her white linen mobcap was set askew over riotous tight brown curls, big brown eyes still blurred with sleep and barely visible under her horribly smashed spectacles. Libby wondered that she could see anything at all through the thick lenses cracked so thoroughly that it looked as if tiny, industrious spiders had spun intricate webs inside the glass. The frames were injured too, bent out of shape so that they sat atop her nose in the most comical fashion imaginable.

Unfortunately, the stocky sixteen-year-old could barely see past her hand without eyeglasses, thereby causing a great dilemma when she'd dropped them while aboard ship on the crossing. She'd panicked, then effectively crunched them underfoot. Sometimes, and to Libby's supreme exasperation, Alice was the most timid, superstitious, easily excitable creature ever born. John had been the one who'd employed the young cockney girl, designating her as Libby's lady's maid just after their wedding, and despite her flightiness, Libby had gradually become quite fond of her.

Truth be told, her undeniably kind husband, with his immeasurable capacity for generosity, had felt sorry for the child, who'd made the crossing from England at twelve years old, alone and without family. Alice did not possess the keenest wit, to be sure, but she was sweet and loyal, and would do anything to please Libby. Libby had almost managed to rid Alice of her thick accent, except when the girl was excited, or groggy as she was at the moment, when she'd lapse back into the speech of her birth.

"They don't make traveling hacks so good 'ere as back 'ome, do they, mum?" Alice often intimated to Libby, with not a little pride, that she now considered Philadelphia her home, America her country, and had been less than enthusiastic about returning to London, where she'd eked out a terrible existence in the East End along the docks. Alice put her palm at the small of her back and stretched languorously before pressing her face against the glass window. She yawned as she peered, squinty-eyed and blinking, into the night. "Look there, ma'am, it seems 'is lordship's be 'avin a party."

"Yes, it does appear that way. Please, Alice, try to remember to speak correctly," she added absently, but her thoughts were on the festivity that seemed to be going on inside. A strange way indeed for a man to mourn the wife he professed so beloved. Henrietta had been dead for only a matter of months, Libby thought with cold disapproval, frowning as she retied her bonnet ribbons and pulled her skirt away from the door, wishing the ridiculously inept driver would hurry up! Never one to wait patiently, she was within moments of throwing the door open herself, which she preferred anyway. She suffered waiting on the nitwit driver only out of a lingering loyalty to John, who'd always insisted on propriety and a well-ordered household, where the servants were expected to do their jobs and Libby was expected to act the lady and let them.

"Aye, poor Miss 'enrietta, I mean Henrietta." Genuine tears filled Alice's eyes, magnified and round behind her wrecked glasses, for she was a kindhearted sort and had loved Libby's best friend as much as Libby had. But who had not? There was just something about Henrietta, some indefinable vulnerability, an inner sweetness that endeared her to everyone she met.

Libby turned her attention back to the house. She had lost John to influenza only three years ago, and Henrietta had been ever at her side to help her through the initial months of her widowhood. Now she was gone too. Though Libby had managed to work through the initial shock and grief, she could never let herself dwell on Henrietta's untimely death for long without getting so choked on emotion that it was hard to hide her distress. She quickly turned the subject.

"Now, remember, Alice, my parents have no idea I'm in England yet, and I don't want them to, or Mama'll make Papa bring her up here at once. No one is to know I am their daughter. Under no circumstances are you to mention my kinship with the duke and duchess."

"Yes, ma'am, but I sure like 'is Grace's coach and team," Alice said. Quickly recalling her lessons, she corrected herself, then went on slowly as if concentrating mightily, "Oh, I mean His Grace's, and it's better'n these here nags that you hired to bring us here. It rides a far sight more smoother, and has those furry throws to keep a body warm in the winter."

All true, Libby thought, feeling chilled through to the marrow herself, after hours and hours of the long, damp drive. On the other hand, she wasn't fond of all the pomp and circumstance she was subjected to during journeys made under her father's ducal crest either. She adored her father, of course, respected his aristocratic lineage, but considered herself an American first, like her Carolinia-born mother always had. Since their hard-fought victory in the revolution, Americans were no longer forced to kowtow to the English nobility. They believed in justice and equality for everyone, and Libby was proud to be a part of that.

That was one reason she had chosen to wed John, who'd been so much older than she; actually, well into his sixties when they'd married, he'd been older than her father. But she'd admired him greatly, because like her cousin, Geoffrey Kingston, of Charleston, he'd fought for liberty, had used his newspaper to fight the British with no fear for his own life. He'd been a close family friend when she'd come to Philadelphia for her schooling, then gradually became her mentor. Even before they'd wed, she had admired him more than any man, except for her father.

"Well, we've arrived at last, Alice, so there's no need to complain. Gather our things and we'll get out and stretch our limbs."

Alice nodded obediently, and Libby again perused the manor rising in front of them with its many multi-paned casement windows that lit the misty night like rows of smoky beacons. Indeed, some gala event was raging in full glory inside the room on one side of the entry, where she could see dark shadows flitting across the bright light. She sobered. Was she right? Was there someone inside Lasserthon Manor capable of murder?

Far away, thunder rumbled and rolled, seemingly in a head-over-heels tumble across the vast moorlands. A fitting background for her melancholy mood, she decided as the gaunt-faced, humorless driver finally thrust open the door. The sour, unpleasant odor of cheap rum hit her in the face like a nasty wet slap, and Libby averted her head, considering herself and Alice very fortunate indeed that he'd not plunged them, unfortunate horses and all, into one of the oily black bogs lining the muddy turnpike.

As she stepped down onto the cobbles, a fiery display of lightning danced across the dark horizon, then bolted down to the ground like a jagged spear of fire thrown by Thor. In the brief flash of light she could see a rainstorm, slashing down in a roaring attack on the moors, a visible torrential downpour. It occurred to her to wonder just how far one could see when gazing out across the endless wastelands, as thunder cracked loud enough to shudder the door panes. The horses shied uneasily, causing the coach to lurch like a sick drunk, and Libby felt sure the storm would sweep in upon them within the hour.

Fresh damp wind swirled in over them, pregnant with the scent of impending rain, as she stood waiting for Alice to step down from the carriage. Wispy shreds of mist cavorted around Libby's feet in restless pirouettes, and she found the temperature had dropped considerably now that night had fallen to inky, impenetrable black. The air hung heavy with the moldy, earthy smell of wet, and bogs, and cold, fluid air that precedes violent storms.

Libby waited until Alice stood beside her, again pleased she'd elected to hire the private coach. Her parents would have sent the finest of their burgundy coaches, each emblazoned alike with the Thorpe coat of arms in gold and silver. Or they would have met her themselves, every eye watching their every move, as if the carriage carried a wedding party of glittering gods and goddesses. She had thought it rather fun, of course, when she was a little girl, but down deep, even then she'd harbored a secret sense of guilt when she'd seen how everyone bowed and backed away when her father emerged from the door.

"Gad, this place looks spooky, like it's got ghosts up there in the top rooms where it's so dark," Alice was whispering, looking fearful indeed. "They say ghosts walk at night on the moors, you know, and get people if they go out alone." Shivering violently, Alice grasped the small silver cross she wore on a chain around her neck and quickly wound her cloak about her shoulders. As the maid complained that the wind was going to whip off her cap, Libby hardly listened. She studied the house to which Henrietta had come as mistress. Lord Lasserthon was enjoying himself. Was this the way he behaved as a bereaved widower? Resentment flooded her, and she let it rush as it would, hot and stinging. She was quite pleased now that she'd not apprised Henrietta's husband of her arrival. She had caught Lord Lasserthon unaware, and she was certainly seeing how he lived when he was not expecting an old friend of his deceased wife.

"It appears no one has noticed our arrival." Libby bunched the soft suede of her russet traveling skirt in her hands and climbed the steep staircase to the front door, leaving the driver to unload their trunks and traveling valises.

The portal was massive and well kept with potted cedars on either side of the entrance. Libby grasped the brass, horseshoe-shaped door knocker, found it quite heavy as she released it against the door plate. It fell hard, clanging loud and sending muffled echoes pushing through the shroud of fog.

Almost instantaneously the oak door swung inward. A man stood before them, in silhouette against the candlelit entry hall. Libby recognized him at once as Greeley, the prig of a butler that Henrietta had found so amusing. Henrietta had had a dry wit about her and made Libby laugh with some of her outrageous observations. In one letter Henrietta had called Greeley the politest gargoyle this side of China, and Libby hid her amusement at the aptness of the description, for the man before them did indeed have the look of those great stone mammoths that hunched themselves over the ramparts of many English estates, including her own family's Thorpe Hall. He stared down at her, broad forehead wrinkled, heavy jowls covered with thick black sideburns that nearly touched his chin. Tiny black eyes gleamed from underneath unruly, bushy brows, and he wore wrapped about his neck the most inordinately long length of white linen. To her way of thinking, it looked more a bandaged throat injury than a mere cravat. Truth be told, he did look a trifle frightening, but according to Henrietta's account, the butler of Lasserthon Manor was as harmless as an attic mouse.

"May I be of assistance, madam?"

"Please inform Lord Lasserthon that Mrs. John Thornhill has arrived from America. You may tell him that I'm a friend of the late Lady Lasserthon."

She'd surprised the formidable butler with her identity. She could tell by the way his dark eyes flew over her face in careful scrutiny, before flicking briefly to the shivering Alice.

"Please follow me, Mrs. Thornhill."

Libby, trailed so closely by Alice that she was almost riding on her hem, walked along in Greeley's wake, very glad to be out of the chill wind before the storm swept across the moors and pummeled the ancient manor with its fury.

Chapter Two

The inside of Lasserthon Manor, Libby found, was warm and filled with pleasant, comforting smells that made one glad to return home on cold, inclement evenings. The unmistakable scent of beeswax mingled in the expansive foyer with the sweetness of the urn of red roses atop a table beside the door. Even more welcome, enough so to cause some hunger pangs in Libby's stomach, were the mouth-watering odors wafting from the kitchen. Roast pork, if she was not mistaken, and some other savory dish perhaps made from apples and cinnamon spice.

All in all, Lasserthon's house seemed pleasant enough, with its well-oiled mahogany tables that reflected gleaming branches of candlesticks in their glossy surfaces. Straight chairs, upholstered in fabric of swirled greens and browns, lined the entrance foyer, and a wide oak stair with white banisters rose from the back of the hall. A cheerful fire burned in a fireplace near the front door.

Indeed, Lasserthon Manor was not the cold, gray fortress Libby had expected and that Henrietta's correspondence had described. Henrietta must have loathed the place so much that after a time she could enjoy no aspect of it.

The imposing Greeley came to a halt in front of a pair of white double doors. The butler awaited them there, standing in profile, looking at the closed doors. In that hunched pose he resembled, all the more, a stone creature that had dislodged itself and crawled down from the highest of ramparts. Across the hall, behind other closed doors, the frivolity of Lord Lasserthon's party continued with unabated enthusiasm. She could hear many different voices caught up in animated conversation, with an occasional loud burst of convivial laughter.

"Kindly wait in the parlor, madam, if you please, and I will apprise his lordship of your arrival."

The parlor turned out to be a fairly large room, but one made cozy by its homey decor, despite it being very nearly dark. Only one branch of candles burned atop the mantel, throwing out a faint yellowish circle of light near the hearth, which seemed very strange indeed as a place to deposit newly arrived guests. Several sofas upholstered in dark blue brocade framed the fireplace, where a peat fire seemed to be merrily entertaining itself, with an energetic display of snapping and popping and sprays of glowing sparks up the chimney.

Glancing about, Libby perused the interior, her gaze lingering on the white porcelain bowls of newly bloomed peonies arranged on various tables, all upon oval-shaped crocheted doilies. Most of the furniture looked comfortable and rich of quality, and she especially was impressed with an exquisite painting of the English countryside that was affixed to the wall between two windows. In one corner, a pair of wingback chairs had been placed to encourage intimate conversation; another was positioned in front of a glass-encased bookcase that invited one to sit and read a good book.

Despite herself, Libby had to admit the room charmed her. On the other hand, she was cold and tired, and her hands and feet felt like ice. Alice, never one for ceremony, made a beeline for the crackling blaze.

"Oh, ma'am, the fire feels so good. Come close, now, and warm up yourself." Alice shivered as she boldly lifted her skirt and leaned forward to warm her bottom. "Oh, I do wish I'd o' worn my heavy woolens, but who would've thought there'd be a winter chill in the air when it's nearly into May? Why, I bet our buttercups be bloomin' soon back home along the garden."

Libby hastened to the hearth herself and joined Alice before the fire. Her toes felt a bit numb, as if studiously pricked by evil elves wielding sharp needles. Her sheer white stockings and leather boots had proved to be too little insulation for so many hours inside the drafty coach. She contemplated throwing up her own skirt and undergarments with the same reckless abandon as Alice, but negated the idea quickly enough when she heard a faint movement. It came from behind her and, startled, she swung around and stared with not a little astonishment at a man who now stood a few footsteps away. Her composure was destroyed, and her jaw dropped in a most unladylike fashion.

The man was tall and quite large-framed, and though impressive in that regard, those attributes diminished considerably under the charm of his smile. "I've startled you," he said with great understatement.

"Why, in truth, you did." Libby did manage to regain her poise quickly. "I had no idea anyone was nearby." And no one had been moments before. Where in heaven's name had he come from? Thin air?

"I was looking for my cuff pearl. I fear I must have lost it earlier this evening when I came here in search of a book. Afraid I've not had much luck locating it, however."

Libby examined his handsome face as he spoke, and somehow, just why she wasn't sure, she felt certain he was lying about losing his cuff pearl. He hadn't been looking for anything when she'd walked into the room. No one had been in sight or she would have seen them, even in the dim reaches where the shadows were deep and dark.

Just as inexplicably she sensed the man might be dangerous, so for just a moment she didn't reply, shocked by her sudden, strong negative reaction to him. Warily she watched him step closer, into the circle of flickering firelight. He was dark of complexion, but she felt it due to much time spent bareheaded in the sun. Very tall, lean, but she could see his strength in the way his coat hugged his wide shoulders. Strikingly handsome, exceedingly so, in fact, and something in his eyes allowed that he was quite well aware of his masculine appeal. His hair was as black as any she'd ever beheld, too long in back to be completely stylish, extending well down upon his nape and not hindered by the binding of a ribbon.

Still she was increasingly unsettled by him; there was definitely something that made her want to back away and keep her eyes locked on him for fear he might spring at her. He wore formal attire, and looked easily elegant in a superbly tailored black silk frock coat, worn over a pale blue embroidered waistcoat and black trousers. To her surprise, his white silk cravat hung unfastened around his neck. No gentleman she'd ever known would appear such in public in blatant dishabille.

The pleasantly aromatic fragrance of expensive tobacco drifted on the air, and her eyes dropped to the cheroot he held casually between his fingertips. Had he ducked into the parlor to have a smoke, perhaps bored with Lasserthon's other guests? Though he had done nothing untenable, at least not yet, or said a word that could be deemed insulting, she was nevertheless offended by him. Something in the way he gazed down at her from his great height, so boldly and appraisingly, or perhaps it was the way he held himself coolly and disdainfully aloof. He was smiling at her now, and it seemed undeniably mocking, then became even more so when his regard took in her body from head to toe in an outrageously brazen assessment. This man, whoever he might be, was no gentleman in his manners.

"Please allow me to introduce myself." He stepped even closer, glancing briefly at Alice, his gaze lingering on her for a fraction of a second before he returned all his attention to Libby. At that point the firelight flashed against his eyes, and she realized they were not black as she had first thought, but a dark midnight blue. For a second they gleamed like fire reflected off deep ocean waves, and in that instant, before he uttered his name, she knew exactly who he was.

"My name is Julian Rainville, and if you're of a mind to consider titles worth mentioning, which I assume as an American you are not, I'm known as Lord Edmonton. Furthermore,

I can say without a shadow of a doubt that I've never made your acquaintance. Despite a wealth of other shortcomings, I do have a penchant for remembering beautiful redheads, especially one with eyes as green as yours."

Well now, why don't you just grab me up and throw me down on the sofa? Libby thought, finding his forward behavior utterly contemptible. Edmonton was a rake and philanderer, just as Henrietta had written, and it hadn't taken him two minutes to prove himself so in Libby's estimation. His dark good looks, money, and esteemed title probably bagged him just about any woman he wanted. She'd met other men like him at various points in her life, and she hadn't liked them either.

Libby knew from Henrietta's letters that Rainville was the old school chum of Lasserthon. The one who had subjected Henrietta to his unwelcome overtures. Now Libby could better understand why Henrietta had felt threatened.

However, she had never shared Henrietta's timidity. She took a step backward anyway, preferring he did not stand too close. Edmonton cocked a faintly inquiring brow, but in his eyes he was laughing at her. Caution flooded her as she felt toyed with, as if he were some darkly beautiful spider and she a moth struggling to escape his sticky web. Highly annoyed with herself for feeling such fear, she stiffened her posture and put that unsettling visual image out of her mind.

"How do you do? I am Mrs. John Thornhill. I've only just arrived here in England a few nights past in the company of my maid, Alice." Libby gestured to the girl, who had not budged from the warm fireside. "We're here to visit Lord Lasserthon. We come from Philadelphia. In America."

The moment the last word left her lips, she realized how patronizing she'd sounded. Edmonton, of course, didn't fail to notice.

"America, you say. I believe I might've heard of the place. Didn't some backwoodsmen from that little hamlet conjure up that pesky little Declaration of Independence a few years back?"

The Earl of Edmonton was teasing her. She knew this full

well, if only by the smile he wore, but she chose to take offense. Everything about him irked her, it seemed.

"Precisely, my lord." Her voice intentionally frosty, she went on disdainfully, "And if you'll recall, those self-same backwoodsmen chased you well-trained, well-equipped redcoats out of our country with your titled tails between your legs. If I might be so bold as to mention our victory in the war."

Edmonton laughed but swiftly sobered as recognition dawned on his good-looking face.

"Why, you're Libby, aren't you? Henrietta's good friend from America." He gave a low laugh. "Well, well, I've been wondering when you'd show up. I find your name rather intriguing, I must say. Libby's short for Liberty, is it not?"

Stiffening, and with the distinct feeling that he was making fun of her, she replied coldly, "I was born on the day Cornwallis surrendered, so Mother named me Liberty in honor of our victory over British tyranny. I must say I'm surprised you've been curious about my arrival."

"Henrietta left you all her personal possessions, so I assumed you'd come here eventually to claim them. Didn't Lasserthon write and inform you of the bequest?"

Actually the inheritance was the excuse Libby had chosen to use for coming here to Lasserthon and investigating her friend's death, so she quickly nodded. "He did, of course, but unfortunately, I've been unable to make the journey until now. You see, I own a business establishment in Philadelphia, and I was needed there to run the—"

"You own and run a business establishment?"

She heard the emphasis, his tone of disbelief, and she fixed him with a scornful gaze. "I inherited a small newspaper and printing company from my late husband—"

"You're a widow, then?"

"Shall I answer you, Lord Edmonton, or do you prefer that I wait while you rudely interrupt me again?"

He inclined his head in abject apology, but his eyes were dancing. "My, I do feel reprimanded. You colonial wenches do not mince words, I see."

For a moment Libby's eyes widened, unable to believe how insulting his words had been. She felt her hackles shiver and begin to rise. Prepared to lash out in kind, she unfortunately did not get the chance.

"My dear Mrs. Thornhill, welcome to my home!" The effusive greeting came from the threshold, a man's voice, and Libby turned to find a gentleman striding quickly toward them. He looked quite upset. "I am distressed I wasn't prepared to offer you a proper reception. Why, I had no idea you were even in England, much less expected here this evening."

So here he was in the flesh. Raymond, Lord Lasserthon himself, Henrietta's grieving widower. Henrietta had portrayed him as attractive, and Libby found him extremely so. With curly, caramel blond hair that matched a close-trimmed mustache and abundant sideburns, his eyes were of a similar hue, amber-brown, and brimming with warm solicitude. He wore forest green, both coat and trousers, his waistcoat gold, his cravat neatly folded and held in place with a ruby pin. Quite the opposite of his distasteful houseguest. She glanced at Edmonton, and found him watching her with his usual cynical expression. She returned her attention to Lasserthon.

His face was broadly formed and rather pale and wan-looking, though he appeared more youthful than she had expected. He was thirty-two years of age, certainly not too old for Henrietta, who had come to him as a twenty-five-year-old bride. Libby's own husband had been twice that old at their betrothal, and their match had been quite a comfortable one.

"I'm afraid I was remiss, Lord Lasserthon," she explained politely, watching him closely for any hint of subterfuge. Henrietta had been terribly unhappy with him, had revealed as much, going so far as to fear he meant to harm her. What had this man, with such a harmless, pleasant way about him, done to cause such dread in his wife? "I realize now, of course, that I should have sent word to you in advance, but I was anxious to arrive at the manor before the storm made the roads impassable." Not true, of course, but believable enough to convince him, she suspected.

A rattle at the windows bolstered her contrived story, as did the ticking sounds of raindrops striking the glass with a burst of sudden ferocity.

Lasserthon noticed as well. "It appears you've just escaped that fate, by the sound of it." He smiled, as warm and welcoming as before. He glanced aside at Alice, and Libby immediately enlightened him as to her identity. Unfortunately, Edmonton's ill manners seemed to be rubbing off on her.

"My maid, Alice. I do hope you'll have room for her."

"Of course. I'm glad you've come, truly I am. Henrietta spoke so often of you and so very highly. Why, it seemed every time I sought her out, she was writing long letters to you."

"Yes, she did," Libby agreed, then decided to strike a barb into the courteous conversation and observe which of the two men flinched. "The truth is that she often wrote to me. She took pleasure in telling me all the details of her life here at Lasserthon Manor."

Lasserthon looked away as if deeply moved, but she was more curious to see if Edmonton was alarmed by the knowledge that Henrietta might have revealed her less than complimentary opinion of his character. Her interest was rewarded with his elaborately lazy grin.

"Mrs. Thornhill is a widow," he observed aside to Lasserthon. "She's from Philadelphia; that's a town in America."

Lasserthon looked quizzically at his friend, but when he looked into Libby's gaze, his brown eyes brimmed with a deeply shared empathy. "I'm sorry. I didn't realize. I hope your loss wasn't as recent as mine."

"My husband passed away nearly three years ago. He was ill for some time before his death."

Lasserthon nodded, very sad, as if he fully understood the pain she'd suffered. Edmonton stared unwaveringly at her. A movement behind Edmonton caught Libby's attention, a slight quivering of the velvet draperies. Someone is hidden there, she realized, jolted to her core by the revelation. Just beneath the gold fringe decorating the hem, she detected a pair of lady's pink slippers, the toes adorned with black velvet bows. Edmonton had not been looking for a cuff pearl in the dark parlor; he'd been looking for a hidden corner in which to seduce his latest paramour. Though Libby did not consider herself an innocent or prudish in the least, she was shocked by the sheer audacity of the tryst.

She turned to Edmonton, her gaze clashing with his eyes, and she saw no guilt in those gleaming navy blue depths, no fear of discovery. He knew she knew, she realized, and he was daring her to expose his debauchery.

"You've met Edmonton, I see," Lasserthon was noting now, and Libby gratefully returned her attention to her host. "Julian's been a frequent houseguest here this past year. He keeps us all amused. In fact, he suggested having this dinner party tonight. He tries hard to buoy my spirits. I fear I haven't done well since Henrietta was taken from me."

Libby stood very still. Yes, Henrietta had been right to fear Julian Rainville and his unacceptable attentions. He was quite obviously a predator who could not be trusted. Even now he stared openly at her; it seemed to Libby as if he was daring her to reveal his crimes. Was she the next woman he meant to entrap against some dark windowsill? Had he made similar advances against Henrietta, here inside her own home, he, who purported to be her husband's close friend? Had she threatened to expose him? Would that have become a motive for him to harm her?

"My guests and I have yet to sup," Lasserthon told her, his smile eagerly sincere. "I do hope you aren't too weary from your journey to join us. Everyone in the village thought the world of Henrietta. I know they'll be anxious to meet you."

Libby forced a smile. "I will be delighted to join you and your guests. I would feel better, however, if I could have a few moments to freshen myself. It's been a rather long journey from Liverpool."

Lasserthon nodded and told her of course she could, but a melancholy expression soon stole away his smile. "I'm willing to offer you Henrietta's private bedchamber, unless you feel it would be too upsetting for you. I've left her room completely untouched, you see, so you could go through her possessions at your leisure. She stated quite unequivocally that she wished you to have everything."

"Actually, I think I'd feel comforted staying in her room."

"Come, then, and I will show you upstairs myself. I'm most anxious to talk with you, Mrs. Thornhill. I've not met a single one of Henrietta's friends from America. She did think so very highly of you."

Lasserthon was so engagingly artless, he made it hard for Libby to suspect him of any foul play, much less a crime as heinous as his own wife's murder. On the other hand, his despicable houseguest fit that role without Libby having to exercise much imagination. But looks could be deceiving, she knew that full well, and she wasn't a person to make instant judgments on a person's character.

"Dinner's soon to be served," Lasserthon said aside to Edmonton. "I suppose we'll see you there."

"Of course." Julian set his vivid eyes upon Libby, eyes that revealed nothing now except polite interest. "I'll look forward to your delightful company again, Mrs. Thornhill."

Libby did not answer as she took Lasserthon's arm and allowed him to lead her toward the door.

"I do hope you'll entertain the idea of staying here at Lasserthon for a more lengthy visit. I'd be pleased indeed to have you. I know it must appear unseemly to you, but I find that if I fill the manor with guests, it's so much less lonely without Henrietta here with me."

Libby was touched to hear him say that, and relieved too that he'd extended the invitation, for she'd been determined to finagle one if he had not.

"I'll certainly consider your kind invitation. I do have commitments in London within a month or so, but my plans are incomplete at the moment."

Lasserthon seemed genuinely pleased by her response. "That will work out admirably, then, since we'll all be heading down to London for the Season before too long ourselves."

As they were leaving, Alice in their wake, Libby hesitated in the doorway and glanced back at Julian. His stare was unnerving, as was the way he inclined his head in mock salute.

She said nothing, allowing Alice to shut the door behind them, but she could not help but wonder who the woman was he'd secreted in the window and if he'd seduce the unfortunate lady with his dark good looks, as she feared he might have done with poor Henrietta.

Chapter Three

As Libby walked with Lasserthon up the elegant staircase to the second story, she found little to brand the manor dark and foreboding but plenty more of the tasteful decor she had seen thus far—several beautiful brocade settees, an occasional wing chair alongside a small polished table, a mirror or painting here and there, a potted plant. Henrietta's bedchamber turned out to be down the hallway far to the back of the house, and Libby could not fail to notice how Raymond seemed reluctant to linger on his dead wife's threshold. After instructing a young maid to light the fire and put fresh linens on the bed, he immediately bid her good-bye and went down to join his other guests.

Libby hesitated, somehow reluctant to enter the room where Henrietta had spent the last months of her life. Her heart twisted when she stepped inside softly and watched the maid hasten about her duties. The room had obviously been left much as Henrietta had kept it, and Libby decided to quickly wash and change her clothes, not yet ready to face the task of going through Henrietta's personal belongings. She didn't look around much, couldn't bring herself to do so. Later that evening, or even tomorrow, would be soon enough to face the heart-wrenching task.

Her baggage had already been deposited at the foot of her bed, no doubt at Greeley's direction. Libby set Alice to work unpacking, and the girl was soon shaking out the plum-colored silk gown Libby had chosen to wear down to dinner. Libby took her time washing and rewinding her hair into a neat coiffure at her nape before she stepped into the fresh gown and allowed Alice to button up the back. Surprisingly, she felt very much refreshed and ready to face Henrietta's husband and his guests, even Edmonton. Libby dismissed Alice to take her supper in the kitchens, then hastily made her way downstairs, where she found that Lasserthon was graciously holding the dinner hour for her convenience.

"There you are, dear lady." Lasserthon had obviously been watching for her because when she appeared at the portal, he instantly came out of a deep red leather chair and strode briskly to meet her. Ever solicitous the man appeared to be, but she wondered if he'd treated Henrietta even remotely as well as he was now treating her. Judging by the misery stamped so visibly between the lines of Henrietta's letters, she thought not.

Around the drawing room, Lasserthon's assembled dinner guests turned from various conversations, the gentlemen rising to their feet at her appearance. She glanced around, noting that everyone there was appraising her person, every detail from head to toe, no doubt searching for faults. She bore their scrutiny with a friendly smile, encompassing everyone. It occurred to her again to be thankful none present knew that she was the daughter of the Duke of Thorpe, one of the richest heiresses in England. There was little question of how she'd be received if her kinship was made known. Mere mention of her father the duke, and those around Libby became embarrassingly deferential. Therefore she chose to travel incognito under her married name so that at least she would know that any friendships cemented were because of her character and not because of her wealth.

Libby arranged a calm smile on her face as Henrietta's husband took her hand. He squeezed her fingers briefly, as if meaning to give her courage. He was indeed the epitome of an affable, relaxed host.

"Come, let me introduce you round. Nearly all my neighbors have joined us tonight. You truly chose an opportune evening on which to arrive."

Libby agreed wholeheartedly but for entirely different reasons. Without seeming to, she took in the room and its inhabitants with critical objectivity. Julian, Lord Edmonton, was not difficult to single out. He stood by himself near the fireplace, holding an empty brandy snifter cradled in his left hand. He looked tall and dangerous, especially when he gave her a grin that struck her as ironic, mocking. Ignoring him completely, Libby vowed not to notice him further this evening.

"Everyone, please, come near, if you will. My guest from America has joined us." He lightly touched Libby's elbow and drew her farther into the room. "May I present Mrs. John Thornhill. As many of you know, she was my beloved Henrietta's dearest friend in Philadelphia. She's only just arrived this evening, but I hope you'll help me convince her to stay on for a nice long visit."

"Hear, hear! And welcome she is too." This ebullient cry came from a portly old gent who was squinting at her from behind great horn-rimmed spectacles. His eyes were pale blue and watery and appeared immensely enlarged through his glasses. Libby had a feeling his vision was even poorer than her unfortunate maid's. He was perhaps in his fifties, with a belly indicative of a man who enjoyed his ale and good food, and lots of it. When he stopped before her, she realized belatedly that he was obviously already well into his cups.

"Mrs. Thornhill," said he, leaning into a bow so deep that Libby feared he'd topple forward. She observed the shiny bald spot at the top of his pate as he went on. "You honor us with your visit. As justice of the peace of this fine parish, I humbly welcome you to the village of Lasserthon."

"Jasper's held his position for nearly three decades now, and with great success," Raymond explained, clasping the man's shoulder in a friendly fashion. "May I introduce the honorable Sir Jasper Landers."

Libby was slightly disconcerted as the honorable Sir Jasper grabbed her hand and began to work it up and down like the most obstinate of pump handles. His craggy, florid face, however, expressed pleasure that appeared quite genuine. She tried to ignore the rather robust breath that poured from him for fear of inebriating herself on the fumes.

Unobtrusively she sought to remove her hand, still lost inside his giant paw. "How do you do, Sir Jasper?"

"Well, indeed, my dear. You're quite lovely, I must say, dear me, quite." He waited, beaming as if he actually expected her to reply to such an inappropriate remark, while everyone else looked acutely embarrassed.

"She certainly is." Edmonton interjected his wholehearted agreement from where he stood, warming his back at the fire. He hadn't come forward with the others. "Quite a ray of sunshine on such a wild, stormy night."

Libby pretended he hadn't spoken. The truth was, however, that she was pleased Julian had saved her from making a response to the drunken old man. Sir Jasper was struggling to adjust his cravat now, sticking a finger between the starched fabric and his hanging jowls and jerking the necktie outward as if it were a tight noose. The effort caused him to become unbalanced, but Lasserthon reached out a hand and steadied him when he staggered to one side.

"Sir Jasper, perhaps you should sit down," Raymond said in concern. "I suspect your gout's acting up with all this damp weather."

"Aye, aye, this blasted toe makes walking near impossible without my cane, especially in this damnable fog." Sir Jasper instantly realized he'd used profanity in the presence of ladies. "Forgive me, Mrs. Thornhill, ladies"—he included the others with a bleary glance around—"but I do suffer a great deal of pain on nights like this."

Perhaps Sir Jasper would be the obvious person with whom Libby should ply her long list of questions about Henrietta's demise. If only she could corner him when his tongue was loose and active from spirits and before he succumbed to alcoholic stupor. She watched him circle his arm around the waist of a woman standing nearby, one Libby assumed to be his wife. He brought her forward with a great deal of pride, as if he wished to show her off. Surprisingly,

she was small, bookish, and rather plain; at least Libby thought
so until Mrs. Landers smiled. The sweetness of her expression transformed her completely, as often happens with people blessed with ordinary beauty. Slightly shocking, however,
was the gown she wore. Bright red, actually scarlet, and she
held a fan made from black feathers. A small cluster of red
roses encircled her smooth chignon of graying blond hair.

"How do you do, Mrs. Thornhill? I am Evelyn Landers,
and I'm most pleased to make your acquaintance. We live
quite nearby, actually only a short walk down the road from
the manor. Our house is well known for its rose trellises, and
I must admit my gardens are my pride and joy. I'd be pleased
if you'd join me for tea tomorrow so that we can become better acquainted. Henrietta and I were very close, you know.
We all miss her dreadfully."

Henrietta had mentioned Evelyn by name in a letter and
indeed described her as a friend. Libby warmed to the woman at once, hoping Mrs. Landers would tell her if Henrietta
had confided any specific fears during the last days of her life.

"I'd be delighted to call, Mrs. Landers."

"No, no, please, call me Evelyn. Everyone does."

"Then I am Libby."

Evelyn's smile widened, and she appeared quite artlessly
pleased by Libby's acceptance of her invitation.

Lasserthon guided Libby toward a second couple who
hovered nearby. "This is the vicar of our parish, the Reverend Joseph Curtis and his wife, Betty. Joseph has the Anglican church in the village, where my family has worshiped
for generations. Henrietta particularly enjoyed the services.
She commented on more than one occasion about the lovely
stained-glass windows of the church. She had quite the eye
for art, you know."

Had Libby actually heard his voice catch when he mentioned Henrietta? She wondered if Raymond's reactions
were contrived, then chastised herself at the extent of her
cynicism. Still, it behooved her to hold certain suspicions. If
Henrietta hadn't been happy with him, there had to be good
reasons why she was not.

In her eyes, the vicar seemed too young to be ordained. He was tall, blond, and handsome in a way Libby hadn't often found clergymen to be. Everything about him seemed remarkably fragile, from his slender face and narrow shoulders to his long, cool fingers that closed around Libby's hand like bones. His face was pale, completely unlined as if he always kept himself shielded from the sun like the ladies of Charleston, where her mother had been born. The sun in South Carolina was as hot and searing as the moors of Lasserthon were wet and clammy. Libby wished she was there now, enjoying the warm seaside climate. An intense longing to visit Palmetto Point came over her. The plantation of her mother's family was the place she'd grown up, playing on rice levees and riding horses. She'd go there, she suddenly decided, as soon as she finished visiting her parents in London. Perhaps she could persuade her younger brother, Burke, to return to America with her—if he was back from his never ending trip to Italy.

The vicar's wife, Betty, was pleasant-looking but somber as she gently shook her black curls and murmured how tragic it was to have lost Henrietta.

"Yes, it was shocking," Libby answered, her eyes wandering to Julian. "Sometimes I can hardly believe it's true."

Julian, however, was not listening to the introductions. Instead his eyes stayed riveted on a young female guest, a pretty blond-haired woman who sat upon a couch near him. Perhaps the lover who'd hidden in the drapes, Libby conjectured, but couldn't glimpse the lady's slippers to find out for sure. Betty, she observed, was innocent of any indiscretions in the parlor. Her pumps were a staid black leather with not a ribbon or bow to lessen their severity. Her simple dress of black bombazine was just as drab.

"It was just so horrible." Betty kept shaking her head, causing a few tendrils of her thick, dark hair to escape her black velvet snood. Her chocolate brown eyes were filled with sorrow, an emotion that appeared undeniably sincere. "Henrietta loved to walk, for the fresh air and exercise, and often would stop by the parsonage for a spot of tea."

It was sounding more and more to Libby as if Henrietta spent most of the days before she died thinking of ways to escape the confines of Lasserthon Manor. Betty also extended an invitation for Libby to drop in for a visit, which Libby accepted without hesitation. During her brief stay in the village, she intended to become acquainted with as many' people in Lasserthon as she possibly could. One of them must know something, or might at least let slip a scrap of information about the true state of Henrietta's marriage.

Next an elderly couple, the Tanners, proudly proclaimed they'd been married for well nigh fifty years. Curiously, it seemed they'd also grown in resemblance during the many decades they'd been together. Both were short of stature and slight, with thinning gray hair and soft-spoken gentility.

"They've the largest landholdings hereabouts, after Lasserthon Manor," Raymond informed her, and the Tanners nodded vigorously in an impressive display of synchronicity.

Sir John Fordenbury was a heavy, unattractive man who, for some reason, gave Libby a quiver of unease. He looked to be about sixty, said little other than the expected amenities but seemed inordinately eager to introduce his fiancée, Miss Mary Louise Baird.

Very interesting. His betrothed was the blonde in whom Julian was showing such interest. Libby examined the young woman closely as she was presented. She looked barely into her twenties, and she wore carnation pink and a guilty look on her face. Sure enough, a quick glance told Libby the young woman also wore black velvet bows on her pink pumps. Mary Louise was not unaware of Libby's interest in her footwear and immediately blushed so deeply that her face almost matched her gown. Extremely young and naïve, Mary Louise seemed precisely the sort of lady a man like Lord Edmonton would want to seduce. How could he be so vile as to compromise such a victim and with her betrothed husband just across the hall?

Blithely, with unabashed gall, Julian met Libby's glance of contempt, his lean, dark face set with a knowing smile, as if he was enjoying Mary Louise's plight. Libby was relieved when dinner was announced and Raymond offered her his arm. Lightly she lay her fingertips upon his forearm and allowed him to escort her across the foyer into the large dining parlor.

The other guests fell into line behind them in the appropriate order, but Libby could not stop thinking about Julian's revolting behavior. She was absolutely appalled. Not that she wasn't aware such dalliances occurred daily in polite society, on both sides of the Atlantic Ocean. But Julian had been so blatantly reckless in his conquest, as if he took great pleasure in shocking Libby. Indeed, he was obviously a scoundrel with no sense of decency. Had he played his depraved game of seduction with Henrietta, in her own home, under her husband's nose, wooing her with his dark charm? She didn't want to believe it, but somehow she knew it had to be true. Henrietta was such an innocent, so gentle and trusting, but she'd known enough to be afraid of such a man. Then again, he was obviously a master at corruption. Henrietta could have fallen under his spell unwillingly, in much the same way as the unfortunate Mary Louise, like a moth drawn to perish in a gas flame.

The dining parlor was as lovely as it was spacious. Fine porcelain place settings gleamed, crystal goblets shone with ruby red wine, and three gold candelabra set the table aglitter under the glow of twenty-four tall white tapers. All quite lavish, especially the three epergnes filled with purple grapes and polished red apples. Though Henrietta had never confided Lasserthon's yearly income, it obviously was quite significant, surprising Libby, who had assumed, since Henrietta had brought with her a considerable dowry, that Raymond had need of a rich heiress to replenish his dwindling coffers.

With a great show of pleasure and attention, Lasserthon seated Libby to his right. Wasn't he perhaps a bit too accommodating? What was he trying to hide?

Blustering on with his drunken zeal, Sir Jasper took the chair on Libby's other side. His more than tolerant wife, Evelyn, positioned herself directly across the table and gave

Libby another sweet smile. The vicar and his wife sat opposite each other, and Libby noticed that Julian adroitly inched
into position beside Mary Louise while her fiancé took a seat
across from them. The nodding little Tanner twins politely
rounded off the seating arrangement at the far end of the
table.

As Libby arranged her skirts around her legs, she decided
it was probably a very good thing that she could not see what
was going on underneath the lavishly appointed table in the
space between Julian and Miss Mary Louise Baird. She could
only imagine how adept the woman in the black-bowed pumps
would have to be to fend off the advances of such a well-
versed lover. The woman should know better, she thought,
should know that such a flirtation could only lead to disaster.
It suddenly occurred to her to wonder just how many ladies
Julian had led to ruin. Five? Ten? A dozen? A hundred? Her
disgust with him was growing by leaps and bounds, and she
began to wonder just where he had been the day Henrietta
met her death.

Outside the manor house, far out on the moors, the night
shook with growling thunder, the angry rumble intermittent
with barrages of rain that hit the house with the fury of
demons. Libby glanced out the windows behind the table
and found the tall expanse of glass panes blurred by sliding,
sluicing waves of water. She wondered if the rain was as all
pervasive here on the moors as the fog was purported to be.
When she posed the question, Henrietta's husband offered
up the answer.

"Not as much as the blasted fog, which visits us virtually
every day of the year, especially out on the moors."

"Aye, that be true. Many a lad has lost his way home come
Saturday night when he's too foxed to walk a straight path,"
Sir Jasper rasped out with unbelievable insensitivity to his
host's recent bereavement. To the justice of the peace's
credit, however, he realized his blunder at once, turning a
deep purple color that overtook his face until it appeared that
a huge round grape sat perched atop his starched lace cravat.

Those around the table sat in mute dismay, no doubt hoping someone would hastily dispel the uncomfortable silence. Both the Tanners displayed extraordinary concentration as they unfolded the rich white linen napkins, then reached in tandem for their wine goblets.

"Forgive me, Lasserthon, I didn't think," Sir Jasper offered, his bluster wilting like a three-day rose.

Lasserthon handled the man's contrition with grace. "Unfortunately, what you said is true. Many others succumbed to the perils of the moors before poor Henrietta lost her way."

Libby turned when Edmonton spoke for the first time, very interested to hear what he had to say on the matter.

"Perhaps this conversation is for the best. Mrs. Thornhill should be forewarned not to stroll afar without an experienced companion to guide her. Too many accidents have already occurred hereabouts. Another death would indeed be a needless tragedy."

Good Lord, something in the way his eyes pinned her as he spoke seemed almost a tangible threat. Surely she was imagining it, but to her own chagrin, she felt a slight quiver of alarm. Julian was smiling now as if he'd merely shown concern for her safety. Not one to be toyed with, by him or by any other, however, she decided to point out a few discrepancies in the story she'd been told.

"I'll certainly heed your concern, Lord Edmonton, for I'm known to be impulsive at times. I must say, however, that Henrietta was not so inclined in the least. In fact, she was a most cautious person, especially when going about on her own. I find it peculiar and completely out of her character that she should venture out onto the moors, especially if she had been repeatedly warned of the danger."

Her dinner companions showed various degrees of surprise at her remarks, looking at her, then at each other in consternation until Julian spoke again, completely contradicting her appraisal of her friend's behavior.

"Henrietta was fascinated with the moors," he told her, casually lifting his goblet. "She often took long walks on the trails among the heather, every day, in fact, if the weather was fair. Most often she strolled alone, unless Raymond or I were available to accompany her."

"I find that hard to believe."

Rather bluntly put, Libby realized as soon as the words left her lips, especially when Mrs. Tanner gasped as if mightily shocked. Julian gave a low laugh, but his eyes were cold upon her face.

"Mrs. Thornhill is not one to mince words." He glanced around the table. "I discovered that earlier when we first met in the parlor. The truth is, I don't believe she's fully accepted the fact that her friend is gone."

Again their host interjected diplomatically before his guests could fall into a full-fledged duel of words. The idea appealed more to Libby than it should have, but perhaps with loaded pistols rather than verbal repartee. For a moment she visualized with wondrous contentment a mental picture of herself smacking Julian, Lord Edmonton across his smug, handsome face. Then appalled at herself, she quickly thrust the violent image away.

"I suppose Julian's right," Lasserthon said sadly. "Henrietta was prone to take long, solitary walks, though I warned her daily to be careful because the moors were so treacherous."

"Did I understand you to say that you often escorted Henrietta on her walks, Lord Edmonton?" Libby could not stem her desire to confront Julian. She studied his face as he answered her query, looking not uncomfortable at all under her pointed interrogation.

"Yes, I had that pleasure many times. But only when her husband was busy elsewhere."

Yes, I am quite sure that was the case, Libby thought. You've probably made a career of enticing innocent young women out of their husbands' protection and into your clutches. She relentlessly pursued her line of inquiry.

"But on the day she disappeared, am I to understand that neither you nor Lord Lasserthon were available to accompany her?"

Lasserthon looked absolutely stricken as he answered for Julian. "Though I will regret it until the day I die, I rode out that day to give directions to my manager concerning my tenants."

Such an alibi could readily be verified. She turned back to Edmonton. "And you, sir, where were you on that day?"

Julian appraised her thoughtfully, a half smile riding his lips. He was taunting her again, she realized. She could see it in his eyes. But somewhere in those blue depths she saw something else too, something that looked like wariness. "I was riding out on the moors myself the very same day, though I never happened upon Henrietta. Would that I had. If I had, she might very well be sitting here with us, whole and sound."

"You enjoyed your outing alone, sir?"

His eyes didn't flicker. "I always ride alone. Sometimes for hours at a time. It gives me time to reflect."

"Yes, that's true," Betty Curtis cut in with a bright smile, blithely unaware of the accusatory undercurrent sliding in and out of the conversation. "Julian seeks his inspiration out on the moors. He's the most wonderful artist. Were you aware of his great talent, Mrs. Thornhill?"

Libby had not been. Henrietta had never mentioned that Julian was an artist. "No, I had no idea. What sort of work do you favor, Lord Edmonton?"

Julian suddenly leaned back and gave an impatient wave of his hand. "Please, do me the favor of dispensing with the title. Call me Julian. I prefer it."

"I feel the same way," Lasserthon interjected, smiling. "Most of my close friends call me Raymond. I would have you do the same."

Libby returned his smile. "As you wish, of course." She was not finished with Julian yet, so she returned her regard to him. "Perhaps you'll show me one of your paintings before my visit is done. I've always enjoyed watching artists at work."

"Actually," he said, refilling his wineglass from a carafe on the table, "I'm best known for my nudes. Perhaps you'd agree to pose for me, Mrs. Thornhill—after we get to know each other a bit better, of course."

Libby gasped in her shock, stunned by his vulgarity. More startling was the fact that the others laughed at his crude remark. Even the vicar was smiling. Noticing Libby's dismay, he hunched a shoulder in an apologetic shrug.

"You'll get used to Julian, Mrs. Thornhill. He thrives on the outrageous. The truth is, his nudes are quite the rage in London at the moment."

"He sculpts too, and quite brilliantly," Mary Louise murmured softly, then blushed. "I sat for him once myself." Her color went deeper, flooding up beneath her cheekbones. "But I was fully dressed, of course. Sir John commissioned a marble bust of me."

"And I have treasured it," Sir John replied, lifting her hand and pressing her fingers to his mouth.

For a fleeting instant Mary Louise looked repulsed, or at least that was how it appeared to Libby, but the young woman quickly lowered her eyes, making it impossible to know for sure. The old man doted on his lovely bride to be, anyone could see as much, but Libby was sure Mary Louise did not feel anything of the kind.

"Sir John is to announce his engagement at my estate at Brickhill. I do hope you'll join us there for the weekend, Mrs. Thornhill," said Julian, staring challengingly at Libby, as if daring her to reveal what she'd happened upon in the parlor. She would not let him bait her into causing a scene.

"Perhaps, if I am still here," she answered noncommittally, then turned the conversation to the vicar.

"Have you been in Lasserthon long, Reverend?"

"Almost six years. Betty and I were both born in London. We served a time in the country, near the village of Lopenbridge. Are you familiar with it?"

Immediately Libby was alarmed at the mention of a village so near to her father's vast country estate at Thorpe Hall. She noticed that Julian looked quickly at Joseph at the mention, and wondered why. Surely he knew nothing of her kinship with the duke and duchess. Momentarily she considered telling them the truth about her family, then quickly decided against it. She wanted them to treat her as anyone else, especially since she intended to interview them about Henrietta. She nodded, said nothing, trying to gather her thoughts again as Mr. Tanner remarked at length about the flocks of sheep he kept and how the prices were falling in the London markets.

Libby held her tongue for some time afterward, listening closely to the conversation drifting around her, but all seemed normal chat among friends and neighbors. Only Julian seemed out of place among the gathering, a dangerous presence among country squires and simple villagers.

"Mrs. Thornhill runs her own business establishment back in Philadelphia," Julian suddenly said during a lull in the conversation, after Betty had spoken about a church bazaar to be held the following week.

"Indeed?" Mr. Tanner said with surprise as he leaned forward to allow the maid to remove his bowl of creamy leek and potato soup. "What sort of establishment do you run, my dear?"

"I own the *Boston Daily Republic,* a small newspaper and printing company. My husband left it to me."

Evelyn smiled, magically transforming herself into a beauty once more. "How wonderful. I always thought I'd like to write poems and such as that. Do you write anything for your newspaper?"

"I've written articles about various social issues. Henrietta used to contribute articles as well. She is a very good writer." Aware she'd used the present tense to describe her friend, she couldn't bring herself to make the correction.

No one, not even Lasserthon, seemed to know about Henrietta's love of the written word. She wondered why. Had they not talked together during their brief marriage about their likes and dislikes, the things they loved? She and John had spent hours discussing their shared interests, both before their marriage when she worked for him, but afterward too, when she became his wife.

The servants of Lasserthon Hall were well trained and efficient, moving quietly about their tasks, unobtrusively serving the diners from silver trays of braised beef and buttery potatoes. Libby was hungry and ate with enjoyment, but barely touched the burgundy in the tall crystal goblet before her. She preferred to listen and learn while the others imbibed enough to answer her questions without thinking.

She did note as the meal progressed that one servant was very unlike the others. The woman was of Oriental extraction, Chinese perhaps, and was dressed exotically in a scarlet-embroidered black silk pants and tunic. She hovered behind Julian's chair more often than not, providing his every want and desire while he totally ignored her presence. She was older than he, perhaps in her thirties, beautiful with her slanted sloe eyes and straight jet black hair that hung in a queue well below her waist.

"You've noticed Lu Ling," Julian said, drawing Libby's eyes away from the lovely servant and back to him.

"I've noticed that she serves only you."

"She belongs to me."

Scandalized, Libby could only stare speechlessly at him. Lu Ling gave no indication that she understood what he'd said. The room grew quiet. Julian seemed to enjoy bringing conversation screeching to a halt, she thought furiously. She'd never met so uncouth a man. And he purported to be a gentleman, a peer of the realm?

"I assume you're jesting," she said coldly.

"I'm afraid not."

"Then I'm surprised you'll admit to such a barbarous, deplorable thing."

"Have you been to China, Mrs. Thornhill?" he asked, leaning back in his chair, unperturbed, nonchalant.

"No, I have not, but I daresay I wouldn't purchase any Chinese citizens if I did happen to visit their country."

"Her father was selling her on the street outside their gate. I took pity on her. She's made a fine personal valet. I've no complaints."

Shocked enough to lean back against her chair this time, Libby made sure he didn't see her discomfiture. However, for once she couldn't think of a suitable reply. She looked around at the others, wondering how they could so blithely accept his outrageous incivility.

"Julian's trying to shock you, my dear," the Reverend Curtis said kindly. "We've all become accustomed to his ways since he's been visiting. Actually, he saved that girl from a horrible fate. Most of her sisters ended up in the basest of brothels. Lu Ling is most grateful to Julian for saving her from a terrible life."

Libby just couldn't believe everyone could sit there so tolerantly and listen to Julian's crude remarks. No wonder Henrietta had been frightened of him. He was grinning at her, but his eyes looked like cold blue ice, and she sensed that he wasn't amused at her questions as much as he wished her to believe. She had a feeling that he didn't like her any more than she liked him. He was intentionally trying to make her uncomfortable. Perhaps he was trying to drive her away, which only pointed to the fact that he might very well have something to hide.

Lifting her goblet, she finally tasted the dark red wine, found it rather dry but of good quality. For the remainder of the meal, she kept her thoughts to herself. She'd bide her time. Tomorrow was soon enough to seek out the answers she wanted, and she'd start with Evelyn Landers when she joined her for tea.

Chapter Four

After enduring a story by the minute Mrs. Tanner, who looked alarmingly like a hungry baby robin as she chirped and nodded her way through the unremarkable tale of her trip to the market, Libby excused herself from the drawing room, where the ladies of the party had returned for coffee and gossip. At first she thought she might learn some interesting tidbit by closeting herself with the other female guests, but thus far had only heard about the best way to pick summer melons and a fail-safe recipe for plum pudding rounded off by Mrs. Tanner's marketing exploits. She had a feeling she would have learned much more in the company of the gentlemen, who had retired to Lasserthon's study, to speak of much weightier subjects, no doubt.

As she neared the closed door of Raymond's study, the faint rumbling sounds of male voices met her ears. She hesitated, certainly not above compromising her scruples enough to eavesdrop a moment at the keyhole. It would be well worth the effort if she heard mention of Henrietta. Unfortunately, the door was thick of wood and substantial enough to muffle most of the discourse going on inside the room. Disappointed, she moved on to the foyer staircase, glancing around as she did in an attempt to familiarize herself with the mansion.

At the base of the wide steps, she lifted her skirt and ascended slowly to the second floor. She paused at the top, highly tempted to snoop around a bit, for there was no sign of servants, and the house was very quiet. She'd learned a

great deal during the course of her first evening at Lasserthon Manor, but the cause of Henrietta's death was still a
complete mystery to her. The only thing she was certain
about was that Henrietta had not died the way her husband
had told everyone she had. Though Libby now had her
doubts about both Raymond and Julian, nothing incriminating had been revealed by word or action, not yet, in any case.
Then again, her visit had only just begun. Now, after a single
evening in the house, she was even more convinced her
friend had met her death due to foul play.

A heaviness crept over her heart, bringing a sigh of sadness in its wake as she realized how different this first visit to
Lasserthon should have been. Henrietta should have come
running down the magnificent staircase to greet her in the
warmth of the foyer, and the two of them should have enjoyed a wonderful vacation together, sharing everything that
had come to pass since last they'd met, planning excursions
and picnics and all sort of exciting pastimes.

Moving along the ornate banister, she made her way a
short distance, then stopped to lean over the balustrade near
the door of the study below. The men were enjoying a jovial
gathering, apparently enjoying port and cigars and each
other's company. She could hear a loud burst of laughter
now and then. Something told her the subject matter might
be a bit more bawdy than the usual fare of Napoleon's intrigues, London politics, and economic forecasts. Probably
more insulting comments, courtesy of Lord Edmonton, designed to shock his companions. Why the others condoned
such boorish behavior was beyond her. Eccentric artist he
might be, but he was unconscionably rude, his remarks scandalous by even the most open-minded standards, and his
actions even worse. Though never one to jump to quick con-
clusions about a man's character, Julian's behavior had left
her little choice but to find him utterly contemptible. Actually, it almost seemed he wanted her to think him a vile,
loathsome serpent. If that was truly so, why would he?

Reluctantly she turned toward her bedchamber. Tonight

would garner her no more information from the circle of friends downstairs, but tomorrow was another day. She would weasel information about Julian from Evelyn Landers when she went there to call. Delicately, of course, but single-mindedly until she'd found out exactly how Henrietta had felt about him and the other members of her household, even her husband, who at the moment seemed beyond reproach.

When she entered her bedroom, she found it warm with several lamps left burning for her return. Alice had retired as Libby had bade her but had done her job well. The fire crackled merrily, and the soft satin counterpane was turned back invitingly. One of Libby's nightgowns lay atop the bed, a full garment of soft white lawn, and alongside it, a matching robe that buttoned high upon her throat.

The readied bed looked so comfortable and inviting that Libby had to stifle a yawn, more than ready to snuggle under the comforter and into the soft reaches of the feather bed where she could sleep undisturbed for hours. The journey that morning had started at dawn, and had not been one with myriad comforts. Removing her dangling garnet and pearl earrings, she walked across the room, realizing she would not be able to put off much longer the task of going through Henrietta's belongings.

When she'd changed for the dinner hour, she'd forced herself not to think about Henrietta's last hours spent inside this room, but now she could not help it. Henrietta had slept in this very bed, had seated herself at the lovely antique dressing table with its elegantly curved legs. Lasserthon had intimated that he'd not touched anything in here since his wife's death. Libby wondered if that was really true.

Even if Libby had not been told, however, she would have known the chamber had belonged to her friend. Henrietta's favorite color scheme glowed on the walls, where tiny nosegays of yellow buttercups and pink roses tied up with blue ribbons dotted the cream background. It resembled the decor in Henrietta's bedchamber at her father's house on Market Street. A swell of grief struck her, bringing so many memories swimming to the surface. Libby fought her feelings, unable to allow herself the luxury of being ruled by sentiment. She had to keep her objectivity until she had uncovered what really had happened to her friend.

Kicking off her slippers, she stretched her arms and dug her toes into the plush floral carpet underfoot. It was rich of hue and soft of fabric with long garlands of roses entwined with ivy woven in dark blue, rose, and gold. She walked in her white stockings to one of the tall casement windows and pulled back the heavy burgundy draperies.

Wind and weather still ruled violently over the moors. The glass was spattered with rain, making the panes glitter with mosaics of shiny silver against the black velvet night pressing in from outside. In the morning she would gaze over the vista that had faced Henrietta each morning she had arisen in her short stay at Lasserthon Manor.

Suddenly Libby felt alone, morose to the depths of her soul as she dropped the curtain back into place. She struggled to undo the buttons at the back of her frock, and though usually adept at undressing herself, tonight she was tired and emotionally drained and wished Alice was there to help her.

After a momentary battle, she was able to step out of the gown, then quickly removed her chemise as well and slipped the soft nightgown over her head. She sat down at Henrietta's dressing table and loosened the thick coils pinned at her nape. Brushing her hair thoroughly, she braided it over her shoulder, thinking about the last time Henrietta had sat there, doing the same thing. Then unable to stare at her own sad reflection, illuminated with all its pain in the oval mirror affixed with two candles, she put down her brush and extinguished the flames with a small brass snuffer.

The four-poster bed was partially indented into a wall alcove. The footboard angled toward the fire to catch its warmth and was high enough that Libby was forced to use the bed steps. Carved from fine dark wood, the bed was the most masculine piece of furniture in the room, and Libby realized that if not for Henrietta's personal touches—the yellow and white floral overstuffed chairs flanking the fireplace, which had been a wedding gift from Libby, the pastoral paintings Henrietta's mother had painted—the room would have been a dark, unimaginative chamber.

As she settled against the softness of the white satin pillows, she realized that Henrietta's favorite shawl was draped over the headboard, the brown and gold paisley silk one they'd chosen together on a shopping spree long before Henrietta had been betrothed.

Sadly Libby recalled a day when her friend had flown with wind-flushed face into their shared room at Mrs. Scott's School for Young Ladies, flinging off that very shawl and collapsing with laughter upon the bed as she related how the staid, proper Mrs. Scott was asleep at her desk, her snores loud enough to echo down the hall. They had laughed together often in those days.

Libby picked up the soft shawl and held it to her face. Henrietta's scent still lingered in the material. It was strange how certain people had their personal fragrance, one when smelled brought them quickly to mind, and the sweetness of lavender and roses, blended together in bath oil, would forever bring Henrietta's laughing face spiraling into Libby's consciousness. What had Henrietta been thinking when she'd last draped this garment around her shoulders? Had she been contemplating a walk on the moors, as Julian and Raymond insisted was her wont?

Pulling the shawl around her shoulders, she felt comforted until it occurred to her to wonder what her friend had been wearing on that last day. She climbed down off the bed and walked across the room to the gigantic mirrored wardrobe. She turned the handles, and her breath caught when she saw the interior, so neat and orderly, everything on the appropriate hook or folded neatly in fresh-laundered piles. Libby pulled out a pink and white sprigged afternoon frock with the apple green spencer that was worn over it. Beside it hung the russet silk that went so well with Henrietta's dark hair, alongside the dark green velvet they'd chosen together for the snowy balls they assumed she would attend in wintry Yorkshire.

How could Henrietta be gone forever? It seemed only yesterday they'd sat together in wicker chairs in Libby's garden and discussed the newspaper. Henrietta had been so young and vibrant, so good-hearted.

Libby felt her anger start to rise. It wasn't fair. It was all too strange, too unlikely. Henrietta's last letter had been filled with unhappiness. Why hadn't she said enough for Libby to prove wrongdoing? To know where she should look to uncover the guilty party?

She took a moment to bank the glimmering red coals, then got back into bed. She sank beneath the crisp white bed linens. Had Henrietta thrown herself down on these pillows and wept in lonely despair? Or had she lain on these soft sheets waiting for her handsome husband to come and wrap her in his arms?

Libby's thoughts turned to her own husband. She'd loved John, respected him immensely, had learned much about life and business from him, but she'd never appreciated the ordeal of the marriage bed. He'd consummated their marriage, of course, but when he joined her in her chamber, infrequently as it had been, she'd felt little, if anything at all. She'd grown to consider her husband's needs as a burden a wife must bear, though her mother had intimated just the opposite, that the act of lovemaking was so much more wondrous, a special joy shared between a man and his wife.

More a clumsy, undignified procedure designed for John's momentary pleasure, she thought, then was flooded with shame. She'd loved her kind, elderly husband, she truly had, and still missed his wisdom and guidance. But she did not long for a bed partner to paw under her gown in the darkness, and she didn't contemplate marrying again for that very reason.

In Henrietta's case, however, perhaps the marriage bed had been different. Raymond was so much younger than John, and truly quite handsome and gentlemanly in his behavior toward the ladies. Still, Henrietta had indicated just the opposite.

Outside, the rain pelted in a heavier cadence, a lonely, sad song. The thunder had rolled off across the distance some time ago, but she almost shivered, thinking how far out on the Yorkshire moors Lasserthon was, how alone she was among so many complete strangers. Perhaps she should require Alice to sleep on the couch at the foot of her bed for the rest of their stay. Just for company's sake, if for nothing else. Alice would probably be more comfortable here than in the servants' quarters under the nose of the frightening gargoyle of a butler. Alice was afraid of her own shadow anyway.

Her hand stilled when she heard a murmur of voices outside in the corridor quite near to her door. A man's voice. It was Julian's voice, she knew it. She fought her desire to peek outside into the corridor and find out what he was up to, lurking around outside her door. It was a battle she did not win. Within seconds she was out of bed, tiptoeing barefoot across the carpet and stealthily cracking her door.

Julian was outside, all right, several doors down the corridor. He held a single candlestick, and the flickering light caught his face, carving dark hollows around his eyes and mouth, and making him look like the devil she felt he very well might be. He carried his coat over his arm, and his necktie hung loose again. He was whispering to a woman, which didn't surprise Libby in the least.

When he turned slightly, Libby realized that his companion was the Chinese woman who served him. Lu Ling was her name. Was she his lover as well as his valet, forced to serve his needs in bed as well as in other aspects of his life? She wouldn't doubt it, considering the type of man he was. A sudden vision entered her head, of that dark, exotic couple entwined on a bed, twisting, grappling, and a flutter of response deep inside sent a spiral of utter shock through her. Appalled, she chastised herself that she was certainly as bad as he, spying and eavesdropping so shamelessly. Still she could not stop watching the tryst transpiring in the hallway. The blasted man fascinated her, perhaps because she'd never met anyone who'd flaunted propriety in quite the same way. She was not surprised to see him stride off down the hall in the opposite direction, leaving Lu Ling standing alone outside his door.

On his way to his next conquest, she deduced with a disdainful curl of lips, then was inwardly dismayed at the sheer force of her dislike for the man. She was ready to close her door again when she realized that Lu Ling was unrolling a black quilted pallet she was carrying and spreading it out on the floor in front of Julian's door. Libby drew her own door closed without a sound and carefully turned the key against the very strange inhabitants of Lasserthon Manor.

She certainly had never encountered their like before, and she was certain Henrietta must have felt intimidated in the same way. Perhaps she could strike up a friendship with the Chinese woman. That poor soul could no doubt tell Libby many a sordid tale if she was indeed the gatekeeper at Lord Edmonton's notorious bedchamber door. She probably had to have a list in hand to keep all his lovers straight. Libby had to laugh at her own thoughts. But it was true that the Chinese girl would get very little sleep on the threshold of such a well-traveled portal.

Tomorrow when she was fresh again and not so emotionally exhausted, she'd sift through Henrietta's belongings, slowly and thoroughly. Perhaps then she'd discover the answers to all her questions. She blew out the candle on the bedside table and tried to relax, staring unseeingly into the deep darkness. She listened to the drizzling rain, wishing she could hear Henrietta's voice again just one more time.

Julian's dark blue eyes penetrated her thoughts, so mocking and sardonic, as much so as his smile. He was hiding something behind that arrogant visage. She was an astute woman, had always been, and she knew he knew more than he let on about the circumstances of Henrietta's death. God willing, she would discover just what that was. Henrietta would have been both appalled and fascinated with the man herself, would have probably written long passages about him in her daily journal.

Libby surged upright in bed. Henrietta's journal! Of course, that's where she'd have put down all her fears and suspicions! And Libby knew the secret place where Henrietta always kept it. Scrambling to light the candle again, she finally brought the wick sputtering alive, then quickly searched the drawers of the bedside table. Then she saw it. Henrietta's large white Bible lay unmolested in the top drawer.

Quickly opening it to the back cover, she found the clasp and the compartment sprung open. The journal was not there, and Libby's heart skipped a beat when she saw the single folded letter that was enclosed inside. It was addressed to her, but why had Henrietta kept it hidden in the Bible instead of posting it? Had she feared someone had been spying on her?

Eagerly Libby broke the wax seal. The letter was dated a week after the last one had arrived at Libby's home. Filled with excitement that soon turned to dread, Libby began to read.

Dear Libby,

    I don't dare attempt to send this openly to you. I'm terribly frightened now. All is not well. Lord Edmonton grows more and more presumptuous, and Raymond is not the man I thought he was. I'm so afraid now that I hardly venture out of my room other than for meals. Thank goodness that the two of them carouse most of the night and sleep most of the day. I keep my door locked and pray that you'll soon come and rescue me from this loneliness and despair. Oh, Libby, I wish Father hadn't insisted on this marriage. I don't belong here in England. I don't understand the customs, in fact find some of them most horrible and vulgar. I live in fear of my husband coming to me. I wish I could tell you more, but I'm afraid in a way I've never been before. I live for your letters, Libby, with all your news and chatter about our beloved Philadelphia. I have even thought of running away, coming back home, but know in my heart that I could not manage it. I'm so alone here, so alone and so afraid.

The letter ended there, abruptly without a closing, and from the handwriting and smudged ink, Libby knew that Henrietta had been weeping as she wrote the heartrending message. Now she was appalled that she hadn't laid her work at the newspaper in other hands and come at once. Henrietta had been terrified.

Holding the letter crushed against her heaving chest, Libby felt tears well up in her eyes for Henrietta, but at the same time, fear for her own safety burgeoned to new heights. She stared across the room at the door, thankful it was locked securely, then snuggled back under the covers, still holding the letter. She did not extinguish the candle, and it was a long time before she fell into a fitful slumber filled with dreams of mist-shrouded moors and snarling wolves and murderers with cold blue eyes.

Chapter Five

The attics were vast, cavernous reaches that seemed to stretch out forever on the fifth and uppermost floor of Lasserthon Manor. Along the north end, where a wide expanse of windows poured early afternoon light into the otherwise dusky interior, Julian stood in shirtsleeves in front of a large wooden easel. He still wore his evening attire from the night before—dark trousers and dress white shirt, which he had unbuttoned at the throat and rolled the sleeves to his elbows. The cravat and coat he'd worn the night before lay discarded nearby on a blue velvet, camel-back couch.

He was working furiously on his latest project, had been for hours. Highly annoyed, he scowled down at his canvas, paused a moment, then in a burst of frustration snapped the long-handled brush he held and sent both ends spiraling against the wall behind the couch.

No matter how hard he tried, he couldn't quite get it right. Julian planted his fists on his hips and took a deep calming breath. He stared at the work he had done so far. He had the background color, a warm, molten gold, had blocked the woman's face and shoulders out, very rough, but well enough to catch her grace and beauty at the dinner table the evening past.

For most of the night he'd mixed the colors, the exact tint an elusive, unattainable quest, or lounged on the couch, laboring over her delicately etched features on his sketch pad, dozens of candles lighting his work, most of which had long ago been reduced to waxy stubs before sputtering completely out. Not long after the dinner guests had summoned

their carriages and departed for home, Julian had climbed
to the temporary garret studio he'd set up when he'd first
arrived at Lasserthon's house. A studio was a necessity no
matter where he was. Most of his hosts were eager to oblige
him, his hostesses even more so, for a hidden attic lair held
an appeal for more intimate assignations as well as a quiet
workplace.

Though dawn had come and gone hours ago, with the servants stirring awake on the floor below, he had no desire to
sleep. He took up his short palette knife and scraped a bit of
the rust red paint he'd used earlier to duplicate the American
woman's hair color, but it still wasn't exactly right. Her
vivid coloring was unusual enough to evade his efforts.

Muttering an oath beneath his breath, he put down the
palette and took a few steps toward the sofa. Chastising himself for the compelling desire to paint the woman, he was not
surprised by the overwhelming obsession that had struck
him from the first moment he'd seen her. She was beautiful,
more than anyone he'd seen in some time, which was the
usual reason that compelled him toward any subject. More
than that, she was interesting, with a quick mind and lively
intellect she didn't mind revealing. He had spent most of the
supper hour surreptitiously examining her face—the elegant
bone structure, the large, expressive eyes, a shadowed green
that reminded him of the deepest shades of the forest, and
full, soft lips that had no doubt captured the imagination of
every man who'd ever seen her.

Usually when someone intrigued him to such a degree, he
found it easy to catch her essence at once, or at least some
part of it. Miss Liberty Thornhill, on the other hand, was
proving as mysterious as a misty-edged dream. He smiled at
her name, then at the memory of her great pride in her em-
bryonic country. He needed more time with her, time to study
the delicate curve of her cheekbones, the hint of strength in
her chin when she tilted her head in a certain way, the long
sweep of dark eyelashes that veiled those incredible jade
eyes. What he wanted, hungered to do, was to touch her skin,

to lightly trace his fingertips over the softness of her naked flesh, her pink lips, to bury his hands in her hair and savor the texture that shone like a length of watered silk.

The mental images he was harboring brought a familiar, but unwanted, tightening deep inside his loins, and he visualized her as he had portrayed her on canvas during the long night, on her knees, head thrown back, her hands holding her fiery hair atop her head. The portrait had already taken form as one of the most provocative poses he had ever envisioned, even in its present nebulous form. From the first instant they'd met, when she'd surprised him alone with Mary Louise in the parlor, he had felt an extraordinary need to touch her. That desire, she had shown him instantly, would never be realized. She had loathed him on sight, and had no compunction about showing those feelings, both to him and to everyone else at the dinner table.

"But that, beautiful lady, only makes me want you all the more," he murmured into the stillness of the attic. A challenge to exceed all others. The excitement of a good chase never failed to beguile him, and this time the prize would be well worth whatever methods he chose to seduce her.

Walking to the sofa, he sat down and picked up the pad of thin parchment from the oriental tea table positioned in front of the couch. He leaned his head back and propped his booted feet on the table and stared down at the renderings of Libby Thornhill's face he'd done with colored chalk. Her hair was all wrong, but she'd worn the long, shiny tresses pinned severely at her nape, a crime to his thinking, when a woman owned such magnificent hair. Braided so tightly and coiled at the back of her head, she had effectively disguised the beauty of the glinting gold and copper strands temptingly interwoven with a darker auburn. He had no doubt it would ripple and gleam if she allowed it to cascade down her back, especially under the light of candles. He had mixed far too much gold into the red, he realized; he had needed only a touch to give it the golden sheen he wanted.

Again he realized that he needed to gaze long and hard at

her, take his time examining every facet of her face and curve of her body. He wanted her here, on this couch, alone, posing as he directed her to. He would have to find a way to entice her cooperation, and as he thought of her reaction to such an improper request from him, he gave a low laugh. If he shut his eyes, he could still see her face, the ever composed expression stolen for one revealing moment when he'd suggested she pose in the nude. He had shocked her last night, more than once, but some inner devil had led him to continue to provoke her.

A bright shaft of sunlight suspended with floating golden motes had moved across the arm of the couch, and as the warmth touched his face, he felt the first twinge of fatigue. Though he was used to long hours and little rest, he needed a few hours of sleep to revive himself. He had learned to survive on far less during his years in the Orient and more lately during his secret forays into the French countryside. Though exhilarating enough, his spy missions were behind him now, at least until the urge to live dangerously hit him again.

Ready to give up on Libby's likeness, at least for the time being, he got to his feet and picked up a rag dampened with turpentine. He moved to the window and gazed into the distance as he cleaned his paint-stained fingers. Fog had finally risen over the rolling miles of desolate moors, but the horizon blended into a pale lavender mist where it met the blue sky.

Hours earlier he'd watched the sun come up and enjoyed the ever changing hues of the light on the strange, empty land. Unlike most people, he loved the moors, loved urging his stallion into a full gallop across the purple heather. He did think better there, where it seemed he was the only living person left on the earth.

Perhaps that's what he should do today. Perhaps there in the vast expanses of heath and bogs and little else, he would know what he should do about Henrietta's lovely, very suspicious little friend. Libby Thornhill had complicated his plans since she had shown up so unexpectedly. Not that he hadn't known she'd come eventually, but he had hoped to be long gone by then, away from her nosy questions and obvious distrust.

There was no doubt whatsoever that she suspected foul play. Her vivid green eyes had seemed to penetrate his mind, delving inexorably into his thoughts where he kept hidden his darkest secrets. That lovely gaze had watched him often throughout the dinner hour, though she tried to disguise her interest. He'd seen her contempt as well. Julian shook his head, remembering how close she'd come to accusing him of murdering Henrietta in front of Lasserthon and everyone else present.

Libby Thornhill was complicating his plans, all right, and he found it especially irritating now that he was so close to persuading Mary Louise to take the final step in his plan. In any case, however, he wasn't overly worried about Libby asking questions and snooping around. She would not be able to prove anything against him. He had made damn well sure no one could.

Spreading his fingers, he ran both hands through his hair, tousling it, then rubbing his tired eyes. Still, she was going to be a spear in his side until he got rid of her. If his hunch was correct, Libby Thornhill was already inquiring around about his past and anything else she could worm out of Lasserthon's neighbors. He had seen the way she had jumped at Evelyn Landers's invitation to take tea at her home. He'd have to find a way to deal with her, and soon, before she got to Mary Louse, who just might let slip more than she should.

So soon after the mess with Henrietta, any suspicious circumstances would cause talk. He would have to be cautious with every move he made. There was no question that Libby was extremely bright, even more so than Henrietta, and he had a strong suspicion that the young American widow had already cast Julian in the role of Satan and his legions of demons all rolled into one.

The best course, he'd come to believe, was to get rid of her as soon as possible. Find some way to drive her out of Lasserthon. Perhaps a few more well-aimed insults would be enough, but he strongly doubted it. Henrietta had spoken of Libby often when she'd first arrived at Lasserthon, and he well remembered one of the virtues she'd named Libby to possess. Determination. He had a feeling Libby would soon show him just how much resolve she had in her pretty little head. If she thought him responsible for treachery against Henrietta, she would never rest until she proved his guilt.

"The American woman leaves the manor."

Julian swung around at the sound of Lu Ling's voice. She stood a good distance away, at the other end of the attic, where a flight of narrow steps led up from the servants' floor. She had spoken softly, in Mandarin Chinese, and he answered in kind.

"Is she alone?"

"No, my lord and master, she leaves from the front drive with her serving girl. Afoot. Do you wish them followed?"

Julian nodded. "Tell Chang not to let her see him but to keep her in sight."

Lu Ling placed her palms together, bowing low to him as she backed away. He watched her leave to do his bidding, then strode across the floor and stood at a small round window that overlooked the front drive.

Far below his high vantage point, he could see Libby Thornhill moving out from under the portico roof with her young maid in tow. She was dressed in a gauzy white dress with a light blue pelisse over it. On her way to join Evelyn Landers for tea, no doubt, and an exhaustive interrogation about Henrietta and him. Yes, he'd have to do something about the inquisitive Mrs. Thornhill, and he'd have to do it soon.

As Libby left Lasserthon Manor she kept Alice close beside her. After reading Henrietta's letter the night before, she had decided it wise not to wander around alone, especially inside the mansion. Thank God, she'd had the wisdom to bring Alice to Lasserthon with her. The girl was no body-guard, to be sure, but any assailant would think twice before attacking two healthy young women at once. Halfway down the entrance road, she stopped and glanced back at the imposing facade of Lasserthon Manor.

The edifice rose against the cerulean of the sky but seemed very different now with the sun shining. Last night it had been dark and ominous. This afternoon the plain white walls seemed stark and inhospitable. More like the stone-cold crypt Henrietta had described. Libby resisted the urge to shiver when she caught sight of a figure high up in a circular window, in what she conjectured must be the attics. She'd slept very little and felt tired, her mind groggy from lack of rest. Still, Henrietta's words chased round and round in her mind, like children in a game of catch-me-if-you-can.

Even now, in the light of day, after a pleasant breakfast shared with Raymond in a sunroom overlooking spacious gardens, she could feel the extent of Henrietta's fear. She believed more than ever that Henrietta might very well have been murdered. If that was true, then she could be in a great deal of danger, and so could Alice.

Glancing at the unsuspecting girl walking at her side, Libby felt a keen reluctance to alarm her maid. The girl was timid anyway, and quite the most superstitious person Libby had ever encountered. Nevertheless, for her own safety, Alice should know of Libby's suspicions.

"Alice," she said, drawing up and bringing her maid to a standstill beside her. "I'm going to tell you something that might cause you some fright, but you must promise me that you won't get overly upset and will listen to everything I say."

Alice peered out at her from under her straw bonnet, her eyes squinting curiously behind her smashed bifocals. "Yes, ma'am? You ain't sick, are you, ma'am? From riding so long yesterday in the cold? I went to coughing last night, deep in my chest, and I hear something's been going around hereabouts. Some kind of ague, or some such sickness as that—"

"No, I feel fine. I feel I must put it plainly to you, Alice. I have a strong suspicion that perhaps Henrietta did not die in the way her husband said. I think she might have been murdered."

Alice's face drained of all color; her jaw dropped as if it were made of granite. Her myopic eyes blinked once behind the cracks in her lens. "Murder? Here, ma'am, at Lasserthon Manor. Oh, God help us, who done it to poor Miss Hen?" She twirled around, her black cape billowing out around her. Her face was filled with complete horror as she stared back toward the great house at the edge of the moors.

"Now, be calm, Alice. There's no reason to be frightened at the moment. You'll be perfectly safe as long as the two of us stick together and remain on our guard. I wanted to tell you simply because I fear the murderer might be someone who lives in the house."

"Oh, oh, God Almighty, 'e's still 'ere? Do you know who 'e is, mum? What if 'e 'urts us? What if 'e kills us too, like poor Miss Henrietta?"

"If we're careful, nothing will happen to us."

"But who did it? Everybody's been kind enough."

"True, Alice, but appearances can be deceiving. You know that. You remember Teddy Dotter, I'm sure?"

When Alice's face paled to an ashen hue, Libby wished she hadn't brought up the man's name. Teddy Dotter had lived in their neighborhood in Philadelphia, where for years he'd been a footman for a family by the name of Smith. A kind, elderly man who'd been like a grandfather to his young employer, had one day, for no apparent reason, picked up a pitchfork and stabbed it into his young master's back. As the stable boy ran screaming for help, Teddy had walked calmly into the street into the path of a swift-moving dray wagon. No one had ever figured out why he'd committed the heinous crime.

Alice shivered until her entire body shook like a pennant on a windy day. She peered back at Lasserthon Manor as if she feared it might sprout arms and pull her back into its clutches. She seemed incapable of speech.

"I'm not sure who did it yet," Libby confided, taking the

girl's arm and propelling her down the road once again, "but I'm not leaving here until I do. Until then I want you to stay in my room at night. There's a sofa at the foot of my bed that will be quite comfortable for you."

"Oh, yes, I will. I want to, but, ma'am, don't you think you should tell 'is Grace about poor Miss Hen?"

"Father won't be able to do anything until I have some kind of proof to give him. I found a letter last night that Henrietta wrote, and it was quite clear she was terribly frightened."

"Did she say who was scarin' her? Maybe it was that big butler with the giant 'ead on 'im, you know the one who opened the door to us?" Alice began to quiver, folding her arms across her chest, her fear causing her atrocious accent to reemerge in full control. " 'e does look like a killer, don't 'e, ma'am? Why, 'e be the one who took me upstairs last night! He could've kilt me in my bed, and no one would've known."

"It wasn't him. Henrietta was fond of Greeley. She said he was a kind man."

"But looks be deceivin'! You said so yourself!"

There was more logic in that remark than Libby wished to admit. In truth, the butler could be guilty, at least as much a suspect as anyone else, but Libby's intuition told her otherwise.

"I believe Lord Edmonton to be the guilty party, but I shall have to prove it somehow before I accuse him formally."

"The 'andsome gentleman with those dark blue eyes? The one with the China girl?" Alice's face looked like chalk. "Oh, Lord help me, I met up with that one just outside your door this very morn. 'e could have stuck a knife in me right there where I stood. He could have put his 'ands around me throat and choked the life out o' me. . . ."

From that moment forward, Libby had a distinct feeling that Alice was going to envision her bloody demise in every room of the manor at the hands of everyone from the lowest scullery maid to Lord Lasserthon himself. She was more interested, however, that Julian had been lurking outside her bedroom.

"What was he doing outside my door? Did he seem upset when you saw him?"

"No, ma'am. 'e, I mean, he, well, he was just standing there, almost as if he be listening at your door. Then he turned and saw me coming, and he smiled and told me I looked handsome in me white kerchief." She frowned. "Are you sure 'e did it? He don't look like no killer."

"Don't let yourself be taken in, Alice. From what I understand, he's known far and wide as a man of low moral character. Please, whatever you do, don't reveal my suspicions, not to him or to any of the staff. I only told you these things so you wouldn't do anything foolish or put yourself in jeopardy by going off alone."

"Oh, please, ma'am, tell 'is Grace. He can take care of everything. 'e'll be angry with you for staying here when there's danger all about."

Actually, Alice was handling the news better than she expected, Libby thought. She was even remembering to speak correctly. "We'll go to London in time, and I'll tell Mother and Father the whole story. Until then, hold your tongue and don't chatter about this. Just listen to gossip and watch for anything that seems peculiar. Remember to stay as close to me as possible, especially when Lord Edmonton's nearby. Together we'll be quite safe, I assure you."

"Why don't you tell Miss Henrietta's husband? He could help us, couldn't he?"

"Because he could very well be the killer himself. Truth is, it could be anybody in the village. That's why we must be careful."

Sober as a mourner, Alice sank into thought but continued to wring her hands for the remainder of the walk into town. Libby was beginning to wish she hadn't told the girl. If nothing else, Alice's edginess could give away their mission. They were new to Lasserthon, however. Maybe folks would think Alice always looked ready to jump out of her skin.

Evelyn Landers met her guests at the front door of her lovely old home. A stucco cottage set among a grove of tall elm trees, the structure rose several stories with tall windows stretching out on each side of the entrance. Lustrous green ivy framed the windows in a picturesque fashion, but Libby admired more the roses the lady had mentioned with so much pride, and rightly so. They were displayed in gorgeous array, huge in dimension, and of every hue in the rainbow. They hung like bouquets from the walls of the enclosed garden as well, where Evelyn led them, having ordered a wicker table to be set up for tea time. A huge blue and white porcelain bowl held more cut roses in the center of the table, and the warm breeze wafted unbelievably sweet fragrances around them.

"I'm truly pleased you felt up to coming so soon after your arrival," Evelyn said to Libby as they seated themselves in the shady garden patio. "You must be weary after such a long journey."

Once more Libby realized with some surprise that she had taken an inexplicable, instantaneous liking to the smiling hostess sitting before her. She could readily understand why Henrietta had spoken so highly of her. There was some indefinable aspect of Evelyn Landers that made one feel comfortable in her presence, as if she'd been a lifelong friend. Libby found herself more relaxed than she'd been since finding the letter, and not a little embarrassed when Alice hung about the table, like a hungry mastiff begging for scraps, squinting at poor Evelyn as if she expected the justice of the peace's wife to stab Libby with her bread knife.

"Alice, you may await me in the kitchen, if you wish," Libby suggested, smiling but with a slight indentation of her brows designed to mean enough was enough. Her nonverbal warning obviously flew right over Alice's head. The girl gave her a horrified look.

"Do you think it wise to be 'ere all alone?" Alice hissed in not so low a tone, as if Evelyn were not sitting right beside Libby and could hear their exchange.

"I'll be perfectly safe here with Evelyn. Run along, now. Please, Alice."

Evelyn observed their conversation with some curiosity, and Libby answered her unasked questions, for she knew Evelyn would be much too polite to question her. "Alice is a dear girl but a bit overprotective of me, I'm afraid. She means well, of course."

"Oh, I think that's grand, that she respects you so much. She seems a good girl, though I wonder how she can see through those horribly cracked glasses."

"She broke her spectacles aboard ship, and we've not had time to purchase her a new pair. Perhaps shortly we can see to that errand in the village."

Evelyn nodded, then upon being asked by Libby about her garden began telling the origins of many of her rosebushes, some of which, she revealed proudly, had grown in the garden for decades, planted before she and her husband took possession of the grange. Libby listened politely, all the while wishing to turn the subject toward Lord Lasserthon and his dangerous friend. She got her chance with Evelyn's final comment.

"Henrietta did so love to come here. She mentioned once that you had a lovely garden spot at your home in Philadelphia. She said she'd often join you there for tea. That's one reason I thought you might enjoy taking tea out here in the fresh air. Especially since we've enjoyed such an early, warm spring this year. I must tell you, Mrs. Thornhill, that Henrietta reminisced about those afternoons spent with you with a great deal of nostalgia."

"Please call me Libby. I already feel as if we've been friends for a long time." Evelyn gave a gracious nod, and Libby continued. "We were the best of friends. I feared she'd be lonely here in England, so I'm most pleased to learn she had someone so kind with whom she could talk." Libby lifted her dainty yellow cup and swallowed a mouthful of tea, finding it smooth and aromatic, soothing to nerves still ragged from a night spent tossing and turning. Replacing her teacup on the saucer, she added, in as nonchalant a fashion as she could muster, "She mentioned once in a letter that she was quite put off by Lord Edmonton. I must say, after dinner last night I can readily understand her disdain for the man."

Evelyn picked up the delicate scallop-edged serving dish that held artfully arranged oatmeal cookies, shortbread, and iced petit fours. As Libby selected a piece of crisp short-bread, Evelyn nodded. "I could see last night that you were offended by a good many of Julian's remarks."

"And you were not?"

Smiling, Evelyn placed several oatmeal cookies on her own plate. She nodded. "Of course. I've found it hard my-self to overlook some of his more outrageous comments, though I've decided he often makes them for the shock they incur upon his companions."

"That seems a bit immature, doesn't it? For a grown man. A gentleman of wealth and stature. Why do you suppose he'd wish to scandalize those around him?"

Evelyn lifted a slender shoulder in a slight shrug. "Who can say? No one knows him well, and I daresay he doesn't share his innermost thoughts with any of us, unless possibly Lord Lasserthon."

"Is Julian married?" Libby had wondered such more than once but didn't really think so because there'd been no men-tion of a wife at dinner. Even if he was, she doubted he'd in-terrupt his lascivious lifestyle just to please a wife or submit to any decent moral standards.

"Julian's never been married, or betrothed, as far as I know." She paused, studying Libby's interested face. "I do hope you'll give him a chance to redeem himself. He isn't as wicked a per-son as you seem to think. In fact, he's done many a good turn for people hereabouts at one time or another."

Surely the woman jested, Libby thought, barely able to contain the scornful reply lolling dangerously on the tip of her tongue. She wondered if Evelyn had some past relation-ship with the handsome Earl of Edmonton, perhaps herself a victim of his deadly charm. She knew she could not ask, so she kept the conversation casual.

"Julian, a Good Samaritan? What sort of kind deeds are at-tributed to him, might I ask? I had suspected by my own observations and some of Henrietta's comments that he was not to be trusted."

"That's quite true about Henrietta. She shared her fears with me early on, and I revealed to her the same thing I just told you, that it amused Julian to be offensive, for some reason known only to him. As she got to know him better, I believe she gradually became used to his ways."

Libby knew better, but she merely inquired, "Why do you say that?"

"I don't know, really. She just seemed more relaxed in his presence in the weeks before her death. He can be quite charming and solicitous when he wishes."

He hadn't displayed much charm in her presence, but it was interesting to know that Henrietta felt easier with him toward the end, at least from Evelyn's point of view. Had Julian enticed Henrietta into a tryst around that time? Perhaps one she immediately regretted and wished to end, only to have him go into a rage when she dared to spurn him? A lover's rejection had been the motive for many a murder.

"Julian's had a tragic life in some ways," Evelyn murmured as she lowered her teacup. "Though he never speaks of his past, and truly it's mostly idle gossip I've heard from various people. Which I really should not, in good conscience, repeat to you. My husband would be quite disappointed if he found me gossiping like a fishwife. But I do mention it now, only because you find him so disagreeable. He's weathered hardships that may have caused some of his peculiarities."

"Please enlighten me. I know little about him, actually. Are his landholdings nearby?"

"His estates are a half day's ride south. Quite extensive too, as I understand it. He is rumored to be very wealthy, and now that his paintings have been so well received in London, he is the current rage of the *ton*." She chuckled and dabbed the corner of her mouth with her white linen napkin. "Not that my husband and I are always included in such grand affairs. Julian has invited us to his home several times before, though we have yet to join him for any of his weekend affairs. However, we do plan to attend Sir John's engagement party, the one Julian mentioned to you last night. I hope you'll decide to come with us. Though his soirees are said to be quite wild and uninhibited, especially his weekend hunts, I'm sure he will make everything perfect for Sir John and Miss Baird."

"I should be surprised if any party of his was not wild and uninhibited."

Evelyn laughed. "You will not give up your ill opinion of Lord Edmonton any time soon, I'd wager to say."

"If he shows another side, perhaps I'll understand your kind remarks concerning his character, but as of the moment I find him quite repugnant."

"Not many women would agree with you, my dear." She sighed, pursing her lips and shaking her head. "I fear poor Mary Louise is smitten. She's vulnerable to his charms because she has not yet grown to love her betrothed husband. Theirs was an arranged marriage, you understand, and he so much older than she. Actually, it was Lasserthon who introduced them and helped secure the match. I don't know the man very well, but he does seem to dote on the child."

Libby thought that pretty well described her own short-lived marriage with John. Except that Libby had been loyal and faithful during their betrothal and marriage. She had adored him, not only as a mate but as a good friend.

"You referred to a tragedy in Julian's past. I don't recall Henrietta mentioning anything about that."

"I'm not sure she knew. She always talked more of home and how she missed America. She mentioned you often, Libby, and a few other friends. I understood she had no family left there."

Libby shook her head. "Her father died suddenly just months before she left for England." Libby was annoyed that Evelyn kept turning the subject away from Julian's dark past. She searched for a suitable maneuver to get the conversation on track but was saved the effort when Evelyn returned to the subject of her own volition.

"Since I've heard some aspects of Julian's life, I've been more charitable in my censure. Some stories are every bit as scandalous as you might expect, others are not."

"Scandalous?" Libby prompted, trying not to show her eagerness, but eager to hear the sordid details she was.

Evelyn glanced up toward the room that she had pointed out earlier as her husband's study while showing Libby around the garden. "I'd not want Jasper to overhear me telling you these things, but since you are staying a time at Lasserthon Manor and feel so uncomfortable with Julian, I think I should try to alleviate your fears."

"Thank you. I do appreciate your concern."

"Well, the worst thing I've heard is that he shot his own brother-in-law."

So unexpected was the revelation that for a moment Libby could only stare at her. "Shot him? Do you mean in a duel? Did he kill him?"

Evelyn nodded. "He supposedly hit him square between the eyes. Julian's well known for his prowess with a pistol."

"What happened? How could his sister ever forgive him for such a thing?"

"Though they tried to keep it quiet"—Evelyn lowered her voice even more—"I understand that she took her own life."

"Because of what Julian did to her husband?"

"I've always heard that his sister killed herself before the duel was fought. Unlike most London scandals, it's all been kept very secretive and hushed up, but if it's true, it certainly would be enough to cause Julian to become embittered."

"Indeed it would," Libby agreed thoughtfully. "And no one knows the truth about the reason for the duel?"

"None that I know of. The Rainville family was always quite wealthy and powerful, but there was some sort of scandal concerning the family name years and years ago, I'm not even sure when it was. Something to do with his older brother and a woman. The brother died shortly after, I believe, leaving the title to Julian. Whatever it was, it ruined the family name. Julian's worked very hard to reestablish himself and gain back the wealth lost to him. He made a fortune when he was in the Orient, it's said."

"Doing what, I wonder?" Libby had a few less than savory ideas as to what he might've gotten into, including white slavery, after having witnessed the unfortunate Lu Ling groveling to meet his every whim. Anger erupted inside her, just thinking about him keeping the poor woman as his gentleman's valet. It was indecent.

"I have no idea, dear. But you see, he's not had the ideal life. He's no doubt been stamped in some way by his past. I always try to remember that when he utters some disgraceful remark, then smiles at the gasps he elicits. He was at his worst last night, I must say, and I cannot fathom the reason why. He's usually much more civil and proper."

Libby wasn't sure she could believe that Julian wasn't being his usual crude self. It was interesting to know his background, however, even in so sketchy a manner.

"What about Lasserthon?" she asked, leaning back in her chair. "Have they always been good friends?"

"That's a question I cannot answer." Evelyn busied herself by refilling Libby's cup, then poured more for herself as Libby sipped the newly warmed tea. "Actually, Julian wasn't hereabouts so often before Raymond married Henrietta. After she arrived from America, Julian began to visit Lasserthon Manor more often, and stayed for longer periods of time. I always thought he seemed rather fond of Henrietta. You know better than anyone how sweet and gentle she was. Though I really cannot say for sure, because I rarely saw the three of them together. It was only when Henrietta came here that I was able to spend time with her. I do miss her. She was a very agreeable companion."

"I know. I miss her too. More than I can tell you."

The two women shared a moment when their eyes misted, filled with regret over the loss of their mutual friend. Afterward they sat in companionable silence, speaking of the weather and other unimportant topics.

A short time later Jasper joined them with his usual bluster and roar, and the subject turned to far less personal subjects. Libby waited a suitable length of time, then politely begged leave. On the way home, with Alice sticking to her like a cocklebur to wool, Libby let herself digest all she'd learned and ended up concluding that Julian now seemed even more a suspect in Henrietta's death.

As Libby and her maid came up the road from the village, Julian was cantering down the driveway from his afternoon ride on the moors. He dismounted at the portico and handed his reins over to the lad who'd been awaiting his return. He'd timed the arrival rather well, he decided as he pulled off his leather riding gloves and slapped them against his thigh, his eyes on the beautiful young widow from America. Libby Thornhill did not look any happier to see him than she had the night before. If looks could wield a knife, he'd already be in his grave. She loathed him enough to amuse him and made it quite easy to provoke her.

"Good day, Mrs. Thornhill," he said with a slight bow as she approached. Her maid gave him a momentary fright, however, when she came up very close as if she couldn't see him well. When she did recognize him, she looked as if she'd run upon a stampeding elephant. She gave a peculiar squeaking sound and pressed up against her mistress, whispering something that sounded suspiciously like, "It's him, it's him."

Her mistress looked distinctly embarrassed, though she did not look any more friendly. "Forgive Alice, Lord Edmonton. She's rather nearsighted and was startled to find you here." When she glanced at her servant, who looked absolutely terrorized, she added, "Alice is a bit on edge today."

On edge? Good God, the girl's eyes looked ready to explode out of their sockets. She actually shook when he settled his gaze on her. No doubt her mistress had shared her less than complimentary opinion of him.

"Perhaps you could invest in some eyeglasses for the poor girl. She's looking at me like I'm ready to steal your purse."

Alice gasped loudly and took a protective stance near the

black net purse dangling from her mistress's arm. Libby obviously had had enough.

"Alice, really, don't hover so. Please go along and draw me a bath, if you will."

"Oh, ma'am, I couldn't leave you alone here, not now." The chit peered suspiciously at Julian, and he had a feeling that she was trying to get him into focus.

"Do as I bid you, Alice."

Julian grinned at the girl. "That's right, Alice, I'll keep an eye on your mistress for you. Actually, I was just going to invite her to join me for tea. Or do you Americans still prefer to throw your tea into harbors?"

"Only when necessary, my lord." Libby Thornhill gazed up at him, quite level and assessing, with none of her maid's myopic squint. He tried to memorize the vivid green for later that evening when he made a second attempt at her likeness.

Julian was surprised that she agreed to stand chatting with him. It wasn't lost on him that she'd rather catch the pox than suffer his company. Unfortunately, the freckled little maid refused to obey Libby's instruction. He watched, straight-faced, as the maid took the liberty of drawing Libby a short distance away from him, where she commenced what Julian assumed to be an animated, low-pitched list of reasons why she shouldn't be expected to prepare her mistress's toilette. He waited patiently, but the matter was settled when Libby gave her a stern look that finally got the girl's attention. At last the girl dragged off, albeit reluctantly, but kept turning back, just to make sure Julian wasn't grabbing at Libby's worldly goods.

"Forgive me, Mrs. Thornhill, but you do seem to have a rather peculiar relationship with your maid."

"She's merely protective of me."

"You'll come to no harm in my company, I assure you."

"I daresay not, sir, because I have other errands to accomplish. Good day."

Julian watched her walk up the steps and join her maid, who still lingered stubbornly despite her mistress's orders. He wondered if Libby was as afraid of him as her maid appeared to be. There was no question now that Henrietta must have passed along something to make Libby distrust his motives. He would have to find a way to ferret out of her exactly what Henrietta had said. Libby Thornhill was no fool, and he had a feeling she knew exactly what he'd done. The thought disconcerted him.

Chapter Six

At precisely eight o'clock Libby entered the dining room, bracing herself for another confrontation with Julian. Neither she nor Alice had handled the afternoon encounter on the driveway well at all. Both surprised and relieved, she found Lasserthon sitting alone at one end of the long table.

With his usual impeccable manners, Raymond stood, a wide smile on his face as he walked to greet her. Suddenly afraid her primary suspect had fled the premises before she could prove his guilt, she quickly inquired about Julian.

"And where is Lord Edmonton this evening? Will he not be joining us? I fully expected a dinner hour where I would be subjected to his rude remarks."

Raymond chuckled. "I sensed last night that you didn't care for Julian. He's a man who one must tolerate for a time before affection can grow. Henrietta didn't care for him at first either, but she realized eventually that he isn't half the ogre he pretends to be."

Allowing him to draw back her chair, she seated herself, smoothed her skirts, then studied him as he retook his place beside her at the head of the table.

"Indeed? From what Henrietta said in her letters to me, it appeared she grew more leery of him the longer his stay here at Lasserthon."

Raymond made no comment as he signaled to Greeley, waiting at the sideboard, that they were ready to dine. Libby spread the large maroon napkin atop her lap as a savory beef and onion soup was ladled into her bowl. Only after Raymond was served did he respond to her observation.

"I suppose Henrietta revealed a good deal to you in her letters about our life here at the manor."

Instantly Libby became alert, tried to hide her reaction to his question behind a bland expression. She hedged about the truth. "Why, yes, in some regards. She did make mention of Julian's presence occasionally and indicated she found him unsettling."

"He does have that effect on people, especially women like Henrietta. She was incredibly shy when she first arrived here. Perhaps that's why his outspoken manner intimidated her."

When he lifted a spoonful of soup, Libby sampled her own fare and found it perfectly seasoned and delicious. Though she was hungry, she was more interested in the conversation than the food and realized belatedly that Raymond had skillfully circumvented her inquiry as to Julian's whereabouts. She pressed the point.

"Has Edmonton left our company for good, or should we expect him to join us later this evening?"

"Oh, he's still here. I saw him earlier after he'd returned from his ride. That's a daily ritual with him, but I daresay at the moment he's closeted himself upstairs in the attics. He'll probably stay there for the rest of the night."

Baffled by his remark, Libby regarded him, her spoon poised halfway to her mouth. "In the attics? Whatever for?"

Raymond smiled at her quizzical expression. "He works there. When he requested a studio for his use while here, I offered him a spacious chamber on the second floor, but he preferred the solitude of the garret. Why, I can't fathom. Last time I was up there, the place was covered in dust, and drafty as well. I had it cleaned and furnished appropriately for him, of course. Julian apparently likes the peace and quiet. Says his Muse can find him there." Raymond motioned for Greeley to refill his wine goblet but studied Libby as he continued. "On several occasions he's locked himself up there, then gone days without talking to a soul, except for Lu Ling, of course, who takes him his meals. At times he's quite passionate about his work."

Libby decided his latest work in progress most undoubtedly was the poor, infatuated Mary Louise. Libby wouldn't have been surprised at all if the girl was found chained in the attics for Julian's carnal appetites. Her neutral reply bore little resemblance to her inner thoughts.

"He's quite peculiar, wouldn't you agree?"

Raymond nodded as if that was indeed common knowledge to all who knew Edmonton, then delved heartily into the portion of roasted lamb that Greeley had just placed on his plate. While she considered ways of turning the discussion back to Julian, Raymond inquired about her day.

"Did you enjoy your visit with Evelyn? She's such a delightful woman and an absolute wizard at growing roses. I suppose you were quite impressed with her garden."

"Quite, yes. I've never seen blossoms so big, not even in the finest conservatory in Philadelphia. Her entire garden was filled with the sweetest fragrance. She's quite easy to get to know. She told me all sorts of stories about you and her other friends from the village."

Raymond tensed noticeably, then covered his reaction by draining his wine and calling for more. Libby watched him take the decanter and refill his goblet, then hers, sensing his discomfort and wondering why he feared what she might have heard. Perhaps she had settled upon Julian too quickly and Lasserthon himself deserved further investigation. The revealing moment was fleeting, however, as he smiled at her, once again appearing perfectly relaxed.

"And what notorious secrets did Evelyn reveal to you about our quiet little hamlet?"

Libby smiled at the teasing quality of his question. "Actually, the only revelations that could be construed as such were in her mention of Lord Edmonton's past. It seems Julian was embroiled in a tragedy concerning his sister?" She waited, wanting Raymond either to confirm or deny the tale, and if she was lucky, elaborate with the details. He didn't disappoint her.

"Aye, that was an unfortunate situation indeed. As I understand it, he was off on one of his voyages to the Orient when it all came around about his sister. I didn't know the Rainville family well at that time, but I can remember hearing rumors that his sister, Victoria, threw herself to her death out of her bedroom window. It was said that she was unhappy in her marriage. Apparently Julian blamed her husband for her death and challenged him to a duel. Of course, guilty or not, the poor man was killed. Julian's most assuredly one of the best shots in England, if not the best. It would take a stalwart man to face him. Of course, in this particular case Julian did the challenging, and in such a public forum, a crowded coffeehouse, I believe, that the unfortunate fellow had little recourse but to meet him on the field of honor."

"I see." Trying to appear only mildly interested, though she wanted to ask a hundred different questions about the scandal, she spread honey onto a warm biscuit that had been offered to her moments before. She realized with some surprise that she was actually enjoying herself. Henrietta's husband was turning out to be a pleasant enough dinner companion. He put her at her ease, and both tonight and that morning at the breakfast table she had found conversation with him easy and entertaining. She had yet to reason why Henrietta had come to dislike him so thoroughly. Then again, it was certain Raymond displayed his most exemplary behavior in her presence. She wasn't foolish enough to be swayed by his accommodating ways and good manners. Henrietta had been a wise woman, and a good judge of character. If she'd become disenchanted with her husband, there had been a good reason why.

"Do you believe that Julian's sister's untimely death might have changed him into the unconventional man he's become?" she asked casually.

"I didn't know Julian well until a few years ago, though we attended the same school when we were lads. We saw each other now and again because of the proximity of our estates. It was only after I wed Henrietta that he began to visit the manor more regularly. I once accused him of extending his visits here for the sole purpose of enjoying the company of my wife."

"What did Julian say to that?" Libby was most intrigued to hear his response. In her mind, Raymond had every right to demand such answers from a man of Julian's disreputable character.

"He said, 'Of course I only come here to see Henrietta. She is a beautiful woman, is she not? Surely you don't think I come to see you?' " Raymond laughed, as if enjoying his friend's quip for the first time.

Libby smiled, thinking it sounded precisely like something a rogue like Julian would say. Her cheeks grew warm with resentment, for it appeared more and more to her that Julian had targeted Henrietta for seduction. Julian had something to do with Henrietta's death. Libby felt it so strongly that she was shaken by her certainty. Even if he hadn't taken a gun or knife and murdered Libby's friend in cold blood, he could have done something else, some unconscionable act that had driven Henrietta out onto the moors where she'd come to harm.

Clenching her fingers around the crystal goblet in her hand, Libby imagined how frightened Henrietta must have been, if that indeed had been the case. Perhaps he'd tried to seduce her, or even worse, forced her into intimacy against her will, perhaps up in the attics, which he locked against others of the household. If that was so, if he'd harmed Henrietta, Libby would never rest until he paid for that crime.

For a while she remained silent, containing her aroused anger and nursing her determination to know the truth. She listened with one ear as Raymond described his day's activities. Apparently he'd ridden to call upon his tenant farms that lay to the east. With a few casual inquiries she managed to draw out the fact that he was likely to follow the same course every day, alternating the farmers on whom he called. A habit that had most likely left Henrietta inside the house alone to fend off his lecherous friend.

Even Evelyn had recounted her concern over the frequency with which Henrietta had escaped her home to visit the village. Was Henrietta so eager to be away because Raymond's work schedule left her unprotected from Julian? If that was so, why then did Henrietta reveal in her letters that she was pleased when Raymond was away? Had their marriage become so untenable? Had this man, seemingly so kind and unimposing, revealed a streak of cruelty to his wife that others did not see? That idea seemed incomprehensible to Libby, but she had Henrietta's feelings written in her own handwriting to verify it, had she not? She vowed then that Raymond could not be erased from her suspicions, not until she proved beyond a doubt that Julian was the sole person responsible for Henrietta's death.

When Libby returned to her bedroom later that evening, after a pleasant game of chess with Raymond in his book-lined study, she shared with her maid all she'd learned that day. As Alice helped her to unbutton the back of her gown, Libby was pleased she had an ally in the house, even one as frightened as Alice. Poor Henrietta had had no one she could trust or confide in.

By the time she'd donned her white lawn nightgown and robe and sat before the mirror, however, she was beginning to regret having mentioned anything to little Alice. The maid's fears had grown increasingly worse, and to Libby's growing annoyance Alice continually ran to the door to make sure it was locked securely. By the third time she did so, Libby told her in no uncertain terms to get hold of herself.

"Oh, ma'am, I just can't stop thinking about it. What if he comes and murders me in me bed!"

"Alice, be sensible. We're safe here in my bedroom with the door locked. Go on to bed, if you like. I can brush my hair myself."

"Oh, I'm sure I couldn't get a wink o' sleep. Me heart sounds like a drum, it does. All I can think about is poor Miss Hen and all her sufferin'."

Libby turned from where she sat at the dressing table and considered Alice. The girl stood wringing her hands, and her chest heaved with her worried breathing. "You've got to stop this, do you hear, Alice? If I give you a drop or two of laudanum to help you sleep, will you stop that pacing about? You're making me nervous too."

"Oh, yes, thank you, ma'am, I know that'd help me go right off to sleep." At Libby's direction, Alice retrieved the vial Libby kept in her small leather medicine chest.

"Not so much, Alice," she warned as the girl took a hearty swig of the remedy, as if she were quenching her thirst rather than partaking of a sleeping potion. With that much laudanum in her stomach, Alice would certainly sleep like the dead.

As the grateful Alice settled down on the couch at the foot of the bed and snuggled underneath a mountain of patchwork quilts, Libby returned to her own thoughts. Briefly she reconsidered her decision not to involve her father. Now that she had additional reason to believe there had been foul play in Henrietta's death, perhaps he could use his ducal influence to bring the perpetrator to justice. She soon dropped that idea for fear her father would drop everything and rush down to assist her, something she knew from past experience he was apt to do. At times he managed to intervene far more than she wished him to, or was the least bit necessary.

The truth was, and despite the fact that she adored him, her father could be the most stubborn man in England. She smiled, well aware that at the same time he was good and kind, and mostly well meaning when he involved himself in her affairs. Her mother was a master at getting around his obstinacy, even when he was in a fierce rage or setting down the most rigid of edicts. It seemed all her mother needed do was smile sweetly and reason calmly, and Libby's father would eventually succumb to her wishes.

Unfortunately, Libby hadn't inherited her mother's knack of appeasing her father, especially not in this particular situation. "What in thunder were you thinking!" he'd roar furiously, a reproof she remembered quite well from her childhood and beyond. True, she'd been a headstrong child and readily admitted it. He'd also disapproved of her marriage to John, wishing her, of course, to have a London Season and wed a suitably titled Englishman, both of which she had adamantly refused to do. She loved America and what it stood for too much to leave it for England's more rigidly class-conscious society with all its rules of propriety.

Sighing, she brought the brush down through her long hair, realizing how much she'd missed her parents. It wouldn't be long before she could travel on to London and see them again. And Burke. The two of them had always been close, since they were little children. It would be wonderful to spend time with him.

When her hair lay in gleaming waves over her shoulders, she found herself still too restless to think of sleeping. She found herself pacing from the fireplace to the window, then back again. The idea that Julian had not been seen since she'd encountered him on the driveway worried her. What if he was off somewhere at this very moment, perhaps stalking some other innocent victim? Or perhaps he was too busy trysting with the love-stricken Mary Louise while her betrothed husband remained completely unaware of what was going on beneath his nose. That, indeed, was the more likely of the two scenarios. She wondered if he was still upstairs in the attic, and what he was doing there.

Libby glanced at Alice. All she could see of her maid underneath the soft quilts was the ruffle on her nightcap and a few wiry brown curls peeking out from under it. She lay unmoving, soft, hissing snores the only sound in the room, other than the quiet crackle of the fire.

Glad for the peace and quiet, Libby paused at the window. Fog had settled in again, giving the effect that the house was the only one left in the world. Underneath the shreds of misty gray the moors lay hidden, dark and vast and endlessly mysterious. It seemed as if she stood at the helm of a ghostly ship navigating its way through a deep, impenetrable ocean. The whole place seemed spooky, especially at night, and Libby folded her arms across her chest and gripped her shoulders. She shivered, experiencing the loneliness that Henrietta had described so vividly.

For a moment she remained where she was, uncertain how she should proceed. Julian's handsome face chased across her mind and made her frown. She couldn't get him out of her thoughts, even when she wanted to. He was so different from any other man she'd ever met. The strange, exotic air he wore about him intrigued her despite herself, as did the sordid scandals that blackened his past.

Everything she'd learned thus far pointed to his guilt, but was that what troubled her? It seemed at times as if he baited her intentionally, as if he was working diligently to make her believe ill of him. Libby straightened from where she had leaned against the window frame, slowly digesting that last thought. Was that the reason he affected her so?

A sharp rap on her door startled her so much that she froze, then spun around, fear catching in her throat. She stared at the locked door, alarmed, but quickly got hold of herself. She was not a cowardly person, never had been. She looked at Alice. Her maid was snoring happily, oblivious to her surroundings.

Suddenly more curious to see who lurked about so late at night than afraid to open the door, Libby picked up the heavy silver candlestick she'd left burning on her bedside table. It could double as an appropriate weapon if need be. She'd open the door, find out what was amiss so late. After all, what could happen with Alice only a few feet away? She was sure she already knew who she'd find outside. How like Julian it would be to creep around in the night, frightening people.

When she stood at the portal, however, she did hesitate, always one to examine the ramifications of her acts. When she pressed her ear against the heavy wooden door, she heard nothing.

Slowly she turned the key and eased open the door. Only the velvet black of the corridor met her vision. She stepped outside, thinking she'd see the illumination of a candle moving away but immediately bumped into a solid form that nearly sent her tumbling. She caught herself by grabbing the door frame. She let out a low cry as a dark figure suddenly materialized in front of her, but when she thrust her candle toward it, she realized with some shock, it was not a handsome blue-eyed rake, but his Chinese serving woman.

"What are you doing here?" Libby demanded breathlessly, but the quilted mat still lying in front of her portal answered her question well enough. "Why are you sleeping outside my door?" Then she became angry when the woman refused to answer. "Answer me! Why are you here? What do you want?"

The woman's eyes were so dark and limpid that they reflected Libby's candle flame in a pinpoint of gold. She shook her head as if she did not understand. Libby had a feeling the Chinese woman could understand a lot more than she allowed, but before she could say more, Lu Ling began to speak, a long, seemingly frantic discourse in rapid, incomprehensible Chinese.

Libby didn't understand one word, of course, but it wasn't hard to grasp when Julian's servant motioned for Libby to follow her. Did she wish to talk to Libby somewhere else, privately, so no one would know? Perhaps reveal something about her master? Full of suspicions, Libby scrutinized the woman's face, looking for craftiness or evil intentions, but Lu Ling only smiled, turning her oval face into the guileless innocence of a child. She was truly lovely to look upon, fascinating and foreign, and very different from anyone Libby was accustomed to.

Somehow Libby felt sure the woman wished her no harm, and unfortunately, Libby's curiosity flooded over her better judgment. Just where did Lu Ling wish to lead her? To some piece of evidence that would shine light on Henrietta's death? It could be. Or it might not be. She might lead Libby straight into terrible danger. To Julian's lair above in the attics was much more likely the destination.

Nevertheless excitement rushed through her, making her heart race. She definitely wanted to find out. Her father had always warned that her curiosity would plunge her into deep trouble, and he'd been correct on more than one occasion.

On the other hand, Libby wasn't stupid, nor was she reckless. She knew better than to waltz off alone with Julian's foreign serving girl. No, of course she wouldn't do that. She'd take Alice along, just to be safe. The two of them together could handle a woman of Lu Ling's size, even if she lured them into harm's way. Even Julian couldn't subdue them both at once, not with them wary of his every movement.

"Wait here," Libby whispered to Lu Ling, then raised an

open palm to explain her meaning. She handed the candlestick to Lu Ling, who took it, nodding and smiling as if quite pleased by Libby's decision. Libby took heart at that, thinking perhaps she could ferret out information about Julian from the maid.

Hurrying across the room by the flickering firelight, Libby unceremoniously shook Alice's shoulder.

"Alice, quick, wake up! Come quick!"

Alice roused and peeped out from underneath the quilt, but her eyes were noticeably blurred from the laudanum. She groped for her spectacles, perched them on her nose, and tried to focus on Libby's face. "What? Where are we goin'?"

"You've got to get up, Alice. The Chinese woman wants us to follow her."

"Who?"

Still groggy, Alice didn't move quickly enough for Libby. She threw back the comforter and pulled Alice's legs off the couch. "Hurry up, now, before she changes her mind! She might want to tell us something about Julian."

"But she can't talk, can she?" Alice was finally waking up now, or at least trying to. "I mean in plain English that we can understand?"

"I only want to see where she intends to take us. Perhaps she wants me to help her escape Julian. He considers her his slave; he admitted it in front of everyone. Perhaps she wants us to help her gain her freedom."

The idea excited Libby and propelled her to continue with her plan while all the time her more pragmatic side was telling her to close the door in Lu Ling's face and make sure it was securely locked. However, she was not one to always listen to her practical side, not when something important beckoned. She did take time to snatch up the silver letter opener from the bedside table. She slipped it into her pocket just in case.

"Alice, hurry now, get your robe on!"

Alice grumbled under her breath, then stumbled sleepily after Libby, obviously still quite affected by the sleeping drug. Libby was pleased to find Lu Ling waiting patiently.

The woman lifted a forefinger to her lips in a gesture of silence, then started off down the hall, beckoning them to follow. Libby smiled, pleased that she had found a way for them to communicate. Still, she had a strong hunch Lu Ling understood everything going on around her very well indeed, and if the woman did understand English, there were many questions Libby wanted to ask her. Well, she'd know soon enough, she thought, following Julian's servant down the hall, the yawning Alice firmly in tow.

Chapter Seven

Halfway down the deserted hallway Libby was brought to a halt by a ferocious case of better judgment. Her abrupt stop brought Alice stumbling into her back, and the sleepy maid let out a startled yelp and just managed to catch her glasses before they tumbled off her nose. Libby groaned as all ten of Alice's fingernails dug painfully into her arm.

"Shh, Alice, you're going to wake up the house!"

All around them the house lay in dead silence, and her whisper hissed fiercely like a yodel down a chimney. She cringed, hoping Lasserthon wouldn't hear the disturbance and rush out of his bedchamber to confront them. Alice was not to be pacified. She was still holding on to Libby like a lifeline to shore. They moved off again, together, very together since Alice was stuck to her like a wood tick. The hall suddenly went dark as Lu Ling turned a corner with the candlestick.

"Oh, lordy, oh, lordy . . ."

"Hush, Alice," Libby gritted through her teeth, wishing she hadn't given Alice the laudanum, wishing the servants hadn't doused the lamps so early, though in truth, it wasn't early at all, she reminded herself. She must be crazy, blithely following Julian's servant into the dark reaches of the house. Why was she, for heaven's sake? Why didn't she just turn back? she wondered as they rounded the corner and found Lu Ling waiting for them at the other end of the corridor. Libby stopped, misgivings ballooning as she resisted Alice's efforts to pull her back the way they'd come. For the most part she wasn't the sort of person to plunge herself into peril, but her intuition was telling her that she was in no danger. She tugged her resisting maid forward.

When they had nearly reached Lu Ling, the Chinese girl disappeared into a narrow-walled servant stair and climbed upward into pitch blackness. Pausing, Libby reconsidered. It didn't take a genius to deduce Lu Ling's intention. She was taking them into the uncharted territory of Julian's attic lair.

Doubt raised its head and plagued her momentarily, as if fate were wagging a warning finger in her direction. No, no, it was saying. Use your head. This is not a good thing to do. Wary, she took a deep breath and wondered what had possessed her to strike off in the dead of night with a woman she didn't know well whose loyalty lay with a man she felt had murdered her friend. Not particularly prudent, to say the least.

Libby stood unmoving at the bottom of the steps. Was it really likely that if she did climb the stairs, Julian was lying there in wait to send both Alice and her to their destruction? Somehow she couldn't imagine it. Then why could she imagine he'd harmed Henrietta?

A better question might be why Julian had sent his servant to fetch her. Because the late hour would assure him that no one would bear witness to his assault? The thought was unsettling, especially when she considered that Henrietta might have fallen for the same ruse.

Almost to the top of the door leading into the attics now, Lu Ling stopped, as if she'd just become aware they were no longer following her. She stood looking down at them, the candle held just below her face. Her skin glowed golden in the flickering shadows, her dark eyes completely inscrutable. Patiently she waited, saying and doing nothing to encourage their cooperation. Though Libby tried to resist her growing impulse to find out exactly what awaited her above, indeed knew full well she should do just about anything else but drag Alice up the stairs rising before her, she could not resist the temptation.

In any case, she surmised—knowing, of course, that she was rationalizing—Alice was her trump card, was she not?

If Julian meant her harm, he'd have two victims to dispatch, and surely that would be too messy. Even Edmonton wouldn't be so daft as to commit a double murder right here under his host's nose. What would he do with their bodies? How would he explain them vanishing so soon after Henrietta's disappearance? The sheer melodrama of the idea caused her to relax, almost laugh, but not quite.

"Come on, Alice, let's see where she plans to take us."

Alice was not bashful about objecting. "No, ma'am, no, 'e's up there waitin' for us. 'e'll murder us, 'e will—"

That's as far as the maid got before Libby clamped her hand over her mouth. "Listen, now. Trust me. We're perfectly safe. Have I ever let anything bad happen to you?"

Alice started a vigorous nodding before Libby's words were out. Libby was aware the girl was probably thinking of the time the city watch had detained them for loitering outside the house of a man Libby had been investigating for a story about English spies. Unfortunately, she hadn't come up with the evidence to prove her suspicions concerning him, and even though they'd been questioned only briefly, Alice had been quite traumatized by the incident.

"Well, except for that time with the constabulary, but everything turned out fine, didn't it?" she conceded. "Oh, truly, Alice, what do you fear? That Julian's going to up and murder the both of us just for the novelty of killing two people at once?"

"Well, you was the one that said 'e been murderin' ladies!" Alice pointed out shrilly, her eyes magnified with fright, at least as far as Libby could tell through the egg-crackled lenses.

Until this last heated exchange their whispering had been low, but Alice's voice had risen dramatically in proportion to her resistance to go on. Lu Ling descended a step or two toward them. Libby tightened her grip on Alice's arm, but the maid dug in her heels like a balking donkey. Finally Libby's tugging brought the girl's capitulation, but she didn't come quietly. The sound of her anxious muttering filled the stairwell.

Libby was beginning to think she shouldn't have painted

Julian in such an ill light to the maid. She should have just kept her suspicions to herself, knowing how timid and superstitious Alice was. And why had she brought up the fact that Teddy Dotter had been a cold-blooded pitchfork killer?

Julian might be dangerous in some ways, but she still did not feel they were presently in danger. On the other hand, she was pleased she had slipped the letter opener into her pocket, just in case her intuition let her down. In any case, they'd come too far to stop now.

When Lu Ling turned and began to climb again, Libby felt a rising excitement as she followed, and Alice seemed to have resigned herself to whatever was to be. At least she wasn't trying to get loose anymore. At the top of the steps they turned to the right and proceeded down a chilly, dark hall until they reached another steep flight of steps that could lead nowhere but into the garret. Alice was slowing down and breathing heavily, but Libby was determined to find out what Julian was up to.

"We're perfectly safe as long as we're together," she reiterated in an undertone. "My goodness, Alice, what do you think he could possibly do to the two of us?"

"He could slit our throats and pitch our bodies into a black bog." Alice's magnified eyes looked enormous. Libby shook her head, but when Henrietta's face drifted into her mind, uncertainty came with it.

Lu Ling already stood inside the attic when they reached the portal at the top that entered directly into the attics, which would be immense in a building the size of Lasserthon Manor. Alice gasped as Libby nudged her inside.

The cavernous reaches that met them were shrouded with shadows except for one area some distance away that was quite well lit. In fact, tapers burned everywhere, in a circle on the floor, many more upon tabletops and wall sconces. The lighted oasis glowing in the blackness made the place eerie and forbidding, as if they'd happened upon some malignant pagan ritual. Where they were the sacrifices, her mind added reluctantly.

Beside them Lu Ling had set the candlestick upon a table

beside the door, and while they stared wordlessly at the dozens of candles beckoning in the distance, Lu Ling moved past them, her silk tunic and trousers whispering softly in the quiet room. When the door slammed shut, both Libby and Alice jumped as if slapped. When Libby heard the scrape of a key, locking them inside, she turned and rattled the handle.

"Oh, oh, oh . . ."

That was Alice's voice, rising in pitch and trembling with horror. Libby slapped the palm of her hand upon the door, ready to beat it down if the woman did not open it. Beside her Alice was tottering on the edge of full-fledged hysteria. When Julian spoke from directly behind them, they both froze.

"Well now, look who's come to visit me. And well past midnight at that. Very improper, Mrs. Thornhill, I must point out."

Julian had stepped out of the darkness into the light. Though his voice held some amusement, Lord help her but Libby had never in her life seen a man who looked more the devil than he did at that moment. He wore nothing but trousers and leather top boots, both black, both spattered with various colors of paint. His chest was bare, a tangle of black hair arrowing into his pants, his massive arms and shoulders showing undeniably how strong a man he was.

Embarrassed by his nakedness, Libby's body reacted. Against her will a raging current of inner turmoil swirled and burned through her with warm, fluid heat that she could neither control nor explain. Luckily Alice's expression distracted her. The other girl's bottom lip hung slack, her face drained and the color of curdled cream. The bulging state of her eyes was even more alarming.

"Good God, is she all right?" asked Julian, following her gaze.

Libby looked back at him, trying to keep her eyes riveted on his face instead of his nude torso, realizing she'd never seen a man in quite the same state of undress. Her husband had been irrevocably old-fashioned about modesty and privacy, and insisted on separate dressing rooms for just that reason. They'd never even shared a common bedchamber, though she knew many married couples did, including her own parents. She blushed when she realized her mind was conjuring up images of marital intimacy and promptly colored heatedly as Julian awaited her reply.

"She'll be all right. You startled her," she answered, pleased by the steadiness of her voice.

Julian had the whitest teeth she'd ever seen, she thought as he grinned, perhaps made so by the dark growth of whiskers shadowing his jawline. His black hair was also mussed and disordered, as if he'd run a hand absently through it, or just gotten out of bed. Again she was thinking about beds. Again she felt the hot rush of blood flooding up underneath her cheekbones.

Julian picked up Lu Ling's candlestick, and under the dancing flame he did appear a most supremely dark and sinister presence, so large and masculine-looking, and of course, totally and completely wicked. Libby could not force her eyes away from him, her heart tripping along at full speed, while beside her Alice was making peculiar snorting sounds, as if she were trying to blow out Julian's candle.

To Libby's shock, Julian threw back his head and laughed with rich enjoyment. The sound rolled out into the darkness surrounding them like the echo of thunder on a stormy night. The fact that he was smiling so agreeably lessened Libby's tension considerably, but she didn't lose sight of the fact that they were alone with him and the door was locked behind them.

"I suspect I'm the cause of your maid's state of shock, since she hasn't taken her eyes off me since she came in here." His hard, sensual lips curved into the most depraved grin, as if he well knew all the boiling currents dancing through Libby's blood. "And you, Mrs. Thornhill, are you as offended by my nudity as your maid is?"

No doubt he'd used that lethal smile to seduce all his victims, willing and unwilling. She was irked by his condescending manner, and her pride finally came along with the realization that she should never have come up to the attics, not for any reason. She hadn't expected him to be unclad, of course, maybe wielding a weapon, knife, or gun perhaps, but not for one moment had the idea of him being half naked even occurred to her. Too bad, if it had, she wouldn't have dared come.

Her heart lurched when he took a step closer to them. Alice pressed her back against the closed door and pressed both hands over her mouth, no doubt to stifle a scream. Julian, however, was not intent on snatching them but merely retrieved his white shirt, where it hung from a nearby hook. Libby kept her eyes glued on his every movement, certainly not willing to turn her back on him. His body was impressive, she had to admit, with wide shoulders and narrow hips. His legs were long, no doubt lengthened by the high knee boots and tight black riding breeches that revealed how hard and molded were the muscles of his thighs. She shouldn't have been surprised, knowing as she did how many hours he spent in the saddle, but he was a much bigger man than she'd thought, his muscular physique disguised a great deal by the formal wear he usually wore.

Her gaze moved to his long tan fingers holding his shirt, big hands that could effortlessly encircle a woman's throat. In his presence, she realized belatedly that he could very easily handle both her and Alice, if he had desire to do them harm. How strange that she still suffered no fear, even as she stood, feeling quite insignificant and vulnerable in front of him. Perverse, indeed, when she suspected he might be capable of murder.

She watched him pull the shirt down over his head in one quick motion, but he didn't bother with the drawstring, and the way the linen neck fell open halfway down his chest, revealing a dark tangle of crisp hair, seemed more decadent and immoral than when he'd stood before her naked from the waist up. His eyes pinned her as he picked up the candle, and she was arrested by the intensity of his gaze. For the first time she wanted to turn and run. Instead she took a deep inhalation and forced herself to meet his stare without showing fear. Alice, on the other hand, still had her face buried in her palms.

Julian paid little attention to the trembling maid, however, but kept his attention trained solely on Libby. His eyes would occasionally catch the light and flash a brief glint of midnight blue.

"Are you afraid, Mrs. Thornhill? Now that I've got you up here all to myself? Are you thinking that this is my den of iniquity, where I bring innocent ladies such as yourself in order to take advantage of them?" Alice gave a sick-sounding moan into her cupped hands. Julian smiled. "Are you thinking I might throw you down right here on the floor and ravish you?"

Alice made another strangled little whimper, as if he already had his hands around her neck, but Libby's courage rose quickly to rescue her. She did not like to be toyed with, and she realized that was exactly what he was doing with them.

"You might try to do so, sir, but be assured I won't abide any such assault without a fight you'll not soon forget."

Julian's smile came as slowly as a sleepy thought. "Yes, indeed, I do think I could count on you to put up a good struggle. You've already shown more guts than good sense by coming up here alone."

"I'm not alone," she reminded him. "Alice is here."

He lifted a dark eyebrow. "Against her will, by the looks of it."

Libby glanced again at her maid. "Quit moaning, Alice. He's not going to hurt us. Or are you, Lord Edmonton?" she asked, studying his expression, though somehow she knew he had no intention of injuring them.

"I really hadn't planned to do bodily harm. It's too late an hour for me to resort to ravishment. That sort of thing takes time, you understand, especially with two ladies involved."

At that point Libby knew full well that he was only teasing them. She almost smiled but caught herself, not wanting to encourage him. The man had become disarming, but he was too dangerous to underestimate. She didn't think he wanted to molest either of them, but that didn't mean he wasn't responsible for whatever had happened to Henrietta.

"Would you care to sit down?" His politeness was ludicrous under the circumstances, and Libby felt a deep sense of the sheer impropriety of standing there with him dressed only in her nightclothes while he bowed as if they were meeting in the receiving line at a society wedding.

Glancing around, Libby wondered where he had in mind for her to sit. She could see no furniture, not a stick of it, but then again, the place was very dark. An odd place for an artist's studio, she decided, thinking it would be a lot more conducive to Julian's more rakish endeavors.

"Perhaps first you should tell me why I was brought here."

Julian seemed genuinely surprised by her question. "Brought here? I assumed you wished to pay me a visit on your own."

"In the middle of the night? Dressed like this?" She gestured at her attire without thinking. When his eyes lowered to her body, she wished she hadn't brought the fact to his attention. Although her nightgown was quite modest, the soft lawn fabric reaching high upon her neck, and the robe worn over it even more chaste, touching the floor, she suddenly felt as though the fabric were completely transparent. Or more vividly, that Julian possessed some uncanny, demon ability to see through it. She fingered the buttons closing the throat of her robe and found them tightly secured.

"Indeed I do find it surprising you'd come here undressed as you are. Tell me, Mrs. Thornhill, are you in the habit of flouncing around strange houses and visiting gentlemen in your nightclothes?"

"I've never flounced anywhere in my entire life," she snapped angrily. "Furthermore I did not come here undressed. I am dressed for bed."

"I'll take that as an encouraging sign of a deepening in our relationship."

Libby ignored the way he was grinning and turning her words to his advantage, but with effort. The truth was, she found him amusing. What on earth was the matter with her? "You're evading my question. I'd really like to know why your serving girl brought me up here."

"I'm really afraid I couldn't say. On the other hand, I can't deny it was quite an inspired idea. Would you like me to ask her so we'll both know?"

His benign reaction to her accusation acted to lessen her indignation, but she was sure he knew exactly why Lu Ling had brought her all the way up here, had indeed ordered it himself, the truth be known. Julian moved to the door. He spoke softly in Chinese. Lu Ling opened the door at once and answered him, her eyes downcast.

Julian listened to her for a moment, then turned back to Libby. "She said you opened your door and started yelling at her. She didn't understand what you wanted, so she brought you up here so I could explain for her."

Libby arched a disbelieving brow. "Well?"

"Well, what?"

"Well, go ahead and explain why she was lingering outside my door. It seemed to me that she had unrolled her pallet and intended to sleep there in the hallway."

"She did so because I asked her to."

His unexpected admission stunned her. "You told her to?"

"That's right."

"Whatever for?"

"Perhaps I was afraid you'd wander off and get lost on the moors."

"Why would I do that?"

"Why, indeed, would anyone?"

Libby frowned slightly, but she had, perhaps incautiously, lost her fear of the man before her. She was in his territory, safe and sound thus far, with no threatening machinations on his part, and she should certainly take advantage of it. Alice was with her, after all. She changed the subject, not sure she believed him about Lu Ling's presence but more interested in other secrets he might be harboring.

"Raymond told me this is where you paint when you're here at Lasserthon."

"Is that why you came up here? For a private viewing of my work?"

Libby could not quite fathom how strange everything was turning out, but she nodded. Why not let him think that? Julian reached out his hand as if to lead her deeper into the dark reaches around them, and she hesitated, but only for a moment. She put her hand inside his, although Alice was pulling on her other arm and whispering for her not to let him touch her. His fingers were warm and strong as they encircled hers.

"Lu Ling will pour tea for us. I do encourage you to persuade your maid there to drink it down at once. It's a special blend that will certainly calm her nerves. She still seems a trifle upset."

Libby thought that upset was quite a mild way to describe it. "Alice has always been a rather excitable girl."

As he led her across the floor toward the candlelit arena, he gave a low laugh. "Does she think I'm going to hurt her? It that why she's trembling like a leaf?"

"Perhaps she's heard of your reputation with women."

She was disappointed when he only smiled. "Why don't you tell me what she might have heard about me on such short acquaintance, Mrs. Thornhill?"

Libby hesitated, realizing then he was quite aware she had been inquiring around about him. "I'm sure you know without my having to tell you. We all know full well that you were not alone in the drawing room the night we arrived here." Pointedly she glanced around into the dark shadows of the attics. "I do hope we haven't interrupted you again?"

"No, not at the moment. Please, sit down."

He'd led her into the circle of light, and she saw that there was a blue curved-back sofa on one side, half hidden by a dressing screen painted with red Chinese symbols. His easel stood a bit farther back in front of some tall undraped windows. Libby seated herself on the cushioned couch, motioning Alice to join her.

Alice obeyed, seeming to relax since Julian indicated no intent to bludgeon or strangle her. Libby arranged her robe to cover her ankles, a bit scandalized to find herself in such a place with a man of Julian's notoriety. She had never done such a thing—in truth, wouldn't dream of doing so and would be horrified if anyone found out where she was at the moment.

Julian had moved away and was sorting through a half dozen or so canvases stacked against the wall. He chose one and returned with it. "I assume you'll enjoy seeing this one. It's not quite finished, as you can see."

Libby's throat clogged when Julian turned it where she could see. It was a portrait of Henrietta. So real did her dear friend look, so calm and serene, so alive, that Libby felt tears begin to burn. She bit her lip and looked down, overcome with emotion.

"Forgive me, I've upset you. It took me a very long time to capture that particular look, but she wore it often, especially when she first came here."

"She looks very sad." Libby forced her eyes back to the portrait so that she could examine it in more detail.

"Yes, almost haunted at times. I know you must miss her terribly."

Not sure what to think of the fact that he'd willingly turned the conversation to Henrietta, she nodded. Her feelings were very close to the surface, and she was glad when Lu Ling chose that moment to return with the tea tray. Julian propped the painting of Henrietta on the easel where Libby could look at it.

As Lu Ling knelt at a low table in front of the couch, Julian lounged down on the other side of Alice. Alice immediately scooted toward Libby, as far away from him as she could get, but Julian only smiled at her. Heaven help her, but he was a handsome man, not in the normal fashion, true, but with an unusual ruggedness that certainly did have its appeal. She tried to ascertain what it was about him that so intrigued her, for she'd known many good-looking gentlemen, had had many suitors before she chose John to wed. When she realized she'd been staring at him for too long—very rudely, she feared—she quickly glanced away.

"Tell me, Mrs. Thornhill, what is it about me that you find so distasteful? Since you've made it perfectly clear from the beginning that you dislike me."

Again his forthright manner surprised Libby. In truth, though, she hadn't hidden her distaste at his behavior. "I hardly know you well enough to dislike you."

"Well enough, it seems."

Since he continued to press her, she decided to resort to honesty and was even more blunt than she had intended. "I've never cared for those who amuse themselves by shocking other people's sensibilities."

"Is that what you think I do?"

"I think that's what you attempted to do with me. Do you deny it?"

"Of course not."

That irresistible smile again, threatening to melt her distrust away. She reminded herself that he no doubt used the same charm on Henrietta and Mary Louise, and countless other adoring women.

"Now I trust you are being honest?"

"At the moment, yes, I am."

Libby watched Lu Ling pour pale brown tea into three beautiful little black cups painted with golden Chinese symbols. They had no handles in the oriental fashion, and gradually the pungent flavor of the brew wafted up around them. She decided that sparring with Julian could be quite entertaining, and would cause no real harm, especially with Alice as a buffer between them. She noticed Alice had relaxed somewhat, actually a great deal, it seemed, since her head was nodding. From the laudanum, no doubt, Libby realized, shaking her maid's shoulder a little. Alice sputtered awake with a jolt that knocked her glasses askew.

"She seems to have subdued her terror for me quickly enough," Julian remarked, propping one booted foot atop his opposite knee. "Does she always doze off with such alacrity?"

"I gave her a dose of laudanum earlier, and she's still suffering its effect."

Julian sipped his tea, observing her over Alice's head, whose chin now rested again on her chest. "Do you always drug your more excitable servants?"

"Of course not. She was edgy about . . . coming here to a new house and all."

"Edgy is a bit tame, don't you think? From what I've noticed on the occasions we've met, she's never a step or two from outright dementia."

Libby couldn't help but laugh because the description was so apt, especially since they'd arrived at Lasserthon Manor. Julian wasn't smiling but observing her so intently that she took a sip of tea for the sole purpose of busying her hands. It had a smooth, velvety taste, very warm and soothing. She watched Lu Ling rise in her graceful way, then bow to Julian before she backed away and disappeared into the shadows.

She examined the tiny cup, wondering what the foreign symbols meant. Libby's thoughts went to Lu Ling and her presence in Julian's life. She raised a question that had bothered her greatly since she'd first seen the Chinese woman kowtowing to Julian's every whim.

"Do you ever feel the slightest twinge of guilt for owning another human being?"

"I see little difference in Lu Ling and your own nervous little maid here. Both are expected to take care of our needs."

"I don't happen to own Alice. She works for me. I pay her quite well for her labors."

"Merely semantics. The Chinese do things differently. I am honoring Lu Ling's wishes. I treat my servants well. You'll see that when you come to Brickhill this weekend."

"I haven't said whether or not I'll join you at Brickhill," she reminded him, then returned to the subject of Lu Ling. "Are you telling me she wishes to be your slave, so you're merely humoring her?"

"That pretty much says it, I suppose."

"Pardon me, sir, if I don't believe you."

Their eyes met, and she saw something move deep inside Julian's. What? Anger? Or was it amusement? "You're very outspoken. More so than Henrietta was. Does your honesty ever get you in trouble?"

Libby ignored the question, or had he meant it as a veiled threat? She was glad, however, that he had brought up Henrietta's name again. She gestured at the easel. "Did Henrietta agree to sit for that portrait?"

"Not this late at night," he answered, leaning back and resting the bottom of his cup on the arm of the couch. "She never came up here during the daylight hours either, come to think of it. Actually, few women have had the temerity to walk willingly into my inner sanctum."

Alice stirred at that and gave him a groggy sidelong look of distrust. Soon, however, she was happily dozing. Libby reached out to give her another shake, but Julian stopped her with a raised palm.

"Please allow me." He poked Alice's arm with his forefinger. She came awake with a sputter, saw Julian, and immediately pressed even closer to Libby.

"Alice, please, try to stay awake," Libby said sternly.

"Yes, ma'am."

"Are you enjoying your stay thus far at Lasserthon, Mrs. Thornhill?"

"Yes, though I wish Henrietta could have been here to greet me. That's what we'd planned, you know, for her to show me her new home."

"May I give you some advice?"

"You can give it. My taking it is another issue."

"Why don't you cut your stay short and travel on to London? You'll accomplish nothing by staying here longer except subject yourself to extra pain and mourning."

Libby couldn't believe he had so bluntly asked her to be on her way. "I think it's up to Lord Lasserthon to tell me when I've outstayed my welcome."

"Raymond won't do that. He enjoys the company of beautiful women, even more than I do."

Libby wondered that he had the gall to say that, when he was the one consorting with Mary Louise behind the draperies and under her betrothed husband's nose. She gave him an arch look that said as much.

"Is there any particular reason you wish me to leave?"

"I'm afraid something will happen that we'll both regret."

"It seems to me that you flatter yourself, Lord Edmonton."

"Things have a way of happening. Look at tonight. Who would have thought you'd seek me out like this?"

Was he teasing her? Or was he that arrogant? Probably the latter. She had no time to accuse him because he suddenly stood up. The open neck of his shirt revealed the molded muscles ridging his chest.

"Would you like to see more?" he asked, disconcerting her for a moment.

She blushed. "I beg your pardon?"

"Of my paintings. I have one of you."

"Of me?"

Julian smiled slightly. "I've not had much luck, though I've been trying. I'll finish it now, if you'll agree to sit here a little while longer. Preferably in the nude, though I have a feeling you'll decline that suggestion."

"You're quite right."

"I can only hope to someday change your mind."

For an instant she didn't know whether to laugh outright or be insulted by his outrageous remark. The gall of him! She somehow had the inclination to believe he was merely needling her sensibilities for no other reason but his own gratification. In a totally unfathomable reaction she was enjoying their unconventional conversation. In that lay the danger of his seductiveness. In her letters Henrietta had declared much the same response to Julian.

"Does your wife mind for you to dally with women the way you do?" she asked calmly, curious to know for sure if he was wed. She did not think so, for she'd heard no one mention such, but it would be one way to broach more questions about his personal life.

He leaned back and gazed speculatively at her. She forced herself not to waver in her gaze. "I don't have a wife, Mrs.

Thornhill. I've never found any particular need to find myself one."

"Isn't that unusual for a man such as yourself, a man with a title to bestow? Who will inherit your name and property? Aren't you concerned with such matters?"

"I might ask you the same question. Did your husband not give you a child before he left you a widow?"

The question startled her, but sorrow came swiftly as she shook her head. It was a never ending regret that she had never been able to conceive. She had wanted children desperately.

"I'm sorry. I see I've upset you."

"Not really. I readily admit that I did wish to bear a child, but it was not meant to be. My husband was ill for most of our marriage, I regret to say."

Julian watched her, but his eyes held nothing but a look of compassion. "That must have been terrible for you."

Nodding, Libby sipped more of her tea, not liking the turn of the subject. She was more than just startled by Julian's next remark.

"You really should never have come up here."

Alert, she examined his face. "Are you telling me I am not safe with you?"

"The truth is that anything could have happened. It wasn't wise for you to come here alone."

As Libby opened her mouth to indicate Alice's presence, he interrupted. "Even reinforced with your maid, though she does have a rather intimidating snore." He smiled, one so wry with humor that Libby was disarmed. "If I was of lesser moral fiber," he continue blithely, "I might have forced you into any number of compromising situations, despite little Alice here. I still could, if you like, just to prove my point." He lifted a brow as if challenging her to urge him on.

"Are you actually saying that you may still assault me, just because I was so unwise as to visit you here?"

"Perhaps, if you're of a mind to cooperate."

Not offended at all, because she knew full well that he was not serious, she tilted her head to gaze thoughtfully at him. "Perhaps you overrate your prowess. I am not easily seduced."

"I'm finding that out, I suspect, but it seems you've thrown a gauntlet at my feet, Mrs. Thornhill. Be advised, I'm not one to ignore a challenge, or the fact that a beautiful woman has come to visit me, looking quite provocative in all those frothy nightclothes. At the moment I'm hard pressed to remember that I am a gentleman."

"I was under the impression that you were quite proud that you were not one."

His eyes grew serious enough to cause her smile to fade a bit. "Just remember that every man you meet is not above reproach, and I will include myself in that generality."

She watched him turn to his easel, remove Henrietta's painting, and place it aside, but she had sobered a great deal. He was more than correct in his assessment. She should never have come up here, with a maid or without one, and what was worse, she knew better, had known better when she first felt the urge to follow Lu Ling. The situation could very well have gotten out of hand.

The realization was even more forceful and, yes, humiliating, for the fact that Julian had pointed it out to her, as if she were a child, much as her father might have. She was a grown woman, a married woman, now widowed, and she felt like a chastised schoolgirl. She should get up and leave right now; if she consulted her good sense, she certainly would do so without a moment's hesitation.

Instead she remained very still, watching Julian sort through his artwork, not wanting to leave yet. She found him beguiling, true, but he was also revealing things about himself. And she was finding his character a lot more palatable tonight than she had the previous evening, but perhaps that was his sole intent. She also was confident that he had no desire to hurt her, so she drank more tea and watched him rise from where he'd squatted down to choose a particular canvas. He turned to look at her, and their eyes locked. A strange, unknown excitement was building inside her, something she had not experienced often in her life of wealth and privilege. Danger. That's what she felt as he delved deeply into her heart with his navy blue eyes.

As Julian continued to stare at her, Libby felt fear, deep inside but not fear of bodily harm, fear of what might happen between them. What was most curious and inexplicable was the odd sense of longing that impelled her to find out. What would it be like if he did touch her? Did force her to his will? She did not want that to happen, there was no question about that. But how would it feel to be overpowered by such a dark, powerful force as he was?

Appalled at herself, she thrust her thoughts away and quickly formed others more conducive to propriety. Still unsettled as he moved closer, she decided it wise to keep Alice awake and watchful. She shook the girl's arm, and Alice sputtered and lurched back to alertness, but Libby was not so naïve as to know she should leave the attics.

Her reasons for staying were attempts at rationalization, but then again, she'd always been a highly inquisitive sort, and she was more than interested in what Julian might have in store for her. She would watch his every movement, and if he did show a propensity to harm her, she would leave at once. Until then she would relax and hope that he would somehow make it abundantly clear to her that he was in no way involved in Henrietta's death.

Chapter Eight

As Julian lounged down on the sofa next to Libby Thornhill's groggy, nearsighted maid, he was thinking how astonishing it was that the American widow continued to sit so serenely and sip tea. It did appear as if the remarkable young lady before him was more than comfortable visiting a man she openly considered a philanderer, and incredible, dressed in her nightclothes. She was turning out to be completely unpredictable, which only acted to intrigue him more by the moment. He asked her if she would like more tea, and she politely replied that she certainly would.

Leaning forward, he did accommodate her, transfered the cup and saucer back into her hands, noticing that they were no longer trembling, any more than her gaze was. If she was uneasy in his presence—and she must be, under the circumstances—she was damned good at hiding it.

For some time he'd expected her to rise gracefully, offer up a suitable excuse before sweeping from the room with haughty grace, her terrified maid dragged firmly in tow. She had done no such thing, however, but sat with him in companionable silence. She was not going to be intimidated, which he'd intended, his sole intention driving her away from the manor and on her way. Swiftly he reconsidered his options, sorting through them one by one, until he realized if he couldn't scare her off so easily, he'd have to win her over. He really didn't want, nor had the time, to resort to more drastic methods of ending her nosy inquiries.

Drinking from his cup, he savored the warm tea as he continued to observe his lovely guest. Again he marveled that she sat there beside him, thinking it impossible, dressed as she was. He never would have expected her to flaunt propriety, but on the other hand, he did know, full well, exactly why she had. There was no doubt either that she was a fashionable, elegant lady, well trained in what was acceptable behavior and what was not. She suspected him of foul play concerning Henrietta, and was quite correct to do so. She needed to prove it, and Julian had a feeling there was little she wouldn't do to ferret out the truth. More interesting was just how far she'd inch out on that dangerous limb to prove her theory.

Slightly amused by her recklessness, it occurred to him to push her a bit and see how resolute she was in her quest. He leaned forward over the snoring maid and fixed his gaze on her face. She met his eyes in the straightforward, unapologetic fashion he'd come to expect from her. Good God, this woman had more than her share of courage. Few other women were willing or able to meet his keen regard without a maidenly blush, or worse, the bloody simpering he hated while the lady pretended to be an innocent coquette, which most women of his acquaintance were anything but. Most ladies who traveled in his circle knew exactly what they were doing. There was little they would not attempt to get what they want, including lying and cheating. He wondered if the American woman was cut from the same cloth.

The outspoken Mrs. Thornhill said her mind, true, quite well, with a bluntness that was somewhat startling. Fact was, from what he had seen of her, he was beginning to admire females bred of colonial stock. First Henrietta, who had charmed him so quickly, and now the beauteous Libby in her staid and frilly nightgown. While their gazes dueled, the entrenched desire to paint her welled up again, so forcefully it was hard to stop himself from going for his brush. Now, under dozens of flickering candles, when her eyes glittered and the bones of her face were cast in classical perfection. That set of her chin was determination, he realized; she looked like a woman who'd never give up something she wanted.

He lowered his gaze to the white robe, full and flowing,

swathing her figure much too thoroughly for his purpose, the high, buttoned neckline a good deal more concealing than the purple gown she'd worn across from him at the dinner table. At the same time she had an innocent, youthful look about her with her bright hair plaited down her back like a small child's. A deceptive illusion, for underneath those flowing folds was a grown woman, a luscious one who tempted him just about as much as any ever had before. One who would enjoy uncovering his secrets and bringing him to his knees in submission.

"I have to paint you. You can't refuse me."

Obviously surprised by his sudden declaration, Libby replaced her cup on the tea tray and said, "So you suggested last night. My answer hasn't changed. Certainly not."

"Why not? What time could be better? I'm burning with inspiration to capture you while you sit here before me looking incredibly magnificent, with Alice snoring peacefully but ready to awaken and defend your honor if necessary."

To Julian's surprise, Libby laughed, low and quite seductively pleasant. His expression faltered when he saw how her amusement transfigured her face. The delicacy of her high cheekbones, chiseled so finely, the jaw just as fragile but tempered, no doubt by the underlying strength he sensed within her. There was that indefinable look of aristocracy in her face and the noble way she carried herself, which made him conjecture about her heritage. Where had she come from? Where had she lived and grown to womanhood before marrying the old man she'd taken for her husband? Had she been forced into the marriage for the Thornhill wealth, because Julian did not doubt, not for an instant, that a woman such as she would have had a swarm of suitors buzzing around her like honeybees on an arbor of blooms.

Her past interested him, and he would make it a point to find out where she'd been and what she'd done until she showed up on Lasserthon's doorstep as Henrietta's avenging angel. He had a feeling she might be keeping a few secrets of her own. She fascinated him, and she would sit for him, no matter how opposed she was to the idea. And she'd do it tonight.

Libby Thornhill had disrupted his plans to take Mary Louise, true, but he had come up with another, better way to get what he wanted. That could wait; at the moment he'd enjoy Libby Thornhill's company until she came to her senses and fled him.

"Though I cannot pose for you myself, I'd enjoy seeing more of your work," she informed him now, shifting her head slightly, as if she'd noticed, and resented, his long contemplation of her. Julian realized he had been staring too intently, but the creamy texture of her skin drew his eyes, so soft-looking that he could barely contain his desire to run the tips of his fingers over that dewy-smooth cheek.

"My husband and I were both patrons of the arts," she said, glancing sidelong at her unconscious servant. Alice's head was lolled back on the couch, mouth open, puffing out soft snores in a way that reminded Julian of his favorite basset hound. "We've quite a good selection from English artists in our collection, but we catered more to American painters, of course. I must say I'm surprised I haven't seen yours of yet, you being the rage of London and all . . ."

"You don't have to disrobe. Your face alone will do."

Her chin tilted again, and excitement filled him as she stared hard at him, her head at just the quizzical angle he meant to portray. Her eyes caught the glow of the light, searching, assessing. Sunlight on oak leaves, he decided. Perhaps it was ocher he should add to catch that golden glow. With the long, half-burnt tapers behind her, surrounding her with an aura while the edges of the canvas remained dark. He felt a familiar rush of excitement, and knew it was more than just his artist's zeal. He wanted her. He had wanted her from the first moment she'd settled those glorious eyes on him.

"I was up most of last night trying to envision your eyes and hair," he said earnestly. "The colors have eluded me until this moment. If you'll agree to sit here now, for only a little while, I can capture them. Your eye color is most unique."

"Many others have green eyes," she said with offhanded

dismissal, but he sensed she was more embarrassed than pleased. She absently fingered the long, loosely woven braid, pulling it over her shoulder until it hung against her breast.

"May I unbraid your hair?"

Turning incredulous eyes upon him, Libby shook her head and gave a laugh, which this time sounded a trifle nervous. "There you are again. No true gentleman would make such a request of a lady."

"That's a bit naïve, don't you think?"

Libby studied his face for several moments before she said, "I am truly amazed, sir, that you've not been called out by some enraged father or husband. . . ."

When her remark faltered, and she looked momentarily abashed by her own words, Julian deduced at once that she'd managed to uncover some of the uglier tidbits littering his past. No doubt in every vile detail. Anger rose inside him with swift, rushing abandon, though why he felt such rage he couldn't comprehend. He knew she was investigating him, and that particular duel would not be the most unpleasant story she'd uncover about him. There were dozens of unsavory tales linked to him, most of which were true.

Tamping down the roil of unwanted emotions, he said quite calmly, "Why do you find it so surprising that I covet you as a subject? You must know you're an attractive woman. Artists are attracted to things of beauty."

"I would suspect, Lord Edmonton, that you find any woman at all worthy of your brush, especially those willing to remove their apparel to accommodate your nudes."

Julian smiled. "When a woman is willing and I find her interesting, why not? I find the female body a beautiful thing, especially naked, both as an artist and a man. Now, if you'll allow me, I have a question to ask of you."

Extreme wariness branded Libby's demeanor, but to his surprise, she nodded.

"Last night you were openly hostile to me. Not because of some of the things I said that no doubt offended you, but from the moment we met. I'd like to know why that is."

"Now you're the one being disingenuous, my lord. We both know Mary Louise was hidden behind those curtains."

"I apologize for offending your sensibilities. Still, that's little reason to deny me the pleasure of painting you. You did come up here tonight, did you not? I suspect that means your disapproval isn't all-encompassing."

She watched him with an interested expression but one that told him she would never believe a word he said. A very smart girl indeed.

"As I said, I'm flattered by your interest," she answered with a dismissive wave of her hand, "but I'm sure there are other, more suitable subjects who would enjoy the honor of sitting for a portrait."

"Ah, but that's the dilemma I face. Once I get to know a person, with all their many flaws and failures, it takes away their aura of innocence. I like to paint a woman when first we meet, when I know nothing of her but the soul I see shining from her eyes and the passion promised in the softness of her mouth."

When he moved his regard down to her lips, they parted slightly. Then she leaned back and crossed her arms over her chest. "Does this sort of flowery drivel really work for you, Lord Edmonton? I should really think most women would see it for the attempt at seduction it is."

Julian wanted to laugh because she regarded him with curiosity, as if she expected him to answer that barbed question. He wondered if she was as calm and unaffected by their intimate tête-à-tête as she pretended to be. Her chest rose and fell, her small breasts lifting the gauzy fabric. By God, she would pose for him; he would not give up until she did. If not here, then at Brickhill.

"Come now, Mrs. Thornhill, don't be stubborn. You're here. I'm here. Alice is here as chaperon, albeit an insensible one. Sit where you are and we'll talk as I sketch. Perhaps you'd like to ask me about Henrietta's time here while I work."

As he'd intended, that hook proved too enticing for Libby not to nibble. Though she hesitated a moment longer while Alice gargled a bit and twitched a foot, no doubt in the throes of a bad dream where Julian was either strangling her or plunging a knife into her heart. When the maid settled into a new stanza of soft, buzzing snores, her head dropped over to lie against Julian's shoulder.

In a turn of subject, he said with droll humor, "She will surely die if she opens her eyes and finds herself touching me."

Libby's eyes glowed with amusement. "She would quite probably faint dead away."

"She peers at me through those bizarre glasses of hers as if she expects me to grab her by the throat."

"Perhaps I should awaken her . . ."

"Have a heart, Mrs. Thornhill, let her enjoy the peace. She'll be hysterical again as soon as the laudanum wears off."

Libby seemed ready to protest, but when he grinned, she surprised him by capitulating. "All right, I suppose it won't hurt to allow you to do a couple of sketches. But just for a little while, and only of my face."

"Splendid. Would you agree to step up here beside my easel? Where the light will show you to best advantage?"

He watched the long folds of white lawn sift down around her when she stood. His gaze slid slowly down the length of her slender body, well hidden and mysterious, but with that tempting hint of womanly curves that urged him to find out just how shapely she was. Someday he would enjoy her satiny flesh, but unfortunately, it wouldn't be tonight.

Libby felt a tingle of anticipation as she stepped up closer to Julian Rainville. She no longer felt intimidation, but her nerves fluttered alarmingly when he stood only a handbreadth away. It was not his person as much as the danger of the moment that rattled her, but then again, he was the danger.

Still, her feminine intuition told her he had no intention of harming her. Despite all the things she'd heard about him, all that she suspected him capable of, he now looked at her out of artist's eyes, hard, objective, intense. She was glad when he turned away to select a canvas, feeling almost a physical release as his blue eyes left her, as if he had dropped a rope with which he had reeled her toward him. He gathered several small pots of paint and arranged them on a table behind his easel. He was focused now, on his work, and if that was the case, perhaps his tongue would loosen while his mind dwelled elsewhere.

A loud scraping sound filled the attic as he dragged a high bench from the shadows outside the ring of candlelight. Alice shifted and lay down on her side on the couch but did not awaken. Libby climbed atop the stool as he bade her, arranging her robe modestly, thinking she had surely lost all remnants of her senses. What on earth was she doing here in the middle of the night with Julian? He no longer seemed to notice her, however, as he concentrated on selecting a pencil.

"Raymond told me you were here most of last night, and often work for days without anyone seeing you. Is that true?"

Julian glanced at her. "Yes, but little good it did me. I've destroyed a dozen sketches of you already." His eyes went again to her hair. "Is there nothing I can do or say to convince you to loosen that braid? I want to touch your hair. I want to bury my hands in it and let it sift through my fingers."

The thrill that jolted its way through Libby's body so affected her that she wondered how she'd feel if Julian actually did what he had described. Though she steeled herself against his masculine allure, it was the sheer potency of it that staggered her. His blue eyes came back to her face, fixed there, forcing her to his will, almost magnetic in their intensity. Appalled, she fought the urge to let him do whatever he wished with her. "I'm sure you'll survive without unpinning my hair. My principles have been compromised enough this evening."

"You must learn to live dangerously. Coming up here was a good first step; undoing your hair would be the next."

"And removing my clothes would be the next, I suppose."

"Precisely."

They both smiled, and Libby found herself actually wanting to reach up and work her hair loose. My, oh, my, she thought, her good judgment was not exactly a force to be reckoned with tonight. Where had her common sense disappeared to? She was not an untried maiden like Mary Louise, certainly wise enough in the ways of the world not to swoon at the sugared words of a roué. She had handled profligates such as Julian during her courtship days, and beyond, when such men thought the wife of an old man would welcome their advances.

Not a man like Julian, not a man with eyes so blue they seemed to glow as brilliant as Carolinian seawater, she thought. Not with her sitting in her nightgown in his dark studio. She felt the slow, unmistakable heat of embarrassment moving up her neck to burn into her cheeks. Never would she have believed herself capable of something so witless. He still might very well be the one who had harmed Henrietta. In truth, everything pointed to it.

As Julian bent his head over his palette, she stared at his black hair. It looked very thick, very soft, and gleamed with a silver sheen in the candlelight. She realized that she had a good opportunity to study him, and did so without hesitation. His skin was darker than most men she knew. Tanned by the sun, perhaps from riding in the moors. She wondered if everyone in his family bore his dark good looks. She'd inherited her hair from her mother, though Trinity's was more the color of copper. Her green eyes came from her father, the Duke of Thorpe. Were all the Rainvilles so tall and well built, with the ability to charm anyone they met?

Julian mixed his paints with complete absorption. She had no feeling of endangerment with him ignoring her so totally. The scrape of his palette knife was the only sound in the vast, quiet attics, and she stared at the short, flat instrument he handled with such familiarity, wondering how he'd come by the odd power he seemed to wield so effortlessly over others. She'd seen him employ it last night, seen the fascination with which others watched him, the incredible latitude given him when he was openly outrageous. Is that the way he bewitched the women he seduced, wooed them with words and glances of honey until they were so enamored they did whatever he asked? How many women had sat upon this very stool and allowed him to have his way with them?

A shiver of alarm convinced her of her vulnerability. She glanced at the couch. Alice looked as if she'd be of little help if the need arose. She lay on her back, mouth open but at least she wasn't snoring any longer. Nevertheless, Libby felt at least a small sense of security with an ally so close by.

"Lift your chin toward me and focus your eyes on that candle there," Julian ordered brusquely, pointing with his charcoal pencil at a candlestick affixed to the wall behind him. Libby lifted a surprised brow, and when he met her eyes, he inclined his head a bit more respectfully. "If you please, Mrs. Thornhill."

Agreeable to his more deferential request, Libby obeyed, but she could not keep her attention upon the pinpoint flame very long. Her gaze kept straying back to Julian, wishing to scrutinize him without his awareness of her interest. And interested she was.

The room became still, so much so she could hear the wind outside, a soft sound almost like a low tide. It reminded her of Palmetto Point, the Carolina plantation on which she'd grown up. She and her brother had loved it there, where they were free to run and play as their mother had before them. She hoped desperately that Burke would be able to join them at their parents' London house for Christmas. He was often away on mysterious sojourns that no one seemed to know the details of, but this time she hoped he'd show up. She really wanted to see him.

"Now, there's the secretive little smile I'd like to portray. What were you thinking?"

For a moment she'd almost forgotten where she was, but she was inexorably drawn back to the present when she met Julian's riveting cobalt gaze. "I was thinking about my family. I'm looking forward to seeing them."

"Tell me about your family, Libby, love, if it will keep you looking so much like an angel flown down to earth."

"Tell me about your family," she countered within a heartbeat, certainly not ready to reveal her relationship to the Duke and Duchess of Thorpe. "Do you have close relatives? Children? Mistresses?"

Julian was looking at the canvas again, working his brush

in swift downward strokes. His brow was furrowed in concentration, but he did answer. "No relatives. No children."

She noted that he did not include the last, nor did he elaborate on why he had not. "I find it surprising that as a peer of the realm, you have no wish for a male heir to carry on your title?"

Looking up, he considered her a moment. "Of course I do, but there's time for that. I've noticed that wives can be demanding. I prefer to enjoy my freedom as long as I wish it."

"Marriage isn't a prison sentence, you know," she offered lightly, but she suspected that he thought of it precisely as such. He was no doubt wise to pursue such a course; the wife of the Earl of Edmonton would be a miserable woman indeed.

"Do you recommend the institution?"

"My husband was a dear man. I loved him very much."

"And a lucky one. How did you come to choose him from the hordes of suitors who no doubt sought your favors?"

"I'm flattered, but that's overstating it a bit, I must say."

"I would wonder if it weren't true." Suddenly he was looking at her again with pure objectivity in his eyes. She felt like a bowl of fruit arranged in a still life, but she did notice how black his eyelashes were when he looked down again, how long and straight. Perhaps that was the reason his eyes seemed to glow when he fixed them on her. They were truly magnificent eyes, she had to admit. And his hair was so thick and silky-looking, and she liked the way it swept back in wavy disarray at his temples.

Oh, Lord, she thought, mentally taking hold of her shoulders and giving herself a sharp shake. She had to remember why she was up here with him instead of admiring him as if he were a piece of glorious artwork hung in the Royal Academy of Art. She was allowing him to beguile her, and she would not have it. She would not!

"Why don't we talk about Henrietta?" she demanded abruptly, then realized her tone had the sting of a needle prick.

Julian stopped in the act of loading his brush with paint and turned to her. The look of absorption faded from his eyes but was replaced with complete inscrutability. "Of course. If you like."

"What did you really think of her?"

"I really thought she was a lovely woman. I have missed her."

Shock coursed through her, then a streak of anger. "That's very strange since she was afraid of you. She told me so."

"Indeed?" He'd assumed a cautious mien, though his smile came slow and easy. "Why, do you suppose?"

"She said you pursued her when she had no desire for your attentions."

"I pursued her because I enjoyed her company. It's a game we play here in England that perhaps you colonials don't indulge in. The man chases the woman long and hard while all the while she pretends she doesn't want him to. Usually it works out admirably for both players."

He'd gone back to work, and she sat still for a moment longer. She wanted to deny that such behavior went on across the Atlantic in Philadelphia, but of course could not. Every soiree or ballroom was filled with ladies pumping their fans and flirting with gentlemen they pretended to find disagreeable company.

"Was Henrietta happy with her husband?" she asked casually, but she watched him carefully as he answered.

Julian didn't look up. "Did she not tell you that in her letters?"

An evasion, pure and simple, but Libby was not ready to relent. "I was interested in your opinion on the matter."

Julian did look up, and again she was jolted by those eyes. This time they filled her with disquiet. She could not read his expression the way she had at times in the past. He was shuttered against her, as if all his thoughts were unworthy and must be hidden.

"My opinion on the matter isn't important. Why are you asking so many questions? Do you suspect Henrietta's death was not accidental?"

Of course he would deduct as much, by her leading questions, if nothing else. Why shouldn't her suspicions come out into the open? "After listening to the explanations given, I think there are questions that should be asked."

"I hope you'll find peace once you realize that everything we've told you is true. We were all as grief-stricken as you are."

Libby did not pursue the matter further. She wouldn't get anything else because he was on his guard. She sat still while he worked, watching him as he mixed various shades, sometimes using his brush on the canvas, sometimes using his pencil in his sketch book, for the most part ignoring her presence. Alice snored on, through her nose now, like wind whistling under the eaves. Libby wondered where Lu Ling had gone. That woman could tell her many things, if she could find a way to communicate with her.

When Julian abruptly walked out from behind his easel, she tensed, very wary when he stood so close that his thigh touched her knee. She moved her leg away at once, but when she looked up into his eyes, she forgot about everything but his proximity. She set her jaw, determined not to fall under his spell.

"I need to touch you, to trace my fingers along the line of your jaw, to mold the curve of your cheek with my palm." His voice was low and husky, his eyes holding her immobile. Before she could refuse, utter even a word, he had his fingertips on both sides of her face. Tenderly, with a gentle touch, he trailed them down her face, then cupped her chin in his palms. "You have a strong face despite its delicacy. That's what makes you so beautiful and hard to capture, I suppose."

Libby could not move, listening to how low and caressing his voice had become, how warm his eyes were as he stared deeply into her own. The pad of his thumb brushed her lower lip. Pleasure feathered through her, and she was appalled that she didn't reach up and push him away. Had he touched Henrietta like this? Was she witnessing the first stage of his well-skilled techniques of seduction?

When his hands moved down her neck and encircled her throat, the first tingle of fear shot through her. Eyes wide, she forced herself not to move.

"Your throat is long and graceful," he murmured, removing his hands without choking her. She breathed with relief as he picked up her braid. "Dare I ask if you've relented about your hair?"

"No," she said, but as the word still hung in the air, he had the ribbon off, his fingers combing through it and arranging it artfully around her shoulders. She stiffened, angry at the liberty he'd taken, but managed to maintain her dignity enough to affix him with a scornful stare.

"Is this the way you've earned your legend as the seducer of maidens, my lord, by not taking no for an answer?"

"Did you expect me to seduce you? Is that why you came up here?"

"I didn't expect myself to be any different from your other victims." As he came close—too close, because her breath accelerated madly—she refused to lower her eyes. "If you're trying to intimidate me, it isn't working. I'm not afraid of you."

"Perhaps you should be." His voice had grown husky, low, dangerous.

"Perhaps you should be," she warned in turn, determined not to flinch. As strange as it was, she did not fear him, though she had no idea why she did not.

He was so close, she could pick up all the pleasant scents of a man. He smelled a bit more exotic than most, with the scents of oil paint and oriental tea and the faintest essence of sandalwood, perhaps from bath soap, but it was his eyes, always his eyes that made her mouth go dry, made her forget who he was. She reinforced her will in that moment, determined he would not touch her mind, would not manipulate her as he'd done to so many other women. For that reason she did not move as he lowered his face even closer.

"You want me to kiss you, Mrs. Thornhill. Do you have the courage to admit it?"

"How like a man like you to think so—"

Julian cut her off then, his mouth hard on hers, her face held firmly between his hands. The plunder of her senses began, his mouth hot, forcefully gentle, deadly with pleasure.

For the first moment she was shocked, then felt a weakness steal over her, but the realization that she might enjoy it if she let herself caused anger, which in turn saved her from making a fool out of herself. Emotions turned off, she stoically endured the transgression without moving a muscle until he finally had his fill and stepped back from her.

Breathless, she stared coldly at him until she could speak with a steady voice.

"You are to be congratulated, my lord. You have lived up to your reputation. Unfortunately, I am not impressed with brutes who take what they want without permission."

With as much dignity as she could gather around her, she awoke Alice, helped the muddled maid to her feet, then headed with her for the door. As she'd said, he'd proven himself to be exactly what she'd expected, but he was not completely at fault. Perhaps she'd gotten only what she deserved by seeking him out the way she had. More important, she knew him capable of forcing himself on Henrietta, but still she could not fathom how that could have spun out of control and provoked the man to murder her.

Chapter Nine

The next morning dawned bright and clear with crystal blue skies mounded by fluffy white clouds, a perfect day for the onset of Julian's weekend festivities. Not wanting to share his company so soon after their tête-à-tête in the attics, Libby requested a tray brought to her room and procrastinated until the last moment, readying herself for the afternoon ride to Brickhill. Although she had told Julian she was undecided, she had known all along she would attend. She'd heard too much about Julian's parties; the temptation was too enticing to miss it.

As Alice stood behind her and brushed her long hair until it shone, then braided it into the sedate coiffure at the nape that Libby preferred, she contemplated the way Julian had grasped it in his hands and brought it against his face to inhale the scent, and how his lips had felt, so warm and tender, on her mouth. She felt herself shiver at the memory as she pulled on her white gloves and vowed firmly to banish the entire episode of the night before from her mind.

The truth was that she dreaded meeting him face to face again, appalled that he might bandy around the information that she had secretly visited his studio. In the light of day, she was perplexed to fathom what she'd been thinking at the time. On the other hand, she needed more time in his company, to match wits with him until she could draw out the truth, one way or the other. Now that she was beginning to like the man a bit, she hoped her suspicions would come to naught.

As it turned out, she did not have an opportunity to ply

Edmonton with more questions on the road to his estate, for as she descended the main stairs, she found only Lasserthon awaiting her in the vestibule. He jumped to his feet from a foyer wing chair near the dining parlor door, dressed as immaculately as ever for their short journey. She was appalled by the crushing disappointment she felt at the absence of his dark-haired, more fascinating, more dangerous friend. It was the proper time, she told herself with wry self-deprecation, to get a grip on her attraction to Julian before it was too late to do so.

"Good day, Mrs. Thornhill. I trust you slept well," were the first words out of Raymond's mouth as he took Libby's hand and escorted her with his usual aplomb toward the front door.

Since she had spent most of the night tossing from one side to the other, pummeling her pillow and listening to Alice snore contentedly at the foot of her bed, his remark couldn't have been further from the truth. She had finally achieved a fitful rest, only an hour or two at most, and she feared the purple smudges underscoring her eyes would announce the fact to anyone who gave her a glance. She wasn't sure if she would make it through to the evening to come, when the feasting and dancing would no doubt last into the wee hours.

"Well enough, thank you," she lied with a smile, having decided she would not reveal her visit to the demon's lair unless Julian was ungentlemanly enough to inform others of her folly. In that case, of course, she'd have to, and it would be interesting, telling, in fact, to know how many details of their tryst Julian would feel the need to reveal. Again, she was still astounded she'd put herself in that compromising situation, but in her own defense, nothing improper had happened, only a harmless flirtation followed by a stolen kiss. Such things happened daily, or perhaps nightly would be more accurate, both in the *ton* in which her parents and Julian were a part as well as in Philadelphia society. Never, however, had she been the lady involved in such an escapade.

A banished memory came stubbornly back, and she felt the way Julian had held the back of her neck with his fingers, holding her head steady as he kissed her. She felt the same flurry of responses sweep over her nerves and hasten her heartbeat. No wonder he was heralded far and wide for his exploitation of women. Even she, who knew better, who did not trust him, who expected the worst from his every action, even she had fallen momentarily under his spell. One thing she had learned from the experience, however, was abundantly clear—she would never look into his devil's eyes again, and share the fate of a mouse bewitched by a cobra.

"Is Julian not joining us in the coach?" she asked, wanting to know where he was. Alice had appeared from the rear hall, alongside one of Lasserthon's footman, who was carrying her trunk to the luggage cart. She had packed all her things for the weekend festivities at Brickhill, in case she decided to travel on to London from there.

"Julian left well before dawn, as I understand it. He scribbled a note, telling me he had decided to return home early and oversee preparations for this evening. I sometimes wonder if the man ever sleeps."

"He's quite a mysterious figure," she agreed, but she did feel a wave of relief knowing Julian hadn't spent the morning telling humiliating stories about her at Lasserthon's breakfast table.

"I'd hoped you'd grow to like Julian better as you got to know him, but I can see that you haven't changed your opinion."

"He's done little to cause such a change of heart, though I have come to understand through you and others who know him better than myself that he does possess a few good points." Libby Thornhill, she rebuked herself inwardly, you are such a liar. You're beginning to like him despite yourself, and you know it.

"Oh, yes, he's been a great friend to me, very understanding, especially in the early months after Henrietta died."

Raymond had taken her elbow, and he continued speaking as he walked with her outside to where their bags were being loaded into a cart that would follow Lasserthon's well-polished black curricle, drawn by a well-matched pair of grays.

"I predict you'll have a grand time this weekend. No one can quite match Julian's house parties. Though sometimes we all get a bit carried away, he never fails to keep everyone amused."

That was something Libby could readily believe, and as Raymond handed her up into the soft leather seat, then rounded the vehicle to assume the reins, she decided to use the hour-long coach ride to find out as much as possible from Raymond. Though she'd been at Lasserthon Manor for several days, she had spent very little time alone with the master of the house. He had appeared absorbed in his duties concerning his tenants and had been gone from the house more often than not. Poor Henrietta, no wonder she had always been so lonely.

Raymond slapped the reins, and Libby settled the skirt of her pink-sprigged white gown around her legs as Alice and Raymond's valet set off after them in the luggage van. The sunshine was warm and more than welcome where it kissed the top of her head, so much so that she tilted her bonnet brim so that she could feel it upon her face. It was the first truly lovely day since she had arrived at Lasserthon, and the bright sky and gentle breeze did wonders to expel the granite gray fog that usually locked Lasserthon Manor in a death grip.

"You look happy today," Raymond remarked, giving her a sidelong glance as the horses fell into a trot down the driveway. He handled the high-quality team well as the clop of their hooves rang against the cobblestones. "It's wonderful to see you smile like this. You've been very somber since you arrived. I suspect it was difficult for you to sort through Henrietta's things."

Libby nodded. "In another way it gave me pleasure to hold her things in my hands and remember our good times together."

"I sensed from the beginning that you were having trouble accepting her death. I felt you held me responsible, and in truth, I blamed myself as well."

Startled by the way his voice cracked, Libby turned to look at him. He still faced forward, his eyes on the business of driving, but he seemed gripped by melancholy. Again she wondered if he even suspected that Julian might have spent time wooing his wife under his own roof.

Thinking perhaps it was time to find out, she inquired in what she hoped was a nonchalant manner, "Did you not worry about leaving Henrietta alone so often with Julian, considering his dark reputation?"

Raymond emitted a short laugh. His reaction seemed opposed to his earlier sadness, and when he noticed her frown, he explained.

"Henrietta was such an innocent, she'd hardly have recognized his intentions, even if Julian had wished to compromise her integrity. And I do not think he did."

"Would not her naïveté be a reason to protect her from him?"

"Julian wasn't interested in her, I tell you, at least not in that way. My wife was much too sedate and virtuous to attract him. He finds such women boring and more often pursues worldly women who don't play the games of a coy maiden. You'll meet many such women this weekend, for he's invited many of his London friends to join us."

Mary Louise certainly fit the first category better than the less chaste one, and Julian seemed to have wasted no time drawing that poor girl into his web. Libby thought it quite a cruel joke for him to force Mary Louise to announce her engagement in his house.

"It seems to me," she said slowly, eager to judge Lasserthon's reaction, "that Julian takes a great deal of interest in Mary Louise. Perhaps more than he should. I've heard it whispered that she's enamored of someone in the neighborhood other than her betrothed husband. I assumed that man was Julian."

This time Raymond turned from the reins and looked briefly at her, and she realized at once that she had shocked him. He seemed at a loss for what to say, and she wondered if it had been the question, or if he found her staightforwardness less than ladylike.

"I would not know, but I will warn you that Mrs. Tanner

and some of the other ladies of the village have little to do other than spread gossip and conjecture about things which are none of their concern. I am quite certain Mary Louise is completely faithful in her devotion to Fordenbury."

The tone of his statement edged very closely upon a reproach, but the warm smile that followed prevented her from taking offense. Actually, she admired him for defending the poor girl, so she dropped any mention of Mary Louise. It was apparent that Raymond saw no signs of Miss Baird's interest in Julian, or if he had, he refused to believe them of any immoral consequence.

The rest of the journey was spent discussing the village and his extensive landholdings, and he would take the reins in one hand occasionally to point out a distant crofter's hut, then proceed to tell her which farmer lived there, his wife and their children, calling each by name and most affectionately. It seemed to Libby that he was a fair master, with a good relationship with those who tilled his land. There was little wonder, as often as he rode out to visit with them. It probably would have done his marriage a measurable favor if he'd spent half as much time in Henrietta's company. Perhaps then she would not have been so unhappy.

All in all, they enjoyed a lovely drive and an entertaining conversation, but she was pleased when they finally caught sight of the estate known as Brickhill. She peered across grassy meadows as they entered the long road that wound through a deer park to the great house. In time the actual edifice appeared, and Libby was duly impressed with the myriad chimneys and glittering windows. Though not as large and grand as her family's estate at Thorpe, it was very much grander than Lasserthon Manor. As they neared, she admired the huge Georgian structure with its symmetrical wings constructed of burnt-red brick, and she was especially impressed by the large lake that stretched out and mirrored the immense facade at the rear of the house.

"It's quite old, actually," Raymond informed her. "A good portion of the interior had fallen into disrepair during the last decade or so until Julian made his fortune in the Orient trade.

He has spent an ungodly sum on refurbishing the place. You'll see, it's really quite fantastic, and very fitting to Julian's rather unorthodox lifestyle. Especially on the back side, where he's added several galleries that face out over the lake."

"And Julian lives here alone?" Libby asked curiously, noticing the chaise and four being moved down the drive, no doubt on their way to a carriage house hidden by the far wing. Other guests had already arrived, by the look of it.

Lasserthon nodded. "As you know, Julian's lost all his immediate family. Actually, he spends little time here, other than weekends such as this one, when he finds being a host more amusing than his other pursuits."

"Where does he spend most of his time, if that's the case?" Libby realized asking so many questions about Julian might appear strange to Raymond, but he seemed not to notice, happily telling her all she wished to know.

"In London mostly, as I understand it, especially during the Season, though we've had the pleasure of his company a great deal during the last year. He always enjoys the hunt, and he visits Bath to take the waters at times, but more often goes to Brighton. Unfortunately, he was there when that terrible tragedy happened."

"Tragedy?" Libby's interest was immediate. She leaned forward and listened intently as Raymond shook his head.

"You wouldn't have heard of it, of course, but a young lady disappeared there while with her husband. It was quite awful, actually, for the couple had traveled there on their honeymoon. Had been married less than a week, according to Julian. He said it was a terrible thing to witness."

"Julian knew this woman?"

"He'd become acquainted with her previously in London at a ball, or some such event, I believe he said. Apparently her father was an old friend of Julian's family. The husband was completely distraught, as you might well imagine."

Libby sat completely still, trying to rein in her reaction, but the irony did not escape her. The fact that Julian was there when another young woman disappeared might very well have been a coincidence, but then again, it could point out a pattern, a sinister one.

"Did they ever find out what happened to her?"

"No, it has remained unsolved to this day. Her body was never found, though the police conjectured she might have gotten stranded on the rocks and been washed out to sea. They say she enjoyed walking the sands, despite warnings of the danger."

The girl's demise was sounding increasingly similar to Henrietta's disappearance on the moors. Libby felt the sick feeling in her stomach return with curls of nausea as they finally wound around a great water fountain dominating the middle of Brickhill's cobbled front court. As much as she didn't want to believe Julian guilty of wrongdoing, everything continued to point to him. One thing was for certain: despite her growing desire to believe he was not the culprit, she would have to continue to be vigilant now that she knew he could be implicated in more than one unexplained accidental death.

Her resolve only solidified as they rolled to a stop in front of the elegantly curved marble staircase that led up to the front door. If Julian was the killer, if he had harmed Henrietta and the other missing woman, he would pay for it. She gazed up at the magnificent house in which he lived, fully aware this weekend might be her last chance to prove him guilty.

As they climbed down from the coach, she saw that Sir Jasper and his wife had arrived not far behind them. She waited for them to disembark from their gig, glad to see friendly faces, and listened to Evelyn's gay chatter as a Chinese butler dressed in a very English manner, in immaculate gold and white livery, led them through the great hall of white marble to a wide, sun-splashed gallery that ran the entire length at the back of the house.

"I do hope Julian deigns to show up," Raymond murmured to her in a hushed voice, peering up at the huge, ornately framed portraits lining the wall behind them. "As you've noticed, I'm sure, Julian is nothing if not unpredictable. There have been occasions when he hosts a party such as this and forgets to show up. Or perhaps he just doesn't want to show up. For all I know, he could be in London by now, enjoying himself with new pleasures."

Nothing Julian did would surprise Libby, and in a way she hoped he would show up late, if only for the sake of poor Mary Louise. Libby would never understand why he'd wish to host the engagement party for his own lover. Somehow she couldn't help feeling sorry for the girl. Last night Libby had been the one to suffer the intensity of his gaze and debilitating burn of his lips against her skin. She chastised herself for thinking about it, angry she was showing such weakness. When first she'd begun to suspect him, she had thought herself immune from his charm. Last night had proven that she was no better than any other smitten woman. She thought again of the way he had knotted his hands in her hair, but was chilled more when she remembered the brief instant his fingers had encircled her throat. She had not been frightened at the time, but perhaps she should have been. Could he be a killer? Had he restrained his deadly impulses that moment for reasons known only to him?

She'd be on her guard from this moment forward, she vowed as she and Raymond accompanied the other couple out onto a flagstone terrace overlooking a lake and well-manicured gardens. It seemed that Julian had brought a good many foreign servants back with him along with Lu Ling, for nearly all the servants wandering among the tables set up on the terrace were Chinese. A stone parapet separated the flagstones from the grass, but most of the white linen-draped tables held spectacular views of the lake. She detected Mrs. Tanner and Betty Curtis at one such vantage point, and it wasn't a moment before the two women glimpsed them and delightedly motioned for Libby and Evelyn to join them.

"Ah, there are some of our neighbors. Please feel free to say hello to them, if you wish," Lasserthon told her, leaning close. "If you don't mind, I see a friend of mine down by the water. I need to have a word with him before the day's out, so if you'll forgive me, I'll do so now."

"By all means," she agreed as he lifted her hand and pressed a polite kiss to the back of her gloved fingers. "Enjoy yourself. I shall enjoy sitting with Evelyn and the other ladies."

"Until later." Lasserthon smiled quite pleasantly before turning to depart, and Libby wondered again what he'd done to cause Henrietta to feel so unkindly toward him. As far as she could ascertain, he treated everyone, especially the ladies of his acquaintance, with a great deal of respect. Other than his choice of Julian as a good friend, he appeared a hard worker who took his duties seriously and had exhibited few other flaws that she'd been able to detect.

"I was hoping we could avoid Mrs. Tanner today, but it appears we're to be bored by her no matter where we go," whispered Evelyn after her husband had begged off to have a smoke with a couple of cronies. Her smile was rueful, and her eyes glowed with mischief.

Libby laughed, thinking that Evelyn looked wonderful in her pale yellow day dress decorated by a large white lace fichu at the neck, and her cheerful mood was catching. Unfortunately, the twittering Mrs. Tanner was to be endured, but Betty Curtis would be entertaining, though she was adorned in yet another staid, dreary dark gown that she no doubt wore in deference to her husband's wishes. She too put on a wide, welcoming smile, as if she were very glad to see Libby and Evelyn. But who wouldn't feel that way when forced to sit alone with Mrs. Tanner for any length of time?

For a few moments their discourse involved the unusually fine weather, which was truly the best Libby had witnessed since her arrival at Lasserthon. The sun still ruled the sky above, and it would have been hot if not for the gentle breezes blowing in off the lake.

When the subject turned to Julian's estate, she listened with care, surprised to find by their many exclamations that they'd rarely visited him before, despite the proximity of his home to their village. She wondered why he had suddenly become so magnanimous with his invitations, as she looked out over the tiered gardens with lovely meandering flagged walks and towering marble statues of gods and goddesses. Scattered at intervals around the water were benches grouped where guests could enjoy looking out over the water, and many couples were already strolling there.

Although it appeared many guests had already shown up, she realized it was early yet, and if Julian's weekend parties were like those hosted by her parents, most of the Londoners in attendance would arrive later, in time for the evening, when the engagement would be announced, or late the next morning.

Listening with only half an ear to the animated conversation swirling around her, Libby found herself examining the other people milling around on the terrace and gardens below, wondering who they were and what their relationship with Julian might be. She'd heard much about his wild lifestyle, but these conservatively dressed, polite people certainly did not seem the type to carouse in drunken revelry.

More important, she scanned the unknown faces with the terror of running into a family friend. Surely her own family shared a few friends with the Earl of Edmonton, since they no doubt frequented the same parties. That would not do, so she pledged to herself to remain watchful in that regard as well, scrutinizing nearly everyone in proximity but fortunately finding no familiar faces among the increasing throng of guests. She turned her eyes back upon the lake, which glittered a brilliant silver under the glare of the sun.

In time, she realized, and with deep dismay, that she was searching for Julian's tall figure among the people around her. She frowned with supreme annoyance. Irritated by her growing fascination with the man, one who could very well be a murderer, she suffered a self-disgusted flush that heated her face and pricked her conscience. She shut her eyes when she thought of the way she'd felt when alone with him, the shivery, excited thrills he had sent through her. He was dangerous, she knew that, but she craved those feelings again. She'd not felt it often, rarely, in her well-ordered life filled with propriety and gratifying work.

Highly annoyed with herself, she sought to focus her attention on something else, anything. She caught sight of Raymond and found him strolling along with Mary Louise some distance away near where a stand of willow trees hung their thick fronds out over the water.

"Lasserthon seems very fond of Mary Louise," she murmured, her eyes remaining on them as they moved slowly along the lakeside path away from the house.

For a few moments she didn't really notice the silence that fell after her remark. When she did become aware, she glanced curiously at her companions. Betty had blushed, and Mrs. Tanner pursed her beak-like lips in a knowing smirk. Evelyn was silent, but her happy countenance had sobered.

"Did I say something wrong?"

"No, of course not." Evelyn sighed as if reluctant to explain, but Mrs. Tanner lowered her voice to a more sedate chirp, her head bouncing around so happily that Libby knew she was more than pleased to enlighten her. The little woman leaned forward, a conspirator ready to share the worst of confidences.

"You'd have no way of knowing, of course, my dear, but those two have a past together. Since she was little more than a child. It was quite scandalous, actually."

Libby was stunned, for it was quite clear what the woman meant. She turned to Evelyn for verification, finding it hard to believe.

"I'm afraid so," she said softly. "But it's over now. Although Mary Louise had been Raymond's mistress for some time, he did end their relationship when Henrietta arrived from America."

"Some people think otherwise," Mrs Tanner contradicted quickly and with glee. "I myself saw them together in the village not two days before his sweet little wife was lost on the moors."

Still reeling over this dismaying revelation, Libby looked back at Raymond and Mary Louise. They walked side by side but were not touching. She glanced around for Sir John and found him at last, standing alone at a distant part of the terrace wall, watching his intended moving off with her former lover. She wondered if he sensed what had gone on between them, but another question plagued her more.

"Did Henrietta know about them?"

Obviously uncomfortable with the subject, Evelyn lowered her voice to little more than a whisper. "I don't believe so. She never mentioned anything akin to it, though at times I was afraid she might suspect they were more than just friends. I must say that I feel Mrs. Tanner's wrong about the affair continuing once Raymond had married Henrietta."

"I am not wrong, Evelyn, I assure you. I have seen him enter her house with my own eyes, on more than one occasion."

"That could have been an innocent meeting, you know. Mary Louise is not a bad girl. She's had more hardship in her life than the rest of us, so I do feel some Christian charity is in order."

Betty spoke up in the young girl's defense. "Yes, she was orphaned early, and if not for Raymond's patronage, she would indeed have been destitute. It was only later when she was older that she fell into the path of sin. I never heard a word or saw her in Raymond's company after his wedding."

"Or perhaps she was more interested in that handsome friend of his by then." Mrs. Tanner's relish for the subject grew by leaps and bounds as the conversation continued. "It's clear to me that she's now in love with Lord Edmonton. And that one will not hesitate to have all he can, if you understand my meaning. I think it outrageous that he dared hold Sir John's engagement party here at his house with all their sinful goings-on."

"Mrs. Tanner, please, you have no real basis for these accusations. This is Mary Louise's betrothal party. You should be more generous in your observations."

Betty's voice carried a slight edge, and Mrs. Tanner had the grace to look embarrassed at the reproof. After having caught Julian molesting Mary Louise behind the parlor drapes, Libby found herself reluctant to disagree with Mrs. Tanner's less than complimentary assessment of the situation between their host and the soon-to-be bride. The bridegroom was being cuckolded even before the wedding, and it would be interesting to learn what he knew of the situation. She tried to remember the dinner party when she'd met him, but recalled little except that he seemed to dote on his young fiancée, endlessly caressing her arm or her hand as if he couldn't resist touching her.

"Good morning, ladies."

Julian's rich baritone voice came from directly behind Libby, and she was startled by the sheer power of her reaction. She felt herself stiffen in dread, her heart racing so hard she could feel her own pulse—she, who'd always prided herself on her self-control. She set her teeth, more angry at herself than Julian for causing her to act like such a nitwit. She realized she sat in rigid anxiety, not sure if he'd announce her visit to his quarters in front of the other ladies. He was not above it, played by few of the rules adhered to by everyone else, but she would maintain her pride even if he did humiliate her.

"Mrs. Thornhill, you are looking exceptionally lovely today. The sun brings out more gold in your hair."

Because of his direct address she was forced to acknowledge his presence, and she did so, slowly raising her gaze. He stood smiling down at her, tall and aloof, as unsettling as ever. His eyes shone a brilliant blue in the sunlight, full of mysteries, but at the moment openly amused by her wariness. He wore riding apparel, a dark brown jacket with a white shirt underneath and his usual tall leather boots over tight tan breeches. But this day she knew how he looked with his shirt off, and she felt herself flushing again.

"I see you've been out for a morning ride, Lord Edmonton," chirped Mrs. Tanner with cheery goodwill, as if she had not accused him of being a lusty seducer of maidens only moments before.

"A party of us enjoyed a hunt early this morning." He still held a riding crop, but he tucked it under his arm as he pulled off his brown leather gloves. "Actually, I was on my way to change into more appropriate attire."

"Do you intend to have some of us sit for you this week-end, sir?" Mrs. Tanner adopted a coy grin that turned her into the spitting image of a carrier pigeon. "I've heard much about portraits being done here when you have your friends up from London. I do admire your work, you know."

Julian bowed his head in acknowledgment. "Actually, I'm quite determined to persuade Mrs. Thornhill here to sit for me. I'm mightily intrigued by her unusual coloring. Perhaps you ladies could help me to convince her."

Libby was aware that Evelyn was looking at her with a newly assessing eye, and Libby was furious with him for bringing up the subject, though she well knew he could have done far worse.

"You really should, Libby," Betty encouraged, her smile completely unwary. "It's quite an honor to sit for Julian, I'm sure you know by now."

"I'm sure there are many others who would be glad to oblige him. I prefer not," Libby answered, hoping to put an end to it.

"But my dear Mrs. Thornhill, I've already begun your portrait, as you well know," he said, his eyes adopting the most devilish glint. "You must allow me to finish what I've started."

Not sure exactly which way to take his remark, she stiffened, but the other ladies only smiled encouragingly. When she refused to comment further, Julian beamed down at her.

"Mrs. Thornhill, if you please, I'd like to show you something very beautiful. Would you walk with me for a moment?"

The following silence drew out to an oppressive extent, and Libby realized the others were wondering at her rudeness. She could not in good grace refuse such a polite request from her host, and he knew that full well. If he continued to seek her out as he was doing at the moment, perhaps the more likely he would be let some incriminating remark slip. There was little chance in any case that he would try anything untoward, not with so many people milling about.

"You've quirked my curiosity. What do you wish to show me?"

His grin was just as intriguing as his offer had been. The three other women turned smiling gazes upon him, unaware of the cat-and-mouse game he was playing with Libby.

"Ah, but that would ruin my surprise, would it not?"

Libby assessed him with wariness, then capitulated. As she made to stand, he pulled back her chair for her. He was exhibiting nothing but charm at the moment, so she decided to listen to what he had to say. Perhaps it would be interesting to know if Julian was aware of his friend's past relationship with his latest lover.

After she had excused herself from her friends, Julian extended his arm to her, as if he really were a gentleman, and she took it, willing to play along with him for the benefit of onlookers.

"You never fail to surprise me. I would never have thought you'd agree to go off alone with me."

"I'm not afraid of you," she said sharply. "You might as well stop trying to intimidate me."

Julian gave a low laugh, nodding to a couple chatting at the top of the marble stairs. "You are a most unusual woman, Mrs. Thornhill."

"Because I'm not taken aback by your charming ways?"

"Are you saying you do not find me charming? Surely I misunderstood you."

He was teasing her, but the unfortunate truth was that she did find him more than agreeable at the moment. "At times, perhaps, when you forget yourself."

He remained unruffled, his sensual lips curved in a smile, and when she realized he was leading her toward the lake, she searched the turn in the flagstone walk where she'd last seen Lasserthon. He and Mary Louise had disappeared.

She decided to confront Julian outright so she could judge his reaction. "Is it true that Raymond and Mary Louise are lovers?"

If he was surprised by the question, he didn't show it. In truth, she realized, he rarely displayed emotion openly. It occurred to her that he always looked guarded, self-contained. Why, if he did not have crimes to hide? Aloof, sardonic, there were many words that could describe his manner. Did his implacable mask of indifference ever crack? Was it inner evil he kept so well hidden from others? At times she felt he was as despicable as his reputation decreed; while perversely, at others, she found herself liking his quick wit, if nothing else.

"Is that what you've heard?"

"Yes."

"Rumors do abound. Alas, I'm accused of the same thing. Actually, by you, I fear."

"That's more than rumor. I can attest to its veracity."

"Mary Louise is now betrothed to Sir John. I look upon her as such. I'm sure Lasserthon does as well."

"You're very good at not answering my questions, my lord."

"Such skill comes with much practice, I assure you."

Libby did not doubt that, but as they strolled under the shade of the birch trees edging the lake, she kept a safe distance between them. Many others were enjoying the sun-dappled walkway but there was no sight of the two they were discussing. The lake was large and formed a turn that hid much of its length from the house. A tall hedge had been planted alongside the pleasant paths, at the base of which grew lush flowers of every hue. Brickhill was truly a beautiful place.

When Julian stopped and gestured toward a path that veered off to their right, a course that would take them out of sight of her friends back on the upper terrace, Libby shook her head. "You really don't think me foolish enough to wander off alone with you, do you?"

"You were alone with me last night, and nothing remotely dishonorable happened."

Libby lifted one eyebrow, calling him on the remark without uttering a word.

"Well, not as dishonorable as I would have liked."

"I never allow myself to make the same mistake twice, Lord Edmonton."

"There's a bench a few yards up this path. Surely you'll

agree to walk that far with me? As you can see, it's hardly isolated enough for me to embark on a full-fledged seduction."

"I'm sure you do know the most appropriate places hereabouts for that sort of thing," she said, but the spot was openly visible. When she saw another group of guests enjoying the shade underneath a nearby rose arbor, she agreed. They passed a round stone table where two elderly gentlemen played at chess. Both men greeted them civilly, and inquired after Julian's success at the morning hunt, and she felt perfectly safe when she seated herself atop a bench in front of a tinkling fountain.

"All right. You've enticed me here. What is it?"

Julian remained standing. "Is this not a beautiful spot?"

Libby looked around, having been more interested in him than in the surroundings. In her eyes, it did not seem particularly outstanding. There was lush ivy growing on the trellis behind her, but none of the fragrant beauty of Evelyn's rose garden recommended it. Sun dappled the bench on which she sat, dancing among fluttering oak leaves before streaming down atop her head.

"It is pleasant enough, I suppose. But all of your property is lovely. What is it here that you find so entrancing?"

"You."

Libby had to laugh. "I looked the same at the terrace table as I do here."

"That's not true. Here the sun glints against your hair, and the green of the ivy makes it gleam like copper. I want to portray you sitting right here. Since you refuse to sit for me, I'll have to memorize how you look at this moment. The vision has exceeded my most vivid imagination."

"Yes, I realize I must be overwhelming to you, but somehow I suspect you have other reasons for bringing me down here."

"Very true. I'd like to ask you to accept once and for all the truth about Henrietta's death. You've been told the facts, and snooping around the way you have been will only cause more trouble for yourself."

Libby was amazed that he'd verbalized the request so openly, and she could not help but take his words as a threat.

When she opened her mouth to accuse him of just that, she was prevented of the opportunity when Mary Louise suddenly appeared just down the path from them. Walking at a fast clip, the young woman stopped abruptly on the lake path when she caught sight of them in the shade.

"Julian! Please, may I speak with you?"

For the first time since she'd made his acquaintance, Libby could readily read Julian's expression. He was alarmed. Did he care so much for the young girl? It appeared that he did because he wasted no time begging Libby's leave.

"If you'll pardon me, Mrs. Thornhill, it appears Miss Baird is in some distress. I'll look forward to seeing you tonight at the engagement ball. I've provided all my guests with costumes. You'll find yours lying on your bed."

Then he was gone, his long strides taking him down the path in a great hurry. Libby watched with interest when they met. Mary Louise was clearly agitated, and Julian appeared to be calming her as he took her elbow and led her swiftly toward the house. Libby looked around, but the other people in sight seemed to think nothing of the extraordinary incident. She continued to watch them until they were out of sight, very curious indeed to know what had happened. She rose and followed their path back to the house, determined that she would find out that night at the party, if she had to ask Mary Louise herself.

Chapter Ten

Pondering the unsettling scene she'd witnessed between Julian and Mary Louise, Libby followed a young, moon-faced Chinese maid who took her up the lavish main stair and down a long corridor in search of her bedchamber. To her surprise, the girl spoke English, albeit brokenly, and was halfway chatty at that, pointing out various rooms of interest as they walked along, including Julian's private apartments. It was hard to believe she was actually a guest staying inside Julian's home, an eventuality she would have never bet on a few days ago.

As she walked through the wide, carpeted corridor set with elaborate mahogany wall moldings and crystal candle sconces, she was surprised when they ran into so few of the other guests. The upper floors were every bit as lavishly impressive as she'd found the rest of Brickhill, and she was especially drawn to the expansive, sunny galleries, where long velvet benches beckoned her to sit below the tall mullioned windows and admire the magnificent panorama of lakes and green rolling hills beyond.

When she finally reached her destination, she opened the door of her spacious chamber and found Alice busily unpacking Libby's clothing. She whirled around at Libby's entrance, peering intently through her damaged glasses to see who was intruding on her sanctuary, then bobbed a dutiful curtsy when she recognized her mistress. "I'm almost done here, ma'am. I barely found me way here. The house is almost as big as His Grace's."

"Yes, it nearly is," Libby agreed, glancing around as she

tugged off her gloves, taking in the large canopied bed with its cream silk bed hangings and the massive matching wardrobe. Both were intricately carved, made of teak and obviously imported from China. Julian certainly had a fondness for all things oriental, and she wondered how many of his bedchambers were furnished in so exotic a decor. Perhaps later she'd have time to explore a bit and find out.

At the moment, however, she was tired. Although she hadn't been in England long, her efforts to expose Julian as a killer had taken a definite emotional toll, despite the fact she had yet to come up with any proof of his wrongdoing. More disturbing, she was becoming fond of him, no matter how hard she tried to remind herself that he was probably a villain to be despised. There was just some chord that he struck inside her, the reverberations of which she couldn't ignore. Shaking her head, she was more than aware it was his male sensuality that appealed to her, just as he intrigued most woman who met him.

Depressed by her weakness, she collapsed into a comfortable wing chair beside the bed. On a nearby table a large black vase held white roses, perhaps two dozen blooms or even more. She leaned close to the flowers and inhaled the sweet perfume.

"He had 'em brought up, ma'am. I put 'em in water so they wouldn't die, but I didn't like touching 'em, no, I did not. He's a devil, 'e is." Alice wrapped her arms protectively around her waist, as if the delicate blossoms might leap out and attack her with their thorn-studded stems.

"They're just flowers, Alice. I'm sure he provided a similar bouquet for every guest."

"I know he got his eye on you. I seen the way he looks at you. And those roses isn't all he got for you. A girl brought up that box over there on the bed too. I know it ain't my place to say such things, ma'am, but I still think he's not one to be trusted. You told me what he did. The duke and duchess wouldn't like you bein' here at this place, and neither would Mr. Thornhill, Lord rest his soul."

"No, I suppose they wouldn't." Libby sighed, realizing

her answer was a vast understatement, and leaned her head tiredly back against the chair. She watched the young servant cross the room and fetch the long rectangular box that lay atop the quilted satin counterpane. The return to England seemed to have brought out Alice's original speech patterns. The girl had had a most unhappy life until she'd come to them. An orphan with no family, no worldly goods, but she had good common sense despite her flightiness. All of Alice's fears had a concrete basis and had been Libby's too, until she was subjected to Julian's seductive charm.

Still, Libby was not a complete fool. That inner voice of hers, one she'd learned to give credence to, kept whispering that Julian hadn't hurt Henrietta. In other moments it also told her that he knew more about her death than he would ever tell her. Could he be protecting someone? Lasserthon perhaps? Or some other person in the village? Or could it be that both men were merely telling the truth, one that Libby didn't want to accept, that Henrietta's mental state had grown increasingly fragile until the time she had become so distraught that she had wandered afar and perished. Guilt came swiftly and berated her loyalty, and face heated by shame, she accepted Julian's gift from Alice's hands.

Wanting a diversion from such confused thoughts, she tugged loose the red satin ribbon and pulled it aside. The top lifted off easily, and inside she found very thin tissue paper. Inside its crackling folds lay a beautiful length of the finest white silk adorned with tightly braided gold trim.

As she lifted out the flowing silk and held it up. Alice hovered nearby, but not too close, as if she thought Julian might have secreted a serpent inside its creases. Libby recognized it immediately for what it was, but Alice peered in puzzlement at the long rectangular garment.

"What is it?" she asked, completely nonplussed.

"It's a chiton," Libby explained to her, rubbing the thin silk between her thumb and forefinger and finding it luxuriously soft and pliant. "The people of ancient Greece wore these garments, wrapped around the body with the ends thrown over the shoulders." She demonstrated in front of the cheval mirror near the windows, and the silk floated to the floor around her feet. She had visited Greece once with her parents when she was a small girl, and been fascinated with the figures in the museums with their gracefully draped clothing, both men and women wearing robes similar to the one she had donned over her dress. She pivoted, turning to look at the back, and thinking it not much different than the simple fashions now so popular that had been exported from France.

"Perhaps you should let it hang for a while, Alice, to prevent wrinkles from forming. Julian said I should wear it tonight."

"You ain't gonna wear that big sheet, are you, ma'am? Heaven help us if His Grace finds out." Alice's voice was scandalized as she examined the design. "Why, there ain't nothin' to it but a piece of silk. There's no sleeves and no top and no bottom and no buttons to hold it together."

"I suppose he's decided to give the ball with a Greek theme. He told me that everyone will be given a costume to wear."

"Don't trust him, ma'am. 'e's up to no good, I know it."

"Alice, please, I realize that I put quite a fright in you when I revealed my suspicions about Julian, but you've got to remember, that's all they were. I've found no proof against him, no matter how hard I've tried. He may be perfectly innocent, after all."

Alice looked unconvinced.

"You can rest assured that I'll be very careful. If he wanted to hurt us, he had the perfect opportunity that night in the attics. As much as I hate to admit it, I might have jumped to the wrong conclusion and placed blame too readily. Everything is beginning to point to the fact that Henrietta was lost on the moors as was reported."

At that point she noticed another, smaller box that lay in tissue at the bottom of the dress box. A small card of expensive vellum was attached, one of Julian's calling cards. His name was emblazoned across the front in flowing gold script. She turned it over and found a short note penned in strong, slanted handwriting. "I wish to see you adorned as Diana the Huntress, so I have made all things Greek this weekend in your honor. I would be very pleased if you'd wear it tonight. The contents of the small box is a gift for your ever present bodyguard. Please present it to Alice with my compliments." The note was signed with the letter J. Libby could not help but smile as Alice returned from hanging the long length of silk over a hook inside the mirrored wardrobe.

"Julian sent you a present, Alice."

Alice peered suspiciously at the box Libby held out to her. "Why would 'is lordship be givin' me a present? What is it?"

"Why don't you open it and find out? Perhaps it's a peace offering. You've made it abundantly clear you're terrified of him, you know."

"Some little trinket ain't going to make me trust 'im," she said, but she eyed the box with interest.

"So you don't want it?"

Alice hesitated but not for long. "I guess I could take a quick peek, just to see."

Libby was curious herself and watched as Alice took it and quickly removed the top.

"Oh, heaven be praised," Alice breathed with pleasure when she saw the pair of small wire-rimmed spectacles. She wasted no time ridding herself of her cracked lenses. She perched the new eyeglasses atop her nose. "Oh, I can see again, ma'am!"

Libby espied the card inside the box. "He's written you a note too."

Alice picked up the card and looked at it, then handed it to Libby. "Would you read it to me, ma'am?"

Libby read it and laughed. "He says that he presents these glasses to you with his compliments so that you can keep a better eye on him."

Alice looked a bit miffed, but she kept the glasses on and made no further mention of Julian's shortcomings.

Libby yawned. "I think I'll lie down and rest awhile. I've heard Julian's parties usually last past dawn. I'll need a bath brought up later, but if you want to go upstairs to the servants' hall, I won't need you until then."

After Alice helped Libby out of her dress and into a blue velvet robe, she curtsied and left the room. Libby snuggled down underneath the covers and stared up at the canopy, thinking that it was very thoughtful of Julian to find glasses for her maid. Not many gentlemen would do so, would even consider the needs of a servant. Where had he found them? God help her, she was falling under his spell, liking him more and more. She would have to be careful this last weekend she spent in his company, not let anything untoward happen between them. On Monday morning perhaps she should travel on to London instead of going back to Lasserthon. As her eyes drifted closed, she wondered if she might meet up with him there during the coming Season. If he was innocent, they might conceivably enjoy each other's company in the future. Perhaps she might even sit for him, under the proper conditions, if he still wanted her to. With that last thought she drifted into an easy slumber with no bad dreams to disturb her.

"You mean, you just wrap up yourself in this sheet and go downstairs without a proper gown?"

Alice's voice was dubious as she carried the long silk chiton draped over her arm to Libby. She wore her new bifocals so she could see clearly once again, and she looked mightily disapproving as Libby wrapped the gown securely around her, then carefully brought the extra length over her shoulders.

"There, now you can see how it forms a perfectly modest gown." Libby pointed at two gold brooches Julian had enclosed with the chiton. "Help me pin the ends in place. You see, it's quite appropriate if you take the care to adjust it properly. My parents have hosted Grecian affairs on occasion, you know."

Mollified by the announcement that the Duke and Duchess of Thorpe would not object, Alice carefully affixed the pins atop each shoulder, firmly anchoring the smooth fabric in place. Libby gazed critically at her reflection as she turned this way and that in front of the mirror. The draping garment was loose and comfortable, and was truly not so different from her normal clothing except that it was draped instead of fitted. She pulled the gold braid belt around her waist and knotted it securely. The soft, filmy fabric clung to every curve of her body, which some might consider inappropriate immodesty, but Libby loved the graceful draping that fell around her legs.

She did not feel the least bit scandalous to wear it, not when she had wrapped it so modestly. She wore her chemise and white silk stockings as she always did, so she saw no reason not to attend the party attired as she was. Still, it was a sensuous garb, suggestive in the way it clung to the female form, and it was not lost upon her that Julian might have chosen the Greek theme for exactly that reason. His parties were purported to be unrestrained affairs, but that did not mean she would resort to carousing. She was quite certain that neither would her friends in attendance; in truth, the idea of Evelyn, Betty, and Mrs. Tanner partaking in wild debauchery made her laugh. She was eager to see tiny Mrs. Tanner in the flowing robe Julian had provided her.

"This will do nicely, Alice. I feel comfortable enough to wear this to the ball."

Alice looked askance at her, as if not quite sure she could agree, while somewhere in the hall outside Libby's door, a man suddenly shouted with laughter. Libby had heard other guests arriving and settling themselves in the adjacent rooms throughout the afternoon. By the raucous, jovial shouts and bursts of merriment, she feared Julian's London friends had come to have a rip-roaring good time. She couldn't deny she was curious to see just how they'd accomplish that goal.

At the moment it sounded as if many of the guests were departing their bedchambers for the night's festivities, their muffled conversations sounding eager and excited, and Libby felt an unfamiliar twinge of nervousness. She looked at herself again as she sat down in front of a dressing table set with a round mirror. The costume was not revealing, she reassured herself, she was perfectly presentable. Alice had become adept at arranging hair since she'd become Libby's personal maid, and she worked now to make the coiffure just right, her face creased with utter concentration as she braided Libby's long hair into the elegant chignon that Libby had described to her as was worn in ancient Athens.

When Alice was finally done and stood back with pride to admire her handiwork, Libby raised the lid of her jewelry case and selected a long strand of pearls. She draped them through the braided coils and across her forehead as she'd seen done in oil paintings. Once satisfied, she still hesitated, perversely both excited and dreading the coming evening.

The truth was that she'd not attended such a gala in a long time. John had rarely felt up to such affairs, and after his death she'd thought it improper to attend alone, except for a few soirees given by close friends. Now, however, she was flushed with excitement and anticipation in a way she had not been since a young, unmarried girl. What's more, she knew the reason had more to do with spending time with Julian again than with dancing and mingling at Mary Louise's engagement party. She was bewitched, she feared, but not so much that she would lose her head altogether.

"Alice, run downstairs and make sure everyone else is wearing costumes. I cannot imagine my embarrassment if I was the only one to attend dressed like this."

Alice was gone in a thrice, and Libby had a feeling the girl hoped to be able to report that no one else had dared don a chiton. She took a deep breath to reduce her growing apprehension.

Goodness gracious, she was not a blushing innocent at her first season! But that's how it felt, she realized, as if she were dressing up for adult activities for the first time, ready to be presented to society. Much to her parents' dismay, she had refused the usual coming-out ball—in fact, had shunned the London season entirely. At the time she had not wished to be a part of the English *ton* who glided through the halls of Almack's with their noses in the air. She had too much American blood running through her veins and vastly preferred the new republic, much to her father's rage. She feared he'd never quite forgiven his daughter for preferring America to England, and their relationship, so close and loving all her life, had been strained since her wedding to John. Her mother, Trinity, an American born and bred herself, understood and tempered his anger. Her mother had become quite good at handling her father through the years. Lately Libby had come to realize how hurt he must have been over her adamant refusal to live in England. She looked forward to traveling on to London; again thinking she'd go there after the weekend was over. She hadn't realized how much she'd missed them.

Behind her the door swung open and banged on the wall behind it. Alice rushed through the doorway, looking terribly distraught, and Libby jumped up and whirled around.

"What is it?" she cried, alarmed by the ashen hue of her maid's face.

"Miss Baird is missin'! Everybody's in an uproar down in kitchens, and the servants are all sayin' she's run away so she won't have to marry his lordship! That's all the staff's talkin' about, but the party's going on too, just like that poor lady ain't gone and run off."

For a moment Libby stood very still, the most horrible sense of dread slowly rising from some deep, dark place inside her. She knew, somehow, and with absolute conviction, that Julian was responsible for this dreadful turn of events.

"What about Sir John? Does he know she's gone?"

"One o' the footmen said he upped and drove off in his carriage with not word of farewell to a soul. I did hear a groom say 'e was headed back home. They think 'e means to catch up to her and make her marry him, whether she wants to or not."

"Julian hasn't postponed the ball?" Libby asked incredulously, placing one hand on the dressing table to steady legs that suddenly felt shaky.

Alice shook her head until the tight curls peeking out from her cap danced around her face. "The ladies and gents are wearin' the Greek sheets, but nobody's seen Lord Edmonton. Nobody knows where he went, not even his butler and the housekeeper." Her eyes rounded considerably and grew fearful. "Do you think he be the one who took her off, ma'am, took Miss Baird and killed her, like 'e did to poor Miss Hen?"

Libby forced down a swallow through a throat that felt constricted to the size of a dressmaker's pin. She did fear the worst had happened to Mary Louise, but if Julian was at fault, why would he wait to commit the crime at home, with a house full of guests? An alibi perhaps?

A ripple of frigid apprehension shimmied down her spine, revealing quite clearly what she really believed. She did not want to believe Julian was involved, but how could she not? She'd seen him that afternoon with Mary Louise, seen how upset the young woman had been. Unless he was downstairs with his guests, had been with various people throughout the day who could verify that he'd had no part in what had happened. Perhaps Mary Louise had run away of her own volition. Or, perhaps someone else had been involved.

"What about Lord Lasserthon, Alice? Did you see him among the guests?"

Getting a hold on herself now that Libby seemed calm and composed, Alice answered with less hysteria, "Yes, ma'am. He asked about you, when you be comin' down. He said to tell you he was waitin' for you."

"He'll know exactly what's happened between Sir John and Miss Baird, I'm sure." Libby walked to the door, the soft drapes of silk fluttering around her legs. She stopped there, glancing back at her maid, who was wringing her hands, her eyes, greatly magnified behind her new eyeglasses, filled with worry.

"Oh, ma'am, can't we go on to London now? I'm frightened to stay. Ladies ain't safe hereabouts."

Libby took a moment and seriously considered Alice's suggestion. Now that Mary Louise had disappeared so mysteriously, all Libby's initial misgivings about Julian were returning in full force and with frightening certitude. She would go downstairs and find out as much as she could about the situation. If she still felt misgivings afterward, perhaps she should journey to London and present all her suspicions to her father.

"You may sleep here in my room if you wish, Alice. I know you're frightened. If Miss Baird isn't found by tomorrow morning, we'll depart for my parents' house in London."

"Oh, yes, yes, thank you." Alice's body drooped with relief. "His Grace wouldn't like us bein' here with all this evil and killin' and disappearin' goin' on."

"Neither would Mother. It will probably turn out to be some inadvertent misunderstanding, I suspect, and nothing more than that. Perhaps it's only a case of the bride getting cold feet. It never appeared to me that Miss Baird ever held any fondness for Sir John."

"You will be careful, won't you, ma'am?" Alice's trembling voice beseeched her. "I don't trust Lord Edmonton, even if he did give me my new spectacles. I been around men like 'im more than you, men who 'ave that look to their eyes. I seen the things they do to innocents like you, ma'am."

"Alice, I'm hardly an innocent. I'm a grown woman, completely versed in the ways of the world. I know Julian has his faults, some of which I heartily disapprove, and you can rest assured I won't lose my head before I know what part he has in all this. I'm capable of taking care of myself. Besides, I have other friends here, and I intend to surround myself with them throughout the evening."

Alice nodded but did not look or sound convinced. "I'll stay 'ere with you so 'e can't get at you."

Libby nodded, but she was very eager to get downstairs and question Raymond about this latest development. Outside in the corridor, she began to pick up faint strains of music long before she reached the top of the grand marble staircase. As she paused at the balustrade, she realized the party was in full swing. At least fifty guests were already milling about, maybe more. As Alice had said, most of them wore flowing white robes.

Among the moving throng she picked out Raymond's position when he lifted his arm in a wave. He began to push a path toward the bottom of the steps, obviously intending to meet her. She descended quickly, noting with some dismay that many of Julian's female guests had not pinned their chitons modestly as she had but had draped the silk over only one shoulder, leaving the other completely bare and making it readily apparent they wore little, if nothing, underneath their silk chitons.

"Where have you been? I've been waiting for you." Lasserthon took her hand and touched the back of it with his mouth. He looked annoyed, she saw his mood quite clearly, and she also sensed by the red, watery condition of his eyes that he'd been drinking for some time, and too much by the looks of it. The odor of brandy was strong upon his breath, and so potent she was forced to turn her head.

Good God, he was already drunk, very close to complete inebriation. He took her arm, holding on to her much too tightly, obviously unsteady on his feet. She had never seen him thus and certainly did not appreciate the way he was forcing her along with him. Perhaps she'd finally seen the vice that had turned Henrietta against her husband.

"Is it true that Miss Baird has come up missing?" she asked, gazing up at him, then away when his eyes slid over her with open lasciviousness. It seemed as if he could see through the thin silk; the sensation was so strong that Libby had to fight the urge to look down and make sure her gown was not transparent.

"The chit turned tail and ran instead of doing her duty."

"Chit?" Libby was shocked by the term, and the snarl on his face as he'd said it. "What do you mean, 'her duty'?"

Lasserthon's eyes seemed to change right in front of her, grow more crafty, as if he realized he was drunk and wanted to hide his condition from her. "She agreed to marry Sir John, and now she's breached that promise."

"It's true, then, that she left here? Did she speak to anyone or leave a note of explanation?"

"Not that I know of, but what other reason would she have to flee on the night of her engagement?"

"Did she say anything to you about being unhappy this afternoon?"

"I didn't see her this afternoon."

"But I saw you walking with her near the willows down beside the lake."

"You're right, I did stroll with her for a moment until Julian showed up and took her away with him." He smiled blearily. "Maybe he seduced her, and she couldn't face Sir John afterward. Wouldn't put it past Julian, would you?"

Appalled by his behavior and crude remarks, Libby disengaged her arm from his grip. If she hadn't decided to go on to London before, the decision came easily enough now. She'd never set foot in Lasserthon Manor again. "I believe I'll seek out Evelyn and Sir Jasper now. Please excuse me, Lord Lasserthon."

Lasserthon did not look pleased, but she gave him no choice, hastily wending her way away from him and through the crowd. The scents of different perfumes, some spicy, some floral, mingled with the faint odor of warm bodies jammed together as she fought her way through the room, eagerly searching for a familiar face.

She was about to give up hope of finding anyone she knew among all the strangers when she finally caught sight of Evelyn moving through the vestibule toward the front door. As she drew closer, she saw that both Evelyn and Sir Jasper wore their traveling garb.

"Evelyn!" Libby called desperately, and somehow Evelyn heard her voice and turned around to scan the people behind her. She looked worried as Libby reached her.

"Evelyn!" she cried. "Where on earth are you going?"

"Jasper decided we should return home when he heard about Miss Baird. Sir John's quite a good friend of his, you remember. You've heard what's happened, haven't you?"

"I only know that she's disappeared. Do you know what happened to her?"

Evelyn shook her head. "No one seems to. We've been looking everywhere for Julian so that we can explain our hasty departure. Have you seen him?"

"Not yet, but I've only just come down. What about the Tanners and the Curtises? Are they leaving as well?"

"They've already left. We're all quite upset about Mary Louise. She's quite a sweet girl, and it's not like her to cause this kind of worry. I can't imagine what possessed her to up and leave without a word." She shook her head. "First Henrietta and now this. I'm just sick with worry. I pray she's all right."

"Do you have any idea when she was last seen?" Libby hoped she wasn't the last eyewitness to the girl's whereabouts. That would certainly point an incriminating finger at Julian.

"She hasn't been seen anywhere since late this afternoon. Sir John was simply beside himself. I do hope he finds her at home, though I cannot imagine why she would return there without advising him. It's all very strange." She examined Libby's face. "What about you? Do you want to come with us?"

"I arrived with Raymond, but I've decided to hire a coach and travel on to London in the morning."

"Oh, dear, I do hate to see you go. I've enjoyed your company so much the last few days. I was hoping you'd stay for a longer visit. You will come back someday, won't you?"

"Perhaps. I'll be in London for some months before I set sail for America again. You must come visit me there. I'll send you my address as soon as I arrive."

The two ladies hugged as Sir Jasper came forward to fetch his wife, and Libby patted his arm and tried to reassure him, for he did indeed look inconsolable.

"I'm sure Miss Baird is quite all right, Sir Jasper. Try not to be alarmed."

"I do hope so. Fordenbury's sick with worry. He needs his friends around him if she's run off and left him at the altar. He doesn't deserve that, no, he does not."

Realizing the Landerses were in a hurry to depart, she bid them farewell, then turned back to the party. She was not pleased to find herself alone with so many strangers, and it did not take her long to find out, as she walked through the mass of revelers, that they were of a much wilder set than she was used to.

Many of the women wore their Grecian robes pinned so loosely that their bodies were scandalously revealed, and some of the gentlemen wore the short leather tunics and thonged knee-high sandals of Roman centurions. There was much laughing and eating, and as she passed through the various rooms, she found places where men apparently well into their cups were lying on couches, their heads in the laps of scantily clad women.

Shocked, she wondered if Julian had had an orgy in mind when he'd planned the weekend, for that was quickly what it was becoming. She observed a woman holding a wineglass to a partner's mouth, and while Libby watched in dismay, he pulled off her shoulder strap and bared her breast.

Turning away, sickened by the open debauchery going on, she hurried for the steps and the safety of her room, where she intended to call at once for a carriage. She passed a man reeling from drink, and managed to avoid Lasserthon when she saw him standing in a window alcove, his arms draped around the shoulders of two laughing women. She searched for Julian as she moved toward the stair but could not see him. So he was gone too. It now seemed clear that he was with Mary Louise, or had been. Why else would he not be in attendance at a party he was hosting for his friends?

Pleased when she reached the staircase unmolested, she lifted the hem of her gown, and headed up the steps as quickly as she could. She paused at the newel post to look down upon the gathering. The noise level was rising as the party was well on its way to a drunken revelry, and she was astonished despite herself.

Suddenly furious to be caught in such a predicament, alone with only one female servant to protect her, she berated her own lack of judgment as she hurried down the deserted hallway toward her room. It was very still and quiet in the upper reaches of the house, and she realized that everyone must be downstairs. Even the servants were busy providing food and drink for the party. She paused, looking down the hallway where the Chinese maid who'd brought her upstairs had pointed out Julian's apartments as they walked past. She hesitated, glancing behind her. It would be a perfect time to search his rooms. He had not been seen all evening, was possibly far away with Mary Louise.

Nibbling her lower lip with indecision, she decided to see if he was closeted inside his rooms. When she reached his door, she tapped lightly on the panel. Constantly looking up and down the corridor, expecting to be accosted at any moment, she waited briefly, then knocked again, louder this time. There was no answer, and she reached down and turned the knob. The door opened easily.

"Julian? Are you here?" she called softly, peeking inside.

A single lamp burned on the mantel, but the large sitting room was empty. Taking a deep breath to bolster her courage, she stepped inside and shut the door behind her. Her gaze found a pair of double doors directly across the room. They stood wide open, seeming to beckon her onward. She could see one end of a huge canopy bed. Tiptoeing stealthily, she crossed a plush oriental carpet and peered into the dusky bedroom. A fire burned on the grate but had dwindled to a glimmer that left most of the chamber in darkness. No one was in sight.

If she was quick, she could search through his drawers without being seen. If he did return from wherever he'd been, he would no doubt go directly to the party, where his guests awaited him. She began in earnest, heading first toward the wardrobe, which she pulled open and quickly sorted through the clothing she found hanging inside. She found nothing of import, so she moved on to a large chest of drawers. One by one she pulled out the drawers but found only shirts, cravats, sweaters, everything washed and folded neatly.

Undeterred, she crossed back to a desk that stood in front of a window alcove. She found it locked, but a search of the cubbyholes brought her the key. Hands shaking, she inserted it and gave it a turn. Inside there were papers and files, and she thumbed through them, not sure what she was looking for, anything to prove Julian's involvement, or what she really desired, his non-involvement.

Her search stopped abruptly as she found a small wooden box. She pulled off the lid, and felt her heart come up into her throat. Sick, her stomach roilling with horror, she stared down at the large square-cut ruby, the gem glowing blood red in the dim light, tiny diamonds surrounding it like a glittering silver frame.

It belonged to Henrietta. The ruby ring that had been passed down for generations from mother to daughter. The one Henrietta never took off her finger, not for any reason. She would never have given it to Julian, or to anyone else. It had been Henrietta's most precious possession; he would have had to have taken it from her. Oh, God help her, she had been right from the very first. Julian had killed Henrietta; she held the proof of his crime in her hand.

Chapter Eleven

Dressed in the garb of a Roman centurion, Julian walked quietly through dark rooms that would take him to the ballroom. He did not want to be seen entering from outside. Mary Louise had caused him big trouble today, and he'd had no choice but to deal with her once and for all. He hadn't liked it; the whole affair had left a sour taste in his mouth.

By this hour most of his friends would be well into their cups and would hardly notice if he'd been in attendance or not. All he had to do was tell them he'd been there, and they wouldn't question him further. There were others to consider, however, the ones who would give him trouble, namely Libby Thornhill. She would notice his absence at once and would immediately suspect him, correctly, of being involved with Mary Louise's disappearance. He'd have to think of a logical excuse to convince her otherwise, and he'd have to come up with it within the next few minutes.

Through a swinging door that led from a servants hallway into the dining parlor, he found that he'd been right in his assessment. Most guests seemed to be enjoying themselves immensely and hardly noticed him when he did step out of hiding into their midst. His staff was circulating among the costumed crowd with their usual efficiency, carrying trays of champagne and other spirits from his wine cellars, which were well stocked and open to every taste or whim. He nodded to several groups, pausing often to say hello, wanting as many people as possible to see him in case his whereabouts that evening did happen to be questioned.

In the ballroom, where a large string quartet played, many

couples were dancing. Quite a din of conversation and move-ment swirled around him as he wended his way slowly and carefully across the floor until he caught a glimpse of Libby Thornhill near the marble stairs.

She had donned the costume he'd provided for her, a sur-prising development in itself; he didn't think she'd agree to put it on, out of stubbornness, if for no other reason. She looked gorgeous, of course, when did she not? As he imme-diately changed his course in her direction, she rushed away toward the steps. By her haste and obvious flight, he was fair-ly confident that she was not enjoying herself.

"Julian, you devil, where have you been?" Lasserthon ap-peared out of nowhere with two actresses, one blonde and one brunette, both of whom had posed nude for Julian when he was last in London. They both clung to Lasserthon's arms as he commanded Julian's attention. "Everyone's been looking for you. Did you hear about Mary Louise taking off and playing Sir John for a fool? Half the village up and left in a huff out of concern for the girl, and now my lovely little houseguest is about to do the same."

Raymond was reeling drunk, Julian realized, which didn't surprise him in the least. He'd been on fairly good behavior in the days since Libby had taken up residence in Lasserthon Manor, but Raymond never failed to let out all the stops dur-ing weekends at Brickhill. Julian watched him slide one hand down the front of the blonde's chiton and cup her breast, a liberty to which she responded by giggling drunkenly and encouraging him by leaning into the caress.

"What did Libby say? Is she planning on leaving tonight?"

"Who gives a damn? I say, she's a cold little fish in any case, as cold as my bloody wife was."

Lasserthon was nuzzling the throat of the black-haired ac-tress even as he spoke, fumbling to untie the strap holding her dress at one shoulder. Julian turned away and found Libby just rounding the curve of the balustrade on the second floor. He didn't want her to leave, not yet. He knew she would not like the kind of party he'd planned for tonight, but this one had spiraled out of control even faster than usual.

By the time he reached the upstairs corridor, she was nowhere in sight. When he turned the corner of the wing where
kept his own rooms, he saw her entering his own apartment.
He knew without thinking that she was searching for evidence to convict him; worse, he knew she could find it there.
He increased his step but detoured momentarily as a couple
emerged from a nearby room and engaged him in a witless
conversation about their costumes. He nodded and exchanged
a few polite remarks before excusing himself and moving
off down the corridor. He waited to make sure no one else
saw him, then entered his rooms and quietly pulled the door
closed behind him.

Libby wasn't in the sitting room, but he hadn't expected
her to be. He strode straight for the adjoining bedchamber. If
he hadn't needed Lu Ling to help him deal with Mary Louise,
Libby would have never gotten this far. Everything was
falling down around his head, dammit; he hoped to bloody
hell she hadn't found Henrietta's ring. He'd been a fool ever
to take it. His worst fear quickly materialized when he stopped
soundlessly on the threshold and found her standing at his
desk. She held Henrietta's ring in her hand.

"What are you doing in my bedroom?"

Libby whirled around, then stood frozen with fear, staring
at him out of horrified eyes. It was the first time he'd seen her
look afraid, and he didn't like it.

"You did it, didn't you?" she got out in a strangled voice.
"You killed her."

"It's not what you think," he said, very low, not wanting
an ugly scene but furious she'd stumbled onto the evidence
that could tie him to Henrietta's disappearance. Libby seemed
incapable of movement until Julian took a step toward her.
She reacted then, darting quickly toward the door that led
into his dressing room.

Julian caught her easily, though she struggled with all her
strength. He managed to get one arm around her waist, pin-
ning her arms to her sides. When she started to scream, he
clamped a hand over her mouth, cursing inwardly. He could

not let her set off an alarm, not without everything, all his well-thought-out precautions, going up in smoke.

"I don't want to hurt you, Libby, do you understand me? Just shut up and hold still."

Libby struggled fiercely, her screams muffled underneath his palm. Furious with her for putting him in this awkward situation, he lifted her off the floor, evading her kicking feet as he carried her to the bed. He threw her down on her stomach and held her when she tried to roll away. He jerked loose the gold cord belting her gown and bound her hands behind her back, holding her head down so that her cries were muffled in the pillows. He grabbed the cravat he'd thrown on the bed earlier when he'd changed into his centurion costume and quickly bound it around her mouth. She was still fighting him and was turning out to be a hell of a lot stronger than she looked. He flipped her onto her back and glared down at her, suddenly as furious as she was.

"You forced this on me, Libby. I didn't want you to get hurt. I didn't want you to get involved, but you couldn't let it rest, could you? You just had to pry and snoop until you pushed me too hard, didn't you?"

Her green eyes were glittering with helpless fury, and hatred, no doubt, but his eyes were drawn down to her heaving chest and the sheer chemise she wore underneath the thin chiton. The binding ribbons had come loose in his attempts to subdue her, gaping slightly to reveal the soft curve of her left breast. A fierce streak of fire singed him like a lightning bolt, pure lust at the sight of her bound and struggling underneath him.

Halfway sickened by what he was doing, he jerked her gown back into place, grinding his teeth together to stop himself from doing something he'd regret later. He wanted her; he'd wanted her since the moment she'd flung insults into his face the first night they'd met. He'd intended to have her when the time was right, winning her over gradually until he could take her in his own way, and he'd been making progress until this had happened. Now was not the moment

to think about that. He had to get her out of the house without
being seen, and he had to do it now.

When Julian lunged up and stood panting above her, Libby
stopped fighting and lay still. She labored to breathe through
the tight binding around her mouth, but as he stood above
her, looking so dark and terrible and fearsome, his eyes glittering with fury, a new terror gripped her.

"I told you to mind your own business, Libby. Why couldn't
you listen to me?"

Libby stared up at him, where he stood like a fierce centurion of old, in a red shirt and black leather tunic worn under a
molded gold breastplate. He wore knee sandals and a short
red cloak hung from his shoulders, but it was his eyes that
Libby looked into, eyes like blue ice. She imagined him drawing out the short sword he was wearing in a black leather
scabbard on his belt, plunging the blade down into her chest,
or taking her by the throat, his fingers gripping hard, squeezing until her vision went black. She lay motionless, realizing
exactly how helpless she was, sick to the depths of her soul
that Julian truly was the killer, and she had unwittingly placed
herself in his murderous hands.

She watched him run both hands through his thick black
hair, turn and pace a few agitated steps away from the bed,
only to whirl around and come back. He grabbed the bedpost
with one hand and glared furiously down at her.

"Well, you've left me little choice now. My patience with
you is sorely tried, Libby. If you know what's good for you,
you'll do exactly what you're told from this moment forward. Do you understand me?"

He'd gotten down close to her face, so close she could
smell the sharp tang of his cologne. The anger radiating from
him was nearly palpable. He could have dealt with her brutally, ended her life with one stroke of his hand, but he had
not. Why? Perhaps, she realized through her haze of fear, if
she went along with him, someone would look for her. Alice
was already upset and worried; she'd put out the alarm the
moment she found Libby missing. Slowly she moved her
head up and down, forcing herself to remain calm, deciding

she might have a chance to escape if he thought her docile; he might let down his guard.

"Good girl. Now lie still."

Libby did so but could not stop herself from struggling when he approached the bed again, a long black scarf in his hand. He lifted her head, and she knew he was going to wrap it around her throat, tighten it until her eyes bulged and she breathed her last. Instead he wrapped it around her eyes, effectively blindfolding her. She felt him grab her feet, hold them together, and bind her ankles tightly together. Blood pounded through her veins with a renewed terror so fast and hard and awful that she felt her heart would explode.

Blindfolded, gagged, bound, she lay stiff with dread, but she could hear him moving around the room. What was he doing? Retrieving a knife with which to slit her throat? Is that why he'd blindfolded her, so she wouldn't see how he was going to kill her? Oh, God help her, she'd been such a fool, such an utter, stupid, besotted fool. She flinched as she felt his hands grip her shoulders hard; then she was pulled up into a sitting position at the edge of the bed. She groaned as he bent and hoisted her up until she lay over his shoulder like a sack of meal. She wiggled until his forearm clamped down forcefully on the back of her thighs.

Did he intend to take her out of the house? Surely he could not negotiate the crowded rooms without being seen. There were too many people, and they all had full rein of every chamber and hallway, both upstairs and down. He could never get her outside without being detected. She lived on that hope until she heard a small scraping sound and felt a wave of cold air as she was carried out of the bedchamber. A stairwell, she realized as he began to descend, his muscled forearm holding her immobile. A spiral stair, for he carried her round and round in a dizzying descent, narrow because she could feel the wall close on either side of her. A hidden passage, she deduced with a sinking heart, one that connected his bedchamber to God knew where.

Despair built steadily as he carried her down with swift, sure footsteps, carrying her easily as if she weighed nothing.

His strength in itself was frightening, and she didn't fear he'd drop her unless he wanted to do so. Defenseless, hopeless, she lay limply, her cheek against his back, wondering if this was the way he'd stolen Henrietta out of her home. And Mary Louise, had he carried her to a similar death earlier that very day?

After what seemed an eternity of winding steps, he shoved open a second door, and she was taken through what she assumed was a long passage, then finally out into the cool night air. She could not breathe well, but her heart was beating so hard and fast that her body shook with its violence. Somewhere, far away, she could hear music playing and the voices of people having a fine time, chatting and eating, totally unaware that she was being abducted by a murderer. He walked swiftly, his boots making staccato clicks on the cobblestones. Where were they? The courtyard? The front drive?

When he brought her inside another structure, she recognized it as the stable at once by the commingling odors of dusty straw, the rankness of manure and horseflesh. A moment later he tossed her down unceremoniously in a pile of hay, and she lay on her back, every muscle held rigid, listening as she heard a jingle of metal as a harness was taken from a hook. A slow clop of hooves told her a horse was being readied, then led from its stall.

Then he was back, pulling her up and tossing her over his shoulder again, handling her like a rag doll filled with down. The breath was forced out of her as she struck his broad shoulder. He mounted with her, then drew her down in the saddle in front of him, where her back lay against the Roman armor covering his chest. His arms held her tightly in place as he walked the horse outside, and as he kicked the stallion into a gallop, she knew exactly where he was taking her. To the moors. To dispose of her as he had done to Henrietta.

For a long time they rode at a mile-devouring gallop, and she could neither see nor hear anything other than the wind blowing hard against her face. He held her securely, and she managed to grasp hold of the horse's mane though her wrists were tied together. All around her rose the dark earth scents of bogs and decay and dampness, and her fears renewed as she thought of being thrown into such a place, slowly sinking, bound and helpless, into a morass of black mire and decayed vegetation.

When he finally drew up and swung off the horse, she drew all her residual strength together, determined to give one last, desperate attempt to fight free, but he lifted her down easily and this time carried her cradled in his arms as a mother would carry a baby. She could hear the sounds of running water and was certain it came from the rushing currents of a river.

Was that the way she would die, then, trussed up and thrown into a torrent, unable to keep herself above the surface, slowly sinking in a watery grave? Her whole body held tense and rigid, she waited for him to heave her into water, but to her utter relief, it did not happen. He silently carried her out of the cold, and she heard a man's voice mutter something low that she couldn't understand.

"Is the girl still here?" That was Julian's voice. He had stopped, still holding her, but the other man was approaching, his footsteps growing louder.

"No, she be long gone. 'ave you got another lass so soon? I 'ave no way of disposing of 'er till me boat gets back."

"I'll take care of this one myself," Julian answered, and Libby shivered, not sure which would be the more horrible fate.

A short time later she was tossed down again, onto the softness of a bed this time, and she felt his fingers at her brow until the blindfold was suddenly whipped off. She blinked, blinded by the sudden brightness, then saw Julian leaning over her with a knife in his hand. She stared up at him in complete panic, but he merely sliced through the scarf binding her mouth with one quick swipe, then quickly severed the other cords, freeing her hands and her feet.

"I've got to get back before all hell breaks loose when your nosy little maid finds you missing. You won't be hurt here, unless you attempt to escape. If you do try to flee, I can't be responsible for what's done to you."

Then he turned away and without another word spoken strode across the floor and out of the room. Libby scrambled up on the bed on her hands and knees, afraid to believe he was actually leaving her unharmed, but as she heard the key turn, she realized she was a prisoner, locked up to await what horrible fate she knew not.

Chapter Twelve

Several moments after Julian left her alone and untied, Libby scrambled off the bed and searched for a way out of her prison. Chafing her wrists, which ached from the tight bindings, she realized at once that she was being held in some kind of circular structure, a stone tower with curved walls. There was only one window, and she went there first and jerked open the casements, only to find iron rods barring her escape. She wrapped her fingers around them and pulled with all her power but found them set into stone, completely immovable. Outside she could see nothing but darkness and fog rising from the ground far below, but there was no doubt that she was far out on the moors. The gurgling of the stream was still audible, and she put her face to the grate and yelled for help. No one came, neither to save her nor to shut her up. After a while she gave up and wondered if she was completely alone in this strange, isolated place or if Julian had left jailors to guard her.

Most of all she supposed she should feel relief that Julian had not murdered her as she was now certain he'd done with Henrietta and Mary Louise. She knew full well, however, that the fact that he had yet to harm her did not mean that he would not. He had been caught by surprise when she'd found the ruby ring and hadn't had time enough to deal with her. She had to find a way out before he returned. Or had he left? Was he still in this fortress, or tower, or whatever it was? Waiting for some unknown reason before he dealt with her?

The idea chilled her to the bone, and shuddering with renewed fear, she glanced around the room, thinking that she might find a weapon to use against him when he returned for her. Now that she examined the room, she found it quite well appointed, lavish almost, in an airy, feminine fashion. The Chinese motif of which Julian was so fond marked the furniture and carpets, as well as the lamp shades and paintings. The bed was not of oriental design, however, but a large sleigh bed made of oak and hung with red silk panels embroidered with black fire-breathing dragons. There was a small teak wardrobe against one wall, and she walked quickly there, hoping to find something inside with which she could defend herself.

Only one gown hung there, and she stared at it, nausea writhing like worms inside her stomach as she recognized the violet-sprigged white frock that Mary Louise had worn earlier that day when she'd summoned Julian beside the lake. So Julian had brought her to this place too, and the man with the gravelly voice had said she'd been disposed of.

Libby swallowed hard, her imagination running rampant. If the poor girl had already become Julian's latest victim, Libby was next in line to perish at his hands. What other choice did Julian have, now that Libby had uncovered evidence that would connect him with the deaths of two innocent women? He would have to kill her. He would have no choice.

Sobered by the realization, she stared at the muslin gown hanging before her but could not bring herself to touch it. She turned away, envisioning the young woman sinking slowly to the bottom of some sucking, vile black bog, then quickly forced the awful picture from her head. She saw a red enamel trunk at the foot of the bed and searched through it frantically but found nothing but clean blankets and pillows.

There was no fireplace, but a glowing copper brazier atop a tripod stood near the bed, and she warmed herself beside it, at a loss for what she could do. Physical escape was impossible, but perhaps she could use her wits to bribe her way out of this dangerous predicament. Perhaps she could talk Julian out of killing her, even seduce him if she had to. He had made no secret that he desired her, and she had desired him, she thought, clamping her teeth and cursing her own stupidity. She must make him believe that she didn't care, that she didn't believe him capable of such crimes. She sighed and gave up on that tack. It didn't make sense to her, so it certainly wouldn't to him.

When she heard the rattle of a key, she spun around, hugging her arms around herself as she realized how nakedly vulnerable she was. She braced herself to face Julian, to try to reason with him, but it was not Julian who appeared a second later but Lu Ling, carrying a bundle in her arms. Libby's first impulse was to rush forward and attack the smaller woman while the door was open, then make a run for it. That idea was immediately put to rest when an absolutely gigantic Chinese man followed the serving girl inside. He stood at guard in front of the portal, his massive arms crossed over his burly chest.

Libby had never laid eyes on the giant before, but his looks alone were enough to strike terror in the bravest of hearts. He was completely bald, making his head appear as large as a pumpkin, and he wore big gold hoops suspended from both earlobes. His face was grotesquely pockmarked and irregular of feature, as if he'd been pummeled mercilessly inside a pugilist tent. She stared at him, frightened to move for fear he'd grab her. Had Julian summoned him to take care of her? To do the murder that Julian himself had no stomach for? Was he the brute who disposed of Julian's victims?

"Do not be afraid, my lady, Chang will not hurt you."

Libby's eyes swiveled from the man to Lu Ling, her jaw dropping with surprise. Lu Ling gazed back out of soulful, unfathomable dark eyes.

"You speak English?" Libby asked, once the initial shock had left her and the import dawned upon her. She wasted no time beseeching the other woman's help. "Please, Lu Ling, you must help me escape this place! My father is a very wealthy man. He'll give you money, all that you want, if you'll take me to him in London. I swear he will, swear it!"

Lu Ling studied her silently, then moved forward. "My lord and master has requested I give you warm clothes to wear until he can return. They are from my own closet but will fit you well enough. You are a bit taller but otherwise quite slender, as am I."

"Why didn't you tell me you spoke English? Why am I here, Lu Ling? Please, you must tell me these things!"

"I do only what my lord and master commands."

Libby wanted to grab the woman and shake her, but a second glance at Chang convinced her otherwise. "That's Miss Baird's dress in the wardrobe. I saw her wearing it today. She was here, wasn't she? Where is she now? Is she all right?"

Lu Ling's face remained implacable. "Please take the clothes. It will grow cold here in the tower before the morning comes. There are warm blankets inside the chest. I have ordered tea for you and food for your supper. Is there anything else you require?"

"Please, tell me, am I to be killed like the others?"

Lu Ling did show some surprise at that, but the revealing expression was quickly hidden under her usual inscrutability. "No harm will come to you if you do as you are told. My lord and master will return soon."

Libby knew she would find out nothing more as the woman placed her palms together and bowed in the Chinese custom. A different woman appeared in the doorway, an older oriental who wore the same black silk pants and tunic as Lu Ling and Chang. She held a tray covered with a white linen towel, and she carried it to the table beside the bed, then placed her palms together and bowed in the same way Lu Ling had a moment before. She backed away, as did Lu Ling, and Chang followed them outside, then turned the key with a fatal-sounding click. She went to the door and listened but heard only a low murmur as they spoke together in their strange tongue. Her heart fell as she heard the giant guard take his place just outside the room.

She sank down on the bed, still holding the Chinese attire that she was supposed to wear. There was no chance of escape, none whatsoever. Had Henrietta sat here in this very place, terrified, waiting for whatever method of execution

Julian chose for her? No one knew where Libby was or even that she was gone. Except for Alice, who feared Julian anyway. Surely when she realized Libby could not be found, she'd flee the house and get word to Libby's father in London. Oh, God, she hoped so, because if Alice did not realize quickly what was afoot, she was in as much danger from Julian as Libby was.

Ever since Libby Thornhill had shown up at Lasserthon Manor, she had been a thorn in Julian's side. Now, however, his problems had escalated far beyond her nosy interference. He wasn't sure exactly what to do with her, what she'd believe if he chose to tell her the truth, but he'd have to worry about that later. Right now his most pressing problems were taking care of the flighty nearsighted maid and mingling with his guests long enough to have an alibi for the evening.

Dismounting outside the stable, he left his horse in the hands of a young groom, then made his way quickly to the door through which he'd carried Libby, bound and struggling, a few hours earlier. By the time he entered the house and melted in among his guests, he realized that few, if any, of them were going to be witness to his movements one way or another. Most had been drinking since early in the evening, or had already found a willing bed partner for the night.

A few people yelled greetings at him, raising their drinks in a salute to the good time he was providing, and he waved and nodded but kept going. All the while he kept his eyes peeled for Alice's freckled face, more than concerned that the girl might set off the alarm about her mistress before he could silence her. After a few moments of mingling among his friends, he proceeded up to the second floor, managing to exchange a word or two with everyone he encountered. If worse came to worst, and Libby Thornhill had to disappear like the other girls, he wanted more than one person to remember he was carousing among them at different times throughout the evening.

Upstairs, he was relieved to find no one loitering about,

except for one man who was passed out near the top of the steps, an empty wine bottle crooked in his arm. His snores were loud and obscene in the quiet corridor. Julian glanced down at him and circumvented his prone body, heading at a swift clip for Libby's room.

Once there, he tapped a knuckle on the door, and when the portal was thrown wide, Alice stood before him, looking openly distraught. He made an immediate attempt to calm her, launching into the story he'd concocted on the ride back from the tower.

"Alice, you must come with me and be quick about it. Your mistress has taken a fall, and I need you to help tend to her."

"I knew it, I knew something was wrong! Milady said she wasn't goin' to stay long at the party, and it be hours now. I went once and looked for her but couldn't find 'er at all." She paused, staring suspiciously up at him.

"I took her upstairs to see my work. Come, she's still in my studio. You must watch over her while I fetch a doctor."

"What is it? Is she 'urt bad?" Alice asked as Julian took a firm grip on her elbow and pulled her quickly down the hall. He looked behind them to make sure no one saw them leaving Libby's chamber.

"She tripped and hit her head hard against the floor. I think she'll be all right, but I didn't want to move her for fear I'd injure her more."

It didn't take them long to climb a back stair to his studio on the third floor of the east wing, not at the pace he was setting. He thrust open the door for her and let her rush inside, but it took only a moment for Alice to realize she'd been duped. She swung around, her eyes wide beneath the glasses he'd provided for her, the lamplight glinting off the thick bifocal lenses.

"Where's my mistress? What 'ave you done with her?"

"She's not hurt, Alice, but I'm afraid you're going to have to stay up here for a while. I can't have you starting trouble."

"Where is she? Oh, God, oh Lord in heaven, you've done

kilt her, 'aven't you?" Her voice was rising in pitch, becoming as shrill as a banshee's wail as she closed in on pure panic.

"She hasn't been harmed." He grabbed her arm and gave her a shake. "Now, calm down, girl, and listen to me. Don't waste your time screaming because no one can hear you up here, not even the servants."

Julian turned to leave, annoyed he'd been forced to deal with this further complication, but Alice wasn't finished with her hysteria. Her shouted words brought him to a standstill at the threshold.

"You best not hurt Miss Libby! She's not who you think she is!"

Something in her voice, the hint of a threat, arrested Julian, and he turned slowly to face the agitated maid. "What do you mean?"

"I mean she be an important lady, real important, especially 'ere in England. She's got family 'ere that be rich and powerful enough to 'unt you down and 'ang you like a dog, no matter if you be a titled lord or what."

"Indeed?" he said, turning back to study her face. "Pray tell me more, Alice."

Alice hesitated, now that he was watching her out of narrowed eyes. She wrung her hands as if undecided on how to proceed, or was it because she was making up lies to help save her mistress? Then she decided to tell him, and the words came tumbling out with great feeling and loyalty. "No one's supposed to know, but you best take 'eed. His Grace be more powerful than you, and 'e'll 'unt you down and kill you, he will, if you harm a hair on 'er head."

Julian stared at her, not sure what she intended him to believe. Did she wish him to believe that Libby was a member of the English aristocracy? "What are you trying to say, girl? That Libby Thornhill has ties to the peerage?"

"More than just ties, your lordship, she be the daughter of the Duke of Thorpe!"

The last was said with great pride, but Alice's trepidation

at defying him came swiftly on its heels. She began to tremble and stepped backward, no doubt from the look suffusing Julian's face.

He reeled with shock, every muscle turning to stone, and he found himself incapable of speech. Oh, God, it couldn't be true, not Thorpe. He struggled not to show his reaction to the revelation, but could almost feel the blood draining from his face. Alice watched fearfully as his disbelieving eyes pinned her where she stood cowering against the wall. He could not move, could not believe his ears.

"I don't believe you," he finally managed, his voice not his own.

"It's true, I swear it on the Holy Word!" she cried, obviously fearing for her life. "And 'e knows she's in England. He'll soon be sending out men to search for us if we don't show up in London when we should. Ask 'er yourself if you don't believe me, if she's still alive to tell you!" With that, Alice sobbed and buried her face in her hands.

"If it's the truth, why hasn't she told anyone? Why would she wish to keep her family name a secret?"

As he asked the questions, he wracked his memory for any mention of the duke having had a daughter Libby's age. He knew the son and heir, Burke, knew him well, but he'd never heard him mention a sister.

"He only has a son. You're lying to me."

"The viscount be Miss Libby's brother, to be sure. She don't like it 'ere in England. That's why you don't know about her!"

Fury, long suppressed, festering, ugly, began to rise like some dark wraith out of a dank, dark cavern. William, the almighty Duke of Thorpe, was the man Julian loathed above all others in this life. His misdeeds against the Rainvilles were as black as his heart, and Julian's hatred of the man ran deep and cold and vicious. For years he'd been plagued and followed by the duke's vendetta against his family's name. He'd set out to ruin the Rainvilles and had succeeded in ways more horrible than the mere loss of their wealth and prestige.

Clamping his jaw to repress the emotions threatening to overwhelm him, Julian felt his fingers curling into tight fists as he took a step toward the hapless maid. Sensing his rage, Alice rounded a chair and cringed behind its back. Julian stopped at the sight of her quaking, though his fingers itched to grab her and shake her senseless.

"Are you telling me the truth, girl? If you're lying to me, you'll be very sorry of it."

All Alice's bravado disintegrated, and she began to quiver all over, finally realizing her peril. "No, sir, no, I swear to you by all that's holy that I am not. Miss Libby be the daughter of the duke and duchess. She be the oldest, and the only daughter. Ask 'er, my lord, ask 'er and she will tell you."

Furious, Julian turned on his heel and left the maid crouched behind the chair. He took time to lock her in, vowing he'd ask Libby, all right, but even as he strode down the hall to join his guests, he realized that perhaps the revelation, if true, was a stroke of good fortune rather than bad. Perhaps tonight, through chance alone, he'd been given the weapon he needed to bring Thorpe to his knees for what he'd done to the Rainville family. Perhaps lovely little Libby with all her lies and deceptions would turn out to be the key he'd always sought that would unlock the vengeance he'd kept hidden in his heart since he was a boy of ten.

Chapter Thirteen

The first night locked in the stone tower was the worst for Libby. Sleepless, edgy, unable to think of closing her eyes for even a minute, she stared up at the ceiling, waiting for Julian to return. She knew not what to expect; if he intended for her to live or die. For hours she imagined what had become of Henrietta and Mary Louise, and wondered if she was destined to share their dismal fate.

When no one entered her chamber before the sun came up, she succumbed to sheer exhaustion and dozed fitfully throughout the following day. The only time she saw other people was at meals when the servants came with her tray. Everything served to her was Chinese fare, with many rice dishes and exotic brown sauces and spices that she'd never tasted before but found palatable.

Surprisingly enough, under the circumstances, she did find the stomach to eat. Usually it was Lu Ling and the burly guard who entered with the tray, and although they treated her with the utmost kindness and respect, neither said another word about her presence there or what was to become of her. She finally gave up trying to find out, but she did begin to nurture hope when another full day passed without her coming to harm.

In time she donned the silky Chinese clothing provided her, after bathing in the warm water Chang carried in each morning, and found the attire extremely comfortable though it was peculiar indeed to wear trousers under the tunic as a man would and soft silk slippers that had no heels. There were books available to her, so she spent some time reading from the tomes inside a library cabinet that held a selection of histories as well as a few plays of William Shakespeare. Whenever she tried to concentrate on a story, her thoughts would always return to Julian and his forcible abduction of her. Why would he think he could get away with such a thing? She was curious as to how he had explained her sudden absence to Lasserthon and his other guests. That's where he'd gone, she was certain, back home to Brickhill to enjoy his London friends, as if nothing had happened, as if he hadn't abducted two women and held their lives in his hands.

By Sunday night she began to expect his return, deciding that once he had rid himself of his weekend guests, he would feel free to deal with her at his leisure. Her anxiety bounded as the Sabbath lengthened into evening. She sat at a chair pulled up to the window, watching the azure sky dissolve slowly into streaks of mauve and gold that melted slowly into the edge of darkness, as if the sun had warmed the sky and gilded the world with rosy light.

Her vantage point high inside the tower revealed only more of the endless gray moors, dotted with rising mists, and the silver ribbon of river that rushed along below the tower, its rapids playing never ending music. It was such an isolated place, this cold fortress. No one would ever be able to find her there. She would have to gather her wits, perhaps if she was to stay alive, for she had no idea if Julian intended to show her mercy. If he was a killer, why did he do such things? How did he choose his victims? How many innocent women had there been? Shivering, she turned from the window and stared at the locked door. Now that night had fallen, he would come soon, she knew it.

Within an hour after dusk, a key scratched in the lock. Trembling, Libby leapt to her feet, knowing instinctively it was Julian before she saw him. He stopped on the threshold, and she stared at him, unable to move. He was dressed informally, almost casually, a white shirt and brown leather vest over dark breeches. His boots were knee-high and mud-spattered, as if he'd ridden hard through the damp black paths that lined the bogs.

Neither spoke, but their eyes locked, and as his gaze moved to her Chinese attire, Libby sensed instantly that something had changed between them. He wore an expression she'd not seen in him before, a harder edge, absent the usual sardonic humor, a look that sharpened his darkly handsome features and made his navy blue eyes as cold as midnight. Was this his true face? The face he wore when he killed?

If she had feared him before that moment, now she had slipped over the edge of mere fear into the flames of horror. Oh, God, he was a murderer. He was going to kill her, like he'd killed the other girls. Desperately she tried to get hold of her panic, not wanting to believe it, but she was afraid. Clenching her fists, she lifted her chin and forced herself to dredge up at least a faint facade of courage.

"I trust you've been well treated while here," he finally said, still not moving into the room. He seemed reluctant to approach her.

Not exactly what she'd expected him to say, and when she searched his face, that unsettling icy look was gone. Somehow she knew he was as tense as she was, his muscles held in tight leash, though he gave no outward indication. His remark, which showed concern after her comfort, did buoy her hopes, and gave her the courage to ask a question of her own.

"What have you done with Alice? Is she all right?"

After a short pause he nodded. "Alice is fine and will stay that way as long as you are cooperative."

"I don't understand."

Libby hugged herself, trying to suppress the shivers that threatened to course through her. Nothing made any sense, and the entire situation was becoming more unsettling by the moment. She glanced behind him where he'd left the door ajar, wondering if she could dart past him. She immediately gave up on the idea. He was too strong to escape. Had she not felt those muscular arms around her, gripping her and handling her as if she were a small child? And he was quick and agile, to be so big. She wouldn't stand a chance of evading him. Julian seemed to note her resignation, and he gave a fleeting smile before he shut the door and turned the key.

"Here, put this on."

For the first time Libby noticed the black wool hooded cloak he had draped over his arm. When he flung it toward her, she caught it with both hands. She didn't move, watching him with a wariness that weighted her down like iron chains.

"Why?"

"Because I said to, and I don't have time to explain. Do it. Now." His voice hadn't been exactly menacing, but the dark thread of anger underlying his command was enough to make her hasten to obey. She felt that he was fighting to keep himself under control. She did not want him to lose control.

"Are you taking me out onto the moors to kill me?" she asked, trying to keep her voice steady as she clutched the cloak against her breast, as if it would shield her from him.

"Is that what you think?"

His amused smile fueled her bravado, and she responded angrily. "What do you expect me to think? Tying me up and abducting me like this! Locking me up and keeping me here against my will, like some kind of . . . of medieval tyrant!"

"I'm afraid you left me little choice. Now put on the cloak, and do it now. I'm extremely tired, and I don't have much patience left."

There was no question that he meant what he said—his dark scowl was enough to prove it—and she draped the soft, silk-lined garment around her shoulders. Still she hesitated, studying his face for signs of violence, but all she saw was the fatigue that lined his face.

"Oh, for God's sake, Libby, just do what you're told for once. I'm bloody well not going to hurt you. If I was going to kill you, I could've done it when I caught you ransacking my bedroom."

That was true, of course. She'd thought the same thing when she'd replayed her dilemma over and over inside her head. Then again, perhaps he couldn't take the time then, but now could dispose of her without the threat of being seen. He said nothing else after his irritated outburst, just waited for her to obey him, and she knew she had little choice but to do as she was told. He apparently intended to take her out-side, where escape would be more feasible. If he looked the wrong way or left her unattended for a single moment, she would run.

Calming her nerves as much as she could, she crossed the room toward him. He never took his eyes off her, and they seemed to delve deeply into her mind, trying to read her thoughts, her fears. Her breath grew shallow when she stood close enough for him to touch her, and she felt all her mus-cles begin to tense, afraid of what he might do. She was re-lieved when he merely took her upper arm and guided her outside, as if he were leading her into a dinner party.

Outside the room, she was able to see the rest of the house for the first time. She found it to be tastefully decorated, again in oriental decor, with silk tapestries embroidered with blue Chinese mountains and white clouds with tunic-clad peas-ants pulling two-wheeled carts. Thick carpets covered the stone floors with low divans lining the walls. The place lay in dead silence as he led her down the circular stairs into a wide receiving hall below.

There she found more black enamel furniture and red silk, and she felt as if she had entered a dream of the Far East with harem girls and pagodas and turbaned soldiers. It all seemed so bizarre, and it was not lost upon her that she was not blindfolded as she'd been when she arrived. Was that be-cause he knew she'd never have an opportunity to tell the au-thorities where she'd been held?

As she looked around, so that she could identify it if given the chance, it occurred to her that Julian, like the eastern potentates she'd read about, could very well be collecting young Englishwomen, kidnapping them and forcing them to pleasure him. Though fanciful and unlikely, did she not know for a fact that Julian enjoyed a wild lifestyle with carnal tastes he made no attempt to disguise from his friends and acquaintances?

Outside on the dirt driveway, a closed coach awaited them, four black horses restlessly pawing the ground and jingling their harness. The giant Chang sat high on the driver's perch, but she'd not seen Lu Ling, or any other of the Chinese servants, since Julian had brought her downstairs. In the absence of a footman, Julian pulled down the step himself and opened the door. He assisted Libby inside, a most proper and polite gentleman.

Inside, she settled into the corner farthest away from him, not exactly sure what to expect. Julian took his seat across from her, his dark face only partially illuminated by the small lantern affixed outside the door. Again she realized her jeopardy and took a deep breath, determined to stay calm until she got her chance to flee.

The coach lurched forward, then rolled off into the night, without Julian giving direction to his henchman, and Libby's heart began to race as she turned her eyes to the velvety darkness into which she was being driven. She was very afraid again, and though determined to remain as composed as possible, her nerves felt ragged and raw with him sitting so close. He was so big and strong, and though she had felt, mistakenly, that he was not the evil man he pretended to be, she now felt certain of just the opposite. She didn't know him at all, and never had.

After a long period of silence during which he stared unflinchingly at her, she tried valiantly to keep her jumping pulse in check, until he said, quite low and with no detectable emotion, "You've been telling one lie after another since the day you arrived at Lasserthon Manor, haven't you?"

Libby jerked spasmodically where she sat. In the dim light he looked guarded but appraising. She was held in thrall by eyes that glinted like blue stars in a winter sky. She started to answer, found her voice hoarse, cleared her throat, and tried to bluff. She did not particularly want to upset the man who held her life in his hands. "I don't know what you're talking about. I must say I find it highly ironic that you make accusations against my character when you're holding me against my will."

His next remark, quietly uttered, sent her rigid with dread. "Why did you conceal the truth about who your father is?"

Libby could feel her face blanch under the unexpected

charge, but her mind raced and she realized that perhaps the fact that her parents were wealthy and powerful had given him pause in making her his next victim. He had thought her nothing other than an American widow, traveling with her maid. Of course, her high connections would make a difference to a man like him, a member of the *ton* himself, and it would greatly complicate whatever devious plans he had.

On the other hand, she still knew him for what he was; he could not afford to let her go. She felt a bitter flood of bile rise up the back of her throat, and she swallowed it down, sick inside, and began to feel as if she were riding inside her own hearse. She would have to find a way to distract him, then fight him if need be. Her hands were trembling, and she clasped them together and hid them under the folds of her cloak.

"I dislike the attention given when I travel under his ducal crest," she answered at length, after taking a deep, cleansing breath that miraculously steadied her voice. "Therefore, I use only my husband's name with those I meet."

"Do you have any idea how your deceit has complicated my life?"

Libby's brows came together as she considered his rebuke. A prickle of pride arose despite her predicament, and she retorted, "Surely you don't expect me to apologize for making myself so hard for you to get rid of?" She couldn't bear it anymore; if she was going to die, she wanted to know it. "Do you intend to kill me? Is that where you're taking me? I'd like to know so that I can prepare myself to meet my Maker."

"More likely you'll prepare yourself to club me over the head and send me in your place," Julian answered. Then to her astonishment his low, rumbling laugh filled the interior of the carriage. He shook his head and gave an easy grin, his teeth flashing very white for a moment. "Is that what you really think, Libby? That I'm going to kill you? Do you truly believe me a man capable of murdering women in cold blood?"

Libby considered it more than just possible, and she did not share his amusement. Anger rose inside her and rang in her words. "I tell you what I do know. I do know that my best friend, Henrietta, is dead. I know I found her ring inside your room, a ring she would never take off, not for any reason. I know she was afraid of you. I know you tried to force yourself on her. I know that you did the same thing with Mary Louise because I found her dress in the tower room, and now she's mysteriously disappeared. Now I too have been abducted and find myself at your mercy."

"That's right, Libby, you are at my mercy. Maybe you should shut up and think about that for a while."

Julian lay back his head and closed his eyes, effectively dismissing her. As she stared at him, chilled by his words, it occurred her to try to make her move, to throw open the door and fling herself from the swift-moving carriage, but she knew he would never let her escape, not until he was finished with whatever game he was playing with her. Instead she considered the warning he'd given her, felt herself tremble under it until she garnered all her strength. Julian, she vowed, would not find her as easy a victim as he had Henrietta and Mary Louise. She might not be able to escape him, but that didn't mean she couldn't try. For the rest of the ride, she sorted through every idea that she could conceive, determined to be ready when the opportunity presented itself.

Chapter Fourteen

"**W**here are we?"

Uneasily Libby looked out the window as Chang brought them to a rocking halt before a dark, looming structure. Not one light shone from anywhere within, and the cloying, clammy mists crept up from the ground to obstruct her view.

"You'll find out soon enough."

"Why can't you just tell me?" she demanded, nerves worn thin, but was met with silence. Julian had become more withdrawn as they'd journeyed to this place, as if he'd contemplated and readied himself for what he meant to do to her. He seemed angrier than he'd been even when he'd caught her in his room, a controlled, passive wrath that seemed all the more dangerous. She did not want his mood to accelerate into rage, since her false bravery was tottering near the edge of breaking down altogether. She was scared; she was exhausted; and she was afraid he was going to kill her.

Julian took her arm and led her inside through a side door for which he retrieved a key from his pocket. There were no lamps, just deep, impenetrable blackness, but just inside the door he fumbled a moment until he got a candle lit. The flicker of the wick illuminated little around them, but he picked up a large brass candlestick on the table beside the door and proceeded with Libby down the long, narrow hallway, so swathed with shadows that she could make out nothing except the doors lining both sides.

Libby walked stiffly, furtively twisting her hands together underneath the cape. His grip on her elbow was tight, and he said nothing. The place was encased in the silence of a tomb, an analogy that shook her even more. She had the most terrible premonition that this was the last place she'd see in her earthly life, the place where he brought his victims in their final moments. She had to make a move soon, or it would be too late.

A moment later she got the chance. When Julian stopped in front of a closed door near a turn in the corridor, he placed the candlestick on a table against the wall, releasing her arm so that he could insert the key. His head was turned slightly, facing away from her, and Libby slowly moved her hand under the cover of the cloak toward the candlestick. When her fingers closed around the base, she lifted it, found it very heavy, then set her teeth and swung it hard against his head as he bent to unlock the door. He must have felt the movement because he half turned, causing the blow to hit him against his left temple. Grunting in pain, he dropped to his knees, then sideways, his shoulder hitting the door with a dull thud. Libby dropped the candlestick and ran, well aware this was the only chance she'd ever have to escape him.

Fleeing up the cold corridor away from him, she felt her cape slide from her shoulders, but she headed into the pitch blackness that would conceal her. The soft-soled Chinese slippers made no sound as she slowed breathlessly, trying to get her bearings. She could hear Julian cursing somewhere down the hallway behind her; then he yelled her name. Then he was on his feet and coming after her because she could hear the click of his boots against the stone floor. She took off again, desperate to find a way out of the house before he caught her. The hallway turned again, and she advanced through the pitch black, using her hands to feel along the smooth wood surface of the wall.

To her shock a door suddenly opened just in front of her, and a weak, flickering light illuminated the darkness. A woman stepped from the room, a candle in her hand. Libby froze as they came face to face. An awful, strangled sound came from deep inside her throat as the woman's flowing white nightdress seemed to float atop the floor.

"No," she muttered, throat tight, heart stopped. She backed away from the hovering apparition until her back hit the wall on the other side of the hall and stopped her retreat. As Henrietta's ghost swept toward her, Libby shut her eyes and groaned as a spinning dark spiral whirled across her mind, sucking her down, down, further and further until she let herself go without a fight, sliding down a long, inky tunnel away from danger, the ghosts, and the man trying to kill her.

"Look, ma'am, her eyelids are fluttering. She's coming around at last."

Libby heard the voice somewhere very near to her. The person speaking sounded quite girlish and delighted that she was regaining consciousness, a youngster's voice, but she was afraid to open her eyes. She held them tightly closed, terrified of what she'd see.

"All right, Libby, it's time to wake up. You've had a shock, but you're all right." Julian implemented his demand by holding something that smelled of ammonia just under her nose, and she shook her head violently, giving in to his wishes only to keep the vile concoction from choking her. When she finally did open her eyes, she stared up into Henrietta's concerned face.

"No," she moaned, immediately screwing her eyes shut again. "It can't be, it can't be . . ."

"Yes, it can, it's me, it really is," Henrietta's dear voice came to her, and when Libby felt the gentle fingers stroking her brow, her eyes flew wide again. She stared in utter disbelief at her dead friend.

"My God, what's happening, what's happening to me? You're dead, you are!"

"I'm so sorry, Libby. I never meant to frighten you so much. I heard someone outside my door and thought one of the girls had fallen ill and needed me."

Libby tried to brush away the sticky cobwebs clinging to her thoughts, confusing her, and she blinked hard, but Henrietta did not go away. She leaned over her, smiling down into her eyes. Tentatively Libby reached out her hand and touched her cheek. "Oh, my God, it is you, I'm not dreaming."

Henrietta laughed softly and put an arm around Libby's shoulders as she helped her to sit up. "That's right, I'm alive and well. And I'm very sorry you had to find out this way."

At that point Libby realized she was lying on a soft feather bed, and as Henrietta propped up pillows underneath her, she looked around in amazement. She had to be dreaming. She had to be. She was still in the circular room waiting for Julian to come back. Or was that part of the dream too? Had everything she'd seen and done since she came to England been a terrible, haunting nightmare? Would she wake up soon and find herself safely in Philadelphia, in her white lace-draped bed?

But if she was dreaming, and she probably was, then who in heaven's name were the ten little girls hanging over the foot of her bed, each staring at her with wide-eyed curiosity? Beyond them she saw Julian where he sat in a deep armchair beside a crackling fire. He was bleeding from the head, and there was a black-robed priest dabbing the wound on his temple with a linen towel. Oh, Lord help her, none of this could be happening. She shut her eyes, thinking surely that it would all soon fade away as a figment of her imagination.

"Are you all right? Libby, dear, please try to stay awake. I know you're still rather stunned, but we can explain everything."

Henrietta took her shoulders and shook her gently, and Libby knew then that she was not dreaming, that this was real, that Henrietta was real. She wanted to laugh, to cry out with joy and relief, but she could not and wept instead, loud sobs of shock and astonishment and happiness, until Henrietta gathered her in her arms and cradled her head against her slender shoulder.

"How can this be? How can it be? Why? Why?" Weakly Libby kept asking the same question, over and over.

Then Julian was standing beside the bed, holding a folded towel against the side of his head. He looked angry. "If you'd waited another minute before you saw fit to club me, I'd have explained everything to you."

"You can't blame me for this. I was frightened to death. I thought you were going to kill me."

"You thought Julian was going to kill you?" Henrietta repeated, as if startled by the idea.

"Why, yes, I thought he'd murdered you. I read your letters. You said you were afraid of him. Then I found your ruby ring in his room . . ." Her explanation slowly faltered into silence as she stared incredulously up at the face she had thought she had lost to death forever.

"I don't understand, I can't understand this," she murmured helplessly.

"Of course you can't," Henrietta soothed, dark eyes brimming with sympathy. "How could you? Let me get the girls back in their beds. Then I'll bring you some chamomile tea and explain everything to you."

As Henrietta moved away, the little girls giggled and whispered together about the exciting goings-on but obediently followed Henrietta from the room. Libby stared dully after them, wondering who they possibly could be, still so dazed and disoriented that she couldn't think straight. Julian had gone back to warming himself beside the flames. Logs were burning brightly and sending out popping, crackling sounds as the room became quiet.

She watched Julian until he moved back toward the bed. He was stanching the flow of blood with the thick pad of linen, but he no longer glared at her. "You really clubbed me a good one. My head's pounding like bloody hell."

"I'm sorry, I think. Where are we?" Then as her senses began to return and her thoughts crystallized, she came up with a more significant question and demanded sharply, "Why did you tell me Henrietta was dead? I don't understand all these lies." She frowned, beginning to wonder again if she really had seen Henrietta.

"It was necessary," he said cryptically. "But I'll let Henrietta explain it to you. I'm dead tired, and now I have to contend with a headache that feels like you drove a spike through my temple."

"Here, I've got your tea." Henrietta had appeared on the doorway, a tea tray in her hands. "I'm sure both of you could use a good bracing cup."

"I'm going to find Brother Simon and share a draught of the burgundy I brought to him from France. I've bloody well had enough of your friend here for one night. You can deal with her."

"Happily, my lord. I've missed her greatly."

Julian didn't seem impressed with Henrietta's glowing recommendation, and he gave Libby one last black scowl before he turned and left the room.

"Despite his gruffness, he's really a very kind man," Henrietta shared conspiratorially as she set down the tray on Libby's bedside table.

"Julian is? You don't mean Julian, do you?" Libby sat up and swung her legs over the edge of the bed, finally ready to accept the fact that Henrietta existed. Still, she couldn't stop looking at her, couldn't stop the pleased smile turning up the corners of her mouth.

"I can't believe you're truly alive." She frowned when she thought of all the months she'd spent mourning her. "How could you do this to me, Henrietta? What a terrible thing to do to your friends, to all of us who love you"—she paused momentarily as she thought of Raymond—"and your husband. Hen, he has suffered terribly, thinking you dead." She shook her head, trying to make sense of it. "Are you having an affair with Julian? Did he convince you to join him in the awful hoax?"

As serene as she had always been, Henrietta lifted the warm kitchen teapot and dribbled it into a cup, but she was very serious as she handed it to Libby. Libby found her hands still were trembling when she took it, and she steadied herself by cupping both palms around its warmth.

Henrietta sat down on the bed beside her and placed a comforting hand on her knee. "It's a long story. Do you think you're up to listening to it all right now?"

"Yes, of course. Please. I find this all incomprehensible. Where have you been? Here the whole time? What is this place? And who are those children?"

Moving down until she could brace her back against the footboard, Henrietta curled her legs up beneath her long white robe. "It is incomprehensible. Never would I have thought myself capable of doing anything so horrible." She gave a heavy sigh. "But I was desperate. I had no choice, and when Julian presented me with an opportunity to leave Raymond forever, I felt I had to take it."

"But Raymond was absolutely destroyed by your death. He's still mourning you . . ." She hesitated, remembering how drunk he'd been the night in Julian's ballroom.

"Raymond is incapable of mourning anyone. He thinks only of himself. He's a devil."

That ended Libby's reproaches, because she'd never heard Henrietta, the kindest person she'd ever known, use a voice so edged with icy contempt. She held her tongue, wanting Henrietta to continue.

"He's not what you think, Libby. I was fooled in the beginning too. I thought he was a wonderful man, a wonderful husband, but gradually he began to show his other side, all the evil he had in him."

A delicate shudder passed through Henrietta's slender form, and Libby took hold of her friend's hands. She clasped them tightly in hers, still finding it hard to accept the other woman sitting before her, flesh and blood, alive, talking to her, smiling at her. No matter what had possessed Henrietta to fake her own death, Libby was only glad she was here, the two of them together again.

"He's so cruel, you wouldn't believe how cruel he can be." Henrietta bit her lip and lowered her eyes to their entwined hands.

"Did he beat you?" Libby asked, her voice thick with compassion.

"Yes," Henrietta answered in not much more than a murmur, "but it wasn't for disobeying him, as some husbands do." She looked at Libby, then away, focusing her gaze on the darting orange flames. Tears filled her eyes and gleamed there without falling, and Libby felt a wave of dread rise as Henrietta began to tell her about her life with Lasserthon.

"He liked to hurt me, I'm sure he did, and not because of anything I did wrong, not for something that angered or displeased him. There was never any reason for his violence. But it always happened at night when he came to me. It always began in bed." Moistening her lips, she hesitated, her voice catching when she began again. "I didn't know what to expect from my husband when we wed, you know, about what my husband expected of me, the intimacies involved. Naively, I suppose, I assumed he would be gentle and kind as he was to me throughout the day. Like you hinted that John was, but he wasn't that way at all, Libby. He'd turn into a monster, a vile, horrid man, when he came to bed. He liked perversions, insisted on doing horrible, unnatural things that repulsed me." She became quiet again, and Libby's heart clutched when she thought of everything she must have suffered at the hands of such a man.

"I didn't even know his tastes were abnormal," Henrietta went on after a moment, "not until Julian told me that no decent man did such things to his wife." She laughed, a terrible little chuckle as she met Libby's horrified eyes. "He even tied my wrists to the bedposts on our wedding night."

"Oh, Henrietta, no, how could he be such a beast!"

"That was the least of his crimes against me." As she sat there, her tears began to roll down her cheeks, and Libby quickly put her arms around Henrietta's shoulders and comforted her as she relived the agony and humiliation of her marriage. Her voice was barely audible, her face buried in Libby's shoulder. "He liked to bite me, and I know it was because he liked to hear me cry out in pain. He had this awful leather riding crop he'd use on me, across my back and thighs, when I refused to do the disgusting things he asked of me."

"No, don't tell me any more, I can't bear it!" Libby cried. Rage such as she'd never known surged up, and she clutched her trembling friend close to her breast, shivered herself as she tried to imagine Lasserthon, with his kind brown eyes

and innocent blond looks, being so depraved, so cruel to a
woman as innocent as Henrietta had been.

"He never hurt me where others could see the bruises or
the teeth marks. He told me the things he required of me
were perfectly normal, that every married couple did the same
thing. Afterward he'd sometimes hold me and kiss me tenderly and tell me he was sorry but it had to be done, and my
stomach would turn and I'd feel like retching."

"Oh, Hen, I should have come sooner. You should have
told me this in your letters, I would have found some way to
help you . . ."

"He began to secretly read my letters, and my journal, and
I became so afraid of him because sometimes he'd get so angry that he seemed like an animal. I tell you, Libby, it was
terrible. His eyes would turn completely black, and he'd act
like an enraged animal. Then Julian came, and in the beginning he watched me all the time, so closely that I began to
fear him too. I'd flee the house so I wouldn't have to see either of them. I'd visit Evelyn mostly, and stay there as long
and as often as I could."

"I read your letters and suspected Julian had a hand in
your disappearance."

"Yes, he did, but he wanted to help me. I didn't trust him
at first. I thought he shared Raymond's tastes, and I mistook
his overtures as attempts to seduce me. But it wasn't like that
at all. He stayed at Lasserthon Manor as long as he did because he knew Raymond's habits with women and feared
for me."

Libby was trying to understand, but none of it was making
much sense. "So Julian brought you here?"

"Yes, though I fled from him every chance I got until one
day he caught up to me on my way into the village market
and offered to deliver me from the hell I was living. I didn't
know whether I could trust him then or not, but I had no
choice, Libby. I was completely desperate, with no one else
to help me. Raymond was growing increasingly brutal, and I
couldn't stay there. I just couldn't, not when Julian offered
me a way to escape."

"Why didn't you come home? Or get word to me? I would've come for you. Oh, Henrietta, I feel so badly about letting you down."

"I had no money, no friends who'd believe me or whose loyalty didn't rest solely with Raymond. I thought of sharing my problems with Evelyn, but Raymond was just too powerful in the parish. If she'd intervened, he would've ruined her and her husband. I was afraid to involve anyone else, because . . ." She suddenly looked terrified as her eyes found Libby's. "I think Raymond might have gone too far with his first wife. I think he might've murdered her."

"Oh, my God, I didn't know he was married before. How do you know he harmed her?"

"No one can prove it, of course, but I suspect it. If he treated her as cruelly as he did me, she couldn't have fared well. I was told she died of a fever, but I don't believe it. And since I've been here, I've found out that he had brutally beaten Mary Louise Baird too. Apparently she'd been his lover for quite some time before I came there. But she's really nothing more than a victim. Any woman he takes up with is a victim."

Libby was startled at the mention of the girl's name. "Oh, my God, she's come up missing too, Henrietta. Just in the past few days. Do you think he might have killed her?"

For the first time Henrietta smiled. "No, she's safe. She left here earlier this very evening. Julian brought her to us. He was forced to act because Raymond slapped her hard enough to bloody her lip, and he did it at Julian's estate with other guests nearby."

"I was there that day and saw her walking with him just before she disappeared, but I thought Julian took her. Why would he take that chance when she was betrothed to one of his friends? Sir John would have called him out for hurting her like he did."

Henrietta shook her head sadly. "There's so much you still don't know. Mary Louise was marrying Sir John only because Raymond told her to. She has been Raymond's mistress for years, since she was little more than a child. When her parents died, she was alone and poor, and he made himself her legal guardian, then forced her into his bed. He abused her as horribly as he did me, more so, I fear. Julian said he was worse with her than with me."

Libby found it incomprehensible that Lasserthon could mistreat so many women without suffering any punishment for his crimes. But it sounded as if he chose his victims with care, young women who had no family or powerful friends who might intercede in their behalf. Except for Julian, who'd offered his help on both occasions. "Why was Julian so interested in all this? By all appearances he and Raymond are good friends too."

"That's something I can't answer. I just know that by bringing me here, he saved my sanity. When he realized what Raymond had in mind for Mary Louise, he gave her the same option to escape."

The tide of relief that swept through Libby was strong enough to rock her where she sat. All her fears concerning Julian disintegrated, blown away by the truth. And he had been right. She'd never have believed any of it, that he'd done the things he had, if Henrietta hadn't told Libby the story herself.

"What about Mary Louise's marriage to Sir John?"

"It's over. Mary Louise intends to sail to Ireland and make a new life there. Raymond was blackmailing her about their affair. Fordenbury thinks she's a virgin. Raymond was threatening to tell him the truth, blame her for their affair. He wanted her to marry Sir John, who shares many of his deviant appetites, but he expected her to remain his lover as well. Mary Louise was scared to death of him. If Julian hadn't intervened when he did, she would have been forced to do everything he wanted."

"But where has she gone? And what about you? You're Lasserthon's legal wife. What will become of you?"

"Eventually Julian intends to convince Raymond to apply for a legal divorce since my body was never found." At that Henrietta gave a rueful smile. "That will free both of us, and Julian will make sure any prospective brides of Raymond know exactly the kind of man he is. In the meantime I'm very happy here. I teach and take care of the girls. I really love them."

"Is this a school, then?"

"Actually, it's an orphanage for girls. Julian's family has always owned this house, and he provides coin enough for the place to stay open. Often he's the one who brings the children to us, oft times out from the London slums. I know his reputation is that of a scoundrel, and that much of it is deserved, but I also know he's done a great deal for everyone here."

Libby was shocked by the extent of her relief. Julian was not the guilty party. She sat there and listened to the rest of Henrietta's story, but her heart sang with happiness. Julian was not the man she had feared him to be, not the ogre that everyone believed, not a killer, not a molester, and those revelations gave her more pleasure than she could ever possibly have explained, even to herself.

Chapter Fifteen

For several hours Libby and Henrietta continued to talk about everything in their lives—about their homes in Philadelphia, about Henrietta's guilt over what she'd done and her fear of being found out, about the school and her students. For much of that time Libby held Henrietta's hand, still incredulous that she had come back to life, that she had suffered so much she would agree to such extraordinary measures, and even more incredible, that the much maligned Julian, Lord Edmonton was her avowed savior.

It was not until the wee hours of the morning that they ended their reunion and bid each other good-bye with promises to meet again soon, secretly but as often as possible. Libby found herself relaxed and happy, in very good spirits but exhausted from lack of rest. She'd dozed only fitfully since Julian had whisked her out of his estate for their wild gallop across the moors. She felt a little giddy, very close to sheer elation when she entered the closed carriage with him for the trip back home. They hadn't spoken a word since Henrietta had told her the truth, but she was filled with enormous gratitude that he was neither the monster nor the killer she'd foolishly come to believe.

Libby studied him as he settled down across from her. He too looked tired, and as he rapped on the roof and the carriage rattled over the gravel and away from the orphanage her remorse at having clubbed him with the candlestick flooded her conscience. He wore a white bandage wrapped around his temples but remained his usual silent, stoic self when she tried to apologize to him.

"I'm truly sorry about hitting you the way I did. Especially now when I realize how kind you've been to Henrietta."

Julian observed her in the dim light, his eyes shuttered, completely absent a trace of emotion. But still the difference in his manner that she'd noticed earlier hung between them. She had imagined he'd be more relaxed and open now that the truth had been revealed, but if anything, he seemed more wary, watching her closely as if she were an enemy to be distrusted. It dawned upon her then that Julian might still be concerned that she'd involve her father in the situation. That he might be charged, or thrown into prison for his part in duping Lasserthon.

"I don't intend to tell Father about this, if that's what's worrying you. I think I owe you that after all you've done for Henrietta." She stared at him, still harboring some amazement about the events of the night. She was relieved, mightily so, but she'd never wanted to believe Julian was capable of such crimes, despite the clues that pointed straight at him. Somehow she felt she had to tell him as much.

"I never wanted to believe you were involved, Julian. I know all about your reputation and wild lifestyle, but I always found it hard to believe."

Julian's smile was coldly scornful. "Don't make a saint out of me because I helped your friend. Most of what you've heard about me is true." His eyes pinned her with such severity that she wanted to squirm; she hated how he could unnerve her with a mere look, but he was not finished baiting her. "I'm sure the great Duke of Thorpe would be horrified if he knew his beloved daughter was alone with me inside this coach."

For some reason, the remark surprised her. Taking offense, she replied archly, "I'm not a sixteen-year-old innocent but a grown woman. I've been on my own for quite some time now. Father knows I prefer to make my own decisions. He doesn't interfere."

"Not all your decisions have been above reproach. If I had been the murderer you thought I was, you could very well be lying at the bottom of a bog with your throat slit from ear to ear."

The graphic depiction gave Libby some pause, but she knew what he said was true. "I'm impulsive at times. I've never denied that or portrayed myself as without fault. I always try to take precautions if I feel I might be in danger."

"Until now."

Cocking her head to one side, she contemplated him momentarily, then said, "Are you advising me I'm still in danger from you?"

"I want to make love to you. I have from the first moment I saw you, as you know full well. This seems like a good time and place."

Libby had to laugh. "You're very straightforward all of a sudden. And your proposal rather lacks any hint of romance, to say the least. I would have expected more from a known philanderer."

"As you mentioned, you're no longer an innocent young girl. You're no longer a married woman, and I find you more desirable than any woman I've met in years. Lastly, you owe me a favor for saving your friend."

She heard the teasing note, but the frankness of his words sent a hot blush into her cheeks. She was not used to such a blatant proposition for intimacy, but she was very aware of him, of the dark interior of the carriage barely lit by the coach light, of the way he was looking at her. "We'll both always be grateful. She told me some of the awful, terrible things Raymond did to her." She couldn't stop her shudder. "I had no idea such things went on. It's quite horrifying really."

"I take it your husband had more civil tastes in love-making."

Not wishing to discuss her relationship with John, especially with Julian, she pulled her legs up and curled them under her cloak as she settled into one corner. She felt completely drained, and she stifled her yawn in her palm.

Smiling a little, Julian said, "You look like a kitten all soft and drowsy."

"I've had a trying few days." She studied him as he

stretched out his legs and propped his boots on her seat. "No one seems to know why you do these things, Julian. Why do you?"

"Don't make me out a hero. I'm not one." He leaned back his head as if preferring to sleep.

"I'm afraid Henrietta would disagree. She told me you've been wonderful to her, and to other women trapped in marriages with abusive men, including Miss Baird." His eyes were closed, and she realized she wasn't going to get much in the way of explanation out of him.

"Do you want to know what I thought? That you were going to kill me, and if you didn't, you'd sell me off to some white slaver."

That regained Julian's attention. He opened his eyes. "I take it you've heard rumors about my being involved in that too. Some of my so-called friends warning you about my baser interests?"

"I overheard Mrs. Tanner whispering about it to Betty. Something about you having your own harem of Chinese women out on the moors?"

"Perhaps I do. I wouldn't trust me if I were you. I'm not the kind of man the Duke of Thorpe would want you consorting with."

Julian had brought her father's name into their conversation again, and Libby wondered why he continued to do so. Did he expect retribution from her family? "What matters is what I think. And I think you're the kind of man I want to be with."

Their eyes held. "That can be arranged, you know. Stay at Brickhill with me for a while. You said yourself you weren't expected in London on any specific date."

Smiling, Libby relaxed back in her corner. "You just warned me not to trust you, and now you invite me to be your guest."

"No, you misunderstood. I've invited you to become my lover."

Libby blinked in disbelief, then wagged a finger at him. "Just when I think you can't shock me any more, you come out with a disgraceful remark like that."

"Have you ever taken a lover, Libby?"

"Certainly not. I was a faithful wife, and since I've been out of mourning, I've been much too busy to think of such things."

"All right, if the idea doesn't appeal to you, we won't become lovers. Stay with me and we'll be good friends until I can change your mind."

"Somehow I don't think that would work."

"You're right, it won't, and the reason it won't is because you want me as much as I want you. I knew it the first time I touched you. You have a tendency to shiver when I come too close, and when I kissed you, you opened your mouth and invited me in, whether you'll admit it or not. Let me kiss you now, if you need proof of how you feel about me."

It was time to turn the subject, so Libby did so. "Why didn't you just tell me the truth about Henrietta that night when I found her ruby ring? Everything would have been so much simpler, and a lot less frightening for me."

Julian looked askance at her, but he was more the way he used to be, some of the distrust she sensed in him gone. "Come now, Libby, can you honestly say you would've believed anything I said at that point? You had me pegged not only as a villain but a murderer to boot since the first moment you laid eyes on me. You would've gone screaming downstairs for Sir Jasper to arrest me, or even worse, to Lasserthon himself."

Libby remembered how terrified she'd been when she turned from searching the desk and found him standing behind her. In that moment she had truly feared for her life.

For a while they simply stared at each other. His eyes were fixed on her mouth for most of that time, making her remember how his mouth had felt, warm and searching, so skillful at parting her lips and making her want him to. Her body reacted at just the memory, quivering and shivering just as he predicted. She spoke quickly, wanting to think of something else, anything else, but her voice still sounded breathless.

"Why are you so secretive about the motives for the good deeds? It's almost as if you're hiding something else from me."

Though he didn't react verbally to her accusation, a veil seemed to drop over his eyes, and she knew she had hit upon something that bothered him.

"Why can't you just take what I did for Henrietta at face value? I've known Lasserthon for years, so I was well aware of what kind of man he was. I knew his tastes were cruel and that his first wife died rather mysteriously. I felt sorry for Henrietta because she seemed so lonely and vulnerable. I didn't want to see her suffer."

"Very well said. That's why she considers you her hero."

Julian shrugged off the accolade. "She owes me nothing, but if you want to thank me for her, come over here and let me touch you."

"So, on a mere whim, you put everything you own and enjoy at stake, including your good name and reputation, your property holdings, to steal a wife away from her husband and home, a woman who is a virtual stranger to you."

Julian lifted his shoulder in a small shrug. "I have plenty of faults, but I've never been one to sit back and let a lady suffer abuse. Lasserthon doesn't deserve to have a wife, especially not a sweet girl like Henrietta, and now he'll have to go back to inflicting his needs inside the uglier brothels in London."

"How many women have you saved, other than Henrietta and Mary Louise? It sounds almost as if you've taken on a mission. The good knight riding to rescue the fair damsel in distress . . ."

When Julian moved suddenly, shifting himself into the seat beside her, Libby knew he wasn't there to talk. Her heart thudded harder, at the very nearness of him, at the smell of his shaving soap and a faint hint of the grape wine he'd drunk back at the orphanage.

"We've chatted long enough, Libby. Now we're going to make love, right here and now."

Libby had to laugh, never disappointed at his technique. "Do you really think I'd be willing to do that, Julian? I'm not a tart, some trollop you've picked up on the docks. And I don't make love with men who snap their fingers in my direction."

Julian lifted his hand. When he snapped his fingers, his smile was enough to melt her bones. The sheer masculine force of him was overwhelming, and his magnetism was nothing new to her. She'd been fighting his effect since she'd caught him with Mary Louise. She knew she should move away, act offended as any lady of quality would. Instead she felt the trembling rush of excitement she'd had the first time he grabbed her and kissed her. She didn't move, not even when he put his arm around her shoulder and jerked her up against his chest.

"If I'd thought you a loose woman, I would've found a way to have you the night you arrived at Lasserthon. That's how badly I wanted you. That's how long I've waited to have you." He was exerting gentle pressure to turn her face toward him, and she found herself capable of little resistance. She wanted him to do this, of course. She had wanted it all along, every bit as much as he had. She craved the heat of his lips caressing her flesh; she longed for her blood to pump through her veins and make her body tingle with need. Inside her head, her better sense rebelled, her good breeding recoiled, but she could think only of how good he felt against her, how hard his muscles were when he held her so tightly, pulling her ever further into his web, controlling her, bending her to his will like a willow in the wind.

Valiantly she gave a try at regaining her senses. "I'm a decent woman, Julian. I will not be ravished inside a coach."

"I have no desire to ravish you. I want to love you, slowly, tenderly, give you pleasure. Then I want you to give me pleasure." He murmured these things against her ear; then his mouth was on the sensitive cord of her throat, just beneath her ear. Her arms and legs rippled with gooseflesh in response, but his hands were busy, pushing the cloak off her shoulders, his fingers working loose the silk frogs holding together the front of her Chinese tunic. She made a weak at-

tempt to thwart him but moaned instead when he succeeded
in his quest and she felt very hot lips on her bare shoulder.

"That's right, my love, relax and enjoy what we have together." The hoarseness in Julian's voice was seductive in itself, and she sighed helplessly, all her defenses weakening,
then dissolving completely under his expertise.

Libby closed her eyes and relaxed in his arms, her thoughts
incoherent as his mouth found her ear. He nibbled on the
delicate lobe, pressed a line of warm kisses under the angle
of her jaw, forcing her head back against the seat. She had
never been kissed like this before, not by a man so skillful at
it, and she found that she was trembling like a virgin, wanting to experience everything he had to offer, but afraid and
excited, her emotions ragged, her heart pounding so hard she
felt her body could not hold it.

Then Julian moved swiftly with her, and she was sitting
sideways across his lap, her breasts heaving with unfulfilled
desire.

"Oh my, Julian," she had just enough breath to mutter,
"you are good at this sort of thing, aren't you?"

Julian's laugh came muffled against her throat, but he was
pulling pins from her hair now, stroking his fingers through
the braids to loosen them. When it finally swung down
around her shoulders, he gathered it in both fists. "I love the
feel of your hair. I love the feel of your skin."

Libby could not resist him, could not keep herself from
sliding her arms around his neck and drawing his head
against her breast. She felt as if she couldn't breathe, as if her
throat had grown too thick, her heartbeat wildly out of control. She felt alive and female and aroused beyond anything
she'd ever known. Though she knew what kind of man Julian was, knew full well she was only the latest in a string of
conquests, knew it would not continue between them, could
not, she wanted this feeling to last; she wanted to know how
it felt to be taken by a handsome, virile male who wanted her
so desperately he panted with it.

"I'm not very good at this, I'm afraid," she felt she had to
tell him, gasping audibly as he grasped her breast in his hand

and tore loose the last frog on her tunic, baring her completely. Embarrassment at her lack of experience flooded her, and she felt compelled to tell him the truth. "My husband wasn't very interested in me in this way, you see, and, well, I've never had anyone do anything quite like this before, not so eagerly. . . ."

Her indistinct words captured Julian's attention thoroughly enough to make him raise his head and stare into her eyes. "What was the matter with him? Was he completely daft?"

Libby laughed shakily. "No, but he was so much older than I, and ill for most of our marriage. I wouldn't be telling you this, but I'm not sure what is expected of me. . . ."

"Merciful God, are you saying that the man never made love to you at all?"

"No, of course not. He did, or tried to, but he wasn't always able to; due to his health, and his age, I suppose. I just want you to understand why I'm not as experienced as you might be expecting."

To Libby's relief, Julian didn't laugh or continue to question her. Instead he stopped, pulling her up against him for a moment, stroking her unbound hair with his mouth atop of her head. She could hear his heart beating as hard as her own was. "Did your father force you to marry Thornhill?"

Surprised by the question, she shook her head. "My parents have never forced me to do anything. I chose John because I loved and respected him. Please don't think we were unhappy together, because we weren't."

He did not reply, and she relaxed inside his embrace, thinking it was very nice indeed to be held by such a strong man, to enjoy his lips warming her brow and temple, his fingers threaded in her hair.

"Perhaps a few more kisses wouldn't be completely out of the question," she suggested when he made no effort to continue, sighing with such deep longing that even she heard it.

Julian's laugh sounded so wicked that Libby turned his head with her hand and stared into his eyes. His face sobered and he pulled her head forward. Her resolve slid away so quickly that she hardly knew her lips had already parted to receive his tongue. He pushed at the silk of her tunic, and she felt it sliding down her arms and off, baring her to the waist for his pleasure. When his mouth inched along the top of her breasts, teasingly moving around each nipple without touching them, she bit her lip and grasped handfuls of his crisp black hair, his lips so hot and exquisitely tender that she groaned aloud, thinking somehow that nothing could feel this good, nothing could give greater pleasure. She was lost to the sheer splendor of each sensation, the gentleness of his mouth and hands and fingers as he explored her naked flesh in a way that no one had ever done before.

His lips came close enough to touch her own, then stopped, and Libby knew in that moment that he would not force her to his will, though she knew he could. If she pushed away now, said no to him, he would stop, and she should, she should say no, because if she did not, they would become lovers. They would have a brief, torrid affair that would mean nothing to him. She would be only the latest woman he'd seduced and abandoned.

"Show me, show me everything," she murmured, eyes closed, her head against the arm he had braced behind her.

He gave a low laugh, one laced with triumph and pleasure, but she didn't care. He had proven himself to have some redeeming qualities, and she wanted to know what it was like to be made love to by such a magnificent man. She wanted him; she wanted to be wicked herself for a change, to feel and do and live without worrying about what others would think of her. At this moment at least, she wanted to uncover the secrets she'd missed, and learn if he could continue to make her feel so weak and out of control or if it got even better.

With her complete surrender, the tautness in Julian's muscles dissipated; she felt him relax. He began to take his time, but Libby in turn found herself tensing up as he lifted her hand to his mouth and burned the palm of her hand with his lips.

"Just the prelude, then, of what will be. Relax, love, and let me show you what a wanton woman you are."

Somewhere deep inside her mind, her thoughts were growing fuzzy and disoriented as he slid his palm slowly down her leg. She wondered how many other women had heard those same tantalizing words, how many lovers his lips and hands had worshiped with such reverence. But she could not deny that his fingers stroked and played over her nerves like a master upon harp strings, awakening razor-sharp desires she had either repressed and denied or never known. The most wonderful moan of pleasure came unbidden, from deep inside her throat, as he continued to delve into her clothes and touch her with his fingertips and mouth.

"Tell me you want me, Libby, that I'm not seducing you against your will."

"I think you are seducing me," Libby answered softly, jerking bodily when his mouth closed over the tip of her breast. "I think you collect women like Chinese art and amuse yourself with them until you grow bored. . . ."

"Rest assured, love, I'm not bored at the moment. Shall we continue?"

"Yes, I think we should."

He smiled down at her, and she knew she wasn't fooling him any more than she was herself. They were well on their way to the love affair he wanted, and she realized with some foreboding, that was exactly what she wanted.

Both from her own realization and Julian's caresses, her breath caught as he lowered his mouth very close hers. He stopped before touching his mouth to her lips, and she quivered with anticipation just as he said she did. He snarled his hands in her hair fiercely, in no hurry, holding her head, caressing her hair, looking into her eyes, until she leaned toward him, unable to bear the anticipation.

Then at last his lips found hers, not forcefully as before, but feathery light, tasting her as if she were the most delectable of sweet confections. She felt a hundred different responses burgeoning inside her, but most of all she wanted more; she wanted him to kiss her fully, to possess her fully, to make her blood run hot. Appalled, she tried to control her desire for him, found it impossible. All the needs she'd longed for were boiling up, igniting into flames.

Filled with guilt, Libby remembered how her husband had fumbled under her nightgown, had lain atop her and tried to perform his duty as husband. More often than not they'd had to stop, and she'd consoled him and told him that it did not matter. And it hadn't. She had loved him for all that he was, not for what happened in their bed.

Julian was slipping his arms around her bare waist, bringing her up against his chest, his mouth burning a trail over her skin, everywhere, his mouth and tongue rippling hot currents over her flesh. She wet dry lips, trying to control her labored breath.

"You're beautiful, so soft," he was telling her, his lips against her throat, but she barely listened as she kissed his temple, his chin, his throat. She wanted to explore his body with her hands the way he was doing to her. She couldn't get close enough to him.

His mouth found hers again, and all her sensations became pinpointed there as the kiss deepened, going far past the soft caressing of her lips into a hard, eager exploration of her mouth that left her gripping his hair in her fists. His tongue searched for hers, found it with an explosion of pure passion, and she reveled in the needs pulsating through her, making every nerve raw and tender and needful of his touch.

He kissed her until she had to stop, had to draw breath and regain her senses. Her chest was heaving, and she laid her head against him, wondering if he could possibly be enjoying their intimacy as much as she was. She lay still in his arms, a mass of trembling desires, waiting for what he'd do next, both wanting him to continue and to stop, but knowing she would never stop him.

Now his mouth was at her temple, his left hand holding her in place on his lap but his right hand working loose the bindings of her silk trousers. When the waist came free, he brought up his hand and turned her face upward where he could capture her lips. As he kissed her, deeply, devastatingly, he cupped her breast, testing its fullness gently in his palm, then began to caress her nipple with his thumb. Libby moaned with mind-less pleasure.

But he wouldn't let her go, his mouth insistent on hers, but his hand was sliding over her flesh, caressing the tips of her breasts until they were hard and erect and so exquisitely sen-sitive that she felt she couldn't bear it. Then his arm tight-ened, drew her up until his mouth fastened wetly over one erect nipple.

Libby felt it as if struck by lightning and lurched in his arms, but he held her tightly. She grabbed his hair as he suckled, wave after wave of pleasure rushing through her, yet he had only begun with his exploration. His hand was sliding down her thigh, taking silk with it, and he caressed her leg, finding the bare skin of her belly.

Then his fingers found the soft curls he sought, and Libby went rigid in his arms as he slid a finger into warm folds hid-den there. No one had ever done such a thing, and she was both appalled and shocked, and tried to struggle but he held her firmly in place.

"I'm not going to hurt you," he said huskily. "Let me show you pleasures you've never dreamed of."

Libby lay still, but she was tense, all the lovely, melting sensations gone. His mouth was on her temple, his breath warm against her cheek. She bit her lip as he began to stroke her, his fingers seeking her most sensitive spot, and then the pleasure began to bud like a new rose, opening slowly, then building and building until she was clutching his shirt, arch-ing herself to meet the exquisite probing. He was relentless in his desire to pleasure her, his head dropping until his mouth found her breast again, and when her body gave in to the response he was coaxing from her, her pleasure came with such unbelievable force that Libby went absolutely rigid as jolt after jolt of pure ecstasy surged through her. She cried out, but the sound ended as a second wave ripped through her, then a third that left her groaning and shivering until it finally subsided, leaving her to collapse weakly against Ju-lian's chest.

Breathing heavily, Libby could not speak, could not believe what had happened. He laughed softly, a pleased sound, as she continued to quiver helplessly in his arms.

"If this is the prelude, I cannot think how magnificent the rest will be," she murmured with what breath she had left.

"Now will you stay with me? Just one night if you'll give me no more."

Libby wasn't sure she could have denied him even if she wanted to. Her body was still so sensitive, she felt if he merely touched her again, she would explode into more of the wonderful, inexplicable spasms he'd extracted from her.

"I'll stay," she whispered, wondering if she would live to regret her weakness for Julian, feeling certain that she would but still unable to deny him what he wanted.

"Good," he said, straightening her clothing and drawing the cloak around her. He kept her on his lap, cradling her comfortably against his chest. "Now, go to sleep until we get to Brickhill. We'll have little time for sleep once I get you into bed."

Libby smiled against his shoulder but did not answer. Still overwhelmed by Julian's first lesson in lovemaking, she closed her eyes and wondered what on earth could possibly be better than what she'd already experienced.

Chapter Sixteen

As the coach swayed and rocked across moorlands lit by a full bright moon, Julian held Libby securely across his lap. She had fallen asleep and felt small and warm, and infinitely good, relaxed against him as she was. She had been exhausted, and he wasn't surprised, not after having spent several days locked in the stone tower and then the unexpected revelations concerning Henrietta. Now, of all things, guilt was beginning to prick his conscience.

He shook such thoughts away, reminding himself that Libby had made it abundantly clear, by manner and word, that she wished him to make love to her. One thing he'd had difficulty accepting, however, was her lack of experience. On the other hand, he'd found something profoundly more pleasing—that a hot and passionate nature lay hidden under the calm, ladylike behavior she exhibited to those around her, one he meant to enjoy as long as she'd let him. As wedded wife she'd obviously not enjoyed the intimacy any woman deserved. Still it was clear to him that she'd loved John Thornhill and he'd not mistreated her, unlike Henrietta or Mary Louise. Or Victoria.

Refusing to let himself dwell on his sister, he shifted Libby into a more comfortable position, with her head against his shoulder. He brushed away a couple of silky strands so he could see her face. She was a beautiful woman, but there was more to her, some indefinable quality about her that completely intrigued him. How her dead husband, how any man, could live in the same house with her, bound to her by nuptial vows, and not spend most of his time in bed with her seemed completely impossible to him.

Unfortunately, she had spoken highly of her parents as well as her husband. He felt a tide of the ancient hatred start to swell and rush toward a shore of rage. He'd fought that anger against her father for so long, years, and he had contained it with iron-fisted control. The cold loathing had lain in a festering, black sore on his soul, waiting the right moment to strike back. Until now he'd never had the weapon of revenge, not until Mrs. John Thornhill walked into his life. She was the sharp, lethal dagger that could pierce the Duke of Thorpe's heart, and fate had tossed her into his lap.

The time was at hand to repay Thorpe for his crimes against the Rainvilles. Julian stared down at Libby, and felt his muscles begin to tense as he thought of Libby's father. She shifted her head, and he saw a glint of red-gold in the dim lamplight. Again he brushed her long hair behind her ear, wanting to look at her delicate features. When he ran a fingertip down the curve of her cheek, so fragile and elegant, she snuggled closer, as if she knew he was caressing her. She trusted him now; she thought him not the villain she had once suspected. But was that true, now that he knew her true identity? His mouth tightened and his jaw clenched as he watched her sleep so peacefully, because the truth was that Julian was indeed the worst man she could ever take up with, the one man who could use her as a pawn in a fight against her own family.

One part of him rebelled and made him sorry she'd have to play a part in his vengeance. She had not done the misdeed herself, but even her innocence in the matter didn't lessen the transgressions of her father, the almighty duke. His gut began to twist and knot up at the thought of what the man had done to his mother and brother, but worst of all, the suffering his actions had indirectly caused his little sister, Victoria. He couldn't hold Thorpe entirely responsible for her agonizing death because that had been Julian's own fault, and the bastard he'd arranged for her to wed.

Libby was caught in the middle, but Julian had every reason to use her to bring her father to his knees. Libby would be little hurt if they enjoyed a brief affair. She wanted him as much as he wanted her; she was a grown woman who prided herself on making her own decisions. She was ripe for the plucking; her naïveté in love affairs something he could plot to his own advantage. He did like her, admired the grit she'd shown, and her courage in the face of fear. She was a formidable woman; she wouldn't cling and cry when she learned the truth about his motives. She might hate him for it, but she would go on with her life in America.

Perhaps for that very reason he was loath to hurt her, but that didn't mean he wouldn't. He'd dreamed of getting even with William, Duke of Thorpe, for far too long. Perhaps he should even go so far as to marry her in the final twist of the knife. He smiled coldly, envisioning the look on the duke's face if that wedding came to pass. Although Julian had not considered marriage a particularly desirable option at the moment, it would certainly cause Thorpe a great deal of pain, especially if his daughter openly defied him by wedding a Rainville against his wishes.

On the other side of the coin, Libby would make him a more than suitable wife, and he'd always known he'd have to wed eventually. She'd be completely in his control, where he could make sure she wasn't hurt any more than necessary. Even better, Thorpe would be livid with rage and completely helpless to do anything about it. Indeed, the idea was definitely worth serious consideration, and now that Libby had agreed to stay with him, he had time to convince her if he decided to go through with it.

Now that his guests had dispersed and there was no risk of running into anyone at his estate, he had ordered Chang to return them to Brickhill. When they finally arrived and rolled to a stop in the courtyard, Libby stirred in his arms but did not awaken. Nor did she open her eyes when Chang opened the door, so Julian kept her in his arms and strode toward the door where Lu Ling stood waiting with a lamp. "Is she ill?" she whispered as she held the door wide.

Julian kept his voice low as well so as not to awaken Libby. "She's asleep. Has anyone inquired after her?"

Her face serene, Lu Ling shook her head. "Only her maid. It has been quiet here since our return from the tower. Did you make her understand?"

Julian nodded. "She talked with her friend for a long time, so she'll cause us no more trouble."

Holding the lamp out to light their way, Lu Ling obediently started down the hall leading to the steps that led into Julian's bedchamber. At the top of the staircase Julian passed her and carried Libby to his bed. She had agreed to become his lover, and he'd be damned if he'd give her time to change her mind.

"Thank you, Lu Ling. You may go."

Lu Ling nodded, then bowed as she silently left them, leaving through the sitting room and closing the door after her.

Julian stood for a moment looking down at Libby, then began to undress her. Her body was beautiful, small and delicate with long legs and a tiny waist, the kind of woman who made a man want to protect her, though in Libby's case she was fully capable of taking care of herself. He almost laughed. She had come close to uncovering and proving his involvement in Henrietta's disappearance. She was not a woman to be toyed with. If he was not careful, very careful, she would see through this new batch of lies he meant to spin around her.

She roused some but did not come fully awake, and when he had her naked and underneath the sheets, he undressed himself and slid into bed with her. He would let her sleep as long as she could, would get plenty of rest himself before he gave her a second lesson in lovemaking. He pulled her into his embrace, and though she stirred again and protested initially, she soon snuggled up close against his side.

As sleep overtook him, he realized with some surprise that Libby was the first woman he had ever allowed to spend the night in his bed at Brickhill. He shut his eyes, thinking she felt very good curled up against him, her silken hair against his cheek. He would have to be careful with her, he thought as drowsiness blurred his mind and soothed his own fatigue. Libby was the kind of woman who could ingratiate herself into a man's heart before he knew what was happening. He would enjoy her company while he had the chance, and make sure she enjoyed it even more. Because when she found out his primary motivation for taking her as his lover, she could very possibly hate him with every ounce of her being.

When he awoke again, early dawn was misting the room with a smoky shower of pearly gray light. Libby was lying on her side, her head propped in her palm as she gazed down at him.

"You take liberties, sir, bringing me naked into your bed without my knowledge."

Julian laughed at the understatement of that observation, then reached for her. Her hair fell over her shoulders in clouds of gleaming golden bronze, and he wanted to kiss her, to feel her pressed full-length against him.

"I cannot believe I am here in the bed of the most notorious rake in all of England, a man vilified as the devil of debauchery, the enemy of all innocent virgins. My parents would simply die."

"But you're no innocent virgin, and you want to be here." He grasped a handful of her hair and pulled her mouth down to him.

"Yes, and very glad that I am."

She spoke against his mouth; then their lips met and mingled, and explored, and ignited, and Julian pushed her back upon the pillows. "It's time for lesson two, love."

He moved until he lay full-length atop her, catching her hands and holding them beside her head. She gazed up at him, smiling, but when his eyes roamed down over her, he could see how her chest was heaving. He lowered his head and feasted on her breasts as he held her immobile, and her low moans of pleasure sent a rush of desire through him. He wanted to show her how good it could be between a man and a woman, had intended to do so slowly, tenderly, but he had not counted on the passion flooding him in a deluge of flame and heat.

When he let go of her hands, Libby began to explore his body as well, sliding her palms around his sides, then up over his back. She held him tightly, positioned herself to receive him, and the racing fire inside him streaked out of control. He rose to his knees and lifted her hips, then entered her, finding her warm and ready, astounded at how much he wanted her.

When he thrust deeply into her, she cried out, but when he paused in concern, she pulled him back into her. She moved with him, slowly at first, and the soft sounds she was making inflamed him further. He shut his eyes, enjoying the feel of having her at last, until his pleasure could not be contained and his climax ripped up through him like a cataclysm in his soul, and the cry that roared up from someplace deep inside of him was as disbelieving as hers had been.

When he collapsed atop of her, she clutched her arms around his head, and he lay panting, his cheek upon her heaving breast, his heart thudding inside his chest, his mind reeling with turmoil. Because, he realized, he'd felt more than he should, more than he could. She already had become more than just a passing fancy, the latest of his conquests. Somehow, some way, she had gotten to him, and that was dangerous. That was the last thing he could allow.

Chapter Seventeen

Stretching her arms over her head, Libby sighed contentedly, slowly swimming her way into wakefulness. Warm and relaxed, snuggled comfortably under the covers, she kept her eyes closed until she remembered where she was and who she was with. A smile touching her lips, she reached out for Julian but touched only rumpled sheets. When she opened her eyes and found him gone, she was struck by her immediate sense of loss.

Turning on her back again, she pulled the pillow that had cradled his head up against her breast and clasped it close to her heart. The essence of him lingered, memories from the night before sweeping her in a sweet deluge. She remembered how fiercely he'd made love to her, then how tenderly. He'd been pleased with her, and she had been astonished how he made her forget everything but him and the desires and pleasures he'd brought to her. He'd taught her many things already, and she felt her face grow warm as a tingling in her loins brought it all back with a vividness she couldn't deny.

How strange that they'd come together this way—she and a man she'd found detestable. No longer did she feel so; instead she felt there was something special between them. Although she'd had little experience with men other than her husband, she did not think there was another man alive who could make her feel the way Julian did.

A soft tap at the door brought her upright in bed, and she quickly snatched up Julian's black velvet robe from where it lay at the foot of the bed, donned it quickly before calling permission to enter. She was disappointed when it wasn't Julian but pleased to see Alice again, safe and sound. Before Libby could get out a word, Alice hurried across the room, her alarm spilling out in a frightened rush.

"I ain't never been so scared, ma'am. He told me nothing but to bring you up this pot o'tea."

"He did? How thoughtful he is." Libby smiled as she tightened the belt at her waist and sat up on the side of the bed.

"But'e be the one who took Miss Hen! What'as he done to you, ma'am?"

Libby realized that poor Alice knew nothing about what had transpired since she'd been gone, and though she now regretted subjecting her maid to such unnecessary fears, she quickly enlightened her with the truth.

"I was completely wrong about him, Alice. Julian had no part in Henrietta's disappearance. The truth is"—she looked toward the closed door but lowered her voice in case anyone loitered outside—"and you must promise never to repeat this, but Henrietta isn't dead. She's perfectly fine, and happily teaching children in an orphanage not too awfully far from here."

"Oh, he done been a messin' with your head, 'asn't he, ma'am? They say he's devil enough to do such things. I should never've left you alone where he could get his hands on you. Just look, your eyes are all red and bleary. What's 'e been doin' to you?"

Libby had to laugh, fearing Alice's description was quite apropos, though in not the way she thought. She'd missed her loyal friend, and she reached out and patted Alice's arm. "I'm perfectly fine. I'm just happy now that Julian's convinced me beyond a doubt that he has done nothing wrong. Henrietta assured me that he's shown only kindness and regard for her well-being. Remember, Alice, you must tell no one about this."

Alice didn't look convinced but stepped away from the bed as Libby stood up and stretched again like a contented cat. "I think I will have some tea, if you please. What about you, Alice? What have you been doing while I was gone?

"He left me locked upstairs in the attics till all the ladies and gents left the party, but there was a Chinaman who brought me food and looked after me. He was young as me and 'is name was Li. He don't talk English good, but I've been teachin' him."

Libby smiled at that and took the cup Alice offered, thoughtfully studying her maid. "It sounds as if you're rather fond of Li."

"I thought all 'is lordship's Chinamen were heathens and murderers, but Li taught me this gamblin' game with dice." As Alice spoke she handed Libby a folded linen napkin.

Nodding, Libby swallowed a mouthful of the soothing brew and asked where Julian was. She was already eager to see him again.

"He's 'avin' 'is breakfast and wants you to join him as soon as you be ready. Bathin' water's on its way, and his lordship asked that you don a riding habit so 'e can show you his property."

"Then I better hurry and dress," Libby said, unbelievably eager to bathe and join Julian. A horseback ride out in the fresh air sounded wonderful, she decided as she glanced out the tall paned window where Alice had just swept back the drapes to admit a flood of bright morning sunshine.

"I think I'll wear my green velvet," she began, then stopped, a thought occurring to her. "Is there anyone else here, Alice? Other guests, I mean?"

"No, ma'am. I've been alone here with just 'is lordship's staff till he come back with you. It be the strangest house, ma'am, with all foreigners and all, but they've been kind enough and most just talk gibberish to each other."

Within an hour, Libby was bathed and dressed for horseback riding and more than eager to spend an entire day in Julian's company. Though she did not miss the irony of the situation, she was enjoying the scandalous affair in which she found herself embroiled. Julian was sitting at the table when she entered the door of the breakfast room, but when he saw her, he rose and strode toward her, as if he was eager to see her too. Despite the fact that Lu Ling stood near the mirrored buffet, he pulled Libby into his arms and gave her a kiss that nearly took her breath away.

"Julian, please," she protested in embarrassment, but she smiled and knew with some chagrin that if she had her way, they would continue the embrace upstairs and forget their ride in the bedroom. Wondering what he'd done to her sense of propriety to make her behave so wantonly, she nevertheless allowed him to seat her close to his right.

"Are you hungry?" He smiled at her, his eyes roving over her face.

"Ravenous," she answered, admiring the breadth of his shoulders in his brown wool riding jacket. She remembered how they'd lain entwined, his mouth pressing kisses in her ear, his hands exploring her body, and couldn't suppress shivers of pleasure only heightened when she realized their wicked, immoral love affair had only just begun. She reached for a piece of toast and spread it with blackberry jam while Lu Ling set a steaming cup of coffee beside her plate.

Across from her chair, the long mirror above the sideboard presented a view of the table, and she was amazed to observe herself sitting so calmly at Julian's side. How could she have been so wrong about him? She'd always been a good judge of character, but this time her intuition had failed her. Indeed, her estimation of him had risen to heroic proportions now that she'd learned his selfless motives. He had probably saved Henrietta's life, or at the very least a miserable life of pain and domination. No matter what happened between them in the future, she would always be grateful to him for that. She smiled and shook her head, and Julian noticed, pausing with his cup halfway to his mouth. He raised an eyebrow in question.

"I cannot get over how wrong I was about you," she admitted softly. "You really had me fooled."

"I daresay I still have a great many people fooled."

"They don't know the truth about you, as I now do." Libby replaced her cup in her saucer and studied him with narrowed eyes. "Why do you promote the idea that you're a reprobate of the lowest caliber when just the opposite is true?"

"Because I am a reprobate of the lowest caliber. Don't color me a perfect gentleman because I've helped a few unfortunate women out of untenable situations. I've earned my unsavory reputation, I assure you."

Libby leaned back in her chair and observed him for a moment. "You act as if you're proud of it."

"Not especially proud. Just realistic. I have my good points, I suppose, as does anyone, but I'm no angel. You know that now, I suspect. Would an upstanding man of character seduce a lovely, innocent widow like yourself?"

"You didn't force me to do anything I didn't want to do."

"True."

They were both thinking about some of the intimacies they'd shared the night before, a few she had never dreamed existed, and she could almost see the desire darkening his eyes. Her body smoldered as well, similarly awakening to what might happen again in the next few hours.

"You ought to be ashamed. You've turned me as brazen as yourself."

Though Libby was teasing him, Julian became serious. "Stay here with me for a few weeks. I don't want you to leave."

She should not, definitely should not, even consider staying longer than a day or two with him. Good Lord, she had done enough already to destroy her good name and strike both her parents with apoplexy.

"Perhaps I'll consider it," she answered, unable to prevent the pleasure that spread over her face. "But I truly can't remain here very long. I truly cannot."

Julian lifted her hand and kissed the back of fingers, and Libby knew then, with his lips lingering upon her skin, that despite her disclaimer, she probably would stay on for a fortnight if he really wanted her to, but that was far longer than she ought to.

After they'd dined, they walked side by side through the sprawling salons of Brickhill. She admired the many treasures he pointed out, much of it artwork and furniture he'd brought back from all parts of the world, from China to India to Africa. She had never see so much Oriental decor and was continually amazed by the vivid jewel-like colors, scarlet and black and jade green, the intricately carved tables and tapestry chairs and divans. It seemed as if she were walking through the palace of a Chinese emperor.

"Where are your own paintings?" she asked as they strolled along one of the large galleries through slanted bars of sunlight streaming down through a long row of mullioned windows.

Julian took her hand and tucked it into his arm. "I usually give them away or leave them upstairs in my studio. The ones I'm pleased with I send on to my house in London."

"You're very nonchalant about your work, seeing as it's the rage of the country." It occurred to her to wonder if her parents had ever purchased his paintings. They were art lovers and acquired many great works of the masters in their estates, including some wonderful portraits of themselves. Her mother, Trinity, was particularly pleased to discover a new talent.

"It's a hobby, nothing more. One I gain some pleasure from at times. I still want to paint you. You'll let me now, won't you?"

"Yes," she said simply, all pretense of dislike and distrust banished now that she knew him better.

"In the nude, I should have added."

"Sounds wonderful."

They laughed and walked on together through other sunlit salons into yet another long, windowed gallery that seemed to dominate Brickhill. As they strolled on toward the stable courtyard, Libby realized the immense portraits lining the wall beside them were members of the Rainville family. Many of his ancestors were dressed in Elizabethan ruff and hose, others in more modern attire. There was a similar gallery at Thorpe Hall, where her own ancestors were immortalized between arched, velvet-draped windows.

Thoughts of her family made her realize that she would soon have to leave and join her parents, but perhaps Julian would agree to come along with her. She would like for them all to become acquainted and wanted her family to know that Julian was not the blackguard they'd no doubt heard him to be. With interest she examined his ancestors, stopping at one end before a painting of a strikingly handsome man holding the bridle of a magnificent white stallion. There was a certain arrogance about the turn of his head.

"Who is he, Julian? He somehow reminds me of you." She smiled. "Except that you are much more handsome, of course."

Julian glanced up at the portrait, and Libby immediately noticed the tension that overtook the leanness of his jaw. She studied his face and sensed he was uncomfortable with her question. When he answered, however, his manner seemed quite easy and relaxed, and Libby wondered if she had imagined his first reaction.

"That's my older brother, Rupert. He died when I was ten years old."

"How sad," she murmured, looking back up at the portrait. "Was it an accident? He looks very young."

"That portrait was commissioned three months before he died in a fall." He kept his eyes riveted on his brother's likeness as he went on. "My mother never truly got over it."

She heard his pain and knew his brother's death had affected him deeply. She questioned him no further on the subject as he took her arm and led to the next portrait. He stopped there, and Libby studied the smiling family portrayed in the gilt frame. His family, she realized, when she recognized him as one of the smaller children. Even then he was beautiful, she thought, even more beautiful than the little girl who sat in his lap on the floor in front of their mother's chair.

"What a pretty little girl."

"That was my sister, Victoria. I'm sure you've already heard about the way she died."

His voice was so steadfastly composed that she was quite sure he had retreated inside himself to hide his emotions over Victoria's tragic suicide. But she remembered well the story Evelyn had told her, and that he'd killed his brother-in-law in a resulting duel.

"My sister died because I placed her in the house of an abusive husband." He didn't look at Libby but kept his eyes riveted on Victoria's face. "I arranged it all, then sailed away to China and left her in his clutches. Later I found out that he had abused her horribly. She took her life to escape him by jumping off the roof onto a cobbled courtyard." He stopped at her gasp of horror. His smile was cold. "It was my fault she died."

"No, it wasn't. How could you have known? I'm sure you thought him an upstanding man."

"That's what I thought, but I didn't bother getting to know him, did I? I was just pleased that he offered for her so that I could be on my way. You see"—his voice grew as brittle as frozen porcelain—"our family name was blackened by scandal. Few people would think of having Victoria in their drawing rooms, much less marrying her."

Libby wanted to ask him about the scandal and the deadly duel, but his mood had grown darker. It was not the time to pursue it, for evidently it had stamped him with suffering. Blaming himself for his sister's death was in itself enough to cause him distress, but he had saved Henrietta's life because of it.

"You mustn't blame yourself, Julian. It wasn't your fault."

Julian looked down at her, then surprised Libby by pulling her close and holding her against him, but there was no passion in the embrace. It was almost as if he was drawing from her warmth and understanding. Her heart was touched by his wordless show of vulnerability, and she wondered anew about this strange man she had taken as her lover. She knew somehow that he held many dark, painful secrets hidden in his heart, many that she would probably never know. Yet the truth was that his past no longer interested her.

There was good in Julian, good that for some unknown reason he masked from everyone. She could help him, if he'd let her, could show him how good life was, how happy he could be, if he'd let go of whatever guilt from the past haunted his present. She was determined to try to reach him, even if they remained lovers only for the few short months she planned to spend in England, because, she realized with a shocking flash of insight, she was beginning to care about him. She already did care, she thought with a sinking heart, and she wasn't sure if that boded ill or well for her. One thing she did know, however, was that she would not let such doubts destroy the happiness she felt when Julian threaded his long fingers through hers and smiled tenderly down into her eyes.

Chapter Eighteen

Julian had spread out a quilted white blanket upon the grassy edge of the lake, and Libby leaned back on her palms and gazed out over a bed of yellow tulips to where a riding path rolled upward into a thick deer park. It was a beautiful spot in which they'd chosen to rest, and with their mounts grazing nearby, she closed her eyes and lifted her face to the sun. Though she'd brought along a bonnet that matched her habit, Julian had already removed it and loosened her simple chignon. Her long hair rippled unimpeded down her back, and she enjoyed the freedom it gave to her while alone with him in a suitably private spot.

"Yes, that's perfect. Hold your head just that way."

Julian sat a few yards away, leaning against a giant oak tree that shielded them from the house. He had his right leg braced up, a large sketching pad balanced atop his knee. He had insisted on drawing her in charcoal shadings, but after a moment or so, she dropped the designated pose and gave him her best provocative smile. "I thought you wanted to paint me in the nude. Have you changed your mind already?"

Glancing up quickly, Julian first showed his surprise, then grinned. "Not a chance. We have all night to work on that. Out here I want you in that green dress with all that glorious hair down around your shoulders and the yellow tulips behind you." His eyes never left her hair. "Shake your head back and forth. Slowly."

Libby dropped her head back and obeyed and then looked back at him. He had stopped drawing, the pencil poised in his hand, staring at her. With open appreciation in his voice, he said, "You know, on second thought, perhaps it is time for me to start the nude."

Laughing at him, Libby shook her head and pointed across the lake to where a team of his gardeners were tending a flower bed and raking the graveled sidewalk. "Not here, I'm afraid."

"I know other places where no one can see us."

"Yes, I'm quite sure you do."

They shared a smile, but Julian seemed intent on getting his vision down on paper, so they settled again into companionable silence. Libby stared out over the water where several pairs of snow white swans paddled in graceful tandem. She could hear the servants working, their voices drifting out over the water. They spoke in Chinese, as did most of Julian's servants. He had transplanted a strange oasis of foreign culture onto English soil, and she wondered briefly why he'd felt that need. She could not help but find Brickhill as beautiful and intriguing as she found Julian himself.

She turned her attention back to him and found him on his knees, leaning forward with his sketchpad on the grass, working furiously with his pencil. It looked as if he might be shading her hair, and a silky black lock had fallen upon his forehead in his concentration. It was so peaceful, so incredibly right, being here alone with him, that a contented sigh escaped her. She thought about the painting she'd seen of him when he was a small lad, and wondered if he'd run through these very fields and splashed and cavorted in the lake with his sister and brother. She decided to ask him as much, suddenly wanting to know everything about his past.

"Tell me about your childhood, Julian," she said, rolling onto her side and propping her cheek in her palm. "What were you like? Did you get in as much trouble then as you do now?"

Julian stopped what he was doing and sat back on his heels. "My father thought I was destined for hell, but my mother insisted that I could do no wrong."

"Most mothers feel that way about their sons, I suppose." She thought of her mother and how close they were, and knew the mother's bond with her daughter could be just as strong. She longed to see her mother again, and her father, even though he'd never completely forgiven her for not marrying an Englishman of his choosing.

"What's that little smile all about?" Julian had put down his work and was walking toward her. She moved over, welcoming him down on the blanket beside her.

"I was thinking that my father would probably be pleased that I was spending time with a proper Englishman, one with a title, no less. He was very much against my marriage to John."

"So you defied him?" Julian lifted a soft tendril of her hair and caressed it idly between his thumb and forefinger as he gazed down at her.

"My father never forbade me; he just used all his wiles to convince me to his point of view. It didn't work, of course, because I idolized John."

"Idolized him? That's high praise from a wife, I must say."

"John was a patriot during our revolt against King George, and I've always admired people who fought and won against such impossible odds. Remember, I was named for their victory."

Julian smiled, but he seemed more serious than usual with the subject as he questioned her further. "Yet your own father is a duke. Surely that gives you some loyalty to your English forebears. They are your family."

Julian was watching her so closely that it was a bit unnerving, and she wondered what thoughts he hid behind those navy blue eyes. "I love my family, of course, but I prefer to live in America. So does my mother, because she was born there in South Carolina, though she won't admit it out of respect for my father's feelings. My brother, Burke, is just the opposite. He loves England first and foremost, and everything it stands for." Libby saw a flare of recognition in Julian's eyes. "Do you know Burke?"

"I know him when I see him," he answered, but was obviously bored with the subject because he leaned down and pressed his mouth against her lips. The kiss was warm and soft, and she found the long, gentle mingling that followed most enjoyable. "What about my parents, Julian? Are you acquainted with them?" she asked when he moved his attention to the side of her throat. Her eyes were still closed, but she felt him pause and his voice was muffled against her skin.

"I've never met them, and I don't give a damn what they think about me, and neither should you. You're a grown woman, one I can't touch without losing control."

She could feel his desire for her as he pressed himself against her, and he was demonstrating that need by unbuttoning the bodice of her riding jacket. When his hand slipped inside and cupped her breast, she felt all the swirling, hot emotions well up and gain momentum as he caressed her nipple with the pad of his thumb. She felt it harden instantly under his touch, and her mouth went dry. She swallowed hard as he brought her up tightly against his side, then hesitantly took a few liberties herself. She slid her hand up the front of his shirt and caressed the bulging muscles of his chest. She had found that she loved to touch his body. She wanted him to touch her even more, but she was not unaware of the servants slowly making their way around the edge of the lake with their tasks.

"I've become absolutely shameless," she said, snuggling closer and wrapping both arms around his hard-muscled waist.

"And why is that?" he murmured, his hand sliding down her thigh, over the soft velvet of her skirt.

"Because I wish we were alone somewhere, out of sight of the whole world. I never expected I would wish for such things."

Julian was quiet, but as he began to massage her shoulder, she relaxed against him. "Tell me about your husband. What was he like?"

"He was very nice, very kind. I admired him first for his strength and courage, but later I found out how wise he was. He secretly printed up patriot newsletters during the war, and was imprisoned by the English for his efforts." She laid her head against his arm and looked up at him. "I grew up in the Carolinas with my mother's family, for the most part where nearly everyone in my family fought as patriots. My Uncle Geoff and Aunt Adrianna, and Grandfather Eldon, even my mother rode as a courier now and again."

"The Duchess of Thorpe rode as a patriot courier?" Libby laughed at the disbelief in his voice. "So that's where you inherited your tendency to seek out and confront killers without a thought to your own safety."

Libby gave his shoulder a playful push. "You weren't a killer, which I was very glad to find out, and I always kept Alice at my side, did I not? Besides, I knew all along, instinctively, that you really couldn't have done such things."

"Lasserthon certainly could, and you came there and willingly stayed without knowing either of us or what kind of character we possessed. In truth, you thought I was the worst sort of criminal."

"I only stayed a few days, if you'll remember. If I'd felt myself in real danger, I would have traveled on to London and asked my father's help."

"I suspect the duke won't be exactly delighted that you're here at Brickhill with a man of my reputation."

"As you said, I'm an adult. What he thinks of you doesn't really matter. It's what I think."

"And just what do you think?"

She put her palm against his cheek and smiled into his eyes. "I think you're wonderful."

Julian took her hand and pressed her palm against his lips, then rolled over until he lay completely atop her. Libby felt the first quiver of excitement, slightly appalled at how desperately she wanted him to make love to her again. She had been in a perpetual state of erotic arousal since she'd come into the dining room and he'd smiled at her, one full of sensual promise. Her body seemed to have become highly charged now that they'd made love, ready to respond to anything he said or did, to his slightest touch.

"Thorpe won't like you being here with me, my love, I can guarantee you that."

Libby was prevented from giving answer to his forbidding prediction by his mouth, greedy and hot as if he meant to devour her, and she lost herself to the deep, draining kisses he was demanding from her. Afterward he pushed himself up onto his knees and pulled her to her feet.

"Come, my love, for you've left little restraint in me," he muttered, righting her clothing. "If we hurry, we'll make it to the house before I lose all control and have you right here for all to see."

Chapter Nineteen

"Surely you've done enough sketches of me, Julian."

Though Libby smiled, her voice did have a plaintive note. Julian had positioned her on a one-armed fainting sofa for yet another nude, so she wore only a black silk robe, so thin it was veritably transparent. "You'll soon have enough for an entire gallery showing, you know."

Julian glanced up behind his easel. "Now, that would be a collection worthy of a king's ransom. I daresay it'd set the Royal Academy of Art back on its heels but break all records for attendance."

"Have you exhibited your work there?" she asked, curious because she'd often heard about the significance of that honor from her mother. Libby had been to one exhibition herself many years ago when one of Burke's professors had a painting selected to hang at the show.

"I've never entered. This is a hobby that gives me something to do when I'm bored."

"Then you must be very bored. You've posed me in a hundred different positions and thought of little else since I've been here."

"I can't help it if you're so tempting a subject. Especially now."

"Now?"

"Before we became lovers, you held back on me. Now I can see the real Liberty Remington Thornhill. Now I can see the sultry siren you hide behind those innocent green eyes. Your eyes shine with your emotions. Beautiful but hard to capture. It's still eluding me."

Libby felt a hot rush of pleasure at his words, but she always felt too warm around him, as if she were always feverish. Her behavior was increasingly shameful. She was, or had been, a respectable woman who'd spent her entire married life maintaining a spotless, conservative reputation. She shuddered to think what would be said about her if her affair with Julian was brought to common knowledge. Her parents would be utterly humiliated. The idea made her feel guilty about postponing her arrival in London for so long.

"I truly must be on my way to London tomorrow. I've been here nearly a month now, and that's much too long. My parents will be worried about me."

Absently, his eyes on his work, Julian shook his head. "No, that's out of the question."

Having to laugh because he'd said the same thing every time she mentioned a departure, she reminded him, "Julian, I can't stay here with you forever, you know. I have responsibilities in Philadelphia as well as in London. You can come with me to visit my parents, if you like. They'll be thrilled to know I'm keeping company with an Englishman for a change." That wasn't exactly true, and they both knew it.

"Not this Englishman," Julian said, putting down his brush and surprising her by going down on one knees beside her. Libby felt her heartbeat quicken at his nearness, felt a slow, liquid languor began to pool in her loins. It was indeed extraordinary, these feelings that he could elicit in her, and she gave an inward laugh when she remembered she'd thought herself incapable of passion. He'd brought her body alive with his tender caresses, but more than that, he'd made her happy. So much so that it sometimes frightened her. She did not think him a man who would want to marry her. More important perhaps, she was not sure he was the kind of man she needed to take as a husband. On the other hand, she knew with some misgivings that she already bore him a great deal of affection; in truth, she adored him. How could she not? She shook away those thoughts, or more truthfully, they were shorn away when Julian opened her shift and placed a kiss on her naked belly.

"My parents are open-minded, and not nearly as intimidating as most people assume," she managed to say, but her mind was involved with what he was doing, her body soft and ready for the passionate lovemaking she knew would come. Flutters of anticipation disrupted her breathing, and she wondered how he would want her this time. Sometimes it was so slow and leisurely, sweet torture, with Julian adoring every inch of her body for hours before he brought her to climax. Other times he would pull her into his arms and take her with such fierce urgency that she'd forget everything in the passionate whirlwind he created in her.

"He's a duke, for God's sake," Julian said suddenly, leaning back and looking at her, almost angrily, it seemed. "Do you think he'll suffer your name linked to a man with a reputation as vilified as mine has been? He'll forbid you to ever see me again." His gaze searched her face, and she wondered if it could really be vulnerability she saw revealed there.

"He can't forbid me to do anything. I'm an adult with my own yearly income. I don't need his permission to take a lover." She brought his hand near her lips and kissed his bent knuckles. "Look what you've done to me, shamelessly consorting this way, and all the while sublimely happy."

Her attempt to turn the subject worked, as Julian said, "I'm only pleased I'm the one who you chose to consort with."

While he murmured, he tugged the cord around her waist, and the silk fell the rest of the way open. He smiled, not taking his eyes off hers as he gently pushed it off her shoulders. He lowered his head to suckle her breast, and Libby placed her hands on his shoulders and leaned her head back. She would surely die if she persisted in this love affair. He was going to kill her by sheer pleasure alone.

"You are a terrible distraction to the artist in me," he muttered, lifting his face to look at her, but Libby drew his head close and captured his lips. He responded, gently at first, but their mouths seemed to catch fire, and the kiss soon escalated into mindless, exciting waves of sensation.

"My God, I can't keep my hands off you," he said at length, pulling back and searching her face, seemingly as shocked as she by their response to each other. Libby hoped he was as enthralled as she, but knew it would be quite impossible. The man before her had known many women, had probably posed them thus, had no doubt used the same words to seduce them. Somewhere in this huge estate he probably had a gallery full of dozens of his portraits of romantic conquests.

Such hurtful thoughts brought a rush of something akin to despair plunging like a blade in her heart, and she fought it because she knew what it meant. It meant she was falling in love with him, something she'd sworn not to do. She knew better than to make such a terrible mistake, she really did, but she couldn't help herself. He made her weak, made her knees turn to rubber, and with little more than a glance.

"How many women have you brought here and painted just like this?" she got out breathlessly, torturing herself with the need to know.

Julian slid his palms up and down her arms, but his eyes glinted with amusement. "I have no idea because I don't keep count. At the moment I prefer to concentrate on you."

"I suppose you have a room somewhere full to the rafters with nudes of your many lovers." She had tried for a light tone, as if she were making a joke, but even she knew she had failed miserably. Her words had sounded jealous, and even worse, possessive. Despite the hurt she felt at thinking about his other women, she knew full well she had no right. "How do you arrange them?" she went on like the worst of shrews, but unable to prevent herself. "In alphabetical order, or perhaps in chronological order . . ."

Julian frowned. "Stop it, Libby. If it'll make you feel better, I've never brought another woman up here. My studio at Brickhill's been sacrosanct until now. I've done nudes, of course, plenty of them, you know that, but I don't keep them. I give them away to whoever wants them. Usually to the lady herself to do with what she will. I don't care whether they're destroyed or not, because it's the process that intrigues me, capturing her essence, not the finished canvas."

Not quite sure she could believe him, Libby felt like a fool for questioning him so relentlessly, but she perversely hoped what he said was true. She tried to raise a smile. "I shall make sure all of mine are burned to cinders before I pack my bags."

"Then I'll have to commit you to clay, but only if you'll allow me to keep the sculpture here where I can enjoy it."

Libby wasn't sure she could deny him anything as he rose and moved across the room out of the circle of light thrown by the single branch of candles. She leaned her head against the sofa and closed her eyes. She could hear him moving around his worktable, heard the splash of water from a pitcher and realized he was readying the clay. She had never seen any of his sculptures, but she had heard they were exquisite.

"Why don't you exhibit?" she asked, drawing her robe back into place. "You would be the talk of the town."

"I've already been the talk of the town, and it's not all it's cracked up to be. Most of what's said has been grossly exaggerated, if not out-and-out falsehood. I'm no saint, by any means, but no mortal man could create as many scandals as I'm given credit for."

Glad to hear that, Libby hesitated, fearing she shouldn't ask any more about him but could not resist her curiosity. "Haven't you ever sought to end such talk by taking a wife? You must have an heir eventually, with your brother gone. I assume you have no other male heirs."

"Not even a cousin, so I have given marriage some thought." He sat down beside her again, and when he reached out his hand, she put hers in it. She had a feeling she'd rise like a phantom at the merest tug and let him lead her anywhere, off a cliff, down into hell, if only he'd smile as warmly at her as he did now. He drew her to her feet and led her to a stool he'd positioned before a sculptor's stand.

"Now, with your permission, I'll show you how titillating working with clay can be." He helped her to remove her robe, and she felt completely, utterly defenseless as she stood naked before him. But she didn't feel embarrassed, and she again realized how uninhibited she'd become. She could tell herself that it was artistic, that she was merely a model, but she knew differently. She longed for him; she burned for him. Now. Yesterday. Tomorrow. Forever.

"You have the most perfectly female form," he said gruffly, his gaze roaming her slender body. "You take my breath away."

She was unprepared for the jolt she felt when he brought his hands to her face. He closed his eyes as he molded her forehead with his fingers, then slowly traced the line of her jaw, the contours of her lips and nose. He brought his hands slowly down her throat to rest lightly on her shoulders. Then as her chest began to heave, he turned to the wet clay and began to work.

Moistening dry lips, she watched him, her attention soon riveted by the swift, efficient movements of his hands, turning the shapeless lump of inanimate substance to human form. He was a study of concentration while he molded and pressed and coaxed it to his will, and she could not take her eyes off him. He was the perfect one, she thought, so dark and beautiful, and she wished at that moment that she had his talent, that she could form his likeness between her palms, make some glorious work of art that would keep a part of him with her forever.

Then he turned back, his blue eyes alive in the candlelight, caught up in the burning zeal of artistic passion. His hands covered with the cool gray clay, he cupped her breasts and tested their weight, then slowly slid his palms down her rib cage to her slender waist. There was something so impersonal as he examined her body with his artist's eye, and at the same time so arousing that her head tipped back, tumbling her hair down her back.

"That's it, love, that's the way I want you. Your head back, your lips parted, as if you're in the throes of passion. God help me, I've never seen anything like you before."

Then his hands were gone, leaving her to shiver, and the exquisite quivers rippled her bare flesh with unrequited need. She could feel the clay that his fingers had left upon her skin, and she felt almost drugged as she watched him through half-closed eyes as he fashioned her torso for the bust, wishing he would come back, would touch her again.

Within minutes he did, this time worshiping her hips, going to his knees in front of her to explore her thighs, inside and out, his eyes following his hands as he touched her, stroked her, followed the curve of her calf to her bare foot. He was touching every part of her, memorizing it for its reconstruction in clay, but she thought no longer of what he was doing but of what he was doing to her.

She was aroused to the point that she felt she could not bear it, and she wanted to feel him against her, inside her. She reached out and touched his hair as he bent his head to caress her feet. He looked up, navy eyes shining with such erotic intensity that she knew he was as affected as she, that he wanted her as much as she wanted him.

"Please . . ."

At her soft entreaty he stopped; then his head was in her lap, his tongue seeking the most sensitive part of her, and she groaned with sheer animal response, arching up against him, her fingernails biting into his shoulders. Then he was on his knees again, all thoughts of work gone, tearing off his velvet dressing gown and dragging her to the floor with him by one arm around her waist.

Then he was atop her, holding her wrists imprisoned, his knees between her legs. "I'm not going to get any work done, not with you, Libby, just lots of half-finished projects," he said gruffly into her hair, but those were the last words he attempted as they both went eagerly after the passion driving them. She felt him poise above her, then thrust deep and sure, and she cried out, not from pain, not from pleasure, but from pure joy. Oh, God help her, she loved him, she thought, she loved him so much that she couldn't bear it. And as he thrust again, his hands cupping her hips and bringing her up to meet him, she watched him until he attained the climax he sought, saw the grimace of need and desire dissolve into joy as he collapsed against her, his cheek against her heaving breasts, their hearts thundering together.

"We've got to stop this," he muttered, his mouth against her naked breast.

Libby put her arms around him and held him tightly, but she smiled, only happy that she was with him and could make him feel the same ecstasy that kept her captive in his house far longer than she ever should have stayed. Because, no matter what he told her or she told herself, Julian was not a man who would be faithful to one woman. She had to accept it, resign herself to it, but now, for this lovely moment, when their hearts beat together as one, she would forget the truth and pretend they would be together without end.

Chapter Twenty

The sky was so deep and blue that it looked eternal, a vast dome over the earth without a single cloud to mar its sun-spangled glory. The air smelled of fresh grass and flowers and the warm breezes that whipped through Julian's hair. In every corner of Brickhill the balmy weather had brought to life the earliest flowers, yellow daffodils, red and white tulips, pink crocus and grape hyacinths, bright forsythia and cherry trees, all splashing their radiant colors against the verdant gray of the deer parks ringing his estate. He'd never seen such early, fine weather, and he was particularly enjoying himself at the moment.

They were very high off the ground, Libby and he, having climbed to the highest peaks of Brickhill's immense rooftop. Libby stood above him on a wooden platform where the rain reservoirs were kept, while he manned his easel a good twenty feet below her on the flat expanse of the east wing. She was dressed in the white Grecian gown she'd worn the night he'd abducted her, and he'd given her a long length of sheer purple silk to wrap around her shoulders.

At the moment it was blowing wildly in the wind, as was her long coppery hair. When she turned her face upward to the sky and held out her arms, as if embracing the wind, the purple silk billowing behind her like the banner of an emperor, Julian's heart trembled and nearly stopped. She'd never looked more beautiful than she did at that moment, and he wished fervently she'd agreed to his first suggestion concerning her attire.

"I still think I'd get a better visual feel for what I'm trying to accomplish if you'd just wind the purple silk around you. The chiton disrupts my concentration."

Laughing, Libby turned and looked down at him. "No matter what you say, Julian, I am not prancing around this roof without a stitch on. You've convinced me to do enough immodest things since I've been here. I have to put my foot down somewhere."

"No one will see you," Julian promised in a last-ditch effort to persuade her. "I've locked the attic door and forbidden the servants to come within a mile."

Libby only smiled, slowly lifting her arms toward the sky. The breeze took the long ends of the silk and fluttered them out behind her like wings in flight. "No, no, no . . . I'm not taking off anything. You've done plenty of sketches of me. You'll never complete any of them, you know. You just do this to get me to undress in front of you."

Julian gave up, but he smiled inwardly as he shaded in her hair. The more he was around her, the more he did want to finish each painting he'd started. In the last weeks he'd had a burning urge to catch her essence in every pose she took up, whether it be sitting serenely across from him at the breakfast table, looking sedate and gracious and lovely, when only an hour before they'd made love like a ship on fire, or when she was sleeping beside him, her silky hair spread across his chest like soft copper flames.

Moreover, he'd gotten to know her better, understand who she was. He liked her wit, liked being with her—in truth, liked having her here at his house. He had not found another woman he hadn't grown bored with after a couple of weeks of constant companionship. Libby was different, unique, but the fact was, and one he couldn't let himself forget, she was the daughter of the Duke of Thorpe.

As usual the thought sent a particularly satisfying feeling through him. Thorpe would be furious when he found out where his only daughter was, and with whom. It gave Julian the utmost pleasure to envision the day he could taunt him to his face that Libby was his lover. He would watch the blood drain from the duke's face, watch him explode with rage, and he would enjoy every minute of the show.

As he glanced up at Libby again, it did not escape him that she would be hurt. On the other hand, he felt she wouldn't turn on him for not revealing his family's past relationship with her father. She cared for him now, perhaps even was in love with him, though she had not said so aloud. She indicated as much, however, by the very fact that she was still with him, continually putting off her deadlines to depart for London. She had no urgent desire to leave him. And the longer she stayed, the more he toyed with the idea of marrying her. He was growing tired of the life he'd been leading, bored with the endless parties and drinking, the many women he'd seduced or who'd seduced him.

Libby wasn't like them. He found himself wanting her more and more, and not enjoying the idea of her sailing away to her beloved America, disgraced in her father's eyes once he found out about their affair. Perhaps he should marry her, settle down, and live here in the country away from the sordid reality of what his life had become. That would be the last, and best, revenge, in the name of his mother, his brother, and his sister.

"I don't think I've ever felt so free," Libby called down to him. "The wind feels like soft velvet brushing on my bare skin. I feel almost as if I could fly off this roof and swoop out over the lake."

Her happy laughter floated down as warm as the breeze, and he felt some of the sheer joy so evident in her voice. At that moment he realized he didn't really want to hurt her, and at the same time he knew full well there was no way that she would not be. He had already driven a wedge between her and her family; Libby just didn't know it yet.

"I'm going to climb higher and see how far I can see!"

Before Julian could object, Libby was pulling herself up a slanted peak of the roof where one of the gigantic chimneys rose into the sky. She was very high above him now, too high, Julian thought with some consternation, slowly placing his palette aside.

"Libby, come back down! You're getting too close to the edge."

The whine of the wind obscured his warning, and suddenly he was gripped by the most awful dread that she would fall. He threw down his brush and headed up to her at a run, but his fears were realized before he got halfway to the chimney. While he watched, her foot slipped on a loose shingle and she lost her balance.

Frozen with horror, he watched her slide down toward the far edge of the roof, scrabbling with her hands to stop herself but to no avail. She screamed, one short, horrible cry, as she went over the edge onto the lower roof below. Then she was gone, and Julian's heart stopped. Then he was rushing headlong back down to the floor, his panic rising in his breast as he jumped down the last few steps and saw her lying in a crumpled heap of purple and white silk. He ran and knelt beside her, and that's when he saw the crimson blood pooling underneath her head.

Paralyzing fear, such as he had never known, took hold of him, and all he could think about was getting her help, getting her to a doctor. Libby didn't move, didn't open her eyes, as he scooped her up and ran for the door, all the while cursing himself for ever having brought her up to the roof in the first place. If anything happened to her, if she died, he'd never forgive himself.

When Libby finally she was able to open her eyes, she was so groggy that she couldn't think straight. Disoriented, she shut her eyes and quit trying to remember what had happened. Her temples throbbed as if impaled by a skewer, and when she tried to turn her head, she groaned in agony.

"Don't move, love. You've got quite a lump on the back of your head."

Julian's voice. He was right, she realized. If she lay completely still, the pickax lodged in her skull did not dig deeper. She opened her eyes again when she felt his weight push down the side of the mattress beside her. He was leaning over her, smiling a little, but there was worry in his eyes, she could see it clearly. Somehow, despite the pain, she realized it was a rare moment indeed if she could detect emotions through the inscrutable mask Julian usually wore.

"I'm sorry, Julian. It was foolish to climb so high."

"I should've warned you about the chimney. Some of the shingles had crumbled. That's what you slipped on." He picked up her hand, and she watched him press it to his lips. Very gentle was his touch, his eyes warm with concern, and it sent waves of pleasure into her heart. He did care about her, there could be no doubt. She smiled a little, and even that hurt.

"You're going to be all right. You've got a superficial cut on the skull and a few abrasions on your arms and legs, but nothing that won't heal up soon enough. The doctor assured me you'd be fine."

"The doctor was here?"

"I sent for him at once, of course." He seemed angry that she hadn't thought he would.

"How long have I been unconscious?"

"Four hours. Some of the longest moments of my life, I don't mind saying."

"So you were worried about me?" she asked, secretly wanting to hear him admit it again.

"I watched you disappear off the side of that chimney and had visions of you tumbling off the roof altogether. If you'd fallen, I'd never have forgiven myself."

"It wouldn't have been your fault if I had. I was silly to go so high. You told me not to. My foot must have gotten tangled in the silk. I tripped, I think, but I can't seem to remember exactly what happened."

Julian was still holding her hand. His face was somber, but when he spoke, his words were the last ones Libby ever would have expected.

"Marry me, Libby. Be my wife. We can elope and be married within the week."

For the first moment Libby only stared at him in complete astonishment. Then her mouth curved slowly with pleasure. It was not as if the idea had not occurred to her, but she had never expected Julian to consider it, much less propose to her. She had expected him to avoid the mention of marriage altogether.

"My, you must feel extremely guilty," she teased, not sure if he really meant it. More important, he had not declared his love for her.

"I'm serious, Libby. I want you to be my wife."

They stared at each other without speaking, and Libby allowed herself to seriously contemplate the idea. She had never been happier than she'd been the last weeks, here in his house, in his company, in his bed. He was a complicated man, one she didn't understand in a great many ways, but he still fascinated her more than anyone she'd ever known. She loved him, she'd already admitted that to herself, but she wasn't sure he was the kind of man she would want as a husband, or as a father to the children she so desperately wished to have.

"I can get the license from the vicar at Wynecoat just down the road. We can be married here, then on our way to London together."

Julian was brushing her cheek with his fingertips, and she felt the warmth seep down deep inside her, into her heart, where she had hidden her affection for him. His eyes were so intense that they glowed down at her, forcing her to submit to his will. She could see that he truly wanted her to marry him, wanted it desperately.

"I can't just elope like that, Julian. My parents would be devastated if I did such a thing when they're only hours away. They'd want to meet you first, to get to know you a bit. And Mother would want to plan a beautiful wedding for us, or at least a reception—"

Shaking his head, Julian interrupted her, his voice gaining a sharper edge, "They'll never approve of me. We'd be wasting our time going to them and expecting their blessing."

"You don't know that, darling. They're very supportive of me in most everything I do. They'll want me to be happy—"

"You've forgotten my less than sterling reputation, haven't you, Libby? Your father will never allow you to marry me."

Libby reached out and took his hand. "It isn't for him to tell me who I will choose as a husband. I daresay you're right about Father, but he didn't approve of John in the beginning, but he respected my wishes. He'll do the same with you. My parents will be much more upset if we elope without telling them. Once they've met you, they'll see why I want to marry you, especially when I tell them how you've helped Henrietta. Once they know the truth, they'll be pleased to welcome you into the family."

She searched Julian's face hopefully because she did not want to run off as if she were ashamed of him, and was relieved when his lips suddenly curved into a wicked grin.

"So the answer is yes? You are going to marry me. Is that what you're saying?"

"Yes, I suppose I am." She gave a rueful laugh. "Though I'm not quite sure exactly what I'm getting myself into."

To her pleasure, Julian stretched out beside her and gathered her gently into his arms. He cradled her injured head against his shoulder. "Just so you don't change your mind. Promise me you'll marry me, no matter what your parents have to say about it."

"That's an easy promise," she whispered, closing her eyes as his lips caressed her temple. She relaxed into his arms and felt at peace with herself. There would be time for them to get to know one another even better before the wedding took place, but she knew, down deep in her heart, with the wisdom that rarely failed her, that despite what he'd been in the past, he would be a good husband to her. At the moment she could not think of anything better than falling asleep every night cradled in his arms, his mouth upon her hair as it was now, feeling safe and secure and beloved.

Julian's arms tightened around her. "If we wait, Libby, it's going to be months and months before we can live together like this. You know how long it takes to plan weddings such as the duchess will insist upon. Do you want us to be apart for months and months? Let's not put ourselves through all of that. We can be happy here together at Brickhill."

"I know," she murmured, sighing contentedly, very eager

to introduce this wonderful man to her family. Even it they did elope the way Julian wanted, what harm could it do? It was their decision, not her parents', and he was right about the long engagement period with all its formalities and fetes and balls, not to mention the pomp and extravagance of a wedding that would be given by the Duke and Duchess of Thorpe. Perhaps Julian was right, after all; perhaps an elopement would be for the best. In any case, her family would end up loving him once they got to know him, for in truth, she thought with a warm current of pleasure, snuggling closer into his arms, who could not?

"Perhaps you're right," she whispered, warming considerably to the idea. "Perhaps we should go ahead and get married here."

Julian turned his head and looked into her eyes. She could see the triumph gleaming in his dark blue gaze, so much that she was slightly startled.

"You'll never regret marrying me, my love, I promise you," he murmured, and as his mouth captured her lips in the most tender kiss she'd ever known, Libby believed every word he said.

Chapter Twenty-one

As Libby sat inside Julian's comfortable maroon barouche, watching the shops and throngs of people in the streets of London pass outside her window, her hand tenderly interlocked with her new husband's long, tanned fingers, she was astonished, and slightly appalled, to find herself wed for a second time. Never in her life had such a wealth of conflicting emotions flicked and flittered through her mind, fighting each other like so many well-armed warriors, all while she sat completely relaxed, a pleased smile on her face. That was the most encouraging aspect of her decision to elope with Julian. She was happy, happier than she could ever remember being before in her life.

After she had accepted his proposal, everything had happened very quickly. Julian insisted upon it, as if afraid she would change her mind if she had long to consider the absurdity of marrying on such short acquaintance. Julian had been so sweetly eager and anxious that she had capitulated and stood beside him in a quaint and wonderfully ancient chapel, whose gray stones were covered with green ivy and yellow roses. The clergyman and his wife were the only witnesses in the ceremony, which had been brief but romantic and tender, enacted under the warm yellow glow of a pair of standing candelabra. They had spent their wedding night at Brickhill, then departed for London, and now that they'd arrived in the city, Julian had become even more loving and attentive.

Even now as she glanced sidelong at his fine aristocratic

profile, her heart warmed with growing admiration and affection. She had never loved a man so, not quite with this overwhelming rush of feelings. It was both frightening and exhilarating, because she had known him for so short a time and because he made her feel so vital and alive. He filled her with joy.

Once Julian realized that Libby was watching him, a sweet, unbidden smile curving her lips, Julian placed his palm over their entwined hands. "It won't be long now," he said, studying her face as if he was judging her mood. "Just a few more blocks and we'll reach Mayfair."

His eyes shone, the lovely inner light she'd grown to recognize, and though he smiled back at her, she sensed another emotion in him, a facet he'd not shown her often. He was apprehensive about meeting her parents, she realized with an innate certitude, and she could well understand his hesitancy. Everything had happened so fast—a whirlwind courtship that was certainly not in Libby's character. She was a bundle of ragged nerves herself, but also very eager to see her family again. Her life in Philadelphia had made visits rare, and since John's death she had regretted so wide an ocean separated her from the only family she had.

Wanting to console Julian, she squeezed his fingers and told him, "You'll like Mother and Father, I'm sure of it. Everyone does. They're both lovely people, not the least bit haughty despite their station."

"That's not the problem, I'm afraid." Julian brought her hand into his lap, then propped a booted foot atop his opposite knee. "They're not going to approve of me, so don't get your hopes up. I'm afraid it's going to be a rather unpleasant homecoming for you."

"You say that because you've never met the duke and duchess. They're quite understanding, and they've become used to me doing things my own way."

"But I know my reputation in London circles, and your father won't be pleased at an alliance with the Rainville name."

He was truly worried, she thought, pleased that he was so protective about her relationship with her parents. "Once they get to know you, they'll love you as much as I do." She laughed. "That is, if you behave yourself now that you're a married man."

Julian gazed contemplatively outside on the storefronts and carriages they were passing as they neared the Thorpe mansion. Quiet lapsed between them, but Libby felt her heartbeat increase as they turned the last corner before she would arrive home for the first time in several years. Libby peered up the street, eager for the first glimpse of the house, but she wasn't nearly as self-assured about the coming confrontation as she had pretended with Julian.

She had no doubt that her parents, her mother in particular, would be hurt that she'd proceeded with the wedding without first informing them. Especially since the ceremony had been held near enough for them to attend, if they'd been invited to do so. She had considered contacting them, of course, but had decided not to, because of the complications that had gone along with it. Libby had no doubt her mother would have argued endlessly and powerfully for her to wait and have a huge wedding with everyone who was anyone in London society in attendance, which was precisely what Libby did not want. Instead she had decided to allow her parents to host a gala reception, if they wished, to welcome Julian into the family.

Upon her finger her wedding ring winked in the sunlight flooding in the window. The stone was quite magnificent, a huge square-cut emerald surrounded by fifteen diamonds. Julian had told her that his own mother had received it as a betrothal ring, and he had seemed very proud to place it on her finger. She loved it. She loved him.

Again the knowledge, the warmth inside her, was so sweet that she stole another glance at her husband, and wondered if she'd forever be enveloped in the strange, wonderful spell he seemed to weave around her. Would he still affect her so much, make her shiver and tremble, make her want to smile all the time, when their marriage grew old, their hair white with age? They'd have children by then, many, she hoped, and secretly she prayed she'd conceive quickly. She'd longed for a child for a very long time, but John's ill health had always made it impossible.

"Here we are," Julian said, moving forward on the seat, for all appearances calm, though she could feel the tenseness of his muscles. His expression was peculiar, a look cast in stone.

"What is it, Julian? Surely you don't fear they'll refuse to receive you?" She tried to lighten the moment. "It's too late for that. You're my legal husband now, for better and for worse."

Instead of laughing, he met her eyes with a most somber look, one that took her aback until some of his strain seemed to drain away. He gave an easy smile. "It doesn't matter to me what they say. What concerns me is how you feel about me."

Libby was relieved and took a deep breath as the footman opened the door. Julian stepped down first, then turned and extended his hand to assist her to the driveway.

"Oh, it's good to be home again," she said happily, gazing up at the large stone mansion rising against the sky. During her childhood they had spent half the year in England, but only a few months here in London, usually just for the Season. Most of the time they resided at Thorpe Hall in the countryside, but between May and August they'd live in the beautiful white mansion standing before her. Now that she stood in the driveway, all the joys of homecoming rushed through her and overwhelmed her with pleasure. Now she had Julian with whom to share it all.

Smiling with anticipation, she took Julian's hand and led him to the wide marble steps that led up from the driveway to a carved stone balcony that rose around to the front entrance. For an instant, at the bottom of the steps, Julian resisted the excited tug of her hand. Libby stopped, a few steps above him, and gazed down questioningly into his face. Startled, she realized that he was not smiling but looked almost angry, his jaw tightening as he gritted his teeth.

"Julian?" Alarmed, she stepped down and placed her gloved palm upon his chest, but he did not look at her.

"I've never been to this house before." His voice was gruff, unnatural. "Rainvilles weren't allowed in the select few."

"Don't be silly," she said lightly, thinking he was anxious because of her father's higher rank. "We're not like that. You'll see how wrong you are after you meet everyone. They'll welcome you as my husband, just as they did John. Perhaps with higher regard, since you're an Englishman through and through."

Julian did not smile at first, then seemed to realize how concerned she was. When he forced a small grin, she lifted her skirts and began to climb the stairs. Her husband followed behind her, and the closer they came to the front portico, the more bubbly she became.

"We should've sent word ahead. I do hope they're here, but since it's barely three in the afternoon, I'm sure they are, at least Mama will be. She does her calling and errands in the morning for the most part, and Papa takes care of his business then as well. They prefer to take afternoon tea alone together."

When they reached the tall front doors with their massive gold door knockers, Libby turned the handle and entered without hesitation. The first person she saw was Joanna, the woman who'd been her chambermaid when she was a little girl.

"Jo!" she cried, the thrill of seeing the dear woman overtaking her completely. She left Julian to close the door as she ran forward to meet her old friend. Smiling, Joanna joined her in a tight embrace, then held her at arm's length to look at her.

"You haven't changed one little bit!" Libby cried, laughing out loud. "I've missed you so."

Joanna was short and stocky, most of her curly gray hair hidden inside the white lace mobcap she wore. She did look exactly the same, with her ruddy complexion and twinkling blue eyes. She had shared many a childhood adventure with Libby, and had taken up for her when she was naughty, many times when she probably shouldn't have. "I've missed you too, dearie. Your mama has been beside herself this last fortnight waitin' for you to come home."

"My parents are here, then?"

"Aye. I just served the two of them tea in the blue and white salon."

Libby gazed eagerly down the wide entrance hall with its black-and-white-tiled floor toward the cozy back parlor that her mother had always preferred. "And Burke? Is he here yet?"

"Your brother's out of the country for a time, but your mother sent him a letter about you arrivin', so he's expected back in the next few days. Her Grace has planned a whole round of parties in your honor."

"Wonderful," Libby replied, though that was the last thing she wanted. She glanced back at Julian, who'd lingered beside the door. Still holding Joanna's hands, she was about to call out for him when her mother's familiar voice came from the salon.

Delighted, Libby turned back in time to watch her mother move into sight at the far end of the foyer. She looked beautiful, but she always did, her coppery hair woven into braids that were coiled demurely atop her head. Trinity Remington never seemed to change or grow a day older, and when she saw her daughter, her smile broadened and she clapped her hands in delight.

"Libby! Oh, thank goodness, you've finally come! I've been terrified something had happened to you!" She started toward her quickly, calling over her shoulder for her husband. "Will, come quick. Libby's finally home."

Libby met her, receiving a tight hug, and she laughed aloud at her mother's scolding words. "You should've sent us word about where you've been and what you've been doing. I've been absolutely frantic. And your father, he's already threatened to send a Bow Street Runner out in search of you."

"I hardly think that's necessary." Libby chuckled at her

mother's reproof. "I'm only a few weeks late. That's fairly good for me, you know."

"But two weeks that left me to deal with your mother's state of near hysteria."

Her father's tall figure had rounded the door and was striding toward them. He was smiling too, and Libby knew neither of them were really angry about her tardy arrival. She clung to her father for a long moment, his bear hug making her realize again just how glad she was to be back home. Neither of them had noticed Julian where he stood aside, and uncharacteristically he continued to hang back, silently watching their family reunion.

It was strange to see him reticent; Julian was not a reticent man, after all, far from it. But now it was time to face the music and put him at his ease. He'd find soon enough that the Duke and Duchess of Thorpe were not the ogres he obviously expected.

"Mother, Father, I have some wonderful news to tell you!"

"Come, darling, sit down and tell us everything. The tea's still hot. I know you're probably hungry after traveling all morning. Here, Joanna, take Libby's cape." Her mother helped her off with her coat, gave it to Joanna, who departed with it toward the back of the house, then linked her arm through Libby's as she'd done so often before. "Were you able to comfort poor Henrietta's husband? How is the poor man? They were married for such a short time, and Henrietta was such an angel."

Smiling, Libby stopped and took both her mother's hands. "Mama, please, listen to me. I've brought someone home with me, someone I want you to meet."

Both her parents looked at her in surprise, and Libby turned and motioned Julian forward. They followed her gaze, and Libby watched with pride as her husband walked toward them with his easy masculine grace. When she looked back at her father, she saw how his face had gone rigid. Her mother gave an audible gasp and took a step backward, one hand on her heart.

"What is it?" Libby asked in concern but soon became alarmed when her father found words, his voice as harsh and cold as she'd ever heard him.

"Get the bloody hell out of my house before I throw you out."

Stunned, Libby looked back at Julian in horror, but he continued to approach as if he hadn't heard the Duke of Thorpe's threat. Julian wore a smile now, but there was no warmth in his face at all; he looked as stone cold as a slab of marble.

"I don't think you'll want to stoop to that, Thorpe, not in front of the ladies."

The duke and duchess stood in shocked silence for a second or two; then Libby heard her mother give a low, sick moan. Libby turned to her, supporting her arm until her father turned blazing green eyes on her.

"What is he doing here?" he demanded harshly, his anger unconfined in its sheer brutality. "Why did you bring him into this house?"

"Father, stop this! Why are you saying these things?"

Her mother's face had drained of all color, so white that Libby thought she might faint, but it was her father's words that wrenched her heart.

"Have you lost all grip on your senses, Libby, bringing him here?"

Libby was stunned by his reaction, at the profanities he'd uttered in her mother's presence. Unable to speak, she turned apologetically to Julian, thankful when he put a supportive arm around her waist.

"Maybe we should go, Libby. I told you I wouldn't be welcome here."

"But why? Why aren't you welcome? What's happening?" She turned frantic eyes to her mother. "What's wrong, Mama? Why are you treating Julian this way?"

Her mother put her hand over her mouth and closed her eyes, as if she would be ill, and Libby's heart fell when her father turned on his heel and stalked toward the stairs without answering Libby's pleas. His wife fled after him, and Libby watched them depart, her face distraught.

"I was afraid this would happen, sweetheart. Maybe we should just go."

Julian pulled her close, and Libby put her face against his coat, trembling, and let him hold her for a moment. Bewildered, slightly dazed, she tried to think what could be wrong, what could have caused such a terrible scene.

"Julian, tell me what you've done to make Father react to you so violently. Tell me!" Eyes serious, she pulled back from him and searched his face.

"I've never met or spoken with your father, or your mother, before this day, I swear it. Perhaps you should ask them why they're acting the way they are."

Libby nibbled her lower lip and looked up the curved staircase where her parents had vanished moments before. "I just don't understand, but I intend to find out. There's simply no excuse for such incivility toward you, and it's completely uncharacteristic of them." She sighed, thinking how furious her father had been, how he'd ordered Julian out of his house. "Perhaps it would be better if you went ahead to your house and sent the coach back for me. Would you mind, Julian? I think it's best if I talked to my parents alone. I'll come there as soon as I speak to them."

"Of course, if that's what you want." Julian cupped her cheek in his palm and gazed down at her, obviously concerned. "Are you sure you want to face them alone? Your father's very angry. He won't hurt you, will he?"

Libby bristled at the insinuation. "No, of course not. He's never lifted a hand against me, or anyone else in the family. I've never seen him react this way. I can't imagine what he's thinking, unless he's mistaken you for someone else. That must be it, don't you think?"

Julian lifted his shoulder in a small shrug, then kissed her on the forehead. She watched him stride down the foyer and exit through the front door before she turned to the stairs, untying the ribbons of her bonnet. She was not looking forward to the

confrontation that would follow, but face it she would, for
she intended to find out what in heaven's name could have
possessed her parents to display such open hostility to a man
they'd never met before in their lives.

Chapter Twenty-two

Libby stood hesitantly at the bottom step, looking up the spiraling white staircase. Worried, and more than a little confused, she reluctantly started the trudge upward. A fierce frown knitted the smoothness between her eyes, erasing all the joyful anticipation she had felt only a short time before. Sliding her hand along the smooth, polished banister, she felt more as if she were ascending a guillotine than seeking out her parents. So astounded was she by the way they'd reacted to Julian, she could barely believe what had happened. Especially the reaction of her mother. Trinity, who was a paragon of grace and elegance and had lectured her children in the importance of civility and self-control.

When Libby reached the second-floor corridor, she paused with her palm resting on the marble newel post. She could hear her father's voice, very angry and loud, booming from her parents' bedchamber at the far end of the hall. Nonplussed, Libby listened to him rage, sorting through the horrid deeds her father obviously believed a man of Julian's reputation must have committed. Truthfully, it was astounding that two otherwise calm and reasonable people could react in such a fashion, even if they loathed the subject of their wrath.

The white double doors of the ducal bedchamber stood wide open, and again Libby was surprised her parents seemed to have no thought for the servants overhearing their shouting match. She'd never known her parents to argue publicly, though when she was younger she had heard a few of their heated disagreements muffled behind closed doors.

When Libby reached the threshold, she peered inside the huge sitting room, draped lavishly, completely in green and gold, the gigantic carved, canopied bed visible through the door that led into the adjoining bedroom. Her father, the Duke of Thorpe, was pacing back and forth, extremely agitated, his face bloodred with fury, his fists clenched into tight balls at his side. His duchess sat watching him silently from the upholstered cushions of a curved gold velvet sofa beside the hearth. She looked ashen and distraught.

It was Trinity, however, who glimpsed Libby first, and she rose at once, as if not sure how to handle the situation. When William noticed their daughter standing timidly in the doorway, he fell silent from his ranting and glared at Libby. He wasted no time in his chastisement.

"How dare you bring that rotten lecher into this house?" His voice sounded alarmingly like the feral growl of an enraged tiger, and Libby had never seen him so angry. "My God, girl, what in bloody Zeus are you doing with that reprobate?"

Libby was grateful when her mother interceded in her behalf. "Now, Will, Libby doesn't know the history between you and him, you know that. Please be reasonable."

"What history?" Libby demanded, her initial shock disintegrating as her own considerable anger came flooding up full force. She stepped into the room but did have the wherewithal to shut the door behind her, not wanting the household staff to hear them since her parents seemed not to give a whit. Unfortunately, and for some unknown reason, her parents had apparently lost all grasp on manners and good sense. The scene downstairs, no doubt witnessed by Joanna, was already being whispered and discussed in the servants' hall.

"What has Julian ever done to you, Father, to warrant this churlish reception?" she demanded coldly. "I've never been so embarrassed and humiliated."

Her father's face fell slack, but his expression of surprise fled quickly as his mouth twisted into an ugly slant. "You're embarrassed, are you?" His voice was harsh, and a tic moved furiously in his cheek as he gritted his teeth.

Libby stared at him in dismay, almost as if he were a stranger. For the first time in her life she was a little afraid of him. "Julian has gone for the moment, but if this is the kind of welcome he'll get here, I'm sure he won't be back. Perhaps I should leave too."

"Oh, Libby, you don't understand, you have no idea what you're talking about," Trinity murmured, sagging onto the couch again.

When Libby met her father's eyes, they bit into her like an arctic freeze, and she completely lost her patience with his unacceptable behavior.

"I'd truly hoped the two of you would be happy for me, but I can see that you've so prejudiced yourselves against Julian that you won't even give him a chance to defend himself against the rumors you've no doubt heard." She took a deep breath, then another, clasping her trembling fingers together, never having imagined in her wildest dreams that she would be met with such a scene when revealing her remarriage to her parents. "The truth is, well, the truth is . . . that Julian and I are already . . . well, we're married, Mother, several days ago at Julian's estate in Yorkshire. And I'm very happy with Julian, or at least I was until we got here and watched you treat him so abominably."

Neither of her parents moved a muscle for the first instant, their faces stamped with absolute shock. White-faced and silent, they stared at her in horrified disbelief. Then her father completely exploded, his words like a doubled fist driven into her stomach. "Then you're a complete and utter fool and no longer a daughter I can claim as my own."

Stunned, Libby blanched. Stricken by his cruel rejection, she couldn't find words, fury forgotten as tears burned and filled her eyes. After all the joy at returning, her life was disintegrating around her. She felt sick inside, trembling, but her father's disgust did not waver. She put her hand on the back of the chair set beside the door, trying to remain upright on her quivering legs as he approached her. She lifted her chin, endeavoring to blink back her tears, but William didn't give her a glance as he stalked out of the room, leaving Libby and Trinity to stare at each other in wordless dismay.

"Libby, Libby, whatever could have possessed you to wed a man like Rainville? You couldn't have known him long enough to make such a commitment."

"I love him," Libby said simply, no longer able to hold back the terrible pain twisting inside her. Tears began to stream down her face, and when her mother held out her arms to her, Libby could no longer contain her disappointment and fled into her comforting embrace. She dropped to her knees and laid her head in her mother's lap. "Mama, please, you don't understand about Julian. I know you've heard terrible stories about him, that he's a scoundrel and a rake, and heaven knows what else you've heard, but he's not all bad, he's really not." She lifted her tear-streaked face and beseeched her mother to understand. "Please, Mama, talk to Father, make him understand that he's wrong about Julian."

Trinity was crying now too, but she shook her head and worked her white linen handkerchief free from the sleeve of her dress and dabbed the wetness from her eyes. "Oh, Libby darling, there's so much more that you don't know. It's not Rainville's reputation that your father finds objectionable. I wish to God we'd told you the truth years ago, but I swear I never saw the need to bring up all the ugliness of the past. Especially after you became of age and made your home in Philadelphia."

Alarmed but determined to know the truth, Libby lifted herself onto the cushions beside her mother. Sniffling, she took the handkerchief that her mother offered and struggled to bring herself under control. "Then tell me now. What has Julian done? He said he'd met neither you nor Father, is that not true?"

Her mother kept shaking her head, then sighed deeply, a sound so full of sorrow that Libby's heart twisted. She lifted her face and gazed deeply into her daughter's eyes, and Libby braced herself, realizing that what she was about to hear would not be pleasant. "We've not met, that's true. It was his brother with whom we were acquainted, many years ago. His name was Rupert Rainville. I don't suppose Julian mentioned anything about him, did he?"

Libby heard the change in her mother's tone, how it had grown hard and bitter, and she tried to recall the man she'd seen in the portrait gallery at Brickhill. He'd been dark and handsome, much like Julian in appearance, and she tried to remember what Julian had said when they'd stood side by side staring up at his brother's painting. "I believe Julian said Rupert fell to his death. There's a life-size portrait of him at Brickhill."

"Why on earth did you ever go to Brickhill?" her mother asked, her eyes searching her daughter's face.

"Julian invited me there for a hunting weekend during my stay at Lasserthon Manor. Many of the people from the village went, as well as Lasserthon himself."

"Did he know you were a Thorpe? Did you tell him your father was the duke?"

"Not in the beginning. I always use John's name when I travel, you know that."

"Oh, poor dear Libby, he's using you, don't you see? He didn't reveal a word about his past, did he?"

"He told me some things. I know what a cruel childhood he suffered, and I know he's not been the most upstanding of gentlemen. He's done some despicable things, and he admits he'd led a sordid life until now, but he can be most kind and generous too. He loves me, Mama, and I love him, desperately so. He's my husband, and I thought you'd be pleased that I had chosen an Englishman for my husband."

"You don't understand, sweetheart. You don't understand why we can't be happy for you."

"Then tell me! Please, I can't bear this. What happened to make Father hate him so?"

Her mother pushed herself to her feet, then paced a couple of feet away. Clearly distraught, she wrung the scrap of lace-edged linen between her fingers while she paced to the window and stood there a moment, staring outside at the garden. Without turning around, she started to speak. "It's difficult for me to speak of this, even now, after all these years have gone by. But you must know the truth, Libby darling. We've kept it all a secret for much too long; even your father and I haven't talked about it. That's why it shocked us so when we saw Rainville downstairs in our foyer." Finally she turned back and faced Libby's bewilderment. "I just cannot believe this has happened. What on earth are we going to do?"

Though Libby was becoming more and more impatient to understand what had happened in the past, obviously well before she was born, she waited without interrupting, glad when her mother came back and took a seat beside her.

"Libby, this will be hard for you to hear, I know, but you must listen carefully and try to understand our feelings. You do remember, don't you, that your father and I were betrothed when we were children."

"Of course. Your wedding was delayed by the rebellion against George the Third. You were enemies when he traveled to Charleston to end your betrothal." Through Libby's eyes, the story had always been romantic and thrilling, and at Libby's urging, her mother had often told the tale of how they'd fallen in love. Now, however, her mother's face was shadowed by less happy memories.

"We fell madly in love, of course, aboard ship on the way back to England. I'd always loved him, though, since I was a little girl, though I wouldn't admit it then. When we realized we wanted our marriage to be upheld, your grandfather, then the Duke of Thorpe, refused to allow it. He considered all of us—me, your Grandfather Eldon, Uncle Geoff, all of us—to be traitorous rebels, particularly me. He thought me unworthy to be a duchess. It was war, you have to understand that, Englishman pitted against Englishman, but Will and I were so much in love that we didn't care. Your Grandfather Adrian did everything he could to separate us, but it didn't work."

Trinity paused in her story, absently tucking a wayward strand of her red-gold hair behind her ear. Her expression became sorrowful, her eyes so haunted that the hairs at Libby's nape prickled with foreboding. She'd known most of the story that her mother had related thus far, but the narrative had always ended at that point with her parents marrying despite all the odds against them. "What does this have to do with Julian? I don't understand how he could possibly be involved."

"Rupert Rainville was a good friend of Adrian's, and I'm sorry to tell you this, but he was a terrible man." Her voice tightened. "Just brutal, with no redeeming qualities I ever knew. I was afraid of him, and Will absolutely loathed everything about him."

"But, Mama, surely you know that doesn't mean Julian has his brother's wicked character. He isn't perfect, but he's not a loathsome human being, not brutal in the least, I swear that to you. If only you could spend time with him, you'll see that what I say is true—"

"There's more to the story, Libby. Please, just listen to me." She clasped her hands in her lap and drew a cleansing breath before she went on. "Rupert Rainville tried to kill me."

Appalled, absolutely speechless, Libby stared mutely at her mother. Trinity took her hand and gave it a comforting squeeze.

"I know this must be painful for you to hear. It's painful for me to relate, but you must be told the truth about everything. Rupert tried to throw me down the marble staircase on the terrace outside the music chamber, the one that descends to the carriage drive. He caught me there, one night in the dark, and he dragged me to the parapet. He was holding me over the drop." She swallowed convulsively, staring into space as if she was reliving the moment of terror. "He was going to throw me to my death, and would have if Will hadn't stopped him in time. The very worst part was that Will's father had bade him to do it, to be rid of me so Will could marry the English heiress Adrian had chosen for him."

"Oh, no, Mother, how horrible!"

"Your father pulled him away from the stairs, and they grappled together, there, at the top of the steps. In the struggle Rupert went over the edge. He did die from the fall, broke his neck. I was all right, but that was the night we all were forced to flee to the safety of the Carolinas. I've told you that story. How we all had to go before we could be arrested—your Grandfather Eldon, Will's mother and sister, Geoff, all of us who believed in the Americans' right to liberty. I didn't want to go, but I had to, because of what had happened with Rupert Rainville. I had to leave your father, and we were separated for nearly a year before we could be together again." Tears sparkled in her eyes, and she dabbed them again as she finished. "You were born in Charleston while we were apart."

Libby could not move, trying desperately to absorb the details of the sordid tale, disbelieving that her parents had chosen to keep the truth from her for so long. "Why didn't you tell me all this before? I knew most of what happened during the war."

"What good would it have served?" her mother answered, tiredly massaging her temples. "The duke died the same night we fled England, had a massive heart attack after Will confronted him with his part in Rupert's attempt to murder me. I wanted nothing more than to erase it from my memory, but Will's never forgotten, never gotten over his bitterness. He never forgave the Rainville family for what Rupert tried to do to me. He's never acknowledged their existence since that day. And now, don't you see, now his only daughter is married to the brother of the man who tried to kill me. Don't you see how painful this is for him? For both of us?"

Of course Libby could understand, a lot better than she had at first, but she also saw the foolishness in blaming the whole family for the evil Rupert had done. "Julian told me he was only ten years old when his brother died! He had nothing to do with any of it, as terrible as it was. He didn't even know who I was, until later, when I went to Brickhill."

Trinity studied her daughter's face, and her voice was very quiet. "He's out for revenge, sweetheart. Think back, Libby, can you tell me he asked you to marry him before he knew who you were, or was it after you revealed your relationship to the Duke of Thorpe?"

Their eyes held for the space of a heartbeat, and Libby's horrible expression told her mother the answer.

"Oh, Libby, can't you see what he's done? He's used you, your innocence about the bad blood between our families, all to get back at your father. Didn't you see the way he looked at Will, how triumphant he looked? He knew this all along. He knew, I'm telling you. If he wasn't using you, why didn't he tell you the circumstances of his brother's death? That he died here at our house? A terrible scandal followed Rupert's death, and Will made sure everything came out about Rainville's involvement in the murder plot. His family bore the brunt of the censure and were completely ostracized here in London. Be it fair or not, they suffered for Rupert's murderous acts."

"Julian said he loved me." Though Libby repeated the words firmly, doubt had begun to fester inside her heart as she thought back over the weeks she'd been with Julian. Now that her mother had pointed it out, she realized that he hadn't mentioned marriage until he'd learned her true identity, and there was no doubt that he'd pressured her into the elopement after her initial rejection of the idea. Had he wanted the marriage legalized before her parents could tell her the truth? Could he truly have used her so vilely for his own revenge?

Earlier, downstairs, he had known full well how he would be accepted by her parents. That's why he'd shown no surprise or outrage when her father had flown into a rage and insulted him. He had looked smug, triumphant, just as her mother had pointed out. Outside just after they'd arrived, he'd stopped at the base of the stone stairs. Libby had noticed a difference in him then, though he had explained it away, but now she knew that was the very spot where his brother had perished. Oh, God help her, it was true, all of it. He had used her to hurt her parents, to wreak the worst kind of vengeance on her father. She'd been a fool. She'd believed he'd loved her and wanted to marry her.

Her heart began to ache, as if some cruel hand was clutching it tighter and tighter until it ruptured and bled. Trembling, she felt grief rising inside her in a great and terrible well of despair. She could not stop the tears, did not try because the pain was too harsh. Her mother put her arms around her, and together they wept for the past, for the present, for the pain of love betrayed.

Chapter Twenty-three

At his Berkeley Square house some blocks east of the Thorpe mansion on Park Lane, Julian was doing some pacing of his own. Now that night had fallen and the hour had grown late, he found himself prowling restlessly back and forth across the lush Chinese carpet of his study, waiting impatiently for Libby to defy her parents and come home to him. At first he had not given the length of her absence much concern, fairly confident in Libby's affection for him now that they were wed. He tended to his pending correspondence and took care of a few business matters that had been piling up since he'd been in the country. Now, however, he was beginning to fear that the duke and duchess had convinced her to stay with them.

Too much time had passed not to make him feel a bit anxious—she'd been with her parents nearly four hours—and that was too long. He had hoped that she would have been angry enough to turn on her heel and leave her father's house with him, but he should've known she wouldn't act rashly. Libby wasn't heedless about anything, except perhaps in her relationship with him. Even so, that had taken a good deal of tender persuasion on his part. She loved her family, dearly loved them, and Julian had seen the pain in her eyes when she bore the brunt of her father's fury.

Perversely, and with a twinge of guilt, the memory of Thorpe's rage evoked a cruel pleasure deep inside Julian, and he wouldn't say he was sorry the man had been hurt. Julian's hastily concocted plan of retribution had come very easily to fruition after years of yearning for such a foolproof manner of injuring the almighty Duke of Thorpe and all in his household.

Still, Libby too had been hurt in the process, and he couldn't say he enjoyed watching the joy of her homecoming drain from her face only to be replaced by acute distress. Despite her suffering, the end had been worth the means, and he wouldn't apologize. Thorpe was a vicious bastard for the things he'd done to Julian's family and Julian had just begun to torment him. The fun and games designed to cause him pain would be endless now that Libby was a Rainville. The mighty duke would have nothing to look forward to except grandsons bearing the name and lineage he loathed above all else.

Julian smiled, cold and contained, and pulled his gold watch from his vest pocket, increasingly eager to show Libby that the London home he could provide for her had all the grandeur of her ancestral house. He would escort her himself through the spacious rooms that he'd had prepared for her comfort. Lu Ling had already arrived and advised the London staff of their duties for the round of parties and galas he and Libby would be attending as a married couple, and Alice had come with her in the baggage wagon and immediately been put to use unpacking his Libby's belongings.

As he stared down into the coals on the grate, he pondered the miracle of having a wife, tussled with the sheer unexpectedness of being a married man. Lady Edmonton. He was having trouble believing that he had actually wed her, but he couldn't say he was sorry he had. Libby was lovely, a warm, wonderful woman any man would be proud to have walk at his side. Not only was she beautiful, her intellect challenged him, and in a highly entertaining manner. He'd found her suitable for him in every way, except for her family ties, and the most surprising was the eager and passionate lover she'd become. Yes, indeed, Libby did please him. She pleased him a great deal. But the fact was he'd have married her anyway, even if he had not found her so fascinating. She was his vengeance personified; she was his weapon to bring down Thorpe.

Some intuition made him turn from his contemplation of the darting flames, and he found Libby standing in the doorway watching him. Julian tensed, instantly aware by the somberness of her face that she knew the truth. Her parents had told her about the scandal that had ended up destroying everyone he loved. He wondered if they'd colored the tale to their own advantage. Her first utterance assured him that they had.

"You used me."

Julian had found early on that Libby was not a woman who minced words, and she didn't waste time now with any unnecessary preamble. She stood completely motionless, her face very pale, the sweet smile he'd seen so often of late nowhere to be found. A slithering worm of unease invaded his gut. If her parents had influenced her, he had expected a barrage of wrath, not this cold, empty calm. He would have to make her understand. Once she knew what had really happened, then she would relent and stand with him against Thorpe.

"Yes, I used you. But then it became more than that."

His confession appeared to hit her like a slap across the cheek. She took a step backward, but her gaze never wavered from his face. The hurt and betrayal in her eyes smote him to his core, and he moved toward her.

"There's nothing else to be said, then," she told him, backing away from his approach. "I was foolish enough to flutter right into your web of revenge, wasn't I, Julian? What a naïve fool you must think me, to believe all your lies, to actually think you really wanted to marry me. How you must have laughed inside when I agreed to elope."

"It wasn't like that."

"I think perhaps it was exactly like that." She turned around, intending to leave, but Julian reached her first and spun her back to face him. Now anger—pure as a flame—flushed her face. She jerked her arm away as if repulsed by his touch. Before she could reach the door, Julian slammed it and shot the bolt.

Libby stopped, then gave a mirthless laugh. "What now,

Julian? Are you going to lock me up again? Or are you planning another abduction in the stone tower?"

"It worked last time." He gave her a big grin, hoping that the easy humor, the laughter they'd shared during their last weeks together, would ease the electrifying tension. It didn't. Libby was too hurt, too angry.

"Why don't you sit down, Libby, and we'll have a little discussion? I don't see why we can't behave like two grown adults. We are husband and wife now."

"I must say I'm a trifle surprised you wanted to hurt my father so much that you'd actually sacrifice yourself on the altar of marriage. I wouldn't have thought you'd have it in you."

"Please sit down. Dinner will be ready soon. Roast duck and walnut stuffing, I believe."

Libby spun around and began to pace the room, much in the same way he'd done while awaiting her. Her dark green cape of silk, which she hadn't taken off, obviously not having planned to stay long, swirled angrily out behind her, and Julian leaned against the door and crossed his arms across his chest. They'd have it out tonight once and for all, and he'd be damned if either of them would leave this room until they did.

"The truth is, my love, I didn't have to marry you at all. Actually, your father would've been every bit as displeased if we'd just enjoyed a fly-by-night affair. Once we'd spent some time together, I realized I actually wanted you to be my wife. That's when I proposed and you so graciously consented. I didn't force you into anything. You could have said no, and we would have arrived here unattached, so to speak."

"Perhaps you should've shared our family history with me before now," she snapped furiously, green eyes sparkling wrath. "If you had, I assure you I wouldn't have stayed in your company any longer than I had to." She stopped in a swirl of silk, hands on her waist, and sent him a stinging glare that might have sent a lesser man staggering.

"I think you'd have stayed with me even if you'd known. I didn't have to marry you, Libby. I wanted to. I also had been waiting a very long time to stick a knife in your father's back—I mean that figuratively, of course—and I have no intention of denying it. Fate threw us together, and I took advantage of the opportunity."

With an incredulous look on a face flushed pink with color, Libby turned on him. Julian had never seen her look so beautiful, with her eyes flashing fire the way they were. "You make it sound like some picnic you'd planned. Didn't you think how I'd feel to know you'd used me to hurt my own parents? Don't you feel any shame for what your brother did to my mother?"

"What my brother did to your mother is still an unsolved mystery. I've heard what the duke says happened, but the truth remains that Rupert was the one lying dead at the bottom of the steps that night, not your mother. Killed at the hands of your father, who conveniently told the authorities he was saving his wife from an attack."

"Why would he lie about it?"

"Who knows? All I know is that my brother's death wasn't enough for the mighty Duke of Thorpe. Your father had to have more vengeance, more Rainville heads had to roll, so he used every vestige of his wealth and power to make sure all of us suffered. He ruined us, Libby, and took great pleasure in it. Did he tell you about that when he was accusing my brother of murder? Did he tell you he set out with cold, calculating method to grind my family and everything they had under his heel?"

The anger Julian had suppressed for so long began to unfurl with all its hatred, and he found himself shouting the words at her and was only infuriated further when she jutted her jaw and gazed haughtily down her dainty Thorpe nose at him as if he were some slimy snake. Somehow he gained control of his temper, then of his voice, enough to speak again in a normal tone.

"Your beloved father made damn sure that my mother was never again accepted in polite society. Then he made certain no banker in this city would ever deal with us again. He didn't quit with his schemes until we were completely bankrupt and penniless. My mother died of grief, over my brother's death, over the fact that everyone she knew had cut her, broken in heart and spirit because of your father's need for revenge."

Libby was staring at him, and he heard himself laugh, dryly and without mirth. "That's right, Libby dear. Thorpe didn't mention any of his sins against my family, did he? He didn't tell you how he bought out our tenants and robbed our properties until we nearly starved because of him. I was ten then, and Victoria was little more than a baby, five years old. Don't talk to me about truth and honor, Libby, because your father can't use those words without choking on them."

When he saw the most horrible expression of misery overtake her face, he regretted the way he'd told her, but nevertheless, everything he said was true. If Thorpe hadn't lied to her about what he'd done, she would have understood Julian's motives from the beginning.

"Mother told me about what happened. She didn't tell me that Father tried to ruin your family."

"Maybe she doesn't know. She left him for a year after my brother died." No matter how angry he was, or resentful she was, Julian couldn't bear for her to look so stricken. He went to her, and to his surprise, when he pulled her against his chest, she didn't fight the embrace.

"I'm sorry you were hurt, Libby, I swear I am," he whispered, closing his eyes and stroking her hair. "I didn't do any of this to make you unhappy, but don't ever ask me to apologize for going after your father, because he doesn't deserve mercy or pity." Julian sat down in an upholstered wing chair near the fireplace and drew Libby down onto his lap. She laid her head against his shoulder, and neither of them spoke a moment. He expected her to weep, but instead she sat up, her eyes dry as she searched his face.

"I have to know, Julian, you must tell me the truth. Did you pursue me, seduce me, only to hurt my father? The weeks we spent together at Brickhill, was it all part of your plan?"

"If you'll remember, you concealed your true identity from me. I didn't know until . . ." He hesitated, thinking first to lie to her about Alice, but he found he did not want to lie anymore. "I first knew your kinship to Thorpe on the day you found Henrietta's ring. Alice blurted it out when she was threatening me with the duke's wrath, and I saw the irony of the situation at once. And I considered using you to hurt your father, but I already liked you enough by then to want to keep you around. I knew that even a friendship between us would enrage your father. We became lovers because I wanted to make love to you. I never had to ask you to marry me, though I knew it would kill your father to have me in the family."

"Then why did you?" She was watching him closely, her eyes deep and distrustful.

"Because by then I knew that if we didn't elope, if you weren't legally bound to me, your father would convince you never to see me again. I wasn't ready to let him do that."

A long time passed while they held locked gazes. Then to his immense relief, Libby relaxed in his arms with her cheek against his chest. Only then did he realize how afraid he'd been, afraid she'd choose her father over him. He tightened his arms around her, relieved. Despite her anger and feelings of betrayal, she wasn't going to leave him. He had won this first battle with her father, but it wouldn't be the last time they exchanged fire. All he cared about at the moment, however, was having Libby here in his arms where she belonged, and his vendetta with her father be damned.

Chapter Twenty-four

The window was slightly ajar, and a warm breeze wafted the white net curtains inward and filtered over the long rosewood breakfast room table of the Duke of Thorpe's mansion overlooking Hyde Park. Other than the sound of a maid beating a rug on a clothesline in the backyard, the room lay in complete silence. At that moment the duchess was nursing a pleasurable daydream of inflicting the same damage with the wicker rug beater atop her husband's thick skull.

They sat together, as they did nearly every morning, side by side, having decided long ago that they preferred the intimacy of conversation to a length of thirty feet separating their place settings. Today, however, it didn't matter how close they sat, they weren't speaking to each other. The row they'd had the night before after their daughter had left the house in tears still stood between them like a thick brick wall, and for the first time in over ten years, they had not resolved the disagreement before they went to sleep. Instead Will had stalked out of the bedchamber they shared and slept in a guest room on the third floor and well away from Trinity.

Spreading a dollop of soft butter on a flaky scone the cook had taken out of the oven only moments earlier, Trinity regarded her handsome husband, who sat in stony silence reading the morning newspaper. He completely ignored her, something she was not used to and didn't care for, but she had her pride too. Besides that, he was dead wrong and should be man enough to admit it.

The hard slant of his jaw intimated that he was still furious, as did the fierce crackling he gave to the newspaper when turning the page. His verbal ranting had turned to an icy silence so intimidating he had the whole staff tiptoeing around like frightened children. Her golden eyes narrowed on his stern face, she took a bite of the warm bread, then dabbed the corner of her mouth with her napkin.

He was sulking because she had taken Libby's side in the matter. She'd experienced impressive doses of his temper a good many times in their wedded life, but rarely concerning her own misdeeds or even the unacceptable actions of their two children. The fact that he had actually felt the need to leave their bed was a dire demonstration indeed, for though married a very long time, they shared a deep passion for each other that showed no signs of burning out.

He was pretending to read, but she knew he was staring at one spot of the folded newspaper much too long to be digesting the contents. Will was as upset as she about their estrangement, but he was simply better at not showing it. She tasted her tea, found it too hot, and set the cup back into the saucer. All morning she'd been waiting for the appropriate moment to broach the incendiary subject again, and she supposed this was as good a time as any.

Taking a moment to choose her words with utmost care, she kept an eye on her husband because she knew he had every reason to be angry. She herself had been shocked by Libby's abrupt announcement of her marriage, and even more stunned that her daughter, who was usually so self-controlled and socially proper, much more so than her mother had been at her age, would even consider such a radical impulse without at least consulting them. It was even more galling to Will that the calamitous deed had taken place in England under his very nose.

For most of her life, it was true, Libby had insisted on her own counsel, but her wealth of wisdom and personal restraint had kept Trinity from worrying about her too awfully much. But this, this was an unbelievably foolish decision. However, it was done, and if her darling daughter was finally going to live in England, so close to them at last, Trinity was going to make sure she was not estranged from her family. Libby was wed to an Englishman. Will had to take succor in that, even if she'd chosen the worst possible candidate for wedlock in the length and breadth of the British Isles. Putting off the next round of their discussion a moment longer, she started to take another sip of tea, then jerked bodily, her cup rattling dangerously in the saucer, when her husband suddenly exploded from the chair, nearly knocking it over backward.

"That bloody devil has already announced their nuptials!" he shouted at the top of his voice, his face turning scarlet as Rainville's latest insult brought a rocket of festering ire shooting to the surface. The young maid standing in readiness at the gigantic carved sideboard nearly fainted, then retreated with all due haste out the swinging door to the servant hall that ran along the back of the dining room. Trinity had the urge to do the same as her husband threw the folded newspaper down on the table, overturning his coffee.

"Read it yourself, Trinity. Now an annulment will be hell to pay. Goddamn him! He planned every bit of this to get back at me!"

While her husband stalked down the side of the table and the servants all kept their distance in a huddled knot behind the swinging door, Trinity calmly blotted the spill with her damask napkin, then picked up the offending paper. The announcement was short and to the point but gave the particulars of the marriage, especially emphasizing the fact that Libby was the daughter of the Duke of Thorpe, and even worse, that the couple had eloped.

Trinity's frown knitted her brows as she read through the article a second time. Despite Libby's belief otherwise, it appeared Julian had indeed concocted a plot of revenge with her poor daughter as the staked goat. Why else would he have gotten the marriage announcement into the morning papers so quickly, when the couple had arrived in London only the day before? He must have sent word by letter before they left Yorkshire. She wondered if Libby had seen the paper yet. Her sigh whispered its way up from deep inside her heart. Libby was going to get hurt before this catastrophe

quit shaking their world. She could only hope Julian's devi-
ousness was something Libby could learn to forgive. At the
moment she was too in love with him to see his faults, and
Trinity knew how that could be. She would forgive Will anything, she supposed, even his pig-headed stubbornness, which
he was exhibiting with a great deal of flourish at the moment.

"At least they're wed, Will darling. He could have set her
up as his mistress and flaunted that in our faces."

William whirled around, turning on her in a way that surprised her. "What are you thinking, woman? This marriage
is the worst thing that could ever happen to any of us. It'd
take a small fortune to buy him off, and from what I've been
able to find out, he doesn't need the money. I guess I'll have
to bribe the bishop to get Libby her annulment."

Despite his undiminished display of anger, Trinity couldn't
believe he'd stoop to such underhanded machinations. "You
can't be serious."

"Oh? And why not? I'll do that, or whatever else it takes
to end this debacle Libby's gotten us into. I'll visit Sir Ian's
office today and have him draw up papers ending this farce
as soon as possible. Rainville's a cad, and as soon as Libby
realizes how he's been manipulating her to get to me, she'll
come to her senses."

Weary of trying to reason with him, Trinity shook her
head. "Aren't you forgetting, Will, that Libby is twenty-six
years of age and a widow with her own annuity? Also, in
case you've forgotten, she's a citizen of the United States.
Our laws won't affect her decisions."

"Not to mention the fact that I love Julian and want to be
his wife."

Trinity and William both turned toward the voice, and
found Libby standing near the door, lovely in a black-and-
white-striped day gown. She was glaring scornfully at her
father, whose face took on the black fury of a thundercloud
about to hurl bolts of lightning to earth. Hoping to defuse the
situation before the two could exchange hateful words they'd
regret later, Trinity got up and walked to meet her wayward

daughter. If a reconciliation was to be had between them, it would be up to her to facilitate it.

"Libby darling, come in and join us. I'm so glad you're here. We need to sit down and talk about this. That's what we've always done when we've had problems between us. Would you like something to eat? A poached egg, or a scone with honey perhaps?"

"I haven't been able to eat a bite since I left here last night. In fact, I've felt queasy all morning." Libby was matching her father glower for glower, and Trinity shook her head, thinking they were far too much alike. Though they adored each other, they'd clashed many times over the years, especially since Libby had come of age and demanded a say in her own affairs.

"Then at least let me pour you a cup of tea. That should settle your stomach. No wonder you're ill, if you haven't eaten anything since yesterday. I think the best thing is for the three of us to discuss this in a rational manner instead of yelling at each other."

"I'll warn you now, Trinity," William said curtly, looking at his wife. "I forbid you to interfere. Good God, you should be as opposed as I am to our daughter's alliance with a liar and a murderer."

"Listen to yourself, Father," Libby cried furiously. "Julian's no murderer. He's not Rupert; he's not his brother. And he's not perfect, but at least he told me about what happened all those years ago. You and Mother hid the whole scandal from me, and now that I've talked to Julian I can understand why. Now that I know the truth, I find it reprehensible what you did to Julian's family."

"What I did to him?" Her father stopped, seemingly speechless at the affront. It didn't take him long to regain his voice, and his wrath. "His brother tried to murder your mother, did he mention that? Does she mean so little to you that you don't care what she suffered at his hands?"

"William! Please! We won't get anywhere as long as you're hurling around accusations!"

Trinity's tone was edged with quiet anger, enough to draw

her husband's attention away from his daughter. She gave him a withering stare until he turned away and gazed out the window. Gathering her shredded nerves, she returned her regard to her child, at the moment just as peeved with Libby as she was with William.

"Now, Libby, why don't you be kind enough to sit down and tell us what you came here to say, and in a civil manner, if you can find it in yourself? And without blaming your father for everything. I do hope you can bring yourself to show a little respect for the man who raised you."

Libby flushed until her pale cheeks turned a rosy hue, but she plopped down in a chair beside Trinity in a rebellious pose reminiscent of her adolescent years. Indeed, obstinacy ran deep and sure in Thorpe blood.

"I'm sorry if I've been rude, Mama, but he has no right to try to force me into an annulment I don't want."

"I'm your father, goddammit. I have a right to do whatever I damn well please. And you'll do as I say because I know what's best for you."

Trinity looked at her husband with not a little chagrin. "Perhaps you should rethink that remark, husband, in the context of our own betrothal and marriage."

As she had intended, her husband's face reacted as he remembered what his own father, then the Duke of Thorpe, had done to separate them, thinking Trinity unworthy as an American rebel to become his duchess. In truth, his inability to accept their relationship was what had impelled him to hire Rupert Rainville in the ill-fated murder attempt, which even now, after two decades, was throwing their family into turmoil and strife. It was truly ironic that even in death, Will's father, Adrian, could still work his evil upon them.

Husband and wife locked intense gazes for a long and heated moment. Then Trinity intentionally gentled her voice, knowing full well how painful the past was to William. "I'd be very pleased, Will, if you'd only sit down for a moment and let Libby say whatever it is she's come to say. I'm quite sure you can control the anger you feel if you'll only try."

No one else could have gotten by with such a rebuke of

the powerful duke, albeit a tender one, but their love had only grown stronger with each passing year. They were partners in every sense of the word, though at times her husband needed a gentle reminder on that count.

William did not look pleased, but he did sit down. A clotted silence then descended. While Libby toyed with the silver napkin ring in front of her, Trinity poured her tea, then refreshed her husband's coffee from the silver coffee urn beside her. "Would you care for a piece of toast, Libby dear?"

Libby shook her head, still frowning, still furious. Trinity seated herself again, aware that Will would not look at his daughter. He adored his first child, had petted and pampered her from the first time he ever saw her, which had been almost a year after her birth when he'd come to Charleston after the war to fetch them home. They'd never been apart since, not for longer than a week. That separation, when she carried Libby inside her and the war raged on around them, was the loneliest, most painful year of Trinity's life. She would not, would not, allow Libby to suffer such a fate. If she truly loved Julian, and if he loved her, then she should be with him.

"Libby, I think it's time for you to speak your mind. As you can see, your father is now willing to listen. Did you have a discussion with your"—she stumbled on the word only because it felt so alien on her tongue—"husband."

"Yes, of course. We talked at some length last night. He told me everything that happened, and I was shocked to learn what Father did to destroy the Rainvilles."

William's jaw was grinding so hard that Trinity was afraid she was going to hear the crackle of teeth splintering, but somehow he was managing to control himself. For how much longer, however, Trinity couldn't imagine. He was a volatile man when pressed beyond endurance, and extremely protective when it came to members of his immediate family. She knew that he felt his daughter had made a terrible mistake, one that would harm her irreparably, if not destroy them all. She smiled encouragingly at Will in an attempt to soothe him, but his eyes looked like two hard green flints ready to spark flames. It was time to take his side, if only to placate him, but what she said was true.

"Please don't take offense, Libby, but as the one who was assaulted by Rupert Rainville, your father did nothing that night except save my life, and yours too, since I carried you at the time. As I set out for you yesterday, they fought and during the struggle Rainville fell. But he intended to throw me to my death; he laughed and taunted me with it. I'll never forget how terrified I was. If it hadn't been for Will, I'd have died that night at his hands."

"I know, Mother," Libby said gently, apparently dismayed by the idea of her mother having been in such danger. "I shudder to think of you going through such a horrible thing. But Julian was just a little boy, far away at Brickhill. He had nothing whatsoever to do with Rupert's villainy. What happened after his brother died is what has caused him to become so bitter. He explained everything to me last night."

"Nothing happened to his family afterward, not that I'm aware of. Except, of course, for the scandal. It was an ugly affair that came out while I was in the Carolinas. Your poor father was left to face it all by himself. It was difficult for him too, you must know that." Trinity stood up and moved behind her husband's chair. She placed a comforting palm on Will's broad shoulder, remembering distinctly how much he'd suffered as he'd faced the gossip and humiliation of the murder investigation alone. He reached up and squeezed her fingers, and she knew he had calmed down enough to listen.

Across from them, Libby watched the affectionate display, well aware of the united front they'd taken against her. "I'm surprised you don't know, Mama, truly I am. According to Julian, and I believe what he says, Father took it upon himself to ruin the Rainvilles during that last year of the war when you were in America. He says Father made sure Lady Edmonton, Julian's mother, was shunned by everyone in society, and that he set out to destroy Julian's family business and banking associations by ostracizing anyone who dealt with the Rainvilles. He ruined them, and poor Julian was left to watch his father die of drink, and his mother waste away, heartbroken and alone."

"That's absurd, Libby. Will would never intentionally harm innocent people, would you, darling?" Trinity glanced down at her husband for confirmation and was startled when he thrust back his chair and walked away without answering. A terrible dread began to rise inside her, a growing foreboding that sent a shudder through her.

"Julian says that's exactly what he did. That his family was ruined, never accepted again by polite society. The estate at Brickhill fell into ruin, and that's when Julian went to sea to make his fortune. He arranged a marriage for his younger sister, whose possibilities had been reduced to nil by the scandal. Unfortunately, it was to an abusive man. She committed suicide to escape him."

"Oh, Lord, no, how awful!" Trinity exclaimed, shaking her head.

"And I suppose your husband"—William nearly spat the word at Libby, his tone heavy with sarcasm—"blames her death on me as well."

"No, he does not. The truth is he blames himself. He's carried the guilt nearly all his life. He's still carrying it."

"Pardon me if I don't burst out in tears."

"Will, please," his wife reminded him softly. "We need to settle this. Libby is our only daughter."

"Julian did nothing to deserve what you did to him, and neither did his mother and sister. Why did you try to ruin them, Father?"

"Honey, I'm telling you that your father never did such a thing. Will wouldn't—"

"I did it because I was so full of rage I couldn't think of anything else. Your mother left me, and I thought I'd never see her again. Rainville had destroyed my family, and I wanted to return the favor."

Shocked, Trinity had trouble comprehending the idea. "Will, they were innocent people. They did nothing—"

"They bore the Rainville name. Furthermore, I don't particularly regret it. Julian's proven himself just as low for marrying my innocent daughter in an act of revenge. He's no better than I."

Disbelieving that such a callous confession came from the mouth of her beloved, kind husband, Trinity watched him stamp angrily out of the room. Nothing more was said, and when Trinity looked back at her daughter, she saw that Libby was fighting tears. They shone in her eyes, then spilled over until she laid her head down on her folded arms and wept.

"There, there, Libby. Things will work out. Your father isn't over his anger yet. Julian and Will don't really know each other. They see only the bad things the other has done. It's up to us to make them see the good in each other."

"No, they hate each other! They'll never see anything except what they want to see!"

"Oh, yes, they will. If they love us the way they should, we'll be able to make them listen to reason. Does Julian love you?"

Hastily, sniffling softly, Libby brought her burst of despair under control. She wiped away her tears, putting on a smile, although a weak one. "Yes, I know he does."

Smiling at Libby's pleasure at knowing the man she loved cared for her, Trinity sat down and hugged her daughter. "We can resolve this if we just put our heads together. We must think of a way to make sure they learn to like each other. Your father is stubborn, true, more than stubborn, but he loves you dearly. He'll come to see reason in time, I'll make sure of it."

"Oh, Mother, I've missed you so."

"That's the best reason I know to accept your marriage to Julian. We'll have you here in England with us. But you'll have to work on Julian too. It's obvious they both bear blame. Do you think you can convince him to forgive Will's interference in his family's life?"

"I think so, but he's very bitter. He's pleased that Father's so hurt, I could tell. He sent ahead to have the announcement put in the papers. Have you seen it?"

"Yes, I'm afraid so."

"Julian has already agreed to let me have a dinner party

for you and Father at our house, but I think he did so only because he was sure Father would refuse the invitation." She looked pleadingly at her mother. "Do you think there's any way you can convince him to come?"

Trinity was not sure, not at all. "Of course I can. We'll be there, darling. And your brother too, if he's arrived in town by then."

"Oh, it would be wonderful to have Burke there too. Julian said once he'd met him. Perhaps he could be the neutral party in all of this. He'd help us, I know he would."

Libby's eyes had begun to shine once more, and Trinity gave her beautiful daughter another encouraging hug, but over her shoulder she was not smiling, not confident at all. In truth, she was very worried that she would never, no matter how much she cajoled and pleaded, convince her husband to set foot on Rainville property.

Chapter Twenty-five

"I do hope, my darling Will, that you won't wear that horrid scowl this entire evening."

At Trinity's remark William, fifteenth Duke of Thorpe, Viscount Remington, glanced across the plush velvet interior of his finest ducal coach at his wife, who sat watching him, her eyes alight with a golden twinkle. Her smile never failed to move him, had enjoyed the magical property of melting his heart since the earliest days of their courtship, when they were young and so much in love.

Tonight, however, even his beloved Trinity could not disarm the anger and disappointment seething inside him. She had, however, with great patience and single-minded determination, persuaded him to attend a dinner party at his daughter's new home, even after he'd sworn in the most vociferous of tones that he'd never, ever, under any circumstances, set foot in Julian Rainville's house.

"Well, I'm not in a particularly jovial mood," he finally answered. "That's for damn sure." The annoyance in his voice lent credence to his remark.

"A bad mood? You? Surely not you, Will?" Trinity's dimples had deepened, a sure sign that she fully intended to summon up every ounce of her considerable charm to entice him out of his sullen humor.

"I doubt I'll ever have a moment of good cheer again until Libby comes to her senses and lets me annul this travesty of a marriage."

Her smile fading somewhat, Trinity inhaled a very deep,

drawn-out, what-in-heaven's-name-am-I-going-to-do-with-you sigh before fixing him with a stare that Will recognized only too well. Her cajolery was over; her glorious eyes pinned him where he sat. "Will, you must listen to me. You've got to be reasonable about this mess. Libby is our dearly beloved daughter. I will not allow us to become estranged from her. Especially now, when she's willing to make a life here in London. Since John's death that's what we've always hoped she'd do."

"The fact that she's aligned herself with the spawn of the devil takes away some of my enthusiasm."

"Julian is not a devil, nor, as Libby pointed out, is he his brother, Rupert. Julian did nothing to harm me or you, or anyone else that I know of. Actually, Libby says that he's a very kind man and most undeserving of the gossip whispered about him. Why do you blame him for what his brother did to us years ago? Julian was little more than a child when Rupert died."

"Perhaps he's not a cold-blooded murderer like his brother, but I can tell you one thing. He's only using Libby to get to me. Anyone who doesn't believe that is a fool." A wave of anger rolled over Will, roiling and boiling inside his gut until he had to grind his teeth together to control it. "He admitted as much, the bastard."

"He also readily admitted that he loved our daughter and intended to treat her with respect."

Will refused to give an answer, irritated anew with his wife, who should be more upset than he. She was the one nearly thrown to her death down that marble staircase, not he. He glared out the window, and they lapsed into an uncomfortable silence until the driver brought them to a smooth stop at the front of Libby's new home on Berkeley Square.

Once they had stepped down to the street, Trinity tucked her hand in the crook of his arm and together they climbed the stone steps. She probably just wanted a grip on him in case Julian opened the door, he thought sourly. The house boasted a good address, at least, and seemed quite fashionable and well kept. He wondered if Julian had obtained the wealth displayed in the heavy gold door knocker his wife was now lifting through his reputed illicit Orient trade. Most likely so, he decided as Trinity let go and the heavy ring fell with a hollow clang. While they waited, she turned and warned him with one last admonition.

"Please remember, Will, that this is now Libby's home. Julian is her husband, whether you like him or not. I do hope you'll find it in your heart to respect your daughter's hospitality. I'll ask you to do it for me, your wife, if you cannot find any other reason to be courteous at the dinner table."

Unused to being chastised by his wife, or opposed—they usually agreed on most matters, or at the least, hashed out a suitable compromise if their wills did clash—Will gave a curt nod but made no promises as the door was thrown open. Libby herself stood before them, her face beaming, looking absolutely beautiful in a high-necked dark blue velvet gown trimmed at both sleeves and hem in white lace. Obviously delighted to see them, she took hold of their hands and drew them into the foyer. Will found himself smiling down at her, his inability to deny his daughter's wishes almost as strong as his weakness toward his wife's wants. Both the women in his life were too charming for their own good.

"Mama, Papa, I'm so glad you've come! Julian's waiting for us in the drawing room."

Libby's delight at their presence was so contagious and bubbly that Will found himself relenting somewhat from his heretofore implacable stand. She had always been so special in his heart, his beautiful little angel who'd been born with his wife's gorgeous red hair. He'd missed her birth and the first few months of her life after Trinity had fled England and the evil plot of his father's, a fact he'd never get over if he lived to be a hundred. Ever since those dark days of despair, he'd tried to make up that year-long separation, and at the same time had hated the Rainvilles with every ounce of his being.

Even now his gut was twisting with conflicts, all manner of raw emotions resurfacing when he entered the elegantly appointed drawing room and saw Julian, looking completely relaxed and unrepentant as he rested an elbow on the black marble mantelpiece. Reflexively Will's jaw formed into a hard, dangerous angle, and Trinity must have sensed his growing tension, because she squeezed his arm in warning.

"Good evening, Lord Edmonton." Will watched in stiff dislike as Trinity left his side and moved forward to greet her new son-in-law. Julian smiled and bent to kiss her hand. Will wanted to grab her away from his touch.

"Welcome to our home, Duchess," Julian was saying now, and Trinity was replying:·

"Oh, no, we'll have none of this formality. You're part of the family now. Please, call me Trinity."

"Yes, Julian, please do," Libby encouraged, looping her arm through her husband's and smiling up at him. It made Will sick to his stomach, and he watched, disgusted, wondering how his daughter could be so blind as to the rogue's true motives. Julian, Earl of Edmonton was known in every gentlemen's club and drawing room in London as a rake and philanderer. Good God, his name was synonymous with ill repute and loose women. The parties held here in this very house were whispered to regularly devolve into nothing less than decadent orgies. Now his own daughter had been dragged down into that low-class, vulgar, gutter lifestyle. Not for long, he assured himself, and with not a little determination, not if he could prevent it.

"Papa, please sit down." Libby left her husband and came to grasp his hand, leading him to a sofa that faced the crackling coals. "How do you like Julian's house? Isn't it beautiful?"

"It's our house, my love," Julian reminded her, moving forward and lifting Will's daughter's hand to his mouth. He kissed it, first the back and then the open palm, and William grimaced with distaste. He glanced away.

As Trinity sat down close beside him and put her hand on his forearm—probably to keep him from storming out, he thought, an action that had indeed crossed his mind—the young newlyweds took their place on a nearby love seat. Silence fell like a heavy iron weight, and they sat crushed under it for several long moments. The two men stared unblinkingly at each other, as if that were the chosen way to call each other out. A duel, Will decided with narrowed eyes, that would certainly end Edmonton's hold on his daughter.

Valiantly and in a falsely cheerful voice, Trinity made the first effort to relieve the tension as tangible and suffocating as thick black smoke. "Oh, Libby, I have wonderful news. Burke sent word today that he will be home in the next few days. He wants me to see to opening his London house, so I hope you'll go there with me tomorrow and help me get the servants started on cleaning and airing the rooms. I'm so eager to see him. It's rare for Will and me to have both of you here in London at the same time."

Libby smiled with pleasure. "Of course I'll help you. I can't wait to see him. It's been so long. Where's he been this time?"

"On the continent, in Rome for the most part, I believe. He's not very good at keeping us informed about his whereabouts."

Trinity went on to explain how Burke lived in the house Will had owned before he assumed his title, one that was only a few blocks away. Unbeknownst to Trinity and everyone else, Burke had been traveling incognito inside French borders in search of information about Bonaparte's troop movements. His mother didn't know about his work for the government, and would never know how dangerous was her son's work. William had borne that worry alone, but he was proud that his son was serving the crown so selflessly. He'd be glad when Burke was safely home; he'd been gone far too long this time.

"Then he'll be here for the Season? Will we go to Thorpe in September?" Libby asked happily.

"Of course. We always do. You and Julian must come as well." Trinity turned her gaze hopefully to Julian, then smiled with relief when he nodded in affirmation. William was not so delighted. He sat stone-faced, not looking forward to having a Rainville at Thorpe Hall.

A footman entered the room—no, he realized with some

shock, it was a Chinese woman. She announced in heavily accented English that dinner was ready to be served. Julian stood up and politely offered his arm to Trinity. William stood and walked to Libby.

"Papa," she whispered, taking his arm and squeezing it affectionately. "I'm so glad you came tonight. I was so afraid you wouldn't."

"I came here to please you, Libby, but I won't pretend I'm pleased with your choice of a husband."

"That's just because you don't know Julian yet. You'll change your mind in time." Libby's remarks were supremely confident, and he did notice that she seemed radiant, her eyes glowing with happiness. As he seated her, her gaze lingered on her husband, who was taking his place at the head of the table. Will sat down across from Trinity, as uncomfortable and ill at ease as he could ever remember being.

Trinity and Libby obviously noticed and quickly set about to fill the awkwardness with banal chatter about the cooler weather, about what would be involved in preparing Burke's house for his arrival, but William was more interested in observing Julian's behavior. More often than not the younger man gazed at his wife, and did, though Will hated to admit it, seem to dote on her. But that didn't mean he really did. How else would the man act in front of his wife's parents? It would take more than that to convince Will the man had a sincere or trustworthy bone in his body.

"Why don't you explain to my wife and me how you convinced our daughter to elope without telling us, Rainville?" he suddenly demanded in a much harsher tone than he'd intended.

The rest of the conversation screeched to a dead halt. The frown Trinity threw at him was indeed one to behold. Libby looked upset, but Julian only smiled at her, patting her hand, ever the gallant, Will noted with bitter scorn.

"I don't know how I happened to be lucky enough to win her love. She's made me a very happy man."

"Is that because you care about her or because wedding

her gave you the best method to avenge yourself on her family?"

Libby intervened, her face distressed. "Papa, please! Don't start this, not when everything was going so well."

For a moment William did feel remorse at hurting his child, but there was something in Rainville's eyes, some inner light—amusement, triumph, he wasn't sure which—but he couldn't stop himself from detesting the man sitting there gazing smugly at him. He knew full well, too, there was no love lost in Julian's regard.

"You're completely wrong, sir. I care deeply about your daughter. Surely you, above all others, realize how easy it is to love a woman as lovely as Libby. I had little need of an ulterior motive."

Both ladies relaxed visibly, and William held his tongue after that, fully aware that if he continued to attack his host, he would become a boor in the eyes of his wife and daughter. So they ate in virtual silence, with the two women making stilted, uncomfortable attempts to alleviate the situation. The poisoned glances he was receiving from underneath his wife's long lashes promised him another heated argument when they reached home later that evening.

"Julian's thinking of entering some of his work at the Royal Academy of Art." Libby was very proud of her husband; it was quite clear in her every word and expression. "I'm sure he'd be pleased to show you some of his paintings after dinner, if you'd like to see them."

"Actually, I've seen several of your paintings, Julian," Trinity said. "You're really quite wonderfully talented. The piece I saw last year was procured by Lady Wellton and portrayed a young woman standing at a window looking down at the street. The look in her eyes quite haunted me for days, I must say."

"That was a portrait of my sister, Victoria. Lady Wellton was her godmother, and after Victoria's death she wished to have the painting."

"Oh, dear, I'm very sorry. I shouldn't have brought up such a painful subject."

"No, actually, painting Victoria helped rid me of a few demons I'd been wrestling with. I've always blamed myself for her death. I should have been here for her instead of thousands of miles away in China."

Even Will heard the catch in his throat, which the other man quickly disguised by lifting his wine goblet. Will had heard gossip that Julian had shot his sister's husband in a duel, and he wondered why he'd offered up the challenge that resulted in the man's death.

The subject matter turned toward more innocuous subjects afterward, with Trinity asking many questions about Julian's work. He discussed it articulately but with a passion that could not be hidden.

"Perhaps you'd let me do a portrait of you, Duchess. I think one with both you and Libby would be quite magnificent, with your similar coloring."

"Oh, yes, that would be wonderful," Libby said, excited by the idea. "Wouldn't it, Papa?" she added hopefully.

"I've not seen any of Rainville's work."

"Then allow me to show you now. We're nearly finished here, aren't we? Would you ladies excuse us?"

Both ladies looked completely terrified by the idea of their two big, angry husbands closeted alone together, but William welcomed the opportunity to say to the man what was on his mind. He pushed back his chair at once, eager to get to the real reason he'd come to dinner. "That sounds like a good idea. I could use a smoke. Trinity, Libby, we'll join you shortly."

Julian too was glad for a moment alone with his wife's father. He didn't like the duke any better than William liked him, but he would make an effort to be civilized, if only for Libby's sake. She wanted them all to be one loving family, an eventuality that Julian felt quite sure was a complete impossibility.

He led the duke into his book-lined study, then shut the door behind him. "Would you care for a drink? Port or brandy?"

"Brandy'll do if you've got it." William settled into a big

maroon leather chair and glanced around the cozy room with its rich cherry paneling and blazing fire. Julian poured them both liberal portions in twin brandy snifters, then handed a glass to William. Despite his determination to act the gracious host, he felt nothing but cold contempt for the man who'd caused such misery for his family. Thorpe had succeeded in many ways, and Julian would never forgive him for those transgressions. But he'd also sired the woman Julian had come to love. Libby was his wife now, and he would continue to make the effort, at least tonight, because it was so important to her happiness.

"I suppose now that we're alone, we can shed the pretenses and be completely honest with each other," he said, seating himself in the chair directly across from William. "I see no reason for us to feign a liking for each other now that we're out of the presence of our wives."

"Precisely. Shall we get down to business?"

Julian observed the duke over his snifter, well aware of the underlying anger in the other man's eyes. He was not in any way, however, expecting his father-in-law's next remark. "How much will it take to persuade you to annul this ridiculous marriage to my daughter? Name your price, and I'll be happy to meet it."

With inhuman effort Julian kept a tight rein on his smoldering rage. Somehow he managed to speak calmly. "You're not only insulting me, you're insulting Libby. I'm glad she's not here to witness this outrage."

William's face went scarlet, and it looked like it was taking some effort for the duke to control himself. He was a powerful man, perhaps a bit taller than Julian and not quite as lean, but still strong and muscular, despite the fact he was no doubt nearing fifty. He would be a dangerous foe, both physically and intellectually.

"As you said, Rainville, there's no need to play games any longer. You courted Libby for revenge against our family, and we both know it. I want my daughter out of your clutches, and I'm willing to pay any amount to free Libby from your influence."

Julian had to smile at the sheer gall of the man's offer, which only seemed to infuriate the duke further. "I'm not interested in your money. I want your daughter, and that's all I want from you. I've got her now, and there's not one goddamn thing you can do about it."

Provoked beyond belief, William lunged to his feet. Julian rose too, slowly but more guarded. They stared at each other, both itching to send a fist into the other's face and pound him into the ground. Julian spoke first.

"Now I'm going to make you an offer I daresay you can't refuse. Your disapproval of our marriage is making Libby unhappy, and I don't like that very much. Since you obviously have no intention of listening to reason or thinking of Libby instead of yourself, it appears I'll have to force you to."

"I'd like to see you try it, my friend." William's words oozed challenge.

"Then watch now, my friend."

Julian moved across the room to where an easel had been set up. A covered painting was propped on the display, and he carried it back to William. He kept his eyes locked on William's face. "I suggest you welcome me into your family, Thorpe, from this moment forward, with open arms and a smile on your face, or I'll display this painting at the Royal Academy of Art for all of London to see."

Slowly he turned the portrait of Libby around, the one in which she sat on his bed, her arms lifting her hair in glorious masses of silk, the most transparent of thin white silk molding her naked breasts. He took the utmost pleasure in the way the Duke of Thorpe's red face slowly drained until it was as chalk white as Dover. Then, quickly, before Julian could react, William moved, swinging a doubled fist hard against the side of Julian's head. Julian ducked, half deflecting the blow but not before William's knuckles had connected brutally against his left eye.

Roaring with rage, he grabbed the duke's lapels and swung him hard around. He managed to land a blow of his own, a short jab to the nose that brought blood spurting out and spattering crimson drops across Will's snow white shirt and cravat. Then they were grappling in a deadly duel of strength, both struggling furiously for leverage as they hit a side table and knocked it over, the brandy bottle and glasses hitting the floor with a tinkling shattering of glass. They went down on it, and Julian grunted as his father-in-law drove an undercut underneath his chin with enough power to snap his head back. His own fury intensified, and he wanted nothing more than to beat the Duke of Thorpe to a bloody, shapeless pulp.

When the door was flung wide, Julian had drawn back his arm for another punch, but at the sound of Libby's horrified scream, he stopped his fist in midair, his other hand clutching the front of her father's shirt, and looked toward her and her mother as they rushed into the room. William's ire proved not to be subjugated so easily, and despite Trinity's cries for him to stop, he let go one last blow into Julian's stomach that left him bent over double and groaning with pain.

"Papa! How could you? How could you do this?"

The awful tone of Libby's voice brought both men abruptly to their senses. They got slowly to their feet, and Julian touched his right eye, which was already beginning to swell as William retrieved his white handkerchief and held it to the blood trickling from his nose. Neither had time to say a word before Libby burst into tears and ran from the room.

Her mother still stood in the doorway, drawn up to an imperious height and looking every bit the Duchess of Thorpe. She was paying no mind to Julian. Her attention was riveted on her husband, and even Julian was taken aback, not certain he'd ever seen such open anger on a woman's face. Her unusual gold eyes flashed sparks that could easily ignite anything they touched to flame, but luckily were not aimed at him, so Julian righted his waistcoat and straightened his torn cravat with as much dignity as he could muster.

"I'll bid a footman to show you to the door," he said politely to the duchess. "I believe my wife has need of me upstairs."

"Thank you, Lord Edmonton," Trinity replied just as formally, and as graciously as possible under such bizarre circumstances. "And please, my lord, allow me to apologize for my husband's uncivilized behavior. He has obviously forgotten his good manners this evening."

Julian nodded and left them to the argument foreshadowed by the duchess's quiet fury. His primary objective was soothing Libby and explaining away his part in the absurdly inappropriate, inexcusable fistfight with her father.

In their bedchamber, he found her lying across their cream-colored satin counterpane, her head buried in her folded arms. He went there and sat down beside her, surprised to find that she was no longer weeping.

"I'm sorry, Libby. I lost my temper. So did he." He sighed and jerked loose his necktie and flung it to the floor. "I warned you that we probably couldn't forget our differences this soon."

Libby raised herself on one elbow, then struggled up onto her knees. To Julian's pleasure she came into his arms, her hands locked around his waist. "I'm just so disappointed. I was sure the two of you could overlook your difficulties once you spent time together. What happened, Julian? You came to blows so quickly."

"It's probably better if you don't ask."

"I have a right to know, Julian." Her gaze lingered on his injured eye, and she raised her fingertips and gently touched the puffiness. "It's going to turn black, I'm afraid. Does it hurt awfully much?"

"No," he lied, when the truth was it felt as if his whole eye socket had been forced a good three inches back into his brain. The duke wielded quite a punch.

"Oh, Julian, I had such high hopes when Papa agreed to come here tonight. And dinner went well enough, I thought. Please tell me what happened to make him hit you."

"Your father offered me payment to annul our marriage," he said, reluctant to hurt her. "I took offense."

"Oh, how could he do such a thing? How could he offer such insult? Is that when you hit him?"

"Well, actually he swung first. But only because he beat me to it."

"Don't take up for him. His behavior is completely unforgivable. Oh, my poor darling, I should never have insisted on having my parents to dinner so soon. I should have listened to you."

As she leaned her head against his shoulder, he relaxed, holding her, stroking her back, his lips on top of her head. As always the feel of her in his arms, the way she molded herself so intimately against him, sent his body rock hard in craving for her, and she responded eagerly, threading her arms around his neck and raising her face for his kiss. At that point he decided he'd wait until the morning to mention his own threat about the nude painting. Or maybe he wouldn't have to mention it at all, he decided as he lowered her back on the bed and began undressing her. A few moments later he'd forgotten all about the fight and the throbbing in his eye, as her soft lips opened up to him and he thought only of the satiny softness of her skin and the lovely fragrance of her silky hair.

Chapter Twenty-six

By the raised windows and the sight of Alice vigorously shaking a white dust cover on the front steps, Libby recognized her brother's residence. It was on a shady street near a small park, only blocks from her own new home, and she was glad she had sent her maid over earlier that morning to help with the cleaning.

The house was large and built of red brick, quite spacious with many tall windows and a broad front porch, and Alice greeted her mistress, then sneezed from the swirling cloud of dust raised from the sheet she'd been flapping.

"Is Mama here, Alice? I'm eager to speak with her."

"Yes, ma'am. She's in the drawing room, havin' 'er footmen move in the new chairs she brought over for the viscount to use."

"How's it coming? Is the house nearly ready? Burke might possibly be here this evening, you know."

"Yes, ma'am, 'cept for a few o' the guest rooms on the top floor 'e won't be needin'."

Pleased to hear things were moving along quickly but more anxious to speak with her mother about the disgraceful scene enacted between their husbands the previous night, Libby left her maid to fold the canvas cover and went in search of Trinity. As Alice had indicated, her mother was in the drawing room, arranging two red-and-blue-striped wing chairs on either side of the fireplace. The windows were standing wide, and the balmy breeze meandering into the chamber had just about dispelled any musty mildew odors.

"Mama? It looks like you're nearly done."

Trinity was dressed in an afternoon frock of green-striped lawn, and she nodded in agreement as she wiped her hands on her long apron. "We're making progress, but there's still much to be done. I want everything just right for Burke. He's stayed away much too long, and I intend to scold him about it." Her mother smiled, and Libby was pleased to see that her spirits had revived somewhat because Julian had told her how angry she'd been the night before. Libby turned when a footman spoke to her mother from the doorway behind her.

"Pardon, Your Grace, but which bedroom do you wish your trunks taken to?"

Libby turned shocked eyes to her mother as the duchess directed the manservant upstairs to the largest guest bedroom.

"Mama? What has happened? You haven't left Papa, have you?" Stunned, Libby couldn't believe that could be true. In all her life she'd never seen a married couple as devoted as her parents were.

"No, of course not. I've merely decided to stay here with Burke for a few days and help him get settled."

Despite the explanation Libby knew something dire had happened to make her mother leave her father's house for even one evening. "Oh, Mama, this is all my fault, isn't it?"

Trinity observed her daughter for a moment, then pointedly dismissed the two servants who had carried in the new furniture. "James, Michael, you are probably needed upstairs, if you please. Come, Libby, sit down. We really need to talk about what happened."

Tugging loose the ribbons on her bonnet, Libby obeyed and took a seat across from her mother. "I guess you know that Father tried to bribe Julian into annulling our vows. Is that what you argued about?"

Trinity's elegant eyebrows knitted in a small frown, but she still looked much younger than her years, more like Libby's sister than her mother. But Libby could see the anger in the set of her mouth and knew full well that her mother knew about her husband's bribe and was quite furious with him.

"He told me. I will apologize to you in his stead, darling.

He is a stubborn man but usually much more circumspect and wise than he's behaving at the moment. His behavior verges on the ridiculous, yet he cannot seem to let go of his anger. I suppose Julian told you everything."

Trinity searched Libby's face as if trying to gauge her feelings, and Libby nodded. "He was insulted. He said Father threw the first punch. I was glad Julian was able to restrain himself as much as he did."

"I'll certainly be the first to admit that Will is acting irrationally where Julian is concerned, Libby, but I must say he did have good provocation to blacken Julian's eye. Even I might have hit him a lick if I'd been there, I'm afraid."

Startled, Libby looked askance at her mother. "What do you mean? Julian did nothing to provoke Father. He merely defended himself."

Trinity raised both eyebrows and shook her head. "Men can be most infuriating, can they not? Well, daughter, brace yourself for unwelcome news because your husband was not as innocent in the fracas as he pretends to be."

"What do you mean?"

"I mean that he attempted to bribe your father too, in a different manner but one that was just as offensive. I suspect he failed to mention it to you for that very reason."

Libby thought back to breakfast when Julian had encouraged her to stay home instead of joining her mother, and now she realized that he might have had reason for it. "What did he say?"

"It's what he did, darling. I hesitate to bring it up, actually, for fear of embarrassing you." Libby turned in her chair when her mother got up and shut the open doors. "It appears," Trinity began, taking a deep breath before she went on, "that you've been sitting for Julian. Apparently in some rather personal portraits?"

Libby could feel the blood running up her neck into her cheeks, her face burning as she avoided her mother's gaze. "Julian didn't tell Father I posed in the nude? He wouldn't. He couldn't humiliate me in that way. He promised me."

"I truly hate to be the one to have to tell you this, dear heart, but he didn't just tell him, he showed it to him!"

Stunned to the core, Libby collapsed back into the chair, unable to believe it. She said as much, and her mother responded with an even worse revelation.

"I'm afraid it's true, Libby. Unfortunately, he not only showed it to Will, he threatened to show it all over London if your father didn't accept him into the family gracefully."

For a moment Libby could do nothing but stare speechlessly at her mother. Then anger began to roll up, larger and larger inside her as the sheer audacity of Julian's action hit her. She jumped to her feet and stalked up and down the newly aired Persian carpet, so furious that she nearly choked with rage.

"How could he? How could he do this to me? What was he thinking?" She stopped in her tracks and whirled back to her mother. "He actually showed it to Papa?" At her mother's nod, she hid her face in her palms and groaned aloud. "Oh, Lord, I can never look him in the eye again. How could Julian do this to me?"

After a few moments of watching her daughter pace and fume, Trinity said calmly, "I suppose he meant well, just as your father did when he offered to pay him off. Neither are thinking very clearly, it seems. It's incredible, really, two men who are ordinarily most kind and thoughtful."

Libby hugged herself, looking distraught and sounding doleful. "Oh, Mama, how can I face Papa after he's seen that, after he knows that I . . . ?" Words failed her, then she had another thought. "Which one did Julian show him?"

Trinity had to laugh. "How many are there?"

Libby blushed beet red and squirmed as she answered. "Well, he is my husband, but he promised faithfully never to show them to anyone."

Her voice full of irony, Trinity sniffed. "I'm not sure your father got much of a look at it before he tried to throttle your husband."

They chuckled together, visualizing the scene, but both of

them quickly grew sober. Libby was still too angry to find much amusement in anything.

"Darling, that's why I decided to stay here for a few days. Sometimes, rarely, 'tis true, but at times I have to find a way to get your father's attention. Perhaps having me here instead of at home with him just might bring him to his senses a little more quickly. He's got to quit blaming Julian for what Rupert did."

"Then I will do the same," Libby decided on impulse, still so furious with Julian that she could barely breathe. "I'll send Alice to pack what I'll need. Perhaps with both of us here, they'll listen to reason."

"Precisely, dear." Trinity smiled and gave Libby a quick hug. "And it'll give me a chance to spend a few days with my daughter and my son."

Libby sighed, some of her wrath subsiding, and more annoying, she hated the thought of not being with Julian, even overnight. But look what he'd done! She vowed, then and there, that she would find those nudes and burn every last one in a gigantic bonfire. And he'd threatened to show it all over London!

"Julian's going to be angry about this," she conjectured aloud, but she lifted her chin and agreed with her mother's decision, "but that's just too bad. Once he and Father agree to stop this feud between them, then we'll both return home."

"That's what I'm hoping for," Trinity admitted.

"Papa's going to go into a rage," Libby predicted, and they nodded together, both knowing William very well. "What about the ball you've planned to welcome me to London? Will you still have it?"

"The evening's been planned for months. It'll go on as intended. You and I will attend, of course. We'll just let Burke escort us from here. No one will suspect either of us are doing anything other than helping Burke get settled. We'll have to be discreet, of course, because we don't need any more scandal. I had considered formally announcing your marriage that night, if our husbands would cooperate."

"Oh, Mama," Libby said again, "Papa's going to be so furious with you . . ."

Her words ended when they heard her father outside in the foyer, demanding where the duchess was in no uncertain terms. His voice sounded calm but dangerous enough in tone that Libby suspected the servants, Alice included, were scurrying posthaste toward the kitchens. She was not exactly eager to see him either, not after what Julian had shown to him the night before. When the door was thrown open, the duke had no eyes for her but glared at his wife, as if ready to murder her.

"Hello, darling," Trinity greeted him mildly, rising to her feet. "Burke isn't here yet, but I'm sure he'll soon be."

"What in the devil do you think you're doing? I command you to come home at once."

Libby watched her mother's delicate jaw harden, almost imperceptibly but enough to be a warning sign. "Libby's going to be staying here with me for a time," her mother announced to her father. "I'm sure that doesn't concern you as much."

The duke swiveled his eyes to Libby. She stared at his slightly swollen nose and cut lip, wounds inflicted by her own husband. "I hope you have enough sense to leave that bastard after what he did last night."

Trinity answered for Libby. "I think both of you acted in a horrendous manner last night, but we've already discussed that in some detail. Libby, darling, why don't you take a moment now to speak with Alice about fetching what you'll need from your house?"

Glad for an excuse to leave the room, Libby walked past her father and carefully slid the doors closed behind her, lingering there only long enough to hear him demand again that his wife come home where she belonged. She wondered how Julian would react when he found out that she would join her mother in the act of defiance. Then she clamped her jaw, unwittingly in much the same way her mother had earlier, and decided it really didn't matter what he thought. How dare he show that portrait to her father? The rush of rage that came in the wake of that thought propelled her on her way to find Alice and arrange for the temporary move out of her husband's house.

Chapter Twenty-seven

Burke Kingston Stephen, Viscount Remington, the only son and heir of the Duke and Duchess of Thorpe, found himself very glad to be back home in the city of London. For nearly a year he'd worked incognito in France, making his way through the cities and countryside while he performed his clandestine services for the crown. His mission had been more than successful, and he'd been able to provide his government with a good deal more than they'd expected concerning Bonaparte's troop movements. The fact that Burke spoke flawless French and Italian, languages learned during a very enjoyable year of his youth studying in Venice and Rome, had helped him immensely as he masqueraded as a Venetian nobleman's son. He'd found the experience both exciting and dangerous, but that's what he liked about it, the sheer exhilaration of walking a tightrope between friends and enemies in his deadly intrigues.

This time he'd pitted his wits against a French beauty who'd made no secret that she suspected he worked for the English. He'd enjoyed toying with her attempts to expose him, but even though Mademoiselle Renate was certainly capable of uncovering him as a spy, she'd failed to do so. Grinning, he remembered the last dance they'd enjoyed together at the home of her brother, an adjutant to Bonaparte himself, and from whose safe Burke had successfully burglarized French military documents earlier the same evening.

Truth be told, he was eager to return to his work and cross swords with the lovely Brigitte again and planned to do so as soon as he was given permission. For the moment he was pleased enough to be in safe, familiar territory, where he could relax his guard and rest his nerves before plunging again into the dark world of spies. He was eager too to see his parents, and thankful that his mother had no idea that he engaged in such perilous activities.

On the other hand, his father was well aware of his activities and backed him completely. Neither of them thought it wise to tell the duchess, but he doubted if Trinity could say much against his furtive work since she herself, as a young woman, had ridden courier for the Americans in their revolution against King George. However, that was before she married his father and settled down to her role as Duchess of Thorpe, and dutiful wife and mother. Still, she'd object to Burke's placing himself in such jeopardy, so they kept his true whereabouts from her, if only to prevent her worry.

More than even his parents Burke was eager to see his older sister, who was slated to arrive from America. He hadn't seen Libby since she'd been widowed. She'd been so sad and lonely at the time, except for her close relationship to her friend. Although she had seemed content to remain unmarried and run her deceased husband's printing establishment, Burke had personally thought her too young to wear drab widow weeds forever. Perhaps, he'd begun to think on his voyage home, now that she'd returned to England, he might play the matchmaker and find her a suitable gentleman who could make her happy and content to remain in London with her family.

As he was sorting through a list of various friends who might be suitable for that purpose and would appreciate the attributes of a woman as bright and beautiful as Libby, the hired hack pulled up at the curb in front of his stoop. Leaning forward and peering out the glass, he was surprised to see the windows of his tall brick town house ablaze with lights. Recalling his request for his mother to see to opening his house, he climbed out, paid the driver, then ascended the steps to the front portal.

The front door was unlocked, and once inside the gold and white wallpapered foyer he doffed his top hat, placed his white gloves inside, then hung it on the polished oak coat tree at the right of the front door. The familiar smells of the house assailed him, varnish and furniture polish and beeswax candles along with a faint musty smell reminiscent of dust and old books, no doubt lingering because the place had been closed up for so long.

In addition, and faintly, he caught the barest hint of his mother's favorite perfume, sweet gardenias, wafting no doubt from the white silk shawl draped over the hook beside his hat. He smiled, pleased to hear her voice drifting to him from the nearby dining hall, and though a bit surprised she had remained there through the dinner hour, he strode briskly to the wide double doors that stood open to the foyer.

When he stopped in the threshold he saw that not only was his mother partaking of a meal within the elegant confines of the room, but Libby was there too. Both ladies sat silent at the moment as one of the ducal footmen served their fare from a silver platter. Sitting directly in front of the doors, Libby was first to see him.

"Burke!" she cried in delight; then she was up and running to meet him. She threw herself into his arms, and Burke hugged her tightly, grinning over her head at his mother, who had risen and was on her way to join her two children. He quickly enveloped her in his hearty embrace, enjoying the way both women were laughing and asking him the same questions at the same time.

"Oh, Burke, it's so good to see you," Libby was telling him eagerly, stepping back as she tilted her head up to study his appearance. "But you look tired, and so much older than you did last time I saw you!"

"I'll take that as a compliment since you've always seen me as a baby brother."

His mother tightened her arms around his waist for another quick hug before she followed her daughter's lead and thoroughly examined his appearance. The two women in his family resembled each other, were both beautiful with red hair of different shades, and heart-shaped faces that were startlingly alike.

"You were gone much too long this time, darling. I simply don't understand your never ending fascination with those Italians. I've finally gotten Libby back to England, and now it's you who's gallivanting off to southern climes where they don't even speak English. How long will you stay in London this trip?"

"Several months, at the very least," he answered easily, suddenly glancing around the room in search of the duke. "Where's Father? It's rare for him to let you out of his sight at the supper hour." He grinned, for his father's affection for his mother was well known among their friends and acquaintances, and indeed throughout the town.

When Libby and Trinity exchanged significant glances, Burke braced himself, fearing all was not as it should be. A chill climbed with cloying dread from the base of his spine, and he immediately questioned, "He's all right, isn't he? He's not ill?"

"Oh, no," his mother reassured him at once, pursing her lips and shaking her head, as if quite chagrined with her husband. "He's hale and hearty, and even more stubborn than usual."

Burke laughed aloud, having experienced his mother's annoyance with his father's obstinacy on past occasions. Though quite happily wed, they did not always agree. "Might it be that the two of you have had a disagreement of some kind?" He turned to Libby for enlightenment. "What's happened, sis? You've no doubt been designated the impartial observer and peacemaker for the problem?"

When he darted a teasing smile at Libby, he found her face a good deal more stricken than their mother's. Frowning, he waited for one of them to explain what was going on, now fearing a more serious rift between his parents.

"Come sit down with us, and we'll explain everything," his mother told him, threading his fingers through hers and leading him toward the table. "James, please bring a place setting for Burke."

Burke nodded at his mother's oldest retainer, a trusted man she'd brought with her from the Carolinas many years before. The old man smiled as if pleased to see him, then moved off to do his mistress's bidding.

"Well, I must say, the two of you have got my house in good shape for my homecoming," Burke remarked as he pulled out a cherry Queen Anne chair and seated himself beside his mother. Above them the crystal prisms of the chandelier glittered with a recent dusting in soap and water, and the glossy surface of the cherry table reflected the gleaming branch of candles sitting between them. "The place has never looked better."

"I wanted everything to be perfect for you," admitted his mother, glancing at Libby, who had taken a chair across from Burke, "but, well, things just haven't quite . . ."

When his mother's explanation drifted into uncomfortable silence, Burke finished for her. "Haven't quite turned out, I suspect, or Father would be here with you, right? So which one of you is going to tell me what's happened?"

As Burke picked up a carafe of water and poured his goblet full, he waited for a reply. Both women seemed unwilling to apprise him of the crisis, whatever it was. Finally it was Libby who spoke up, the torment in her voice somewhat startling.

"I'm afraid it's a rather long story, Burke."

"I'm not going anywhere. I live here, you know." His attempt at levity fell flat, though both women made a small attempt at smiles. He leaned back in the chair and studied his sister's woeful face. "All right, I'll ask the questions. First off, why is Father angry, which I suspect is the case here? Did the two of you cross him together, or is one of you supporting the other in something of which he disapproves? God knows, we've all borne his wrath on occasion."

"Don't make him sound like such an ogre, Burke. In most cases when he's obstinate, he's merely concerned for our well-being." His mother always took up for her husband, even when they were the ones having the disagreement, arguments for the most part that didn't last more than a few hours—one reason Burke found it hard to fathom her being here so late in the evening.

"Does he know you're dining here tonight?"

His mother gave a small nod, which made the golden strands in her copper hair glint under the candle's glow. "The truth is, Burke, and please don't get upset, both Libby and I have moved in here with you."

Burke laughed, thinking she was joking. His smile faded hastily enough when both ladies merely looked at him. Neither appeared any more pleased with the arrangement than he was. The last thing he'd expected was to have his mother and sister as houseguests.

"What exactly does that mean, Mother?"

"It means I've decided to stay with you for a few days until the duke returns to his senses."

"The duke?" Burke knew full well his mother never, but never, referred to her husband in that way unless she was extremely put out with him. "I take it he's done something really bad, like run over Peppy with his carriage."

Peppy was his mother's favorite spaniel, and Libby did smile at his quip, albeit sadly. "All this is my fault, Burke, you see, I've wed again and Papa won't—"

"You're married again? Good God, doesn't anyone in this family send me word of anything? Why didn't you write and tell me?"

"Actually," his sister began again, "it happened rather suddenly." She paused, seemed almost embarrassed. Indeed she was, for her face had slowly deepened under a rosy blush. "It was more like an elopement, you see, and we only got married a week or so ago."

"Ah-ha, so that's the rub. Father didn't like the idea of you running off instead of having the family involved. Well, I'm surprised you're letting that bother you, Lib. You've always had a stubborn streak, even when we were little." He paused again, feeling forced to pump every word out of them like he was plumbing a dry well. "So, who's the lucky man? Or is that a big secret too?"

"I suppose you'd say that I'm the lucky man, but that may be a matter of opinion."

The deep baritone had come from behind Burke's chair, and whoever he was, he didn't sound as if he considered himself the least bit fortunate to be the bridegroom. Burke watched as Libby blanched, then came to her feet in alarm. He pushed back his own chair and stood up, paling himself when saw who had joined them. He stared at Lord Edmonton, who was completely ignoring him, his gaze pinned on Libby instead. Even more astonishing in Burke's eyes, the tall, elegantly attired gentleman wore a rather impressive shiner on his right eye.

"If it is permissible, I'd like a word with my wife. I was a bit concerned earlier this afternoon when I found out she'd ordered her maid to pack her clothes and moved out of my house, lock, stock, and barrel." Julian uttered the words calmly, or perhaps it would be better said, so tightly controlled that his voice sounded as brittle as an ice-covered limb.

In Burke's considered opinion, however, if Julian's anger was leashed at the moment, it wouldn't be so for long. Libby's husband looked ready to explode with the force of Mount Etna. Burke decided it might be a good time to try to defuse the tension.

"Lord Edmonton, I believe, isn't it? It's been awhile since we've met."

For the first time Julian seemed to become aware that diners other than his wife sat at the table. Angry dark blue eyes swiveled to Burke, and Burke detected within them the tiniest flare of awareness before Julian lapsed into the charade both of them had played since their last rendezvous over a year ago.

"That's right, Viscount. I understand you've been out of the country."

Burke nodded in affirmation, wondering what in the bloody hell kind of family hornet's nest he'd walked into. He was astounded Julian even knew his sister, much less had married her, but that wasn't surprising since he hadn't had contact with Julian of late. Two years ago, however, Julian had been his contact in Paris. He suddenly wondered if Libby was aware that her new husband had worked secretly for the crown. Libby hadn't said a word, but when Burke turned back to her, her face was flushed again, but this time she wasn't embarrassed. She now looked as angry as Julian did.

Beside them, Trinity emitted a long, weary sigh, then suggested quietly, "Libby, dear, why don't you show your husband into the drawing room, where you can speak together privately? Burke and I will wait here."

"Yes, Libby, that's a goddamn good idea. Why don't you show me into the drawing room?" Julian's tone was so mocking, Burke came on guard, not certain he should let his sister closet herself anywhere with the man, be he a former colleague or not. However, when Libby's eyes flashed a very familiar brand of green anger and she tossed the linen napkin to the table much in the manner of a gauntlet, Burke felt fully confident, as she led her husband away, that she would give as good as she got. Libby was no shrinking violet, that was for damn sure. It occurred to him to wonder if Julian had known what he was in for when he ran away and married her.

A few moments later as the drawing room doors slid quietly together across the hall, Burke turned all his attention to his mother. "All right, Mother, perhaps you should enlighten me a bit about what the devil's going on around here. From the beginning, if you please."

Trinity drained the contents of her wineglass first—not at all a good sign—then began the sordid tale of Libby's impulsive, hasty wedding, and only five minutes into the somewhat mystifying but entertaining tale, just about the time she mentioned his father had thrown the punch that had blackened Julian's eye and was now sulking alone at their country estate at Thorpe, Burke knew he was in for an eventful, if not particularly enjoyable, next few months.

His whole family was up in arms, every one of them simmering just beneath the boiling point, and since there were two furious, self-righteous ladies staying in his house, Burke was caught smack dab in the middle of the war, and whether he liked it or not, between them and their equally incensed husbands. So much for his peaceful, relaxing sojourn in London. In truth, he might be in less danger in France stalking Napoleon himself.

Chapter Twenty-eight

After Julian discreetly drew the doors together behind them, Libby turned to face him as he approached where she had taken her stance near the fireplace. Despite the anger frozen on his face, she had to fight her desire to rush straight into his arms. Before she could give in to the impulse, however, her humiliation about the nude painting slammed her like a hammer blow. The ensuing anger quickly killed the urge.

"Mother told me what you did to Father. How could you, Julian? You promised me you would never show those paintings to anyone. I would never have posed for you if I thought you'd betray me like this."

Julian stopped before he reached her, standing behind a navy blue damask settee, and Libby was glad he kept his distance, not sure she could resist his advances if he actually got close enough to touch her. She was angry, yes, indeed furious with him, but she could not shelve her feelings for him like some dusty, unwanted book. She was no longer sure she could trust him, true, but that didn't mean she didn't love him. She certainly couldn't deny that, wouldn't, not to herself or to anyone else. Worst of all, now she wasn't the least bit certain he hadn't married her merely to wreak vengeance on her father. The idea pierced her like a needle in the heart, and her teeth caught at her lower lip as she fought to keep her emotions in check.

Julian was watching her closely, as if trying to ascertain her thoughts, but he was obviously not up to playing games either. He waited a moment, choosing his words with care but didn't deny her accusation. "Yes, I showed a painting to him, but only after he tried to buy me off in the most contemptuous way possible. As I told you, he offended me. I reacted in kind."

Outraged, Libby bristled like a cornered cat. "Is that to say then that you don't think it offensive to show a man a nude of his daughter?"

"I was wrong to do it, of course. He made me angry, and I suppose I wanted to show him how it felt." He paused. "More than that I wanted him to quit trying to separate us."

"So you chose blackmail and humiliated me to the utmost by doing so? Julian, I can't begin to imagine what you were thinking—"

Julian slammed his palm down on the back of the couch. "I was thinking I was bloody sick and tired of your father ruining my life and meant to stop him once and for all. Pardon me if you aren't able to understand how I felt, but at the time it seemed my only recourse."

"I must say, you chose a bizarre method of showing him how much you cared for me."

"And you've chosen a bizarre way of acting like a wife! By the way, love, just out of curiosity, have you left me for good, or do you intend to return home when, and if, the whim suits you?"

"This is no whim, Julian. Can't you understand how I feel? You had a fistfight with my father, nearly broke his nose, for heaven's sake, then attempted to blackmail him in the ugliest possible way. In the process you've made it hard for me to ever look him in the eye again."

Julian's expression grew so frigid in the next moment that Libby braced herself for the abrasive onslaught that would surely follow, but his voice remained quite mild, almost too calm. "You're coming home with me right now. Do you understand me, Libby? Ring Alice and tell her to pack your things."

Libby hadn't expected him to issue a command and expect her to obey him. Her hackles rose. She certainly wasn't used to being ordered around as if she were some slave girl, as if she were Lu Ling.

"No," she answered, slowly and succinctly, selecting her words with care, "not until you and my father apologize to each other and quit acting like mortal enemies."

"Don't you understand anything yet, Libby?" Julian barked out furiously. "Thorpe hates my guts and he always will. We've tried to appease him and it didn't work, and it won't work in the future. He'll go to his grave loathing me, and so will you, if he has anything to say about it."

Gazing at his incensed face, Libby couldn't say he was wrong, but she knew Julian was just as much at fault as her father. Both of them were being unreasonable and stubborn; both would have to give in, at least a little, if they were ever to suffer each other's company.

"Mother and I hope to convince my father to announce our marriage at the ball Mother's having next Saturday. Will you agree to come there with me, Julian, and give Papa one last chance to make things right between you? Perhaps if you'd apologize too, for showing him the painting, if both of you would—"

"I'll be damned if I'll apologize to him. I'm just sorry we didn't get to finish the fight he started. Don't expect me to show up anywhere at your bidding while you're living here. When you decide to come home with me and act like the wife you're supposed to be, rather than Papa's precious little girl, then I might be willing to listen to this plan you and your mother have concocted. Listen to me well, Libby. Make your choice, me or your father, or you won't be seeing me at any goddamn ball, or anywhere else you're likely to be." He paused, but his jaw was so rigid that Libby dared not breathe. "If you don't come home by Friday, I'm leaving for Brickhill without you, and you and your whole family can go straight to hell."

Turning without another word, he stalked out the door and down the hall, heaving the outside door shut with a slam that reverberated through the house. Slightly stunned by the ultimatum, Libby walked to the window and watched Julian fling himself into his carriage, fighting her tears as he drove off into the foggy night, perhaps out of her life forever. She had no doubt that he'd meant every word he'd said, and though she knew him to bear some of the fault for the awful predicament, she couldn't blame him for being enraged. It wasn't right the way he was being treated by her father, but it wasn't right either that he'd kept all knowledge of the feud between their families away from her before they had wed. And it wasn't right either that he had threatened to walk away forever if she didn't estrange herself from her father. God help her, what could she do? she thought helplessly, tears welling as she sank into the large chintz chair beside the fire. Withdrawing her handkerchief from her sleeve, she dabbed her eyes and stared down into the grate, where the coals glimmered like so many glowing red eyes, desperately trying to find an end to this terrible fight that was pulling her apart.

"I take it Julian found the door. By the sound of it, he took most of it with him."

Libby turned at the sound of Burke's voice and found her brother approaching her chair.

"Feel like company?" he offered with a grin.

Nodding, Libby sniffed and blew her nose as Burke shut the door. He pulled up a straight chair, turned, then straddled it, resting his folded arms on the back as he gazed at her.

"Not having a very good honeymoon, huh, sis?"

Despite herself, Libby had to laugh with him. Burke had always been able to cheer her, no matter how low her spirits. She had always been the serious child, the one who contemplated everything and wondered why and how and wherefore, while Burke just ran and played and enjoyed the moment for what it was. Now she envied him that.

"Oh, Burke, I've gotten myself into the most terrible fix. What am I going to do?"

"Yes, it's bizarre indeed. Usually it's me that you have to bail out with Father. Why don't you let me return the favor for a change and intercede in your behalf?"

Tearfully Libby observed him with renewed interest. "Do you think there's something you can do to help?"

"I might be able to talk with Father. I know Julian a bit too. I could put in a good word if you like. Act the intermediary perhaps."

Startled, Libby frowned. "You know Julian? Where did you meet?" She paused, then demanded, "Have you known all along about his brother's attempt on Mama's life? If only someone had told me about that, all this could have been prevented."

"I didn't know about Rupert Rainville until Mother told me a few minutes ago. I was as shocked as you were."

"Yet Julian didn't mention it to you either?"

As she watched Burke, she began to sense a certain evasiveness on his part, especially when he answered. "We aren't close friends and actually haven't spent a lot of time together. In any case, neither of us talked about our families when we did happen to meet."

"He didn't seem to resent you? Because Papa ostracized his family in the past?"

Burke shook his head.

"Did Mama tell you about the painting?" she asked, her eyes sliding away from his intent gaze.

Burke nodded, then laughed at the blush that ran up under her cheekbones. "Actually, I was more shocked that you'd let him paint it in the first place. You've always been so stuffy and prim."

"Stuffy and prim! I have not. I just tried to behave with decorum."

"That's right, you've been stuffy." Before she could object further, he told her, "I think I'll ride out to Thorpe in the morning and try to reason with Father. Mother thinks it'd be a good idea, and she's writing a letter for me to take along, no doubt an attempt to mollify his temper a bit. You know how Father is. He flies off the handle and makes a scene, but later when he thinks about things, he becomes more reasonable. Especially if Mother's angry with him. He hates that, you know."

"Yes, I know, but Burke"—Libby stopped, incredulous her father had actually fought with her husband—"he blackened Julian's eye. I've never been so shocked. In all my years I've never seen Father actually hit anyone. Usually he just gets that awful icy look in his eyes until everyone agrees with him out of fear for their life." She gave a pitiably half-hearted chuckle. "Julian was wearing that kind of look when he stormed out of here a minute ago."

"I can't say I blame the poor man. You're not much more than newlyweds, and you've already left him. Can't be much fun for a new bridegroom, I'd wager. I'd be in a damned rage too if my wife walked out on me. Especially if I cared about her."

"It's not much fun for the bride either," Libby answered with a rueful twist of her mouth. "He's leaving town on the day before Mother's party when he knows I want him there so Mother can formally announce our marriage."

"Wish I could tell you what to do, Lib, but you've got to make that decision on your own. I can talk to Father, and I can't promise you, but I think he'll come around eventually, if you'll give him enough time."

"Even after Julian hit him?"

He nodded. "It'd be different if Father hadn't gotten in a good punch himself."

Despite his grin, Libby remained solemn. "I hope you're right, Burke."

Burke stood up, then pulled Libby to her feet. "Come on, Mother's still waiting for us in the dining room. She'll know what to say to make you feel better. She always does."

Libby went with him, but as she sat down and listened to her mother asking Burke about his travels, she didn't feel the least bit better. Nor would she until she was with her husband again. If he didn't come back, she wasn't sure she could bear for him to leave London without her.

Chapter Twenty-nine

The green fields surrounding the village Thorpe were a misty patchwork in the distance, half hidden by the rolling hills and thick deer parks. From his vantage point in the tallest of the twin square towers rising above Thorpe Hall, William could gaze out in every direction and survey thousands of acres along the River Redling, most of which had been under the ownership of the Duke of Thorpe for generations.

The day was warm and beautiful, but he was not enjoying the sunshine gilding his realm; nor was he enjoying anything else in his life at the moment. His dark brows knitted, his mouth hard, he followed the stone walkway to the east wall, which rose five or six stories above the interior courtyard. All he could think about was Trinity. The first time he had brought her to the tower and presented the magnificent view of his properties, they'd both been so young and so madly in love. He had brought her up to his favorite spot, wanting to impress her, determined to thwart his father's plans to annul their marriage. It wasn't long after that day that Rupert Rainville had attempted to hurl Trinity to her death.

Squeezing his eyes shut, he relived that horrific night, as he'd done a thousand times, the moment he'd thought he'd lost her forever—first to death when Rainville had almost succeeded in his murder plot, then later and even more devastating, when he found her gone with her family, back to the Carolinas and out of his life. He had been left behind, bereft, alone, unable to believe she'd actually walked away and left him as if they meant nothing to each other.

In the following year he'd felt like a mere husk of himself, as if he wandered through a dreamscape searching for something real to hold on to. He had ostracized Julian's family—damn right, he had, and by God, he wasn't ashamed of it. He had no use for anyone who bore familial kin to the murdering bastard who had put him through hell on earth. Why couldn't Trinity and Libby understand that? His motives had been pure. What else should he have done? Gathered the Rainvilles gently to his breast?

A commotion and ringing of shod hooves below in the courtyard caught his attention, and when he placed his palms flat on the wall and peered down at the cobblestones, his heart leapt. Thinking the new arrival was Trinity, that she'd changed her mind and come to him, he hoped to see a ducal carriage rattling to a standstill. Disappointed, he realized it was a lone horseman who had appeared, at a swift pace in a clatter against the cobblestones.

His mood blackened considerably, his anger with his defiant wife oozing up again, at least until he recognized the newcomer was his son. Pleasure bloomed within him, for he'd not seen Burke in over a year. So the boy had made it back in one piece, thank God. As Burke dismounted below amidst a flurry of servants running to welcome him home after so long an absence, William cupped his hands around his mouth and yelled down to him with his own greeting. When Burke looked up, Will waved and motioned for him to come up.

Within minutes the two men were embracing, and William smiled at his tall, strapping son, very proud Burke was serving his country so well despite his fears for his safety.

"Welcome home, son," he said, then eagerly inquired, "When did you get back in England?"

"Just yesterday." Burke took off his brown leather riding gloves and leaned back against the interior wall. Most people said he was a dead ringer for William, and it was true. It seemed that Will looked into his own reflected image, but one whispering up from days long past, when he was a young man in his twenties. Again he thought of Trinity and the problems they'd faced when they were Burke's age. Burke obviously noticed how his smile abruptly disintegrated.

"I spoke with Mother last night. She misses you. She wants you to come back to London."

William clamped his teeth, still furious with his wife for refusing to obey him. She could be the most stubborn, hard-headed woman alive when she so chose. Unfortunately, Libby had taken after her in that regard. "If she misses me so much, she could have come to Thorpe along with you. That's what I asked her to do."

"So you haven't had a change of heart about announcing the marriage at Mother's ball, I take it?"

"That's right, I haven't, so don't try to change my mind. I suspect that's why your mother sent you out here, is it not?" He shook his head, a sudden burst of anger ripping through him. "Julian is no good, and Libby should never have wed him. She acted rashly, and now she's having to pay for it."

Burke braced a brown topboot on the stone bench built along the inside perimeter of the tower and braced an elbow on it. He gazed thoughtfully at his father, then shook his head. "Actually, it was my idea to come here to see you."

"Well, I'm glad you did. You can ride with me into the village tomorrow morning. I've got business there, and you can keep me company."

"Of course," Burke answered, turning his regard out over the landscape, where the sun was just beginning to sink down to the horizon like a golden ball into a glorious sea of pink and purple. Darkness would fall quickly after sunset. "First, there are a few things I think you should know. Perhaps what I'm going to tell you will help change your opinion of Lord Edmonton."

William swiveled a quick look at Burke, green eyes narrowed, lips pressed in a tight warning. "I truly doubt if anything you say could make me think well of that reprobate. You've surely heard the kind of man he is, the way he consorts with every manner of loose women and wild, drunken parties where God only knows what all goes on." He thought of the portrait he'd seen of Libby and felt his stomach turn over and a sour taste of bile wash up the back of his throat at the mere idea of his daughter being legally bound to such a man.

"What if I told you he worked with me against Bonaparte?" Burke smiled at William's astonished expression. "That's right. He was a government spy, the man I contacted in Paris at one point. He did the job very well, I might add, well enough to get me out of the country and headed back home."

"I find that hard to believe."

"I thought you would, but it's true, I swear to God. I don't know how much he's involved as an agent at the present, especially now that he's wed to Libby. Until last night I'd neither seen nor talked to him since I left him in France."

"You saw him last night?"

"Yes, he was at my house, trying to get Libby to return home with him. Both she and Mother are staying with me now, in case you didn't know."

"I know your mother is," Will snapped, furious all over again, but had to ask, "And did Libby go home with him?"

Burke shook his head. "She's staying there with Mother in the hope that the two of you will reconcile enough to be half-way courteous to each other." Pausing there, Burke grinned. "I saw the shiner you gave him. Very impressive for a man your age. Julian's a formidable opponent."

"He deserved worse. I'd like to have horsewhipped him." William studied his son for a moment, still unwilling to believe Edmonton had an ounce of honor in him. "He's known everywhere as a philanderer and rake. My God, the stories I've heard about him sicken me."

"He has led a wild life. He admits it, but he must have some good points or Libby couldn't have fallen in love with him. She's got a good head on her shoulders, you know that."

"At times she does. Not this time."

Silence dropped between them as William glowered again, pricked mercilessly by his daughter's utter folly, his eyes fixed steadfastly on the steeple of the village church. He was having trouble digesting the news that Julian actually worked for the crown against the Sicilian. He'd never have given it an ounce of credence if Burke hadn't been a firsthand witness to the fact.

"Well, I'm going down and wash some of this dust off my clothes. I'll be riding back tomorrow if you've a mind to accompany me. I promised Mother I'd attend her party. I hope you'll change your mind and do the same. It would please her greatly, you know that."

"I've things here to take care of," he answered in curt dismissal. "She's perfectly capable of hostessing a fete by herself."

"All right, if that's what you think is right, though I do predict you'll regret all this one day." Burke said this mildly, but his remark still angered his father. Before William could retort, Burke went on, "Oh, and by the way, I've a letter here from Mother. Do you want to read it, or should I just tear it up and toss it in the fire?"

William turned to him, more than eager to see what Trinity had to say for herself, but trying not to show it. "Of course I'll read it. I'll join you later and we'll dine together."

Burke nodded and withdrew a folded parchment from his inside coat pocket. He handed it over to his father, then left William alone to contemplate his wife's entreaty.

William held the letter for a moment, quite certain it was an appeal for him to relent toward their daughter's husband when he finally broke the wax seal with a fingernail. He sat down on the stone bench, opened the fine, thick vellum, and began to read the words set forth in his wife's familiar, neatly slanted handwriting.

My dearest Will,
   I would like to say that I am still very angry and that you are acting in the must stubborn and unreasonable manner imaginable, but despite all that, I cannot deny that I miss you desperately. I'm sure you are quite aware of that too. Perhaps that's the precise reason you took this unexpected journey to Thorpe without me. I do wish you were here to help me sustain poor Libby, whose husband

has also given her an ultimatum in which he demands that she choose between him and you, my dear husband.

I know how you feel, and please don't think I don't have the same terrible memories of Rupert Rainville as you do. I was the one who was in fear of my death and heard the cruel, evil words he uttered in those last minutes before you managed to find us. The difference is, I believe, that you have put from your mind the role your father played in the situation. I know, dear one, that my last sentence has angered you, but please don't wad up this letter quite yet, though I am sure you are inclined to.

I beg you to remember instead the way your father treated us when we were young and loved each other so dearly. When all we wanted was to be together as husband and wife, to have our family and live a happy life. Do you remember those days out at Thorpe, when we floated down the river in the boat, when we locked ourselves in linen closets just to steal a few kisses away from the eyes of the servants? I remember those moments of young love vividly, as if they were only yesterday, and they remain some of my fondest memories of our blessed life together. We faced impossible odds then, didn't we, my darling, and look at us now. We are still together and very happy, other than a few squabbles now and again that send you off to Thorpe without a care for my feelings. I say that to you with the gentlest of rebuke, of course.

What I am trying to say, what I want you to remember, William, my heart, is the way your father schemed and connived to keep us apart. He thought I was unworthy of you because I was a colonial, unworthy to become your duchess. He wanted you to wed the woman of his choosing, a woman of high connections and privilege. But you defied him, Will, because you loved me. That was enough for you back then, was it not? Then what I must ask you is, Why is it not enough for our daughter simply to love this man she has chosen to wed? Why must you approve him first and try to force this annulment against the will of both Libby and Julian?

Don't you see it, my love, you are playing out the same role as your father did in our lives, and he almost destroyed us. Much more than Rupert Rainville's one act of violence against me. Please think about these things, Will. Try to remember how you felt once upon a time, then come home soon. I miss you terribly, and Libby is as distraught and unhappy as I've ever seen her. With much the same misery that I suffered when I was forced to set sail for America without you all those many years ago. I'll pray that I'll be with you soon, and we'll be a loving family once more.

Your devoted wife,
Trinity

William stared down at the letter in his hand for some time, then carefully refolded and placed it inside his coat pocket. He leaned his head against the wall and gazed silently at the lingering sun until its fading rays slowly extinguished and disappeared, darkening the world around him in the black, lonely night.

Chapter Thirty

A lone in one of the guest bedrooms of Burke's town house, Libby lay abed, staring morosely at the green silk canopy. Inside she felt queasy with a loneliness as fierce as she could ever remember. Julian had gone back to Brickhill. He had warned her he'd leave London without her if she did not return home, and now she was sorry she hadn't. She should never have left him in the first place, never let her father's actions force her decisions.

Her mother had meant well, of course, with her suggestion to hold themselves separate from their husbands until the men saw reason, but Trinity had been so wrong this time. Neither man had allowed themselves to be coerced into accepting the other, and all the estrangement brought was unhappiness to everyone, including her mother, though Trinity tried valiantly to hide it as she went about making last-minute decisions concerning the ball.

Now, as her mother slept peacefully in the room next door, Libby lay struggling with her misery, her regret, reliving all the mistakes she'd made. She had plenty of time to think about everything that had happened, to gauge each incident against the others, to live in William's viewpoint, then in Julian's, then her mother's and her own, over and over again. All she had come up with was that she loved Julian to distraction, she missed him dreadfully, and she wanted to be with him, back at Brickhill where they'd spent such happy weeks together.

She realized with a sudden flash of insight that she had already made her decision. Already she knew she was going to

follow him there. She should never have left him in the first
place. She only hoped that he would welcome her back without too many recriminations. Placing her hand upon her
belly, still flat but soon to be swelled with their baby, she
smiled. She hadn't told a soul yet, but she was now sure she
had conceived. Julian would be shocked to find her with
child so soon, but he would welcome the news, she knew he
would.

Who could know, perhaps once their son or daughter was
born, then both men would mellow, would accept each other
for the sake of the child. The feud had festered much too
long to heal without everyone making a serious effort to end
the hard feelings. Time, that's what it would take, time and
endless patience.

A sound caused her to sit up in bed, holding her bed-
clothes up against her breast. She puzzled over the small
clink she'd heard for a moment until a second stone hit the
windowpane, and she realized someone was throwing peb-
bles at her window. Hoping beyond hope that it was Julian,
she tossed back the covers and ran barefoot across the floor
to see. She flung open the casement and peered out, searching the shadowy yard below for her husband. When she didn't
see anyone, her heart fell but flew joyfully heavenward again
when Julian suddenly stepped out of the shadows of the grape
arbor at the side of the house, his face illuminated clearly in
the moonlight as he gazed up at the house.

Her heart clutched, overjoyed when he beckoned in no
uncertain terms for her to come down. Without a moment's
hesitation or thought to do otherwise, she whirled around
and grabbed her robe. Slipping her arm into the quilted
sleeve, she crossed the room and edged open her door. Nothing but nothing would stop her from going to him this time.
He hadn't gone away without her, he hadn't been able to,
and her heart swelled with love and pleasure.

Tiptoeing past her mother's door, she saw that no lamp
glowed inside and was glad her mother was asleep so she
wouldn't have to tender explanation. The house lay in inky
blackness except for the pale moonlight streaming through

the tall, undraped windows on the staircase, but she hurried anyway, down the back stairs and through the hall to the back door. She threw the bolt and eased outside, not wanting to awaken the servants sleeping downstairs.

Holding onto the iron rail, she descended to the ground, then hurried across the grassy lawn, through the dark shadows under the trees, toward where she'd seen Julian from her window. She didn't see him until he stepped out of the darkness and grabbed her.

"Oh, Julian, I'm so glad you came for me. I thought you'd gone home without me. I'm sorry, I'm so sorry I ever left you. . . ."

Julian's mouth muffled any further recriminations, and she twined her arms up around his neck and locked them together, moaning softly as he lifted her bodily against him and kissed her so long and thoroughly that she was left feeling breathless but alive again now that she was back in his arms. Still holding her tightly against his chest, he backed under the arbor, where the shadows were deep, and sat down with her on the wooden bench. He kept her firmly on his lap, and in the darkness their lips met again, eagerly, greedily, until they both had to stop and heave in great, labored breaths.

It was at that point that Libby started to laugh, with sheer, unadulterated happiness. Julian pulled her face against his shoulder to muffle her laughter and spoke against her hair, his voice gruff but just as amused.

"God help me, Libby, you've got me acting like a lovestruck schoolboy, throwing stones at your window in the dead of night. Thank God nobody's around to see what you've reduced me to."

"You wouldn't say that if you knew how happy you've made me by coming here." She smiled, caressing his face with her fingertips, wanting to touch him, to hold him close. "I was going to come to Brickhill tomorrow. I'd already made up my mind. I missed you too much not to."

"I wasn't sure you would." He paused and took a deep breath before continuing. "It took me awhile to realize how much I hurt you when I showed the nude to your father. I'm going to be honest with you, Libby, and I want you to do the same. I admit I wanted to hurt him, that's why I did it, but the other was true too, I wanted him to leave us alone. I wanted to make you choose me over him, once and for all."

"I have, sweetheart, I have. I'll let my mother deal with Father, and if it's meant to be, then we'll see them in the future. My place is with you. I know that now. That's where I want to be."

Julian pulled her against him, and she laid her head on his chest, listening to the steady beat of his heart. She was content, her entire body relaxed and serene. She was where she was supposed to be. She needed to tell him about the child—this was the perfect moment—but a different thought occurred to her first and she asked, "How on earth did you know which room I was in?"

"I didn't. I've been tossing rocks at one upstairs window after another for a quarter of an hour now."

Libby laughed and so did he; then their mouths mingled in the most tender of kisses that grew so desperate with love and passion they had to break away again to draw breath. "Come back upstairs with me," she whispered, wanting him beside her through the night, wanting to feel his hard body against hers, wanting him to make love to her.

"I don't know if that's a very good idea," he muttered, then gave a low chuckle. "First I toss stones at your bedroom window, and now I sneak into the house like some thief in the night. Leave me some pride. Come home with me now."

Caressing his face, Libby sighed. "All right. Let me go inside and pack a few things. Mother will understand. I'll leave her a note."

"Now, that sounds like a very good idea," he murmured, his mouth burning up against the side of her throat. She arched back to give him better access, closing her eyes with sublime pleasure. When she was able to think again, she opened her eyes, then sharpened her gaze when she caught sight of a light moving through the darkened windows of the parlor.

"Look, Julian, someone's awake. Do you think Mother heard us?"

Julian peered toward the front of the house, then glanced up at the bedrooms. "No, or she would have lit a candle in her bedroom. Perhaps it's one of the servants. Or maybe Burke's come home. Did he go out tonight?"

"He's gone to Thorpe to talk some sense into Father, but he must have come back. We'll wait until he's abed, then I'll go get dressed."

"No need to get dressed," Julian murmured softly, shifting her to an angle where he could more easily slide his hand inside her gown. She sighed as his palm touched bare skin, then cupped over her breast, wondering how she ever could have forced herself to spend a night away from him. She pulled his head down to hers, happily attacking his mouth, and their tongues met with a familiar fire, their need for each other only deepened by the days spent apart.

Julian lay back on the bench, bringing her bodily atop him, and after several most enjoyable moments entwined together, they came up for air again. Libby glanced toward the house, hoping Burke would hasten to bed. She stiffened in Julian's arms, stifling a cry when she saw the flames licking at the draperies in the parlor.

"Oh, my God, Julian! The house is on fire!"

For an instant Libby's words didn't quite get through to Julian where he nuzzled her nape. Then he dropped her hair and followed her frightened gaze. When he saw how quickly the shooting flames were engulfing the parlor, he jumped to his feet, still holding onto Libby. Once his initial shock had fled, Julian told her to say where she was and took off at a dead run toward the front of the house.

Shouting a warning at the top of his lungs, he was almost to the stoop when a heavily cloaked figure dashed down the front steps directly into his path. The figure was dressed all in black, and Julian thought it was one of the servants at first, panicked by the fire, but as the person sped away across the grass, he realized that it was an intruder, one who must have set the fire. He took off after him and just managed to grab

the back of the cloak and jerk him to a standstill before the
arsonist twisted away, leaving the cape in his hand. He got
only a glimpse of the face in the silvered light, shocked to
find he'd been grappling with a female. She darted away, but
when Libby suddenly screamed in terror, Julian forgot about
the woman in black. He headed back to the rear of the house,
where he'd left her. The fire had reached the back entrance,
where Alice and the other servants were scrambling up from
their basement rooms to the safety of the yard. The duchess
was nowhere to be seen.

"Julian! We've got to get Mama out! Nobody's seen her!"
Libby screamed again as the flames blew out the parlor windows in a blast of heat and breaking glass, showering the grass
with jagged shards and catching a nearby elm tree on fire.

"She'll have to get out through the front," Julian yelled to
his wife. "Stay back here, Libby, stay here, do you understand me? I'll get your mother out."

A couple of the Thorpe footman followed at a run as Julian made his way around the front corner of the house
again, and he realized that the fire was spreading fast, already through the entry foyer to the staircase and the dining
parlor beyond. The front door was locked, and Julian stood
back and sent his boot hard against it in a desperate attempt
to break through the lock just as Libby appeared below him
on the lawn, still crying her mother's name.

A second brutal kick finally sent the door flying inward,
and Julian rushed inside, ducking low to evade the dense
black smoke that roiled out into the night from the blazing
inferno inside. Coughing, his eyes burning from the hot
fumes, he bent low and headed for the stairs at the back of
the foyer. Almost at once he caught sight of Trinity in her
white nightgown, clutching the banister as she tried to grope
through the thick, noxious clouds of black smoke.

"This way, over here, quick!"

The duchess heard his voice and immediately tried to leap
over the fire licking along the bottom of the steps, but to his
horror the soft muslin of her gown brushed too close and
burst into flame. Screaming, she stopped and tried to beat it

out, but in her panic, she lost her balance and fell onto the smoldering carpet. Julian was to her in seconds, but not before her entire robe had caught fire. He dragged her bodily away from the fiery stairs, jerking the burning garment off her as he went.

Somehow he got the robe off and swooped her up into his arms, both of them gasping and choking as he brought her outside into the fresh night air. He could hear Trinity groaning with pain from where she'd been burned, and Libby wept with relief as he ran down the steps with her mother cradled in his arms. In the distance he could already hear the bells of a fire wagon, but he didn't stop until he had the duchess some distance from the house. He laid her down gently on her back, and Libby fell to her knees at her side.

"Oh, God, no, please, is she all right? Oh, Lord, look, Julian, look at her legs!"

"Stay with her, Libby, I've got to make sure everyone's out."

Julian saw Alice dashing from the backyard, and he shouted for her to go for a doctor, then turned and ran back toward the house to help the water brigade with a blaze that had already raced through the upper floors in a roaring, devouring inferno, illuminating the night sky in a nightmarish, red-orange haze of smoke and swift-rising heat currents that showered glowing sparks out over the neighboring houses.

Chapter Thirty-one

Just before dawn broke the next morning Julian stood in his own bedroom on Berkeley Square, at the foot of his canopied bed, watching his wife fuss worriedly over her mother. Libby hovered at one side of the bed, clasping Trinity's hand while the doctor administered laudanum to help his patient rest. They'd transported the duchess there because it was closer than her own mansion on Hyde Park. The duke's personal physician had come at once to tend her and had quickly treated the burns with a soothing salve that did seem to have alleviated the pain. To everyone's relief, it appeared the duchess's wounds were superficial for the most part. She would be all right except for some lingering pain and discomfort.

Despite a long, valiant effort to save Burke's house, the entire structure had burned to the ground. Other than a few minor roof fires among the surrounding houses, it had been the only casualty of the conflagration. All in all, the outcome of the fire was better than Julian had expected, but he knew full well it could have been catastrophic. What if he hadn't changed his mind and come there looking for Libby? What if she'd been upstairs in bed and nobody had noticed the fire until it was too late to escape by the burning stairs? The ensuing images that branded themselves relentlessly into his brain were so horrific, so unacceptable, as he realized that Libby and Trinity could have easily perished together in the fire. He could have lost her, lost her forever. His jaw worked with suppressed emotion while he watched her tenderly stroke her mother's hair, and he fought the urge to go to her, hold her close, and tell her he never wanted her out of his sight again.

When he heard the door thrust open behind him, he turned and watched the Duke of Thorpe rush toward the bed, his face stark with fear. Burke came in right behind him, and though Will headed straight for his wife's side and took her hands in his as he sat down beside her, Burke stopped at Julian's side. They stood there a moment without speaking while the duchess attempted to reassure her distraught husband that she was truly all right. When Will pulled Trinity into his arms and held her tightly, his face hidden in her shoulder, Julian decided it was time to give the couple some privacy.

Moving silently across the room, he exited into the corridor and gave orders for Lu Ling to ready extra bedrooms, for Libby and him as well as for the duke and viscount in case they elected to stay the night. He turned when Burke joined him, and as the Chinese maid moved away to do his bidding, the two old friends looked at each other. Burke stretched out his hand, and Julian clasped it in a firm grip.

"It's a damn good thing you happened to be there," Burke said, shaking his head, as if overwhelmed by what could have happened. "Or this could have turned into a nightmare. We all owe you, Julian, all of us. Thank God you got to them in time."

Julian nodded. "I'm just glad everyone's all right. I didn't expect you to get here so quickly. I thought you and the duke were at Thorpe."

"We were already halfway back to the city when we heard about the fire. Father had a change of heart after he read Mother's letter and decided to return for the ball."

"I take it you already know that your house was totally destroyed."

Burke shrugged. "It's too bad, but I rarely stay there anyway. Do you know what started it? Libby said she thought someone might have knocked over a lamp. She told us you saw someone in the parlor just before the flames broke out. Do you know who it was?"

"Initially we though it was you, come home." Julian took Burke's arm and drew him a few feet away. He kept his voice low. "Now I think perhaps the blaze was set on purpose. When I ran around the house to raise the alarm, someone ran out the front door."

The muscles in Burke's face hardened perceptibly. "Are you saying it was the work of an arsonist?"

"I can't say that for sure, but it's beginning to look that way to me. You haven't even heard the worst part."

"Tell me."

"The person fled when I gave chase, and, now brace yourself, Burke"—he paused, brows coming down—"but I'm almost positive it was a woman."

"A woman? For God's sake, what makes you think that?"

"I got hold of her cloak and jerked her to a stop. I barely glimpsed her before she wrested away and fled, but I can tell you she had fair hair and was quite tall for a woman."

To Julian's surprise, Burke's expression changed, first revealing shock, then began to redden with rising anger. "Was it silver-blond, her hair? Could you tell?"

"It could've been. It looked almost white to me, but I can't say for sure. I don't think I've ever seen her before. When I heard Libby screaming, I let her go." He studied his friend, whose jaw kept tensing and relaxing as he dealt with his ire. "You know who she is?"

"I think so. If she's who I think, her name is Mademoiselle Renate. I crossed paths with her in Paris. Brigitte Renate. Did you know of her when you were there?"

When Julian shook his head, Burke slammed a fist into his open palm. "I knew she was dangerous, and I suspected she might spend some time as a spy here in England, but I never would've expected her to do anything like this. She's fluent in four or five languages, and said to be one of Bonaparte's best-kept secrets. If she did come here, I know what she was looking for. I took several important government documents from her brother's house when I was in Paris, but why would she want to burn down my house? That doesn't make sense."

"Maybe she hoped to burn the papers before you could hand them over. She's a French agent, you're sure?"

Burke nodded. "Yes, but by God, she'll not get away with this. I'll track her down now if it takes me forever." Any further conversation was cut short when the duke suddenly came outside into the corridor. He still looked completely ashen in the face but in better shape than he had been when he'd rushed to his wife's sickbed a short time earlier. His face was haggard, his eyes bloodshot when they connected with Julian's gaze, but the fear was gone.

"I need a drink, a stiff one," he said.

"I've got some good Irish whiskey in my study."

Both men followed him there, to the scene where they'd had their fistfight not too many days before. Fortunately, Julian had removed the nude painting of Libby, up to the attic, where he had placed all her portraits under lock and key. Guilt struck him like a blow, and he could still see the look of horror and betrayal in her eyes when she realized what he'd done. It had been a stupid thing to do.

In silence he poured them all a generous libation of whiskey. He handed the glasses around and watched the duke down his with one sharp, backward toss of his head. When Will held out his glass again, Julian refilled it without comment.

"Your wife is going to be all right," he said.

The duke nodded. "Yes, thank God." He hesitated a moment. "I owe you, Edmonton. More than I can ever repay."

"And I owe you an apology for what I did the other night here in this very room," Julian said gravely. It was time to end this ridiculous feud, if for no other reason than to placate their wives, and both of them knew it.

"Trinity said you're the one who went in after her."

"I was there to see Libby." He exhaled, long and hard. "I'm afraid she'd up and left me too."

"She takes after her mother."

Incredibly, they managed to share a brief smile. "Maybe you could give me a few pointers in how to handle your daughter? I'd appreciate it."

"I was going to ask the same thing from you. You see, a

moment ago Libby told me she was going home with you and that's where she was going to stay, whether I liked it or not. She was sorry, you understand, but that's the way it was going to be. You were her husband, after all, and she loved you."

"I must say I'm relieved to hear it."

Will's face sobered and he exhaled deeply, his eyes growing haunted in a way Julian understood all too well. "I mean it when I say I owe you my gratitude. God only knows if they could've found their way out without your help."

"I think," Burke said from where he'd been standing quietly by the fire, empty whiskey glass in hand, "that it's time we all started over and let the past die. That's the best thing you could for Libby and Mother."

The duke nodded, and though Julian knew the older man would no doubt try to forget the hatred he'd nursed for so long, it might take a long time for both of them to fight their way out from under the ugly shadows that had darkened the past. But a life with Libby was worth any effort. The future was now too valuable to him to let their happiness slip through his fingers.

"Burke told me that you worked with him in France."

"That's right."

"Do you intend to do so in the future, now that you're married to my daughter?"

"Not unless I have to." He took a deep swallow from his glass and met his father-in-law's eyes. "Your son's taken my place and done the job as well as I could have. That's fine by me. Of late I've had the desire to settle down and lead a more respectable life."

Recognizing his admission for what it was, a proffered olive branch, Will nodded and drained the remainder of his whiskey.

"You're welcome to stay the night," Julian invited, not at all sure the duke would go so far as to sleep in his house, not this soon in their armistice. "Dr. Harrington said the duchess shouldn't be moved for a while. I've had chambers prepared for both you and Burke, if you should want them."

"Thank you. I think I'll take you up on that offer. Again, I do appreciate everything you've done." Will set his tumbler down upon the polished surface of Julian's desk. "Now I'm going back upstairs and sit with my wife until she's able to sleep."

At the door he turned back. "Libby seemed completely exhausted, so I sent her off to bed. She told me to tell you where she was."

"Thank you."

After the duke exited, Julian showed Burke to his room, and along the way he asked him what he was going to do about the French woman.

"If she's here in England, I'm going to track her down and make sure she's punished. If she's gone back to Paris, I'll go there and find her."

Julian left a man still very angry and eager to seek out his revenge on the woman named Brigitte, but Julian's thoughts were on his own wife now. He walked to the end of the hall to the room he'd directed Lu Ling to ready for them. Inside, the Chinese girl was helping Libby don a fresh nightgown. At Julian's appearance the servant quickly picked up the basin of water they'd used to cleanse away the soot and grime from Libby's hands and face and backed away. As soon as Lu Ling closed the door, Libby walked straight into his arms.

"I was so afraid for Mama," she whispered, clutching him tightly. "But she's all right. Papa held me and told me how sorry he was for the way he's treated you."

"He thanked me for saving her life."

Libby pushed away and gazed up into his face, her eyes shadowed. "Is it going to be all right now, Julian? Do you think it ever can be?"

"It's going to be all right, I promise you."

Sighing wearily, she laid her head against his chest, and he tightened his arms around her when it seemed she swayed upon her feet. "Come, sweetheart, it's almost dawn outside. You've got to get some rest."

Libby went along willingly, allowing him to help her into bed. Then she lay quietly against the satin pillows, watching him strip off his clothes and wash before he came to her. She snuggled up against him when he slid under the covers and gathered her in his arms.

"How are your hands?" she said, lifting one and wincing at the raw red skin on the backs of his fingers.

"It's nothing. The doctor gave me salve if I should need it."

"Look at them. You do need it. Where is it?" She put a finger to his lips when he made to object, "Please, let me tend to you."

Julian gave up, well aware she wouldn't rest until she doctored him. "In my coat pocket."

Retrieving the jar, Libby sat back on her heels and carefully smoothed the oily medicine over the backs of both his hands. Her eyes downcast, intent on what she was doing, she whispered softly, "I'm carrying your child, Julian."

Julian went rigid, his heartbeat frozen inside his chest. "What?" he finally managed hoarsely.

Glancing up at him, Libby smiled at his dumbfounded expression. "I'm going to have a baby."

"Oh, my God, oh, my God."

A tiny frown worried her brow. "You're pleased, aren't you?"

Great tenderness welled up inside Julian, and he took her face between his hands. "I am very pleased," he murmured, realizing that he was more than that as the full ramifications dawned on him, and emotion more akin to elation began to spread through him. "You just startled me, coming out with it like that. You're certain?"

"Very." She smiled, green eyes glowing mischievously. "Now you can't run off to Brickhill without me ever again."

Julian drew her back down beside him and settled her head in the hollow of his shoulder. "Never, my love, never again will I leave you, not if I can help it. Nor will I let you run away from me again."

"We're going to be very happy from this moment on, aren't we, Julian? Happier than we ever dreamed possible?"

"Yes, we are, my love, you and me and our baby."

With a sigh warm with contentment, Libby closed her eyes

and went quickly to sleep. Julian lay awake longer, watching the blackness outside the window turn to charcoal, then to soft, pearly gray. Gently, so as not to disturb her, he slid his hand down and rested his palm upon the flatness of her stomach. A son or daughter grew inside her, a human being they had created together. Absurdly he felt his throat burn with the urge to weep from the sheer joy she'd brought into his life. He shut his eyes and cradled her closer. Libby was his life, his heart, and someday soon so too would be the tiny child she carried within her.

Epilogue

The summer sun rode high in the sky, a brilliant, blinding ball of golden fire above the breeze-rippled water. All around the lake, the flower beds of Brickhill were abloom with white lilies and pink gladiolas, marigolds and purple alyssum, the rose arbors covered with blossoms and buzzing bumblebees. Under the gnarled oak tree near the tinkling fountain, the temperature was cooler, the shade deep and inviting, and Julian stood there in shirtsleeves, in front of his canvas, his brush forgotten in his hand as he watched his wife and son play.

Libby wore summer white, her arms bare, the thin muslin revealing the slim lines of her body, as shapely as ever nearly a year and a half after the birth of their child. She sat in the white wicker swing in which he'd wanted to paint her one day not so long ago, the first day she'd come to Brickhill. Tristan was perched on her lap, and they were laughing, Tristan's chubby little fists tightly clutching his mother's arms where she had them looped protectively around his waist. Love came unbidden but rushing in a current so strong that he had to swallow hard to quell the emotion, making him feel foolish at his own sentimentality.

Everything had worked out for them at last. The duke and duchess were utterly charmed by their first grandchild, so much so that they spent a great deal of time visiting him at Brickhill. It was incredible, in fact. Never would he have expected any Thorpe to be his houseguest, other than perhaps

Burke, but never the father-in-law who hated even the Rainville name.

Poor Burke hadn't seen Tristan since the baby had begun to walk and charm everyone by gurgling out words, too intrigued with hunting down the beautiful but elusive Mademoiselle Renate. She'd evaded him thus far, but on their one encounter she had showed her mettle by having him arrested in Paris, only to intervene and effect his release in recompense for accidentally setting fire to his home when stealing back her brother's papers.

Now they were even, Burke had informed Libby and Julian on his last trip to London, but the glint in his eyes when he spoke of his wily mademoiselle was one that had become all too familiar to Julian since he had met Libby. The man was smitten, and the fact that his lady was his enemy did not bode well for a happy ending to his story.

Most of the time Julian didn't allow himself to dwell in the past, no longer had need to do so. He did not miss the parties he'd thrown, the wild, exciting lifestyle he'd given up for Libby, indeed was so happy at times it almost frightened him. He feared all would be taken away as quickly as it had come to him, that he didn't deserve this splendid life he'd been given, did not deserve a woman as wonderful as Libby or a son as perfect as Tristan.

He looked down at the canvas, pleased by his progress, and he carefully added a dab of gold to Tristan's hair. The boy looked like a cherub with his huge blue eyes and bouncing curls, a mischievous little angel who enchanted everyone around him, much the same way his mother did.

"Papa, push, Papa, push," squealed his giggling, squirming son, making Libby laugh at his antics.

Smiling indulgently, Julian laid down his brush and walked to where his family awaited him. He stopped the swing and bent down to touch his lips to Libby's smiling mouth, then pressed another kiss atop the boy's soft curls.

"Push, push, push," Tristan demanded, twisting in Libby's lap to peer up at his father.

Grinning, Julian drew them back very high and let the swing go, laughing at the way both of them shrieked with excitement. Yes, indeed, all was well in his life. He was very content.

PENGUIN PUTNAM

online

Your Internet gateway to a virtual environment with hundreds of entertaining and enlightening books from Penguin Putnam Inc.

While you're there, get the latest buzz on the best authors and books around—

Tom Clancy, Patricia Cornwell, W.E.B. Griffin, Nora Roberts, William Gibson, Robin Cook, Brian Jacques, Catherine Coulter, Stephen King, Jacquelyn Mitchard, and many more!

Penguin Putnam Online is located at
http://www.penguinputnam.com

PENGUIN PUTNAM NEWS

Every month you'll get an inside look at our upcoming books and new features on our site. This is an ongoing effort to provide you with the most interesting and up-to-date information about our books and authors.

Subscribe to Penguin Putnam News at
http://www.penguinputnam.com/ClubPPI